When The Wild Hunt rides,

the souls of the dead

join their parade.

dark Glitter

Wild Hunt Motorcycle Club

BOOK ONE

INTERNATIONAL BESTSELLING AUTHORS

C.M. STUNICH

&

TATE JAMES

Dark Glitter

ISBN-10: 179686773x (pbk.)
ISBN-13: 978-1-796867732(pbk.)

For information address:
Sarian Royal, 89365 Old Mohawk Road, Springfield, OR 97478

Contact the authors at
www.cmstunich.com
www.tatejamesauthor.com

this book is dedicated to our cats

Chapter One

CIARAH

My years of torment ended with a sharp gasp, my first breath of freedom tainted with the stench of rat shit and stale urine. That's what woke me from seemingly endless torture, the urban stink of a city.

Of course, I couldn't remember any of it.

As I blinked myself awake, my damaged mind pulled a curtain over the memories, a veil to shroud me from the pain. It wasn't something I had the energy to fight—or that I'd even want to if I could.

I peeled my heavy lids apart, the motion like the scraping of sandpaper against eyes too used to absolute darkness. It had been a *long* time since I'd seen even the dim, depressing lighting of an alleyway. How long, I didn't know. My memory was fractured glass, the pieces scattered and sharp.

I let out a small soundless scream when I came face-to-face with the wicked dark eyes of a rat. My back hit a dumpster as I scrambled frantically to get away from the small creature, my panicked gaze flicking around my new environment like a trapped animal. Tall brick walls rose up on either side of me, framing the navy velvet of a night sky.

Where the fuck am I?

It was dark, but streetlights and glowing neon signs lit the neighborhood outside of the alley I was crouched in. Shadows shrouded me, giving me a temporary feeling of security while I frantically searched my memory for where I was … or *who* I was.

My wrists and ankles ached and I could see thick bands of bruising and raw wounds around them, like I'd been held prisoner somewhere. Surely that would be the sort of thing that was impossible to forget? What the fuck had I done to deserve being held prisoner? It must've been something awful though, for me to feel this sick, this detached from my own body.

Hot iron, burning my flesh, scalding me, making me bleed.

I blinked and the random flash of memory was gone, tucked safely away from my fragile mind. It wouldn't do to dish up the demons of my past just yet. Closing my eyes against a wave of fatigue, I sucked in shallow breaths of the stale air, the scent of garbage tainting my tongue, and put a hand to my side. There was a burning sensation there, like a blade buried between my ribs. It made bile rise in my throat as I fought to control the churning of my stomach.

It was hard to decide which was worse off: my body … or my mind.

Fractured memories from different times and places assaulted me in waves. *A rowdy bar, a peaceful glade, the sun shining on the sea.* But they were puzzle pieces with no reference, just bits of color and shape I had no clue what to do with.

Had I been in jail, punished for a crime? That would explain the marks on my wrists and ankles, wouldn't it? But my clothes weren't like any sort of prison uniform I'd ever seen, just a dirty, bloodstained cotton dress and no shoes. The clothing didn't seem anywhere near appropriate for the weather; it was cold enough that I could see my breath misting in front of me, so I clearly hadn't planned to be out here …

My quiet panic was abruptly intruded on by a heavy metal door clanging open just feet from where I was crouched. A young girl in a greasy waitress uniform stepped out and propped the door open with a stray brick before lighting up a cigarette.

Terrified, I remained frozen to the spot, both figuratively and literally, praying she wouldn't see me. How on earth would I explain what I was doing out here? It was clearly the middle of winter and I was dressed in little more than a nightgown.

Oh yeah, and I had no memory of who I was let alone who it was I was running *from.*

“Hey, girl,” she said, spotting me, “what the hell are you doing lurking in this shit-filled alley?” The woman took a drag on her cigarette, blonde hair gathered back in a messy ponytail, stray strands curling wildly around her face.

She took a couple of steps closer to me, and I found myself preparing for a fight, awaiting the first blow with pursed lips and a defiant lift to my chin.

Wait.

The first blow?!

She was just a girl, and hadn't threatened me in any way, so why would I be shaking in terror the way I was?

“Hey …” she tried again in a gentle voice, crouching down until she was on my level, like I was a scared child or wild animal, someone that needed to be soothed and reassured with the basic, primal necessity of body language.

She held her cigarette in long, elegant fingers, using a painted blue thumbnail to flick the ash from its tip before taking another drag.

“I won't hurt you, sweetie,” she told me, and I could *sense* she was telling the truth. Was that normal? Could everyone *sense* the truth in someone's statement? I couldn't remember. But the certainty that she *wouldn't* hurt me made a noticeable difference in my anxiety level.

I’d hate to have to kill her.

Unfolding my arms from around my knees, I opened my mouth to speak, and say what? I didn't know. Maybe hello? It didn't matter, because all that came out was a squeaking gasp in place of my voice.

My throat was raw and scratchy, like I'd just gargled bleach, and the pain of trying to speak made my breath catch and a tear roll from my eye. I felt—although I couldn't remember exactly—that I'd shed many, many tears over my life. What was one more?

"Oh shit, babe," the girl hissed, stabbing out her cigarette and offering her hand to me like she was going to touch me; she stopped abruptly, seeming to think better of it. "Hon, you're in a really bad way. Come into the diner with me and I can get you something warm to drink. Fuck, you're practically a Smurf you're so blue."

All true.

I could *feel* it in my bones, that she was speaking the truth.

The waitress hazarded a smile that made the skin at the edges of her eyes crinkle. Even that move rang with the bright bells of honesty.

My hand trembled so hard, but I couldn't seem to stop it as I moved to push myself up from the ground; I would have fallen flat on my face if the girl hadn't caught me with a hand under my elbow. Everything on me *ached* and it took all the strength I had left to keep myself from throwing up as I pressed a hand to the pain in my side and found my feet. I wondered how bad I must really look to elicit such a response from this stranger.

"Don't worry, sweetie," the girl murmured as she helped me stumble toward the door she'd left chocked open, "we just closed the diner so it's all staff here. The coffee is still hot though, if you like coffee?"

Coffee? Of course I liked coffee. I didn't need all my memories to know *that.* Who the hell didn't like it? Not someone I would easily trust.

In lieu of words, I gave a non-committal shrug.

The girl helped me into the first booth we reached, the bench seat covered in gaudy red leather, and the tabletop patterned with the scratched surface of a checkerboard. The building smelled like grease and burnt coffee, but it had an easy, homey quality to it that I liked.

"Wait here, I'll be right back," she promised, twisting her hands in her apron and darting out of my line of sight, presumably to get the coffee. Fuck, she *better* be off getting it. The ache in my side was making my teeth hurt, red wetness seeping through the thin cotton of my gown.

I was bleeding.

I pressed a palm to the wound and waited—what else was I going to do? I didn't even know my own name.

The black and white squares of the tabletop mesmerized me as I stared at them, counting how many there were in a row from one side of the table to the other, so I had no idea how much time had passed when a man's voice jolted me out of my daze.

"Caley!" he boomed as he threw open the front door and stalked in like he owned the whole damn place. He was tall and broad, filling the doorframe like the diner was a funhouse, his heavy motorcycle boots tapping a solid sounding noise when he stalked across the sticky floor and stopped sharply in front of my table.

"Who …" he squinted at me, "the fuck are *you*?"

Slowly, I lifted my face in his direction … and it was like looking at the sun.

Warmth flowed over and through me as my lips parted and my heart began to pound inside my chest. I'd never seen this man before in my life, I was sure of it, and yet … there was something soothingly familiar about him, too.

The sharp emerald green of his eyes, framed by dark brown lashes, seemed to see right through me as he glared like I was something the cat had just dragged in. Which, I supposed, I sort of was. *I must seriously look like a hot mess to be getting this sort of reaction from total strangers …*

He had big, muscular arms, traced in ink and brilliant with color. I wanted to reach out and touch them, run my fingers over the curve of his biceps and feel the hardness underneath. He was a beautiful specimen of masculinity—even if he looked like a proper asshole, too.

"Arlo!" the waitress groaned, coming back out of the kitchen with a steaming mug of coffee and a towering plate of French fries. "What are you doing here so early? We had a deal, remember?"

"Yeah, we did. And you broke it. You were supposed to be home almost thirty goddamn minutes ago." The man, Arlo, dismissed me from his attention as he turned his glare on the waitress. Whether or not this was a normal reaction, I found myself leaning toward him, breathing in the sweet, musky scent of *earth.* Was it weird to sniff people? I had the gut feeling it most definitely *was.*

Is this her boyfriend? I wondered, looking between the two. *Her lover?* The man had the air of a controlling asshole; I was immediately wary of him and sympathetic for … Caley? That was her name, right? It matched up to the tag on her uniform, after all. She was curvy and very pretty. I didn't see any reason why he wouldn't want someone as beautiful as her. Certainly she was a good ten levels above my bedraggled state.

"What?" She frowned at him, looking confused, then darted her gaze to the clock on the wall and sighed. "Sorry, 'Lo. It was a crazy busy shift and I must've lost track of time." Caley placed the plate of food and mug of coffee down in front of me, and my belly grumbled loudly.

"Who's this?" the angry looking man demanded, throwing a disgusted look my way. I knew my cheeks were flaming with embarrassment. It was hardly *my* fault I looked like a drowned rat. Or at least, I didn't think it was.

"I found her in the alley out back. She's pretty beat-up and can't talk …" The young girl twisted her mouth into a frown. "I just wanted to get her warmed up and grab her some food, then maybe drop her over at the hospital to get checked out."

Unconsciously, I licked my dry and cracked lips.

Truth.

Each word she spoke was pure truth; I drank it all in like fine wine.

The man grunted, and didn't look at all pleased, but sat himself down in the booth opposite me. For a tense moment, our gazes remained locked. His bright green on my … whatever color mine were.

Eventually hunger overtook my need to win our stare-off, and I tentatively helped myself to some fries, chewing carefully and wincing in pain as I swallowed. Arlo continued to watch me as I ate, and I tried not to cry with the fresh pain lancing through my throat with each bite. But I couldn't … *wouldn't* … stop eating. The salty heat of these fries was like heaven, and I wondered when the last time I'd eaten was. It felt like it'd been years.

Caley gave me a sympathetic look and a small smile.

"Let me finish closing up, okay? Give her a chance to eat." She moved away while I scarfed down every last fry and every single sip of coffee. It was liquid *gold.* I felt immediately better after drinking it, although my side was still bleeding, hot droplets tracing down my ribs.

"Well, this is going to be interesting," Arlo muttered, eventually breaking the silence as I arched an eyebrow in question at him. "This," he gestured a hand at me, "I can't wait to see what Fionn says about *you.*"

"Arlo, you don't really have to tell Fionn, do you?" Caley gasped, coming to join us while rolling up her apron and shoving it into her backpack. "We can just drop her at the county hospital and be done with her, can't we?"

"You know the rules, Caley," Arlo shrugged, standing from his seat and glaring down at me like I'd somehow managed to disrupt his afternoon. "Anyone that sets foot in the diner that's not one of ours gets checked out by Fionn—human or no. Take her to the hospital and then bring her by the clubhouse."

As he turned away, I saw that the back of his leather vest had several patches. There were the letters *MC,* a small patch that said *1%er,* another that read *New Orleans, LA,* and the largest, central image featured a winged skull. The words *The Wild Hunt* were scrawled across the top.

Now, why did the fuck did that one sound so familiar?

It was with a healthy dose of caution that I followed Caley out of the diner to the dark, gloomy black surface of the parking lot. Despite her intentions and words ringing with truth, I couldn't shake the underlying feeling that there was much more going on than what was being said aloud. But of course, what choice did I have? I couldn't stay in the diner forever.

"Take your stray to Our Lady to get checked out," the man, Arlo, told Caley and flicked an annoyed look at me. "She reeks of blood." He snorted and shook his head, less like he felt sorry for me and more like I was an inconvenient annoyance to him. I guess since he was pretty, he didn't feel the need to be nice. "I'll see you back at the clubhouse."

She nodded her understanding, then flipped him off when he turned his back.

"Come on, girl. You need to see a doctor." Using her key in the lock of a rusty looking car, Caley yanked open the door and held it for me to get in. It seemed like a bad idea… to get in a car with a total stranger. Didn't it? My gaze darted around us, looking for alternative options, but what else was there? I had no memory of anything prior to waking up in that alleyway less than an hour ago.

A motorcycle revved its engine loudly, making me jump, and I saw Caley's boyfriend glaring at us from astride the metal monstrosity.

"I promise I don't mean you any harm," Caley coaxed, bringing my attention back to her and away from the piercing green eyes of her biker boyfriend. *True again.* Was it normal for people to tell so many truths? I couldn't remember. Unable to voice my concern, I nodded my head at the imposing man on the bike, and she got what I meant.

"He also means you no harm," she said carefully. There was something strange about the phrasing of that, but I couldn't put my finger on it. Caley smiled softly and reached out a hand like she might touch my arm, pausing when she saw the blood on the side of my dress. "Holy shit. You really *are* bleeding. Come on, hop in and we'll get that taken care of, okay?"

Glancing down, I saw Caley was right. Not only was my side going numb, but the patch of blood on my dress had seemingly doubled in size.

I needed medical attention.

There was no way around that. Nodding, I climbed into

the passenger seat of her car and sat tentatively. My backside was bruised and sore, much like the rest of me, so I needed to shift around a bit to get comfortable.

Caley slammed the car door, then hurried around to the driver's side and slid in, cranking the engine. As she shut her own door, a wave of nausea rolled over me and I clutched at the door handle.

"Shit, girl. You really are in a state, huh?" she commented, pulling out of the parking lot and onto the main road.

Without my voice, I was unable to tell her to stop. To let me out. To ask her what the fuck was happening to me. My stomach churned and I knew it was only a matter of time until I threw up. Clamping a hand over my mouth, I closed my eyes and felt my head swim with dizziness.

The pungent reek of smelted metal, silver droplets rolling down my skin and tracing ragged scars in my flesh. This smell was similar to that … that flicker of *something* buried deep inside my head. I railed against it, crushed the fragment of memory down but it was too late.

Something was really wrong.

The vehicle around me felt like a coffin, hurtling me toward a death I'd somehow managed to avoid for … for a long time. All this pain and bleeding, this dizziness and disorientation and yet I was still here.

But if I didn't get out of this car, I wouldn't be for long.

"Almost there," Caley said, her voice strained as she noticed my distress. I couldn't look at her though. I couldn't look at at anything. Instead, I kept my eyes squeezed shut and thought of that man, Arlo, and his beautiful green eyes, his glorious ink. I made myself imagine what it would feel like to have his big hands on my hips, lifting me up onto the edge of a table, stepping between my thighs …

"Fuck, finally," Caley breathed and my eyes snapped open as the car stopped moving, right in front of a large white building with a sign that read *Our Lady of Sorrow.*

I practically tore the door handle off in my panic to get out.

"Hey, whoa, calm down! It only opens from the outside, hang on."

Caley hopped out of her side and I waited, tense and sweating as she came around the car and opened the door for me. The second she did, I threw myself out and onto the pavement, panting and gasping as the intense nausea rolled and boiled in my belly. My head was fuzzy, my ears ringing with a high-pitched noise that made me feel like I was about to pass out.

"Let me help you inside, girl. You look even worse than you did before." Caley wrapped her arm around my middle and lifted me to my feet with surprising strength for her size. My breath sucked past my teeth in a silent gasp as her arm pressed into yet more injuries, but I ground my teeth together and walked with her into the hospital.

As soon as I stepped foot inside, I knew I'd made a mistake.

The bright lights blinded me and a sea of voices swelled into a cacophony inside my head.

"I told you—I was headed into the office after a late lunch." Lie. That was a lie. A man was staring a woman down near the reception area, one arm held limply at his side, the fingers of his other hand clutching his bicep like he was in pain.

"You're cheating on me, aren't you?" she asked with a small sniffle, and the man scowled.

"Of course I'm not," he snapped back, making me feel dizzy with the force of his words. They were said with such vehemence and yet, the lie was so powerful that it made me sick.

Or at least, *something* was making me sick.

I tore away from Caley's grasp and stumbled back outside, heading straight for a small patch of green and a row of spindly trees. As soon as my feet hit the moist earth, I felt better. Not great, just … better.

"Can you help me?" a thready voice asked, drawing my attention toward the sidewalk. Sinking to my knees in the wet earth seemed to help a little more and I felt my nausea sliding away a bit.

Until I saw the thing that was speaking to me.

"They spray the grass with poison twice a week," the creature said, its thin, bony arms like twigs about to snap. It was female, nude, with ashy skin and sunken cheeks, protruding ribs and legs no wider than its arms. "And the blood," it told me, pointing at the doors of the emergency room, "there's so much blood here, so much iron."

"Wait up!" Caley was shouting behind me, picking her way across the wet grass in heels.

"I'm dying," the creature told me, bending low in front of me, her eyes like stars in a withered face. I imagined she'd once been very pretty. Once…

But everything she said, it was the truth. I could feel her words like flashes of bright heat inside my chest, a small flame for each honest thing that was said. I was grateful for it, too, because the lies … those were the worst. They cut my heart open like blades.

"Babe, what are you doing?" Caley asked, pausing beside me and breathing heavily. "You don't need to be afraid of—"

"Take my spirit," the creature said, interrupting the waitress with a week, reedy exhale. "Put my energy to good use somewhere else."

"Are you …" Caley came around to stare at me … and then at the dying girl … and then me again. "Oh shit … You can see the dryad?"

I kept my gaze on the strange woman with the sunken cheeks, her sallow skin lit by the fluorescent red of the *Emergency Room* sign. I decided briefly to ignore Caley. Of course I could see the woman. Why wouldn't I be able to?

"Give me your hand," she said, reaching out spindly fingers with cracked nails. On her back, a pair of shriveled wings rustled, small bits of silver and gold falling to the grass near her heels.

"Girl, I hope you know what you're doing," Caley said,

putting her fingers in her blonde hair and staring down at the pair of us like we were crazy. Maybe I was crazy? I wasn't sure. There had to be *some* reason I'd been tied up, some reason I couldn't remember who I was. But I did know this—I could help the dryad. That was something I was sure of.

My hand was a pale blue color when I reached it out toward the girl, such a different shade than all the people I'd seen clustered inside the hospital. They ranged from dark brown to pale white, but none of them were blue.

"Thank you," the girl said as her fingers wrapped around mine, her words ringing with so much truth that I felt my heart skitter and jump. "Thank you."

Light flickered at the places our fingers touched, dancing like sparks across our skin, but then … something went wrong.

The light shimmered, darkened, went out, and then I felt it, like a knife in my side.

"Oh fuck," Caley gasped as the dryad girl drew her hand away from me, watching in horror from eyes like starlight. "This isn't good at all."

I grasped my side, fingers digging at the fabric of my loose cotton dress. Through a small hole in the fabric, I could feel it oozing hot and fresh—more blood. Too much. It was wet and warm and red, sticky against my fingers.

"You need to run," the dryad said, standing up and backing away from me like I was cursed. But it wasn't me that she was scared of—it was something else. "You need to go *now.*"

Truth, truth, truth.

Both women were speaking with truth … and fear.

I didn't know why, but I believed them: it was time to run.

I stood up, but Caley grabbed me by the arm before I could get very far.

"You better come with me," she said, her voice soft but her eyes bright.

I thought about it for a minute, but where else did I have to go?

Nowhere.

I had nowhere and for the moment, I was nobody.

I decided to swallow my fear and follow along for the ride, the sunken cheeks and shimmering eyes of the dryad haunting me long after we left the parking lot.

Chapter Two
REECE

The girl I'd been fucking was now fast asleep and drooling all da hell over my pillow. I stared at her for a couple o' moments, smoking my cigarette, and then stepped out into the hall and shut the door to da damn room.

"You aren't leaving another one in dere for me to clean up, are you brother?" asked Donal as I made my way into the common room and paused, staring the vice president of the club down for a long moment. He was my superior so it woulda been prudent to look away, sure, but I was a dumbass on a good day, me.

"I'm just on my way to see Meme," I said with a shrug, and heard Donal cursing under his breath.

"I'd just as soon eat her as I'd feed the bitch!" he called

after me as I stepped outside, boots loud against the wood of the dock. An eerie fog hung over the water, broken up by clusters of Spanish moss and gnarled oak limbs.

I cracked open the old freezer next to the building's grubby exterior and pulled out a container of chicken, popping the lid and grabbing a raw leg.

“'Ey Meme!” I shouted, tossing the container back into the freezer and grabbing a bag of marshmallows to take wit' me. “Come 'ere, girl!”

I moved down da length of the dock and paused, knowing I looked like a fuckin' asshole and not carin' one bit. I made *quacking* sounds to try and draw da gator to the dock and then tossed a few 'mallows out there for her to munch on. Whenever I tried to bring girls out 'ere to impress 'em with da gators, they always asked me how I knew da damn things liked marshmallows. But what kind o' stupid question is that? Everybody know gators like marshmallows.

After a few moments, I saw her, gliding through the water toward me, her dark green head just barely visible in the fog. If I wasn't fae, I probably wouldn't come out here alone in the dark like dis. Meme was small for a gator, but there were others out dere in the swamp—I knew because the club often used 'em to dispose of bodies.

“Hey girl, where you been?” I asked, using the pole at the end of the dock to hook the chicken leg to. I dangled it out over the water and watched as Meme lifted her long, ugly snout out to grab hold of it. With a crunch of bone, she disappeared under the dark waters again.

I stood there for a few, takin' drags on my smoke, when the sound of a car drew my attention back toward the hard packed dirt of the parking lot. We didn't exactly get a lot o' visitors out 'ere in da bayou.

"Looks like even if we stay outta trouble, trouble finds us, eh, Meme?" I tossed a handful of marshmallows into the water and headed up the length of the dock and back inside. I stepped in through the rickety old screen door just in time to see Caley dragging this thin, frail wisp of a girl into the common room.

"She's got iron in her side, I think," Caley was saying as she helped the girl into one of da old couches. I saw right away that there was blood—fae blood, sure—but the stink o' iron was unmistakable.

"And you brought her here, why?" Donal was asking, looking more annoyed than anything else as he stroked a hand down the dark, thick length of his beard.

"Arlo said Fionn needed to see her," Caley began, ruffling up her hair and lookin' like she was in serious need of a nap or some shit. I just hoped all this raucous didn't wake da girl I left in the dorm room.

"Well, Fionn ain't here," I said, moving over to stand next to the wilting fae on the club's couch. Her skin was a pale blue, almost white, but she was clearly still entertainin' some sort of broken glamour. I could smell it on 'er almost as bad as I could smell da iron. Who knew what she'd look like without it? I wouldn't be gettin' human girls for my bed if I wasn't wearin' one, that's for damn sure.

"I found her outside the diner," Caley said, huffing out a breath and wiping sweaty palms on her uniform. "I don't think 'Lo knew she was fae or else he wouldn't have suggested I take her to the hospital …"

"You took her to da damn hospital?" Donal roared and then closed his eyes for a long moment. "May da goddess help you, you stupid girl."

"The glamour's faded a lot since I got her there," Caley said defensively, wrapping her arms around herself. Guess the girl couldn't help herself—she *was* half-human after all. "She wasn't this color and she didn't smell *this* bad until after …" She paused and leaned in close to Donal and me. "Someone is missing this girl *bad*. That iron in her side, it's got a dampening spell. That, and when she used her magic, I could *feel* it—some sort of signal went out."

I turned my attention back to the frail, wispy thing sitting on the couch.

When she looked up at me, her eyes had the force of a goddamn train. I felt like I was just waiting for the collision, that I was looking at somethin' powerful, something old. And those eyes, like two sapphires, dark and thick wit' magic … I could damn near drown in 'em.

"Get yourself under control, *brudder*," Donal mumbled, flicking me in the crotch. That's when I realized that I was holding onto a rock-hard cock inside my jeans. Over this frail thing? I'd break da girl if I tried to fuck her. The hell was wrong with me? "And call your daddy."

"He's my president same as he is yours," I snarled

under my breath, turning away from the girl before I could think too hard about the rapid beating of my heart or the thickening of my cock. No way, no hell.

I was not gettin' mixed up with a woman as troublesome as all that.

I made enough trouble all on
my own.

Chapter Three

CIARAH

Sitting on the strange couch in the strange room, I felt a sense of … sameness from the man staring down at me, the one who turned away with a curse and removed a phone from his pocket. Watching him, I noticed the emblem on his leather vest was the same as the one the man at the diner had been wearing.

A white skull sat atop an iridescent pair of green butterfly wings. The words beneath it—The Wild Hunt—stirred my memory and made me lick my lips.

I remembered that; I *knew* about that.

But I didn't know why.

And the man wearing the vest? Well, it wasn't *just* the design on his back that was making me lick my lips. He had a thick head of red-brown hair, full ripe lips surrounded by a dusting of stubble, and big muscular arms with rounded biceps and scattered black and gray tattoos. They danced when he moved, teased into action by the strong muscles underneath his tanned skin.

He was *mesmerizing.*

"Alright dere, girl. Start spillin'," another man with a long beard said, standing directly in front of me and folding his arms over his chest. He didn't *look* any older than the other guy—the one with the auburn hair that shimmered like rubies when he moved beneath the lights—yet something about the way this other man held himself said he was older, and in charge.

"Donal, quit with the intimidating shit," Caley yawned, slapping the bearded guy on the arm. "Cleary, she can't talk. She's pretty beat-up too. Look at her wrists."

Donal grunted and narrowed his eyes at Caley. "Girl, don't go beatin' around the bush with me. You want Killian to come check her out then you damn well say so."

"Sorry, D." She grinned. "Just trying to be *demure* like Mama always says I should be."

"Your Ma is human. It's different rules for humans." He turned his shrewd stare back to me, darting his gaze down to my raw wrists, then at my threadbare dress and purple-black bruises down my arms. My hand still clutched at the seeping blood in my side, and I was barely containing the overwhelming need to dig out the piece of metal with my fingernails.

"Alright, Reece!" the bearded man, Donal, yelled. "C'mere boy!"

"I ain't your boy, D," the attractive man who'd been on

the phone muttered as he ended his call and rejoined us. His warm brown eyes ran over me in a way that was almost … *lustful*? That couldn't be right. The pain must be messing with my head. “What you want, anyhow?” He ran a tattooed hand through his short auburn hair then scratched at the stubble on his chin. It was clear he was speaking to the other guy, Donal, but his eyes remained locked on mine like we were magnets.

“Need you to call Killian to come check our guest out.” Donal folded his arms over his massive chest and scowled at me, which finally allowed me to break from the sexy red-haired man's gaze.

Reece. It suited him.

He and Donal both were as big, if not bigger than Caley's boyfriend had been, and I raked through my murky mind to figure out if this was normal or not. Of course, I couldn't remember.

“Sure thing, VP,” Reece muttered, pulling his phone back out of his black jeans and tapping on the screen with his long, elegant fingers. I wondered what those fingers would feel like against my skin, running through my hair, touching my—

“Don't worry, babe.” Caley snapped me out of my daydream, plonking herself down beside me on the couch. “Killian is a healer. He can sort you out, and then maybe you can tell us who you are?”

Blinking at her, I turned this information over in my mind. Even if I could speak, I couldn't tell her who I was. I had no idea. How the hell had I ended up in a situation like this? And why was I not in the least concerned that they were talking like I wasn't human?

"Killian's on his way back now and da ol' man will be 'ere in a couple of hours. He's over in Baton Rouge sorting out some politics." Reece's intense gaze swung back to me as he delivered this news to Caley and Donal, and I shifted awkwardly. Even if the bruises all over my body—and the bleeding wound in my side—hadn't been making me uncomfortable, the force of his stare had me practically shaking.

"Fucking hell," Donal spat, stroking his beard. "Forgot he was doing that today. Caley girl, take your broken bird upstairs for a shower. Maybe wash a bit of that iron stink off her before Killian gets back? You know how sensitive that boy's nose is."

"Sure thing, D." Caley hopped up from the couch and extended a hand covered in rings to me. "Come on, hon, let's get you cleaned up."

Eyeing up her offered hand *again*, I hesitated a moment. My eyes flickered over to Reece, almost as though I was checking with him that this was safe? But that couldn't be right. These people were total strangers to me; Caley was the only one I'd known for more than a few minutes. So why would I be looking to this beautiful man for reassurance?

"I'll take her," Reece said suddenly, stepping forward to nudge Caley out of the way. He bent down, sweeping me up in his strong arms and startling a soundless gasp from my aching throat.

"Reece, um …" Caley started, chewing her lower lip and frowning.

"That's not a good idea, boy," Donal grunted in his strange accent. Now that I'd heard a few more sentences out of him, it seemed like a mix of Irish and Cajun.

How on earth did I know what both Irish and Cajun accents sounded like yet I didn't know my own name? This was insanity.

"Yer opinion is noted, VP, but she needs help rebuilding 'er glamour and Caley is too watered-down to do that for her." Reece's chest vibrated against my body as he spoke and I resisted the urge to lean in closer to him.

So far, everything these people had said was *truth*, and a small part of my brain supplied the information I was looking for.

They were fae. Fae couldn't lie.

Not that they didn't, but they physically *couldn't* lie. Suddenly the careful way they were phrasing their sentences made more sense, like how Caley had told me that Arlo *meant* me no harm. Not that he *wouldn't* harm me.

"Yeah, but I think you can at least let her shower alone, Reece," Caley suggested, ruffling a hand through her short hair and yawning heavily again. "We have no idea what she's been through or how she ended up like this, and the last thing we need you doing is scaring her into taking off. Look, she's fucking terrified of you!"

Oh.

I *was* trembling, but not in fear. No, as soon as Reece

scooped me into his arms and pressed my thin, frail body against his chest, the warmth and smell of him overwhelmed me. This woody citrus and spicy scent mixed with the smell of sweat, a masculine concoction that made my chest feel tight and … other things.

I wet my lips as the bearded man—Donal—stepped in front of Reece and gave him a look that could cut.

"You sassin' me again, boy?" he asked as I leaned my head against Reece's chest and closed my eyes. The rapid thump bass beat of his heart soothed my own racing pulse and I sighed, laying a hand against the flatness of his pecs beneath his dark t-shirt. "Don't you go gettin' a big head because your daddy's the president. You have superior officers to answer to, brother."

Donal paused his rant for a moment and when I cracked my eyes, I saw he was looking right at me. With a sigh, he waved his hand dismissively.

"Fine. Take 'er upstairs then but wipe that smirk off your damn face."

Reece made a low growl in his throat that I don't think he meant for anyone to hear, but I *felt* it. It vibrated through my cheekbones and into my teeth. It made me wonder for a brief moment what that growl would *taste* like if I were to put my mouth to his.

"Reece?" a voice asked from my right. I heard the distinctive sound of *want* in the flowery, feminine words. Glancing over, I found a girl with glimmering gold skin and translucent wings, like a dragonfly's. *Pixie,* my brain supplied, yet another tidbit of information that made no sense in its sudden reveal. It was like my mind was a puzzle, and I was desperately collecting the pieces.

Remembering my own name would help substantially.

"Goddamn you, Reece," Donal said as the man in question turned, ignoring the pixie's multifaceted eyes and heading straight for a set of rough wooden steps against the far wall, the ones with no railing. "This is why you should stick to club whores."

I watched as the pixie girl came forward and lifted her lips in a snarl, revealing a row of sharp, gold teeth. It was clear her anger was directed not at Reece but at *me.*

"Sorry about that, girl," he told me as we ascended the stairs and I watched the pixie lunge forward, dropping the blanket she was holding and revealing the smooth gold lines of her naked body. Donal stopped her before she got very far, and then we were up the stairs and on the second floor. "I try to be frank with 'em, but they never listen—it's da magic. They can't help themselves, no."

Truth.

The bright bells of honesty rang with each word that fell from this gruff man's lips. Without really knowing what I was doing, I lifted a finger and touched the rough, torn surface of a fingertip to Reece's mouth.

Energy passed between us, like a kiss of lightning, drawing whatever it was that *he* had inside himself straight into me.

I felt it hit me like a shockwave, coalescing around the iron in my side and attacking it like it had claws. A scream ripped raw and ragged from my damaged throat, sparking the awful realization of a broken memory.

Iron burning my wrists, my ankles, my neck. Screaming but never being heard. Broken but never able to get whole. Pain, blood, darkness.

"The hell are you doing, girl?!" Reece asked as the piece of iron fell from my side and clattered to the floor, blood staining my threadbare cotton dress, dripping across the leather toes of the large man's feet.

When I lifted my head up and looked into his face, it was unrecognizable. Gone was the red-brown hair and short, scruffy beard, the skin teased to a warm brown from the sun … Instead, I was looking at someone else entirely.

"You cracked my glamour, you," he said, blinking in shock. "Oh, and a whole hell of a lot of somethin' else."

My tongue ran across my lips as a warm fire took over my lower belly, pooling between my thighs, making me ache. My nipples pebbled beneath my dress, so painfully tight that they made my breath catch.

What are you? I wondered as my body was wracked with even more intense tremors, my eyes taking in Reece's new form. His hair was now bloodred and his skin, it was a soft, muted gold color. His smile, that was savage … savage and sex.

I could remember sex—brief flashes here and there. I'd certainly had it, plenty of it, but it had been a while. It'd been a great many whiles.

"You feel it, don't you, girl?" Reece whispered, his breath warm against my ear as he leaned in, the scent of tobacco and leather mixing with his own unique smell.

"You just borrowed a bit of ol' Reece's magic."

He flashed a grin at me, his teeth white in the gently shimmering planes of his face. He didn't sparkle so much as he seemed to *burn,* like the sun. Oh the sun … I could hardly remember what that looked like.

But the expression on Reece's face and the feeling inside of me … My body remembered that, even if my mind didn't.

Coupling, heat, tongues and teeth, hands and fingers, cunts and cocks.

"You're gonna need more than just a rebuild of dat glamour, girl."

I wet my lips again, but try as I might, I couldn't speak. Not yet. Instead, I cupped the sides of Reece's face and leaned in, pressing our mouths together. Heat was rolling over me, flames of lust that seemed to burn. The aching want I felt inside of me, it was almost painful.

Our lips brushed slow and hot, tongues teasing before he pulled back and looked down at me, nestled there in his arms.

"They woulda called me a *dia gnéas* back in the old country, you know? Before the famine drove all them Irish outta dere." Reece moved down the hallway and kicked in a door at the end of it, letting us into a large bathroom with a clawfoot tub in the center. The floor was the same rough-hewn wood as the rest of the building, but burned into it were symbols, and as Reece and I walked over them, they *glowed.*

"That's a *god of sex,* in case you weren't caught up on

your Gaelic. *Dieu du sexe* if we're speaking French." Reece paused next to the tub, still looking at me as I squirmed with need and wet my lips. I didn't much care about the blood draining from my side either. Not that or anything else. Whatever I'd done by touching Reece, I felt this primal sexual need that *had* to be satisfied.

Bending low, Reece laid me on the cold, scratched porcelain and then flashed another terrible, wicked grin.

"Dress off, girl," he told me, reaching down and curling warm fingers around my forearms, carefully avoiding the raw, bruised patches near my elbows. Reece lifted my arms above my head and then reached down, taking the ratty dress in his large hands, hands that shone like gold, etched with dark swirls that chased up the muscular curves of his own arms and beneath his shirtsleeves.

I did what he asked because why not? I wanted him, naked and hard and on top of me. My breath caught as the scratchy fabric slid over my body and away, landing in a heap on the floor beside the tub.

Reece stared down at me, his face a wild mask of gold and black, and then he stepped away, heeling the door shut and pressing his fingertips to the wall. Sigils, runes, whatever they were, flared to life all across the faded, splintered wood walls, a match to the ones burning to life on the floor beneath the biker's feet.

I watched him carefully, shivering as I sat naked and bruised inside a tub in a strange shack in the middle of the bayou. *Have I really never been here before?* I wondered as Reece approached me again, shrugging out of his leather vest and setting it aside with a sort of reverence that intrigued me.

All that care … for a piece of clothing?

Surely there was more to it than that.

"Let's put that glamour back in place, girl," he told me as I blinked heavy lids and touched my hands to my breasts. Whatever Reece had done to me with his magic, they now felt heavy and sore, desperate to be touched.

I wet my lips again, but I couldn't make myself talk. I *wanted* to, but my battered throat just wouldn't obey my commands.

Instead, I watched as Reece turned on the rusted old tap and grinned as I shrunk back from the cold water. As it swirled down the drain, I drew my knees up and lifted my face to the small square window across from me, out at a night as dark as pitch and trees dripping with Spanish moss and secrets.

Where am I? I wondered because although I remembered that this was a bayou, a swamp, I couldn't remember what state or province I was in, what country even … what *world.* Because I knew instinctively that things were not always what they seemed …

"There ya go," Reece said as the water began to steam and he leaned in to plug up the tub. "We'll get ya all warmed up dere." He sat back on his haunches and watched me with eyes like the turning leaves of autumn, a warm brown color that said they'd just recently bid their goodbyes to the trees. "You smell somethin' awful, you know dat, you?"

Reece stood up once again and moved to a large cabinet in the corner, opening up the doors and selecting several glass bottles. When he made his way back over and started popping the corked tops, the air was perfumed with the sweet scent of flowers and growing things.

Petals drifted into the bathwater and turned it a cheery pink color. It felt good, that heated water swirling against my damaged skin, but it wasn't enough. It didn't satisfy these new needs that Reece had heaped on me.

"You're one of da gentry that's for sure, yeah?" he asked me, mixing several more ingredients in the water—dried leaves, bits of dirt, ground spices that smelled like cloves, and sweet-scented liquids. "But *what* exactly you are, I can't even begin ta guess."

Reece reached out toward me, running a single finger along a ridge that bordered my spine, teasing rough, ragged flesh that I hadn't even known was there. Glancing over my shoulder, I couldn't even see the awful scar he traced.

"Plucking da wings off a butterfly," he murmured, his eyes going sad and dark for a moment before he flicked them back to me and grinned, slow and sharp, like a gator. A gator. See, I knew what a gator was. "You ready, girl?" he asked, and then, with the last bottle set aside, Reece knelt next to the tub on his denim-clad knees, using one hand to grip my hair and tug my head back. The other, he slipped beneath the colored waters and between my thighs.

My breath escaped in a sharp gasp as he played along that aching, desperate part of me with two careful fingers, teasing the swollen flesh with sure strokes. His right hand kept me anchored as he leaned in and took my mouth, igniting all of that lust inside of me, like fireworks freshly lit. The matches burned, the fuses smoldered, and I was nothing but an explosion of feeling.

A moan creaked past my lips, brushed against Reece's as he chuckled and teased me some more, running a pair of fingertips from my clit down to my ass and back again.

"Whatever you are," he whispered as I bit his lower lip on impulse, "you taste like magic."

Reece thrust his fingers into my opening and oh, it was … it was exquisite, like coming home after a long trip. I was tight, almost painfully so, but the lust he'd fired up in me needed to be slaked, satisfied.

Our tongues slid along one another's as the runes flared on the floor, the ceiling, the walls, across the glass panes of the single window. Reece hooked his fingers inside of me, teased my inner walls while his thumb brushed the painfully hard nub of my clit.

Cracking my lids just a bit, I lifted a hand up to Reece's face and touched wet fingers to his skin. The pale blue color of my flesh shifted, warming into a peachy-pink, like sunshine over rose petals. And as my own appearance morphed and changed, so did his.

The gold of his skin faded away, the redness of his hair dimmed.

Glamour.

The old faerie word for a magic skin, one that sealed the wearer's true form away from the world.

I remembered that now.

Rubbing my cheek along Reece's stubbled one, I dug the fingers of my left hand into the fabric of his t-shirt and scraped my nails down the side of his throat with the other. The gruff stranger worked me into a frenzy with his hand, fanning the flames in my lower belly until they took over everything, igniting me in a sudden blaze that wracked my body and brought a small scream from my throat.

"Oh," I whispered as I shivered in the wake of the orgasm, trembling and blinking through the haze. "Oh."

"Oh?" Reece asked, giving me one last flick of his fingers before pulling away. "Not bad for a first word, eh, girl?"

I stared at him, glancing down at my naked body, fresh and pink, all of my scars and bruises gone from sight. I could *feel* them, but I couldn't see them—not anymore.

Hmm.

Reece was right—not bad for a first word, not bad at all.

Loud male voices made me tense and jump as I cautiously

padded my way back down from the bathroom.

After Reece had resorted my glamour, and reawakened my body, he'd left me to get cleaned up on my own. At first I'd been a bit offended that he hadn't wanted to stay, but the lust quickly melted from me in his absence and I was able to enjoy the warm water in peace.

Reece was right: I did smell awful.

He'd left me with several bottles of floral scented products on the side of the tub so I took my time testing them all out and ended up washing my hair three times. Wherever I had been, shampoo must not have been available … I needed to use almost half the bottle of conditioner and let it sit for a few minutes so I could comb through the tangles, too. Despite the glamour giving my hair the *appearance* of being healthy and soft, I could feel its true condition.

Once clean to the point of wrinkly, I had gingerly toweled dry and dressed myself in the clothes that Reece had left for me.

Tiptoeing down the stairs, I chewed on my chapped lip and debated my options. There was clearly an argument going on in the living room where I had first met Reece and Donal, and it sounded like there were several more men present which scared me on a primal level.

The few fractured memories I had regained spoke of violence, torture, and *pain*. What if these people had something to do with it? Why else would I remember what a bayou was? Or a gator?

"Girl?" Reece's rumbling voice broke through my

spiraling thoughts and I gasped. He stood at the foot of the stairs I was frozen on, looking up at me with an amused, *hungry* look on his face.

My body flushed with heat under his gaze, and my nipples hardened to rocks once more. It had to be his magic. What had he said he was? A god of sex?

“Don' you look at me with them accusing eyes, girl,” he warned, reaching out a huge arm and snagging my hand to pull me the rest of the way down the stairs. “Ah, ah. I know what you be thinking, *bebelle.* But Old Reece ain't never forced magic on the unwilling. What you be feelin' is just because you got the hots, y'hear?”

I couldn't exactly respond, so just narrowed my eyes at him suspiciously. His words rang with *truth* though, so I had no choice but to believe what he said. Whoever I was, or whoever I had been, I was apparently *overwhelmingly* attracted to huge, red-haired Irish-Cajun men with fingers like damn magic.

“Now you c'mon through here so Killian can patch you up. See if he can't sort out that voice situation for you, no?” He arched a brow at me and gestured through to the common room where the voices had all but stopped their argument.

“There she is,” Caley announced as I stepped into the room. “Hey girl, you look way better after a shower! Sorry the clothes are a bit big for you.”

The clothes in question were a pair of cut-off denim shorts which hung loose around my narrow, bony hips, and a teal green tank top. No undergarments had been provided and I was acutely aware of my nipples standing firm like headlights under the heavy gaze of four men and Caley.

"Should be fine once I get her healed." This came from the one man who I didn't recognize, so must have been Killian. Donal and Arlo, Caley's boyfriend, were both standing with arms folded across their chests, watching me.

The new one, Killian, was just as huge as the other guys but with ink black hair and a scruffy shadow of stubble over his face. As he came closer to me, I tensed and flinched back a step. His cold, ice-blue eyes seemed to see straight through me into my soul, uncovering information *I* didn't even possess.

"Don' be scared, *bebelle*," Reece murmured, laying a hot hand on my lower back and keeping me from retreating any further. "Kill is all bark and no bite, unless you ask 'im real nice like. That trick 'e's doin' with his eyes is just checkin' you for damages."

"I apologize," the dark-haired man said in a quiet voice, one that held danger and intrigue. It simultaneously scared me and made me curious. I mean, Reece called him Kill … and I got the feeling it was more than just his Cajun-Irish way of shortening words.

"Let the damn girl sit, Kill!" Arlo snapped, glowering at him.

"You shut it, boy," Donal warned. "You could have really fucking screwed the pooch sendin' her off to the damn 'ospital, ya know."

"I know." Arlo's mouth turned down in a frown as he glared at me. That same level of annoyance and disgust was still there, the same way it had been at the diner when Caley had first found me.

"You better be damn glad ya sister was a quick thinker, or who knows what level of fuckery we coulda landed in from that tracking spell, yeah?" Donal glowered at Arlo and he finally dragged his intense gaze away from me.

Sucking in a deep breath, I realized I'd all but stopped breathing under the combined weight of Arlo's, Reece's, and Killian's stares.

What the fuck was going on? And did Donal just say that Caley was Arlo's sister?

"Here, sit." Killian gestured to the couch and I hesitantly perched on the edge of it. He sat himself down on the coffee table, but he was so huge his knees ended up pressed to mine. "You're pretty badly beat-up, especially for a fae. We heal so quickly as it is … They must have used a *lot* of iron."

Whips tipped in metal, cutting through my flesh like it's made of butter. Blood. So much blood.

I flinched as the memory slapped me in the face. What the hell had happened to me? What had I done to deserve such violence?

"Make sure ya sort 'er voice box, Kill," Reece added, "so she can tell us who she be. And *what*."

"She's fae. What makes you think she's anything *more*?" Arlo scowled, coming to perch on the other end of the couch.

"Ya didn't see 'er without da glamour," Reece grunted. "She ain't no fae I've ever laid eyes on. And she triggered my magic with jus' a touch of 'er thumb ta my lips."

Both Killian and Arlo jerked back and glared at Reece while Donal sighed wearily.

"Reece, you didn't ..." Killian exclaimed, looking mortified.

"Nah, I'm old enough fer a bit more self-control than dat. Old Reece jus' did what was needed for da magic—nothin' more, nothin' less." The heat in Reece's gaze spoke volumes on the *more* that I still so desperately wanted from him.

"Get on with it, Kill," Donal interrupted. "I'm going to take care of some shit, but I expect this one healed and singin' like a bird by the time Fionn gets back. Understood?"

"*Oui*, sir," Killian responded, and the bearded man left us alone.

Curiously, only Reece and Donal spoke with the thick Cajun-Irish mix. Killian sounded French, while Arlo and Caley just sounded straight-up clean American, with maybe a hint of a Southern accent.

"Ready, *cher*?" Killian murmured to me, recapturing my gaze in his frosty ice-blue stare. It sounded like he said *sha* but my complicated brain knew it was *cher.* I nodded hesitantly and his lips pursed. "Alright then, let's begin."

His huge palms cradled my face as he brought his own close enough to mine that everything else was blocked out around us. All I could see was the bottomless, cool blue of his eyes, and smell his crisp, fresh scent. Like early morning frost on a dead still forest.

"This is going to feel strange. Don't fight it." His words echoed around my head and I was unsure if it had been said aloud or not. I tried to nod my understanding but my face was held firm in his hands.

Killian sucked in a slow, deep breath, then as he exhaled it seemed like his breath rushed all through my body from head to toe and everywhere in between. He was *inside* me, exploring every inch of me with ice-cold mist. As he travelled, he paused routinely, paying extra attention to various injuries on my body, both old and new.

Time passed, I don't know how long. All I could see was blue, for miles. All I could feel was cold. But despite this, I felt safe. My mind watched with fascination as Killian's magic worked its way through my psyche, healing my physical form from the inside.

Eventually, he reached my throat and I watched as his misty magic showed me the damage that had been done. My vocal cords were shredded, like wet cheese, and the tissue surrounding my voice box was inflamed and raw. There was no doubt in my mind that without Killian's magic, I would have never spoken again. How I had even managed the small noises Reece had coaxed out of me was a mystery.

Gently, Killian smoothed my damaged throat back together until it was as good as new, then paused. For a timeless moment, his magic stared into my soul and a sharp stab of pain filled my head.

My consciousness slammed back into my physical form and I cried out as the pain chased me. My hands clutched at Killian's where they still held my face firm, clawing and desperate to make the pain stop.

Make it stop!

Even as my fingernails dug into the skin of his hands, he pulled me closer, sealing his mouth to mine and breathing his magic back into me once again. That cold mist raced straight to my head and soothed the pain, wiping it away and leaving me light-headed and dizzy.

Killian retracted his magic almost as fast as he had sent it out, but when we both returned to our corporeal forms, his lips were still on mine. Slowly, his mouth moved but not to pull away as I had expected. Instead, his lips coaxed mine apart and his tongue slipped into my mouth, reigniting the fire in my belly which had started with Reece earlier.

I sucked in a gasp, my breath catching as Killian took the kiss deeper. His hands still held my face firm and his mouth dominated me like he was staking a claim.

"Kill!" A deep voice cracked across the room like a whip, and I jerked backward out of the dark-haired man's grip.

"Sir, you're back already?" Killian responded, with his eyes still glued to mine. His voice sounded breathy and exhausted, and there were dark circles under his eyes.

"Already?" The man grunted. "Boy, you've been healing this *pauvre bête* for near on six hours now."

"What?" I gasped, then flinched at the sound of my

own voice. It was the first time I had really heard it, to my knowledge.

"You heard me, girl," the man replied from his position seated in an armchair across the room from us. Killian stood from his perch on the coffee table and stretched. His arms rose up above his head and almost bumped into the lazily turning ceiling fan, and his shirt rode up to expose a chiseled expanse of abs.

"Look like Kill 'ere sorted out yer voice situation," the man continued, and I refocused my attention on him, rather than on that delicious V just above Killian's low-slung black jeans.

The newcomer was yet another huge man, but magic and danger rolled off him in waves that I could almost *see*. His hair was long, brushing his thighs as he sat forward with forearms braced across his knees. His beard was as long as Donal's but Fionn's hair had a dark, bloodred shade not dissimilar to the color Reece's had gone when his glamour was dropped.

"Um, yes," I responded, but my voice came out in a thin sort of whisper and I glanced up at Killian in panic.

"Don't stress yourself, *cher*," he reassured me, sitting himself down on the couch close enough that our thighs were touching. "It's healed but just needs a bit of use to get back to normal. Right now your vocal cords are still tight from the healing."

"That's good work, boy." Fionn nodded to Killian. "Girl musta been in a right state for six hours o' healin'."

"She was," Killian murmured, and draped an arm over

my shoulders to pull me in close to his side. "Where'd the boys go?"

"Sent 'em out to deal with the *rougarou.*" Fionn spat this word like it was a curse. It wasn't one I was familiar with, so I kept my mouth shut. "Bastards have been acting up again. Forgetting their place 'ere in the bayou."

He stared at me for a long, quiet moment, his eyes the color of mud mixed with blood. *Where did an image like that come from?* It disturbed me that I had a thought like that so readily available and yet … no idea where it originated from.

"*Rouga—*" I coughed out, struggling to get past the feeling of words slipping from the tight, painful confines of my throat. I had the feeling these words weren't just the first ones I'd spoken since waking up in the alley … but my first words for a long, *long* time.

Years.

"Rougarou," I whispered, just to hear myself talk. My voice was as smooth as broken glass in gravel. It was almost as painful to listen to as it was to speak. But to have a voice again? There wasn't a gift in the heavens or the many hells below this earth that could make up for that. "A werewolf?"

I wet my lips and then felt my entire body go stiff when Caley handed me an ice-cold can of soda. This, I remembered. But from where? And how?

I stared at the lid of the can for a long, quiet moment, the sounds of the bayou fierce and wild outside the walls. I could hear the distinct grunting of gators, the calls of night birds, and the terrified squeaks of those who were nothing but prey.

"Sort of," Killian said, his voice kissed with the slightest hint of a French accent. Not Cajun or Creole, but Parisian. *Parisian.* What was Parisian? The thought had popped into my head seemingly unbidden. I didn't know what Parisian was, only that Killian had that air.

Clearly there was something wrong with my brain.

"A rougarou is a *magicked* wolf as opposed to a born one," he told me, leaning back into the couch with his leather vest slung over his shoulders, his muscles smooth and hard, inked with designs similar to the markings I'd seen on Reece's unglamoured face.

"A magicked wolf," I whispered and felt the sudden urge to sing. Something old and ancient flittered through my mind, like the long forgotten words in a crumbling book. I began to hum and the air around me shivered, like pavement on a hot day.

"Whoa, there, *bebette,*" the long-haired man said, leaning over and putting a hand on my knee. As soon as his fingers touched my bare leg, I felt a rush of power and a spark of fear. Whoever this man was, he was powerful. "Don't go throwin' 'round that kinda magic unless you know what yer doing, you."

"What's your name, *mon cher*?" Killian asked, studying me with white-blue eyes, like an Arctic sea, an endless stretch of nothing that somehow meant *everything.*

"My name?" I asked, blinking heavy-lidded eyes at

him. I felt … almost content, sitting here in this strange old room in the middle of a swamp. There were men on either side of me that I didn't know, and as far as I knew it, my entire world had changed.

Years of torture.

Endless pain.

And now … blissful silence. I knew then that even if these men killed me, put a knife to my throat and spilled hot red blood across the tattered floor, that it would be a better outcome than staying where I'd been.

And where had I been exactly?

"I don't think I have a name," I said as the big man—Reece's dad if I'd overheard the conversations correctly—stood up. He snorted at me, adjusted himself, and put his steepled hands to his lips.

"Everything has a name, *petite fée,*" Fionn told me as I took a deep breath and read *truth* into his every word. "We da fae—if you lost your name, then someone probably stole it. That, or you done gone and hid it from yourself."

Fionn walked away and left me to contemplate his words.

Stole it.

Or hid it.

Either way, I was intrigued.

Chapter Four

CIARAH

For years, I'd known nothing but darkness. And not the sort of darkness with stars, not like shadows cast by a smiling sun. True darkness. Real and complete. It was a void, that darkness—at least most of the time. I learned to shut out the pain and the horror, to close my eyes and drift away.

My mind was my sanctuary, a playground of memories that skipped and teased, that twirled away from me like dancers on a ballroom floor. I hid from the whips and the chains, the shackles and the acrid scent of burnt flesh by running as fast as I could after them, trying to catch them like fireflies.

Sometimes, I caught them.

"Ciarah O'Rourke, you get your ass back in here and clean this fucking house!" My mother's voice followed me out the front door and down the steps, into the rain where her shouting was finally drowned out by the rush of water.

Compared to the stink of the city, the rain smelt refreshing, cool and clean against my face. I knew Mom was still standing on the stoop of our house, eviction notice in hand, screaming into the night, but I didn't care anymore.

I was getting the hell out of there—for good.

Nineteen years old and nothing to show for my life, not even a high school diploma. My mom was a heroin addict and her boyfriends were bad enough to make up for the few good ones I'd managed to have. But I could never keep them. They always left and moved on without me.

Well, now look who was moving on?

Crossing the road, I headed toward Frenchmen Street —the only spot in downtown New Orleans that the locals liked to hang out. Bourbon Street was just fucking gross.

Dressed in knee-high leather boots, tight jeans, and an old jean jacket I made my way toward my favorite bar, this charming little dump called Spirits. I was going to have one last night of fun in town—after all, I did love

New Orleans—and then I was going to leave.

It wasn't that this place didn't hold any opportunities, just that I needed a change of scenery. I'd been living here my whole life with a toxic family and missed opportunities. I was too comfortable living in the familiar squalor of my own existence.

All I needed was a change.

I just didn't expect to get the one that fell in my lap, violent and bloody and awful.

I didn't expect to die.

Sliding into my usual spot at the end of the bar, I handed the bartender my flawless fake ID then ordered a hurricane. Pulling out my phone, I powered up the screen and started tapping out a message to my current boyfriend, asking him to come and meet me for a drink. Right before hitting send, I hesitated. If I was leaving this town, I was leaving Brad and all his baggage behind, too.

Deleting my message, I started again. This time, it was a short and sharp break-up message. Thanks for the memories, sort of thing. The last thing I needed was Brad and his psychotic ex-girlfriend causing drama before my new life had even begun. Just the fact that he'd remained friends with the girl was strange enough, but at the end of the day I didn't really care enough about Brad to be jealous. He was hot, and fucking exceptional in bed, but that was about the end of it.

When Brad's message came back, it was nothing terribly surprising. Just a bunch of profanity about what a shitty human I was, but that wasn't exactly news to me. I knew I was a shitty human. So were a lot of people. At least I was trying to do something to change it though.

One hurricane turned into three, and before I knew it, I was making out with a sexy, green-eyed biker in the hallway to the bathrooms. As small as I was, it never did take much to get me drunk and those hurricanes packed a punch.

"We should take this back to my place," the guy panted in my ear as we came up for air. I blinked up at him through the haze of rum and considered what he was saying. Did I want to fuck a stranger tonight? He was more than handsome enough for it, and if his kissing skill was any indication of what was to come, then I had no doubt he'd perform in the bedroom ...

But he wore a leather jacket with a motorcycle club patch on the back—one with a skull and wings that everyone knew to steer clear of—and my mama didn't raise no fool. A useless heroin addicted waste of oxygen she may be, but one thing she did right was teach me to always be suspicious.

"No." I squinted at him, feeling the numbness in my lips from my intoxication. "No, I think I'm done for the night. This was fun, though."

Pushing off the wall where we had just been climbing all over one another, I slipped past him as he gaped in surprise. Clearly, not the sort of guy that had ever heard no from a girl.

Less than a minute after leaving Spirits, the sexy, well-muscled biker was already forgotten, and I made my way a little unsteadily down the street toward the Mississippi. As antiquated as it seemed, I was departing the city of my youth by boat.

Seems funny, that after nineteen years in New Orleans —a city well-known for its crime—I'd never once felt afraid when walking the streets at night, and that night was no different.

Taking a turn off Decatur, I ducked through an alleyway which took me through to the empty French Market. It was one of my favorite nighttime make out spots when I couldn't go home because I knew Mom would be smacked out on the couch, so when I saw a shadow moving to the left of me, I thought nothing of it. Probably another couple making out in the darkness.

Such was my confidence that night that I never saw it coming until it was too late. Until that shadow stepped out into my path and slid a blade into my stomach like a warm knife through butter. Until that knife ripped upward to my sternum and my guts spilled onto the cold concrete at my feet.

My knees buckled, no longer able to hold my weight and I crashed to the ground in a cold shock of pain and blood. There was just so much blood.

"Don't worry, Ciarah," the familiar voice sneered, "stomach wounds are nasty things. They take ages to actually kill a person."

"Caroline," I croaked, her name like a curse on my lips. I didn't need to ask why. Brad's ex had always given me the creeps, and obviously my dumping him by text

tonight had tipped her over the edge.

"I should thank you. You have no idea how long I've wanted to do this." Her voice was excited and breathy, like she was getting off on killing me. Hell, she probably was. "I've dreamed about it so many times, but Brad thought he was in love with you and I couldn't do anything to hurt him. Now though ... well, you've gone and broken his heart which makes you fair game, bitch."

I was facedown on the dirty ground, a pool of my own blood spreading around me, and she grunted with the effort required to roll me over. Deadweight was a hell of a thing, or so I heard.

"Perfect," she panted, once I was on my back and staring up at a hastily drawn pentagram on the roof. Caroline fancied herself a voodoo priestess, like so many other fanatics in New Orleans. No one actually took her seriously though. She was hoodoo, not voodoo. Little more than parlor tricks and con jobs.

Until now.

The deranged chick began chanting in French, placing small objects on the tips of the pentagram that I then realized I was lying on top of. A direct mirror image of the one above me.

This was bad. Was this honestly how I was going to die?

There was no pain, which was a blessing, but my educated brain knew it was because the wound was that bad. My body had gone into shock and all I could feel was cold.

"What ..." I tried to speak, but my voice was no longer obeying my commands. She got the drift though.

"What am I doing? Besides killing you, of course?" Her eyes gleamed in excitement as she bent low, bringing her nose to touch mine. Close enough to kiss.

"I'm damning you. I'm sending your soul into torture. Where or how, I have no idea, but I assure you ... it'll suck." She grinned wide, then kissed me—the sick fuck—while sliding her lethal knife across my neck and severing all the vital veins and arteries that would ensure my death.

The pain was all-consuming, my lips parted to scream, but all that I achieved were bubbles in the spurting blood pouring from my neck and bathing Caroline.

Darkness crept in with merciful speed, but as my life slipped away, the sketchy runes glowed with an ominous light. Hoodoo or not, Caroline's spell was somehow working ... and in my final moment, I knew true fear.

I woke up surrounded by a different sort of darkness, a soft charcoal color that, if I blinked enough, could be penetrated. It was easy, lazy darkness, the black of a winter night in Louisiana.

"Ciarah," I whispered aloud, testing the sound out on

my tongue. Two perfect little syllables—KEER-ah—trailed across my lips and floated around the quiet room. I was sitting upright in a large bed that smelled like black musk and amber, the smoky hint of vetiver teasing my nostrils when I lifted the navy blue blanket to my face.

Pausing, I closed my eyes and listened to the distant stirring of a car's exhaust.

Ugh.

The thought of getting in a car again made me feel nauseous, all of the metal surrounding me, trapping me inside. I felt like … like maybe once upon a time, I hadn't had these issues. Once upon a time, I'd wanted a car more than *anything.*

"I just don't fucking see how *this* girl could be *Le Gardien du Voile,*" a voice said from outside the window, muffled by the echo of motorcycles outside the clubhouse. I thought it might've been Arlo, Caley's not-boyfriend-but-brother, but I wasn't sure.

"Like you would know, you," another voice said. This one was clearly Reece; the accent was unmistakable. "You were born on this side o' da Veil. What d'you know about *Le Gardien du Voile*?" Hearing the differences in the way the two men spoke, it was clear Reece had a bit more skill with French. "Wait till my *Mère* gets a look at her, then we'll know for sure."

"Seems like an easy fucking coincidence. After more than a century of looking for her ass, she just drops out of the sky like it's no big thing? I call bullshit. What a crock. I've probably got the enemy sleeping in my damn bed."

"You always got an enemy in your damn bed," Reece said with a deep chuckle.

"This from the man who had a ballistic pixie on his ass today? I don't fucking think so, bro." There was the sound of a door opening and closing, footsteps … and then the bedroom door cracked open, spilling light into the room. "You're awake," the man said—it was Arlo for sure. He sounded almost disappointed.

"Ciarah," I said, taking several long, deep breaths to open up my throat. "Ciarah O'Rourke."

"Ciarah O'Rourke?" Arlo asked, pausing at the edge of the bed—his bed, apparently—and staring down at me with a strange mixture of fascination and disgust. "Doesn't sound like no Veil Keeper's name to me."

He made a noise under his breath.

"You got a few hours left until dawn; this is your chance to get some sleep before we start grilling your ass." I couldn't remember a lot about who I was—even now, the dream I had was fading away, the edges burning like a sheet of parchment exposed to flame—but I did know this one thing.

Arlo was a prick.

"I've been sleeping for years," I said, and I wasn't quite sure where the words had come from. They were rough, and it was still painful to speak, but it was better than being silent. I'd been silenced for a long time; I wasn't about to keep quiet a moment longer. "What's a Veil Keeper?"

"For the love of fucking Christ," he said, shaking his

head and putting his hands on his hips. I couldn't see him well in the dark, just shades of gray that made up a mountain of a man, but I had to admit that his smell *was* intoxicating. "You gonna keep playing this amnesia crap?"

I just stared at him because I didn't know what to say to that. It felt as if there were two people living inside my brain, two voices fighting to be heard. At this moment, they were both still whispers, barely audible gasps of memory that floated to the surface like bubbles. If I tried hard enough, I might be able to pop one and get a little tidbit, but that was about it.

"Well, if you're done sleeping then get the fuck out of my bed. I'd like to get some sleep before this shit goes south. Go keep Caley company; she's a fucking insomniac."

I moved the covers away from my bare legs and noticed that Arlo's gaze dropped down to them, sliding up to my bare thighs. A small part of my borrowed panties was visible beneath the baggy t-shirt I'd worn to sleep in. I'd shed Caley's denim shorts; they just weren't very comfortable.

Arlo stepped back, closer to the window. A shaft of moonlight peaked through the curtain, falling across his face, leather vest rustling as he shrugged out of it.

As soon as he did, I noticed the color of his skin shifting from sun-weathered brown to a shimmering silver, like moonlight on a dark lake. It reflected back at me and made me blink, my mind taking in the horns that had appeared on the top of his head, a rack of antlers fit for a king of the forest.

"The Horned God," I whispered, but I had no idea where that information had come from. I scrambled to my knees and reached out to him, my fingers curling in his black t-shirt. "You're the new Horned One, the Lord of Death and Resurrection."

"Sure seems like that memory of yours is on its way back," he told me as I leaned close and breathed in his scent, that same muskiness I'd picked up on his blankets. But this close to him, there was the fresh smell of green things, of the wild … of me naked pressed into the dirt while the Horned One pleasured me with his cock.

Ah.

Where did that one come from?!

"You're the Warrior?" I asked, crinkling my brow and pausing as my mind shuffled through information. *The Horned God, like the Triple Goddess, has three aspects. The Warrior, the Father, and the Sage.* That was important. I didn't know why, but it was *vital.* "You have it then," I gasped, my voice and body trembling. "The Spear of Lug."

Arlo's face tightened, and he reached up, curling his fingers around my wrists and prying my hands off of him. With his glamour dropped, his hair was dark and slightly curled, the horns curving up into the shadows, shimmering white as bone. When he touched me, I felt the earth shift and tremble.

"The Spear's been lost for years," he said, curling the corner of his lip up in a snarl. "You sure seem to know a lot about a lot for somebody with am-fucking-nesia."

"I'm not lying," I whimpered as his grip on my wrist tightened. A shard of a memory flashed across my brain, of being bound in iron, of *pain.* I tried to tug my wrist free but he held tight, pressing me backward onto the bed and pinning my hands above my head.

"No," he murmured, hovering over me and running his nose down the side of my neck like he was *smelling* me, "of course you're not. Fae can't lie. But you …" He shifted his face to smell the other side of my neck. "You reek of magic that's not your own."

His nose brushed lightly down the length of my throat and his hot breath caressed my skin. My skin rippled with a memory un-remembered, something ingrained in my flesh that begged for more.

"Please," I gasped, unsure if I was begging him not to hurt me, or begging him for something *else.*

"Don't flatter yourself, *Ciarah O'Rourke*," he sneered my name like he didn't believe it, like he suspected I had found a workaround for the *fae can't lie* rule. "Now, I'm getting in. Are you staying or going?"

His burning gaze raked down my body to where the oversized t-shirt barely covered my borrowed panties, and my breath caught at the sudden, suffocating blast of magic when his glamour snapped back in place.

"Going," I whispered in a weak sounding voice. I hated it. I hated sounding weak. For all the confusion inside my head, I knew without a doubt that I was *not* a weak woman.

Arlo's forest green gaze held mine for a long, tense moment before he abruptly released my wrists and pushed up off the bed.

"Then go. Caley is down in the bar drinking with the club whores. Maybe you can go *join* them." His emphasis on the word *join* made it sound like he was calling me a whore, too. Maybe I was. My body certainly remembered the feel of a man's hands upon me. Remembered the feel of being pleasured, dominated, and worshiped. "Don't forget: when dawn rolls around, Fionn will be back and he'll expect answers from you."

When I reached the door, I paused and looked back at him. Prick, he may be, but I couldn't deny his attractiveness. Now stretched out on his bed in the exact spot I'd just vacated, with arms folded under his head, he watched me like a hawk might watch a mouse.

"How did you lose it?" I asked, chewing my lip nervously. "The Spear of Lug. It was your sacred duty to protect it for *all* time."

"My predecessor," Arlo grunted. His jaw tightened with anger and his green eyes flashed dangerously. "Shut the door behind you, Ciarah O'Rourke."

Arlo never had given me any direction to the bar where

Caley was supposedly drinking with the *club whores,* so I found myself wandering aimlessly through the quiet building and opening doors at random. After my fourth wrong guess, I gave up trying to find this damn bar, and returned to the kitchen I had already passed. It was dark, and dead still. Shards of moonlight dissected the floor and frogs croaked their nighttime song while my fractured brain coughed up another slice of memory.

Hands tipped with claws made of iron raking through my flesh. Waves of nausea causing bile to rise as the deadly metal poisoned my body. Shadows parting to reveal a face crafted of nightmares and despair. Sobs of terror and sick, twisted laughter.

"You lost here, *bebette*?" Reece's molasses voice caressed my ears and I snapped from my memory with a gasp. "Somethin' got you spooked, girl? You be paler than a virgin's creamy white thighs."

"That doesn't make a lick of sense," I informed him, frowning. "Who says you need to be a virgin to have pale thighs?"

Reece's red-brown eyebrows shot up, obviously not having expected me to reply. My voice was still thin and tight but as Killian had promised, it was improving with use.

"Well now," Reece grinned, advancing on me as I took a couple of steps backward, "you mighta proved Old Reece wrong, here. Because *these* thighs are as pale as they come." His index finger trailed up the inside of one of my exposed thighs, reminding me I'd left my borrowed shorts on the floor of Arlo's bedroom. "But you *sure* ain't no virgin. Are you, *cher*?"

His finger brushed lightly over the thin fabric of my panties, igniting a fire that pooled in my belly and caused my nipples to tighten.

"Says who?" I challenged in a breathy voice, trying and failing to keep from pushing my hips forward into his touch. I'd backed up as far as I could go, with my shoulders against the fridge and an enormous Cajun fae in front of me.

"Aw now, *bebette*, ain't no need for you ta be *honte*. Old Reece *know* these things, just as sure as he *know* you more than you seem, *Le Gardien du Voile*." His glamour rippled with a pulse of magic that made my pussy clench and his red-gold skin gleam under the moonlight, before settling back into his human-like appearance.

"I'm not ashamed," I replied, my elusive memories translating his Cajun words effortlessly. "I'm curious. You said you were *dia gnéas*, but I don't have any memory of this. Will you show me? What it means to be *dia gnéas*?"

Reece's brow shot up once more, but his palm cupped me through my unapologetically damp underwear. "Girl, you don't know what you be askin'. When the sidhe come together …" He shook his head, but his eyes gleamed with a wild and primal excitement that I wanted nothing more than to unleash.

"Show me," I taunted. I'd already forgotten my purpose in coming down here in the first place. It hadn't been to seek out sex, but why not? What was stopping me?

"Hmm," Reece said, teasing up the evening's memories with his fingers. The rest of my brain may have been a fractured mess, but I had no problem recalling our moment in the bathtub. "Sadhbh might not be happy if I took advantage of da Veil Keeper," he said, smacking his lips in a way that made the fractured stumps on my back stir, like the beating of long-dead wings.

They might not be visible through my glamour, but I could *feel* them.

"*Sive,*" I sounded out, the word rhyming with the number five. It was a name, I thought. Or some part of me did anyway.

"Fionn's wife," Reece said, sliding his hand up and under my shirt. His brown eyes sparkled with mischief. "She won't like this … but I sure as shit will."

Taking hold of my hips, he lifted me up onto the counter, stepped between my thighs, and captured my mouth with his own.

Chapter Five

REECE

Dis sweet little t'ang was a trap waiting to fuck Ol' Reece. I knew dat and yet, well, I just couldn't help myself. Somethin' old and ancient was living behind dis girl's eyes—whether she knew it or not. Scared the living crap outta me.

But I was going to do this anyway, me.

This girl smelt like ol' magic, this tangy taste that got on the back of my tongue and made me drool like a damn dog. It mixed with da sweet scent of magnolias and dat distinct flavor of a woman that's wet and ready.

"You want me bad, don't you, girl?" I asked her as I stepped between those creamy white thighs. Her skin was soft and warm, her wet panties pressing up against the front of my jeans.

She didn't answer me, cutting off conversation by teasing my lower lip wit' her tongue, encouraging me to take over and guide da kiss. That was okay by me. I lived for dis shit.

Pressing the hardness of my cock against the girl's wetness, I let my right hand move up toward her breast, cupping da tender flesh in my fingers and squeezing until she cried out against my lips. She wiggled her body closer to mine, encouraging me to go hard and fast, fuck her real easy and quick.

But, nah, dat was boring.

Breaking our kiss, I slid her oversized t-shirt up and tossed it aside, examining the human glamour she was wearing like a new outfit. Pretty white skin sparkling in the moonlight, perky ripe breasts, and a full round mouth dat I just had to see wrapped around my cock. Mm. That was a definite. Been a while since I got my cock sucked—that pixie girl woulda bit it right off at da base.

“C'mere, girl,” I said as I stepped back and heard a needy moan slide from her throat. She was like an animal just uncaged, as wild as my Meme down on the dock. An *animal.* All fae were animals. No, we were worse than animals.

Animals don't kill for fun, no.

My hands dropped to my jeans and flicked open the button, dragging the zipper down nice and slow for effect. She watched the entire exchange with sloe-eyes and partially parted lips. Hungry. Dat's what she looked like, dat girl.

Maybe I shoulda been more scared o' her than the pixie?

"You want me to suck your dick?" she asked, her voice this ragged sexy whisper that I liked far too much. Oh yeah, I was really into dis one. Most interesting woman I'd met in a *long* fucking time.

"You don't want to?" I asked, freeing the long, hard length of my cock from my jeans. The girl's eyes followed the motion, her throat tightening as she examined me from her place on the counter. After a moment, she slid forward, her bare feet slapping against the tile floor.

Outside, I could hear Meme grunting, keeping all them males outta her turf. She didn't like 'em near the nest.

But in here? It was dead silent; you coulda heard a pin drop. The clubhouse was unusually quiet—Fionn didn't want a lot partying or hang-arounds with the Veil Keeper in residence.

The Veil Keeper.

Well, Ol' Reece be damned … never thought I'd have *Le Gardien du Voile* suckin' on my dick.

The girl dropped to her knees in front of me, pushed her long dark hair over her shoulder, and wrapped her fingers around the base of my cock. *Oh, shit yes.* Those long, thin fingers were warm, the grip tight. And the magic … I could feel dat ancient energy prickling across her skin and into mine.

My balls tightened and I swear to fuck, I almost blew it right dere. Barely got started and I was ready to come?

Who the hell was dis girl and the fuck was she doin' to me? No *dia gnéas* I ever met finished so damn quick in his life. Eh, at least I had the magic to get it up again, and again, and again. There was no end for ol' Reece if I didn't wanna be done.

The girl—the Veil Keeper always used to be named *Gràinne* although there was definitely somethin' different about this one—leaned forward and put her lips against the head of my cock. Her eyes flicked up ta meet mine, making my throat feel tight. A growl rose up from my chest, turned my mouth into a wild scowl.

My fingers curled in her hair, but she reached up and slapped dem away.

Oh, we had a wildcat on our hands.

"Maybe another time," she whispered, letting her breath play across the wet tip of my dick. I was leaking pre-cum, getting myself ready ta fuck. Between da two of us, we had more than enough wetness to make it work. And we were about to add a whole lot more.

"Whatever you say, *bebette,*" I growled, just before she slid her mouth over the aching flesh o' my cock. Hot, wet heat enveloped me, lips sliding along da length of my shaft, her tongue cradling the underside as she took more, more, more o' me.

I rested a single palm on her head, but she didn't seem to mind that, sliding back and drawing a long, low groan outta me. I sounded like a goddamn gator, me.

"Fuck, girl, you sure are good at dis for somebody that don't remember their own name."

She pulled back, breathing hot against the quivering tip of my cock.

"Ciarah O' Rourke," she said, flicking her tongue in a circle around my shaft that had my hips bucking and my fingers digging into her hair. "My name is *Ciarah.*"

My lids felt heavy and weighted as she took me onto 'er mouth again, her breathing gettin' faster, harder, moonlight streaming across her long, dark hair. I wanted to see her true form, no glamour, but I also knew dat our glamours were da only things keeping a dangerous surge of magic outta the air.

And those wings ... The ragged stumps had been hauntin' me all damn day. Took a special kind of sick to cut off a faerie's wings. And *Le Gardien du Voile* most of all? I wasn't the only one wondering why a goddess hadn't been able to grow 'em back.

My fingers curled tighter in her hair, pulled her closer. My shaft slid deep into her mouth, but not all da way—Ol' Reece was too long for dat shit—and dat extra bit was fuckin' killin' me. I needed to be buried inside dis girl.

The next time she pulled back, I stepped away, her fingernails trailing along the length of my cock and making me shiver. She sat on da floor on her knees and didn't look a bit less like a goddess for it.

I was a lucky man, me. As soon as the rest o' the world found out the Veil Keeper was back, I wouldn't be da only man fightin' to get her into bed.

Reaching out a hand, I helped her to her feet, hooked my thumbs in the waistband of her panties and dragged them down the smooth lines of her hips and off her feet, pausing to press my mouth to the nest of curls between her thighs. She smelled so damn sweet, I felt like my head was spinning.

I stood back up and lifted her again, putting her right back on da counter where she was before. But this time, there was no fabric standing between us. It was just da hard, slick length of my cock resting against her opening.

“Do we need a condom?” she asked, wrinkling her delicate brow like even she wasn't sure what she was askin'.

I raised a single brow, pulling her closer with my greedy hands on her ass, digging my fingers into the soft flesh.

“You da the goddess o' the veil, you,” I told her which was more than enough explanation for anyone. But she sat there for a long moment, those sloe-eyes of hers glimmering like she was processing a whole helluva lot of information.

“The veil,” she said, her glamour shimmering in response to the word.

“You da *cailleach,*” I said in the language of the old country, that place I never been but that dictated every step I took in life. *The veiled one*. “You a new soul, but you also a lost one, girl, no?”

“No condom,” she said again, like she'd found some hidden cache of knowledge in her brain that told her I was tellin' the truth. The fae don't get sick the same way humans do and me, I was *dia gnéas,* I didn't make babies 'less I *wanted* to.

I cupped da side of her face with one, large tattooed hand, my skin shimmering and flickering in response to her magic. Her eyes met mine just a split second before our lips connected, two hot angry mouths sliding together in tongue and teeth and wild lust.

My other hand slipped between us, guiding the head of my cock to her opening. As we kissed, I pushed myself inside, the tight hot walls of her body squeezing mine to within an inch o' my life. She was almost *too* tight. *Almost.*

"*Tu te sens tellement bien, mon cher,*" I groaned, burying myself to the hilt and using my right hand to cup her ass and pull her close. Ciarah moved her mouth to my neck, kissing and licking and biting the corded muscles in my throat, tense and rigid as I tried to control my urge to pound her into da countertop.

I had to move slow, me.

"You feel so good," I repeated in English, not sure that dis girl, dis strange soul inside a fae goddess' body, if she could speak French. Hell, I was pretty sure none of the previous Veil Keepers could speak the language. Why should they when there were two dozen fae dialects they had to learn on da other side?

"Faster, harder," she said as I moved inside her, the slick ridges of her cunt bearing down on me with such force that I almost lost it again. But what kind o' man would I be if I couldn't give dis poor girl her orgasm *first*? "More," she whispered, her breath teasing along my neck.

I felt a presence at my back before she saw him, lifting her face to look at Killian standing in the kitchen doorway behind us. I knew it was him from the signature scent of his magic, dis cool breeze that swept into the room and tried to cool my heated flesh.

Using my left hand, I turned Ciarah's face back to mine and thrust my tongue between her lips, moving inside of her with long, sure strokes until I felt her muscles clenching around me, pulsing in rapid flickers that begged to milk da pleasure straight outta me.

As Killian watched, a dark brooding energy surrounding him and prodding at my spine, I fucked Ciarah O'Rourke into da counter and stole a climax right outta dat borrowed body o' hers. Her head fell back and her glamour cracked like a thin sheet of glass, revealing the blue-skinned faerie underneath.

Those sapphire eyes o' hers lit up as her body locked down on mine and drew an unwilling orgasm right outta me, cutting through my own lust-laden magic and taking what *she* wanted in its place.

Fucking infuriated me, but I couldn't move, no, trapped inside the scalding warmth of her body as her eyes glowed and she stared up at da ceiling like she was seein' something beyond da old walls of the bayou clubhouse.

"The Wild Hunt rides," she said, holding me in place with legs locked together behind my back. I heard Killian move toward us, a growl escaping from between his lips. All around us, I felt the few people left in the clubhouse stir, cracking the thickness of sleep and coming awake for what coulda been their first *real* waking moment in a century. “We ride,” she said again, dropping her face to look at mine. “And the souls of the dead join our parade.”

Chapter Six
CIARAH

The voice that spoke through me was entirely different from the one Killian had given back when he healed my body. Instead of the weak, thin sound of tight vocal cords, this voice was rich, dark, and sensual. It rang true with the pain of a thousand souls, and the joy of a thousand more, and when it uttered those words it felt like twenty three little lightbulbs ignited inside my consciousness.

All at once, I was *connected* to twenty-three souls in a way that was both more and less intimate than the embrace I still held Reece in.

"Ciarah, *bébé,*" Reece panted, his huge hands still gripping my hips while his glamour flickered in and out of view, like he was struggling to hold it. "Ye need t'let me go, *cher.* The Hunt is coming to your summons; we must complete the ride or forfeit our own souls, y'hear?"

"What?" I croaked, in my still healing voice once more. Releasing my legs from around Reece's waist, I allowed him to slide out of me and step back so I could get down from the bench. "What just happened?"

"You're Le Gardien du Voile, *mon cher*," Killian murmured, holding up my borrowed panties by one finger and offering them to me. "You just called your Hunt to arms using magic that hasn't been seen in over one hundred and eighty years."

"Okay, and what the fuck does that *mean*?" I snapped, exasperated, as I pulled on my underwear and retrieved the t-shirt from the kitchen counter.

"Oh ho, the *minou* has a tongue on her, too! But I already knew that, me. We came good and close, Ol' Reece and dat tongue." He winked an eye the color of autumn leaves and I licked my lips, still tasting him.

"It means," Killian responded to my question while holding out a gentlemanly hand for me to take, "that tonight, we *ride*."

"Take 'er to borrow more clothes from Caley-girl." Reece nodded back toward the bedrooms where I had left Arlo. "I see those thighs wrapped around me while we ridin' *Diabhal* and I be likely to crash straight in ta dat dere swamp."

"Who says she's riding with you, old man?" Killian challenged, but gave me a smile that said he was teasing. It did nothing to alleviate my confusion though, as I could still *feel* those twenty-three souls connected to me with silvery threads like spider silk. Two of them were clearly tethered to Killian and Reece, as they glowed faintly with the same silvery substance as the threads. One, I *knew* was Arlo, which left twenty more.

The remainder of The Wild Hunt?

Once inside Caley's bedroom, Killian confidently approached a chest of drawers and extracted a pair of dark denim jeans and a halter-necked tank top, which he handed to me before pausing.

"Caley's unlikely to have any boots that will fit you. She is *moitié humain* and their feet tend to run a bit larger than *sidhe*." He quirked a teasing grin. "It's the fairy in us, *tu sais*?"

"I have no idea what you're talking about." I squinted at him. "But I'm sure I'll be fine in bare feet. It's a warm night. What are we riding, anyway?"

Killian's lush lips pulled into a broad smile. "Seriously? *Mon cher*, the Veil Keeper has been gone for over one hundred and eighty years. Our fae mounts needed to evolve and adapt with the human world, manifest in a way that would be more readily accepted by the human eye. Eight foot tall horned stallions in fae armor probably wouldn't go unnoticed in the bayou."

"Oh." I nodded, as though I understood what he was talking about. Some part of me *did* understand, but chasing those memories was like trying to nail jelly to a wall.

"Get changed, *cher*, then meet us out the front. We must hurry. Once the magic has been summoned, we *must* obey it." His ice-blue eyes were tight with tension and I could clearly see how taut his shoulders were set.

Nodding my understanding, I closed the door behind him and quickly changed into the clothes he had found for me in Caley's drawers. He'd been correct when he said the healing would help to fill out my frame, as Caley's jeans would've now fit me like a glove, if not for the length. It was nothing a couple of rolls couldn't fix though. The halter top was black, and left my back mercifully exposed.

Despite the glamour concealing the scars, I could feel them every time my t-shirt rubbed over the puckered flesh.

Letting myself out of Caley's room, I started down the hallway. A door slammed open just in front of me and I barely stopped myself from crashing headfirst into Arlo who glared at me with furious eyes.

His brown hair was tousled from sleep, and he still had his shirt and leather jacket draped over one shoulder while he buckled the heavy belt around his hips.

"You sure don't waste time, Veil Keeper," he sneered, then turned and led the way outside while dressing himself. "You couldn't have waited until morning to summon The Wild Hunt? I barely got an hour's sleep, thanks to *you.*"

"I'm sorry," I muttered, but not totally feeling like I *should* be apologizing to him. "I didn't do it intentionally. It just … happened."

Arlo gave a derisive snort as he threw his leather jacket on and kicked the front door open. "Sure. Just happened.

The Goddess of the Veil lets her magic control her now. This bodes well for tonight's hunt."

My temper flared at his scornful words but I bit my tongue. If nothing else, it still ached to talk so it wasn't worth the strain to fight back.

"There she be!" Reece announced, as I followed Arlo out into the cool night where several men were gathered, all wearing leather jackets and vests sporting the same patch on the back. The skull over butterfly wings suddenly made more sense.

My step faltered as my feet reached the gravel of the driveway and I realized what Killian had meant about their mounts having adapted. An array of leather and gleaming chrome made up the orderly line of motorcycles waiting for their riders, just as fae mounts once would have waited.

"Ah, I see the way you lookin' at our noble steeds, *bébé,*" Reece smirked as I approached the group of dangerous looking leather clad men. My eyes remained glued to the bikes, like I was waiting to see them change form. Maybe I was? I couldn't remember.

"Don' you worry, Ciarah girl, Old Reece would be mad not t'let you ride his hog … again." The sexy fae in shades of autumn winked at me and my breath caught. What had possessed me back in the kitchen? I barely knew myself, let alone these men, and yet there I was on my knees with his cock down my throat.

"She's not riding with you, Reece," Arlo snapped in his dickish tone of voice. "Last thing we need is for you to fuck up the Wild Hunt by copping a feel and sending the magic screwy."

Reece's eyes narrowed and he opened his mouth to reply, but Killian smacked him in the gut with the back of his hand.

"He's right, *cher*," Killian murmured to Reece in his deep, husky voice. "We can't risk this Hunt going sour. It will be a hard one already, with how many souls must have gone uncollected since we became *piégé*."

"She can ride with me," Arlo announced, and my eyebrows shot up.

"No thanks." I narrowed my eyes at him. "Surely I can ride alone?"

Arlo snorted a laugh and shook his head. "Yeah sure. Get on the damn bike, woman."

Folding my arms under my breasts, I prepared to stand my ground against this chauvinistic asshole but a nauseating wave of *urgency* washed through me.

"The Wild Hunt *must* ride. Punishments must be dealt to those who flout the faerie law." The words spilled from my lips in that powerful voice, rich with sex and magic, and I gasped.

Those silvery strands of silk connecting me to my Wild Hunt glowed brightly, and around me the leather clad men moved soundlessly to their bikes, kicking them alive with low rumbles and waiting with eyes that glowed like fireflies in the swamp.

Arlo didn't wait for me to protest any further. Instead, he simply picked me up and deposited me onto his bike like I was a goddamn sack of rice. Wordlessly, he swung his leg over, and before I could utter a word we were peeling out of the long gravel driveway.

Faced with the appealing options of jumping off a moving motorcycle or holding on to Arlo's waist, I grudgingly gripped the leather of his jacket and held my body stiff to try and maintain a distance between us.

"What the fuck was that?" I yelled in his ear over the loud rumble of twenty other bikes around us. How I knew it was twenty, I wasn't totally sure. But I sensed the two missing were Fionn and Donal.

"Like you don't know," Arlo snapped back, clearly still of the opinion that I was somehow faking my amnesia. Wanker.

As we flew past sugarcane fields, the wind whipped through my hair and streamed out behind me like a flag, the two missing bikers joining our parade from a side street. They took up a position at the front of the group, just ahead of Reece, Killian and Arlo—and me, clinging to Arlo's jacket.

"*Gardien.*" Fionn nodded to me in a respectful sort of way, and his voice sounded inside my head, making it possible to hear him without yelling. "Ye summoned the ancient magic. Send us where you want us to go."

His words triggered one of those elusive memory bubbles to burst and knowledge washed through me of what I needed to do. Twenty-three bright lights were connected to me through strands of magic, interwoven into my very flesh.

The Wild Hunt.

My Wild Hunt.

But beyond those twenty-three lights, there were just as many dead ones, waiting to be collected. One of my hands raised from Arlo's jacket and I pointed in the direction of the closest one.

"And so we ride," Fionn responded, and these same four words were repeated in unison by twenty-two other voices within my mind.

For hours, my Wild Hunt travelled through the Louisiana countryside at my direction, collecting the souls of all the fae who had died on this side of the Veil. With each soul collected, my heart ached for the pain they were feeling. They were so lost, so alone, trapped in this world that was not their own.

Our own.

But that didn't quite ring true to me. Despite my fae body, I still felt a sense of belonging in this human world.

"How many more, *Gardien*?" Fionn asked, as the most recent soul attached itself to our parade. She'd been beautiful in life, and a blue-blooded *sidhe*. How she died, she couldn't recall. Only that she'd been that way for a long time.

My eyelids drooped shut as I searched for more of those broken lights within me, and paused when I found something … different. Unlike my Wild Hunt, who glowed as bright as starlight, or the souls of dead fae, which were the shadowy memories of bulbs blown out, this was something *else*. I reached out to it to take a closer look, and a wave of pain and hatred crashed over me.

"That way," I gasped, pointing in the physical direction of where this poison was radiating from. Without a doubt, this was what that voice had spoken of. A fae law breaker. Someone who deserved to be punished in the worst way.

"Stay with us, woman," Arlo murmured, releasing one hand from his handlebars and gripping mine at his waist. "I feel you weaving back there. Hold on tighter."

He was right. I was exhausted. Blindly following magic I didn't understand had me weak enough that I could pass out any second, but picking gravel out of my skin sounded anything but pleasant so I did as he said and gripped tighter.

"This the place?" Fionn asked, as our entourage pulled up outside a run-down shack in the middle of the swamp. From inside, the distinctive sound of a woman's screams cut through the early morning quiet and I nodded grimly.

"Who dat, dere? This 'ere be private property and y'all are trespassers!" a man demanded, flinging open the front screen door and stepping out onto the porch.

Arlo's broad back blocked my line of sight, so I slid from the back of his bike and approached the enraged man brandishing a shotgun. Once I got a good look at him, my stomach clenched and rolled, while bile threatened to rise in my throat.

His glamour was that of a normal human man, but with the magic riding my eyesight I could clearly see through it to the rotted, putrid creature beneath.

My gaze locked on his and in an instant, I saw his lifetime of crimes laid out before me.

Violence, abuse, theft, rape, and murder.

The fae lived *very* long lives and this vile creature had amassed an extensive laundry list of crimes to his name. Not the least of which included showing his faerie form to human women, in a bid to terrify them while he killed them slowly.

"Asgall Baltair." My voice was low, thick and heavy with the Veil Keeper's magic. I was the Queen of the Wild Hunt, and this was our sacred duty. "You stand accused of crimes against both fae and humankind. You've broken our most sacred laws and threatened our future in this world. How do you plead?"

The revolting creature trembled before me, his fear palpable as he responded with a single word so tightly delivered it was barely audible.

"Guilty." The strangled sound of his voice made it clear he would have lied, had he been able. But we were fae, and fae *cannot* lie. Truth rang in his damning admission, and sickness pooled in my belly.

"Guilty." That ancient voice spoke through me, both repeating and confirming his plea. The man's glamoured face paled to an ashen grey, "The punishment for your crimes is death."

The man began to babble, and Reece stepped forward to kneel at my feet. "*Déesse*, I humbly ask the honor."

"In humility and grace," I said as Reece rose to his feet, sliding a sword from his hip that I hadn't noticed until now. The blade was black as night, the hilt as red as blood. It sang when he pulled it free of its scabbard, like a demon rising from the depths of hell. I would not want to be on the receiving end of that blade. "I grant your request."

Reece stepped forward and spun his blade in a circle, missing the glamoured fae by several inches. But he hadn't intended to hit him with that swing; he was showing off. After all, what chance did this one man have against the Wild Hunt?

The answer?

None.

My heart thundered in my chest as I stood there and watched the large Cajun man drop his glamour, gold skin glimmering, those dark lines tattooed on his skin shimmering like they were metallic. He didn't have wings, but unlike myself, I didn't imagine he ever had.

Our man, the dark and damned, a shadow within a shadow … he turned and ran toward the swamp, but he didn't go far. About three paces away from the water, he spun back and fired off a random shot.

I felt it hit me right in the gut, a smattering of buckshot that took my breath away.

Pain bloomed wretched and furious, taking over everything, murdering my self-control.

A scream ripped from my throat just seconds before Reece's sword severed the fae man's head, killing his glamour, revealing his true form underneath. I didn't know what he was, didn't care. In that moment, I knew I wanted and needed only one thing.

To feast.

The rest of the hunt stayed very still around me, watching, waiting. Nobody moved forward to comfort me or treat my wounds; nobody seemed concerned.

Me … I was broken in two halves, each one at war with the other. *This is my life, all this pain. This is the only thing I've ever known.* The second half of my consciousness whispered gently to the first, pressing soothing lips to my fear, quieting my anxiety.

I was a goddess and goddesses, they did not die.

Blood oozed down my stomach, coated my thighs. It was thick and viscous and red, so bright against the brown earth beneath my bare heels.

"Veil Keeper," Reece said, dragging the corpse to rest at my feet. Just beyond it, connected with a similar silver thread—much like the one that called the Wild Hunt to me—was the angry, wild spirit of the dead man.

He raged at me, screamed obscenities in a language that I both knew and had never heard before in my life. Didn't matter. He had crimes that required remuneration.

Holding my hands out, I reached for his tattered, rotted form, ugly even in spirit.

As soon as my fingers touched his incorporeal form, the energy that was once him started to seep into me, a violent, awful exchange that sent the herons scattering into the skies, the gators diving beneath the water, even the rats scurrying from the clearing.

I was literally *stealing* the creature's spirit, sucking away the essence of his soul. Of course, a soul could never be completely annihilated, but I would drain him so dry that his eventual rebirth would be messy and painful, jagged and white-hot.

As I drained him, I felt the pieces of buckshot lodged in my skin push forward, dropping from my wounded flesh to the ground around me, much like the piece of iron had earlier. The wounds sealed themselves up, left tiny spots of puckered pink flesh that soon faded.

My vocal cords were next, this soothing wash filling my throat, stealing away the pain and the dryness, the uncomfortable tightness when I began to speak. But it was the last bit that hit me the hardest, the itch and tingle of those jagged scars on my back. Without even knowing why, I found myself crying silent tears, tearing the energy from the wrongdoer's body and using it to fuel my hunger.

A strange, stretching sensation emanated from my back, pulling and teasing and beckoning my skin into new shapes, rising up and away from my body in a glorious spread of gossamer flesh. I stared straight ahead, into Reece's umber eyes, and I saw his hands trembling, his tongue playing across his lower lip.

"*Mon Dieu,*" he whispered, "holy shit."

My head dropped back and I felt the play of my own dark hair against my ass, my eyes looking up at a tangled canopy of oaks and clumps of sea green Spanish moss. And as the last drops of energy seeped from the fae's body into mine, I used the tired, achy muscles on my back … to lift my wings.

My memory was already a mess, a canvas with a picture long obscured by splashes of red and green and yellow paint. Each time I stopped to think, it felt like I was teasing one of those splotches with a single fingernail, desperate to scratch it away and see what was hiding underneath.

Because having wings … it was a memory I was having trouble bringing up.

I sat on the edge of Arlo's bed—I had no idea why they kept putting me in there—and tried to orient myself to the new weight on my back, the massive spread of purple, green, and blue wings that looked like stained glass.

The first time I'd seen them in the mirror, I'd let out a scream.

Sitting here now, staring across the room at my own reflection, I had no idea what to think. Any microscopic movement of my back muscles caused them to twitch, to flutter, to bend. And I could *feel* them, too, just like any other part of my body, like I'd grown two new arms right out of my back and knew instinctively how to use them.

Could I fly?

I didn't know the answer to that. I hadn't had time to ask questions either because after draining the swamp man, I'd promptly passed out. I didn't even know how I'd gotten to the clubhouse, waking up in Arlo's bed and smelling that smoky vetiver hint of his all over the linens. There was another scent in the room, too, faint but intriguing, the scent of his seed. Whether or not it was normal to be able to sense that—or to pinpoint the fact that the smell was coming from the trash can next to the bed—I wasn't sure.

But it intrigued me. Oddly enough, it *aroused* me.

"Seriously?" the biker in question snapped, leaning against the door frame, shirtless and glowering at me. "You still haven't put those things away? You'll be getting fairy dust all through my sheets."

"What?" I spun around to look at his sheets, and my wings knocked over the bedside lamp. It hit the floor hard, the base shattering, and I cringed.

"*Seriously?*" Arlo shouted. "That was a fucking joke! We're not pixies for fuck's sake! Just … put your damn wings away before you break anything else. *Please*."

"I …" I shivered slightly under his intense, furious gaze, and felt my wings quiver with me. "I don't know how."

"Oh for the love of …" He crossed the room in two quick strides and sat on the edge of the bed beside me. "You need to just focus on the muscles supporting them.

Here." Reaching his arms around my body, he stroked a firm line down my back with two fingers on either side of my spine. "This muscle."

The touch of his skin against mine was electric, and as he stroked those newly awakened muscles in my back, I could feel my dripping core pulse and clench with arousal. His fingers were strong and sure, and my body *begged* to feel them inside me, even just for a brief moment.

Breath caught in my throat, I arched my back a little under his hand, pushing my naked chest forward to touch his. My hard nipples brushed over his smooth skin, and I saw him suck a sharp breath in.

"Ciarah," he warned. "Pull your fucking wings in, then put a shirt on. You're not gonna win me over with a quick blow job like you did that asshole, Reece."

Despite his words, his fingers still stroked a tantalizing path up and down the base of my wings, turning me on more and more by the second. Was it always like this when someone touched my wings? I couldn't remember, but it felt … familiar.

Focusing hard on what he was asking me to do, I felt a sucking sort of sensation as my wings retracted, folded and sealed beneath my skin, leaving Arlo's hand splayed flat against my naked back while my breasts pressed to his chest.

"Who said anything about my mouth?" I responded, hitching up a knee and exposing my naked, throbbing cunt as the sheet fell away from me. Why I was naked, I wasn't altogether sure, but I wasn't complaining. Whether it was due to my amnesia or not, I was perfectly comfortable in the nude and felt no shame in exposing myself to this man. This *fae*.

Arlo's pupils dilated and his nostrils flared, taking in my scent the same way I had been able to smell his lingering in the trash can. His hand left my back and trailed down the side of my rib cage, brushing the curve of my breast and then skating over my hip to my open thighs.

"Keeper, you don't know what you're doing," he warned in a voice low and thick with desire. "You're provoking the beast in me, and he cannot be tamed. He *will not* be tamed."

His fingers stroked over my swollen sex and I moaned softly, wanting more. *Needing* more. As my eyelids fluttered, the image of his fae self, of the Horned God, faded in and out over his face and it made me *wild* with wanting him inside me.

"*Cernunnos*," I whispered in a voice not quite my own, "it's been too long since you claimed my flesh. Have you forgotten what it was like? To join our bodies as one under moonlight, to be wild and free?"

"*Gardien*," Arlo murmured. "You're confused. This body is new to you, and I am not the *Cernunnos* you once knew." One long finger slid into my wet heat and my walls clenched around it, holding it captive and demanding more.

"*Cernunnos*, lover, betrayer, don't you see how much I missed you?" That voice whispered from my throat, and I shuddered with pleasure as Arlo slid a second finger inside me. He stroked my inner walls with the skill of an immortal, with hundreds of years of practice under his belt. In the back of my mind, I knew I ought to be concerned about the words falling from my lips, but I was too far gone in the exquisite torture of Arlo's fingers inside my pussy.

"Ciarah," Arlo's deep, husky voice caressed my ears with the sound of my own name, "are you in control, or is The Veil Keeper still controlling you?"

A sharp gasp and moan slipped from me before I found the breath to respond, this time in more of my own voice. "I don't even know. But I don't believe I care either. She is me, and I am her, we are two becoming one, and soon it will be irrelevant who is who."

"Do you want this?" His fingers flicked upward, sending pulsing waves of pleasure shooting through me. "Or does she?"

"Do you care?" I countered, meeting his gorgeous green eyes with confidence. "You don't strike me as the type to second-guess yourself where sex is concerned."

"You're right," he murmured, his eyes turning hard and cold. "I warned you that you were playing with fire, and yet here you still are. What happens next …" Arlo scoffed and stood up, withdrawing his hand and all the pleasure it brought with it. "What happens next is … if you want to get on my good side …"

He lifted his fingers to his lips, the tips shiny with my wetness. I watched in abject fascination as he sucked them clean.

"Then get the fuck out of my room and go choose your own."

Arlo turned and stormed out the door, his boots loud against the floor as he went.

I watched him go and then paused, letting myself fall back into the blankets and rolling to one side, gathering them up in my hands and pressing them to my face.

They smelled good, earthy and musky, like Arlo himself.

I did not want to pick another room … but what I *did* want was to get on his good side.

So I would lie here for just a moment longer and absorb his smell, and then I would indeed choose my own bedroom.

But would it be lonely?

Or after so much time in captivity, would my solitude be bliss?

There was only one way to find out.

Chapter Seven

ARLO

"That fucking girl," I snapped, tossing out a hand in the general direction of the clubhouse and storming up to Reece. He had one boot up on an old wooden shipping crate, a cigarette in his tattooed fingers, and a chuckle dancing on his stupid motherfucking lips.

"Dat fuckin' girl is *Le Gardien,* and you'd do best to get dat in your head and remember it, you." Reece stood up and flicked his still burning smoke into the water. "'Ey, Meme!" he shouted, calling for that stupid goddamn alligator again. But I wasn't done with my bitchin' session. If this asshole had time to stand here and feed marshmallows to a friggin' lizard, he had time to listen to me and complain.

"Yeah, the same guardian that our fathers' comrades had sex with over a hundred fuckin' years ago."

"Naw," Reece said, smacking his lips at the gator as she chomped down on a floating white marshmallow and then leapt up to crunch the bit of raw chicken off the end of his hook. "Just da same body, but not da same girl. A new soul be in dat girl, and you know it."

I clenched my damn teeth.

"She keeps fucking callin' me Cernunnos."

Reece threw back his head and laughed, flashing white teeth in a dark night. It was hard to believe, standing out here like this, that I'd seen that fragile fucking girl tear a man's soul to pieces right in front of me.

The hell is this world coming to?

My brothers might want things to go back to the way they used to be—down with the fucking Veil, a return to the Wild Hunt, a destiny laid out like a road map—but I sure as *shit* did not. I liked being a man, as close to human as anyone else in this club, and I liked living in the bayou, fucking club whores, smoking and drinking. I liked the business of hustling and I was damn good at it.

All of this magic shit?

My glamour shifted and cracked, just like that—and I still had my cut on, too. These leather vests, they were more than just colors for us, more than just symbols, they were quite literally a glamour, easy to toss on and take off when needed.

But here I was, standing in mine and it was shattered to shit.

"*Feet pue tan,*" Reece howled, turning his brown eyes over to me. *You son of a bitch.* "You *are* fuckin' Cernunnos, you dang fool, you." Reece shook his head and leaned down to pull a chicken leg out of the cooler, tossing it onto the warped wood of the old deck with a wet slap.

The gator—this six foot son of a bitch—leapt onto the wood and snatched it up before sinking back into the murky waters. The only light we had was the moon, but that was enough. As much as I wished I weren't sometimes, I was faerie.

Fucking. Goddamn. Faerie.

And it ain't as nice as any of that shit on TV or in books and movies.

No, the fae were dark and they were fucked and they were as awful as the lowest bottom dwelling scum humanity could dredge up. Hell, they were *worse* sometimes. A lot of the time.

"My father is Cernunnos," I growled out, but in the mix of wild bird calls, the whir of cicadas, and the grunts of gators, it was a weak noise.

"Your Père *was* Cernunnos," Reece said quietly, and I felt my entire body go stiff as he stood up straight and stretched his arms over his head.

I chose not to respond to that statement. What was the point?

He was right, and I goddamn *hated* it.

"Want to go hit the bars?" I asked and Reece scoffed, shaking his head and giving me a look like I was the craziest son of a bitch this side of the Mason-Dixon line.

"She won't much like dat and I'm not lookin' to make trouble wit' da Veil Keeper, me."

"Fuck the Veil Keeper," I snarled, turning and using the narrow path on the side of the clubhouse to get to the parking lot. Once there, I booted up my hog with a kick and got the fuck out of there before I did something crazy.

Like fuck a woman who was older than time itself …

And whose soul looked back at me with eyes too broken and too young to be so fucking sad.

The only bar in town that I was sure I could find a red-blooded *human* woman at this time of night was Voila Merde, which pretty literally meant *go to shit* in French. The tourists all thought it sounded real purdy, and the locals thought it was funny as hell.

It was a notorious mixing spot for out-of-towners that'd cleared their visit to our turf with the boss … and also the one place in town that the rougarou liked to stir shit up in front of humans.

The sign in front said *No Flying Colors,* but I ignored it and pushed my way inside, my glamour restored with the emergency bottle we all kept in our front pockets, my temper at an all-time high.

"Give me something that'll get me drunk quick," I said as I slid onto one of the cracked leather bar stools and flicked my glance to the right.

A curvy little blonde sat there all alone, sipping some bright blue froufrou drink and staring into her glass like it had the wisdom of the gods. But I'd met the gods. Shit, I was supposed to *be* one in a sense. And let me tell you this —they're just as fallible as mortals.

I studied her as I waited for my drink. She wasn't wearing a *Property Of* jacket, and clearly, she didn't have a man with her. Maybe she'd come down to Voila Merde to drown her sorrows … but I doubted she just wanted to drown them in alcohol.

Most women that came down here were looking for trouble … and sex.

Both of these I *could* provide, but I was much more inclined toward the latter. Especially with that curvy little piece of ass.

The bartender placed a tall shot glass in front of me and said nothing. Part of the reason I liked this place, bartenders weren't chatty. Tossing the shot of Bacardi 151 down my throat, I gestured for another before sliding off my stool and prowling closer to the blonde.

"Here alone?" It might have sounded like I was being polite, checking she didn't have a man on the way, but deep down I fucking hoped she did.

Despite having come here to bury my troubles deep inside some random human woman, all I kept seeing was the silken slide of dark hair, streaked with turquoise green.

That fucking Veil Keeper was in my head, and ruining what *should* have been an enjoyable random fuck in an alleyway.

"Unfortunately yes," the woman sighed dramatically, stirring her drink and batting her heavy false lashes in a way that was probably meant to be provocative. It only served to remind me of a certain amnesiac and her fae-damned doe eyes. This chick's watery blue didn't have a fucking thing on Ciarah's deep sapphire gaze. That woman's eyes seemed to see right through me every time she looked my way. Inspecting my soul, judging it.

Fuck it, I needed to clear my mind of the Veil Keeper and her perfect, creamy skin. Blondie would have to do.

"I was supposed to be meeting a guy, but he stood me up," the woman continued with a sultry pout. "Maybe you want to join me instead?"

Unable to lie, due to my true nature, I simply nodded sharply and slid onto the stool beside her. Had I been human, I would've offered a bullshit line like, "*I can think of nothing I'd rather do.*"

But I could. I could think of *plenty* of things I'd rather do, and all of them involved a mysterious, sad girl who had sat naked and willing in *my bed* just hours ago. And I'd turned her down.

The bartender placed another shot in front of me, which I threw back quickly. Maybe the haze of alcohol might help me enjoy this more.

Reece hadn't lied when he said *Le Gardien* would not be pleased. New soul or not, some personality traits had run true in the Veil Keeper since the beginning of time, and she was well-known for her temper and jealousy. This might just turn her against me, so she would stop fucking *tempting* me at every gods-damned turn.

Was that what I really wanted though?

It didn't matter. It's what I was going to do.

"You know, it's awfully loud in here," the woman said with a coy smile, "perhaps we should go somewhere quieter to … talk?"

She must have known how stupid that sounded. I'd barely said two words to her, and I think it was pretty obvious that *no one* came to Voila Merde to *talk*.

"Let's go," I grunted, tossing back yet another shot and slapping down some money onto the bar.

Blondie grinned like she'd just won the damn lottery and took my hand in her small clammy palm. I didn't blame her, I was handsome as fuck. Probably ten times more so than whatever creepy mouth breather she'd originally intended to meet.

She led me down the hallway, past the grimy bathrooms where I sometimes took chicks for a quick blow job, and out to the alleyway behind the bar. Once outside, she let the door slam shut behind us and I raised an eyebrow at her.

"Your first time to Voila Merde, sweetheart? You're supposed to prop the door open, else you get shut out here." Dumb bitch. The alleyway behind Voila Merde was gated, meaning that if you let that damn door close, you had to either climb the fence or wait til someone else opened the door again.

"Oopsie." She blinked up at me like she had conjunctivitis or something. Clearly, it was meant to be alluring, but it just came across as twitchy. Especially when compared to the Veil Keeper's steady, confident gaze.

Fuck, there I go again. Yep, best thing to do right now is get balls-deep in this random bitch and forget all about the living goddess.

"Whatever, I'll deal with it later." My hands fell to my belt, then paused as I looked at her with narrowed eyes. Something wasn't right here.

The grin this bitch was wearing wasn't one of someone excited to get some dick stuffed in her. It was more … triumphant? Like she'd just lured me into a trap or something.

Ah fuck.

"Well, look here, boys," sneered a voice from behind me and I sighed heavily. Just my fucking luck. "Seems like fairy boy fell for the oldest trick in the book."

"Tyrell," I smiled tightly at the hairy man as I turned to face him. Hairy was an understatement. Aside from having a long beard and longer hair, he also sported a mat of dark hair down both forearms which I had no doubt continued under his clothes. Some rougarou were like that. Never quite able to shed their fur entirely. Part of what made them inferior to werewolves.

"What the fuck do you want this time?" I snapped at him with derision. "That last ass-kicking I handed you wasn't enough? You wanted to come back for seconds?"

Tyrell was a slimy bastard, always pushing the limits of his turf, and all of us Wild Hunt boys had tangled with him a time or two in the past. My knuckles cracked as I closed my fists, already picturing my hand meeting Tyrell's ugly fucking face.

"You caught me off guard last time, dickhead," Tyrell growled—literally, given he was part wolf—and his eyes flicked over behind me.

This wasn't my first rodeo though, so I knew better than to take the bait and look. It was fairly obvious what I would find, anyway. Tyrell knew perfectly fucking well he didn't stand a chance against me in a fair fight, so he probably had backup.

"Couldn't handle me on your own, eh Tyrell? Needed to bring your posse to help out? Don't blame ya. We fucked you up *real* good last time we caught you poaching on our turf." My lip curled at him in disgust. Rougarou were *scum*.

"Let's just say, I stacked the deck." Tyrell grinned like the wolf he was, and casually swung the baseball bat he held in his hand. "Now, are you going to shut your purdy mouth and let me and my boys rearrange that face of yours? Ah, heck. Who am I kidding? Like I give a fuck."

Without anymore dicking around, Tyrell swung his bat at me, aiming for my ribs; I just managed to jump back out of his reach before it connected.

Unfortunately, that placed me right into the path of Tyrell's backup and I felt the heavy crack of a lead pipe smack into my other side from behind.

If I were human, that shit woulda knocked me flat on my ass.

But I was *far* from fucking human.

Ducking low, I avoided another swing from Tyrell's bat and buried my boot in another man's gut, sending him stumbling with with a grunt and a snarl.

Shitty thing about rougarou though—they weren't human either.

The pain of a foot to the stomach didn't drop the man I'd hit. Instead, all I managed to do was infuriate him enough to cause a full shift. And once one of these piece of shit swamp wolves went, so did the others.

With a howl, Tyrell dropped the wooden bat to the ground, the other man's lead pipe following shortly after. Wasn't a relief though. Hell no. I'd *much* rather deal with these pieces of shit in human form. The weapons they'd be wielding as wolves were much, *much* worse.

Tyrell lunged at me, his body that of a wolf, but instead of paws, he still had *human* hands.

When he hit me full force, knocking me to my back on the pavement, he curled his fingers around my biceps and held me there, his breath reeking of booze and rotten meat. When those inch long fangs of his plunged into my neck, I let out a scream that killed the sounds of the bayou for the briefest of moments before the animals resumed their infinite song.

Another rougarou came at me from behind, latching his jaws onto my skull and squeezing hard enough to crunch bone.

Fucking shit! I thought as I heard the blonde woman I'd picked up at the bar laughing.

The acrid stink of magic punctured the air around me, swirling in the breeze of the bayou and mixing with the stale piss and garbage smell of the alley. I was flailing around next to empty bottles, bleeding out near discarded used condoms.

What a way to go.

Wrapping my hands around the second rougarou's neck, I squeezed as hard as I could, snapping bones. The creature released me with a scream, giving me a moment to refocus my attention on Tyrell.

I could hear the blonde woman—one of the swamp witch's handmaidens, no doubt—casting a spell that I knew would fuck me up a hundred times worse than teeth and claws.

For an immortal, I sure as hell was convinced I was about to die.

But I knew from personal experience that there were things much, *much* worse than death.

Grabbing Tyrell by the scruffy fur on the back of his neck, I used all my strength to chuck him against the brick wall of the bar. The bricks cracked along with his bones and dust lifted into the night air, tainted silver by the moonlight.

Scrambling to my feet, I stumbled over to it and grabbed a handful of dust and debris. I wasn't no voodoo master, no black magic manipulator, but brick dust was powerful stuff.

I threw it in the witch's face, interrupting her as she worked to conjure some sort of elaborate set of supernatural *chains.*

But fuck, Reece was right—I was Cernunnos, and nobody challenged the Horned God.

I wasn't discriminatory either—if a man tried to kill me, I kicked his ass. If a woman tried to kill me, I kicked her ass too.

I hit the blonde in the face with the force of a Mack Truck, sending her stumbling back and slumping to the ground, just before teeth latched onto my ankle, another set taking hold of my bicep.

Two *different* rougarou spun me around, dragging me back to the pavement as several more rushed through a brand-new hole in the chain-link fence.

Shit, the whole MC is here ...

I knew then that I was screwed up the ass.

Three, four, even five rougarou, I could handle. But twenty? Thirty? Plus a couple of witches?

Several more of the men latched onto me, dragging me back through the hole and out toward a waiting line of motorcycles.

A woman sat on one, looking down at me with eyes the color of ice.

She said something in French that I couldn't quite hear, too much blood sloshing around in my skull, too many broken bones. I hurt all the fuck over.

Letting my glamour crack into pieces, I reached into

the earth and pulled strength from the ground, sending the long, wild limbs of a nearby angel oak ripping into the cluster of rougarou.

But the witch on the motorcycle, she silenced my magic with an easy wave of her hand.

The world around me went silent and this time, the animals did not resume their song.

Fuck.

I wasn't looking at another handmaiden.

Right now, I was looking at the swamp witch herself.

Oh blessed Morrígan.

The rougarou backed away, leaving me bleeding and broken on the ground. I struggled to sit up, my ribs shifting inside of me in a way that wasn't natural. My head was swimming and all I could taste in my mouth was the copper burn of blood.

"What the fuck do you want?" I snarled, red misting from my lips.

The witch didn't respond, dressed in leather, her mouth curving to the side in a terrifying semblance of a human smile. She stood up off the motorcycle as I watched, making her way toward me. In the human world, a woman riding her own bike, being the president of a motorcycle club? It was pretty slim, unless it was an all female group. And even then, there were those out there with views older than my goddamn grandpa's. They wouldn't like it.

But then, they'd never met a fuckin' swamp witch before.

She said nothing as she made her way over to me,

kneeling low and reaching out a hand that I promptly slapped away. With a slight gesture of her head, she summoned several rougarou to take hold of my arms, pinning me in place. The most disturbing part of the whole situation was that one of them had the body of a wolf … but the head of a *man,* his all too human fucking mouth latched onto my arm.

If I survived this, I was going to need a friggin' rabies shot.

The witch reached out again, and I dug my fingers into the earth.

I was the youngest incarnation of the Horned God, the warrior aspect. I should be able to fight, and I should be able to use the earth as my weapon.

Instead, I was powerless.

For the first time in my life, I was fucking powerless.

The swamp witch licked her lips.

"*Quel animal de compagnie adorable vous ferez,*" she told me in French, still smiling that strange smile of hers. *What an adorable pet you'll make.*

I clenched my jaw hard and waited to see what she might do.

A low, rolling snarl broke the silence and the forest burst back into brilliant, melancholy song.

The witch whipped her head around and snapped something low in French that I couldn't quite hear, rising to her feet as a large wolf stalked out of the shadows, the size of a fucking pony.

A werewolf.

Not a goddamn lousy rougarou, a human twisted into lycanthropy by magic.

The creature I was looking at, he lived and breathed by the moon.

Shifting into human form, the man stood well over six feet tall, his hair a brilliant and shocking silver, like liquid moonlight, his eyes a bloodred shimmer that radiated power.

He blinked several times before pulling his lips back in a wild snarl.

The fuck is this? The hell does the local alpha give a shit about my ass?

Behind him, several more enormous wolves prowled up, staying in animal form and flanking their leader with the flawless synchronization born of their ability to mind speak.

"This doesn't concern you, Raphael," the swamp bitch—I mean *witch*—snarled at the silver-haired man. He wasn't old, despite his unique coloring. Wolves simply carried the color of their pelt over into their human forms, and the Louisiana Pack Alpha was a rare silver wolf.

"Rosinée," the Alpha rumbled in a voice like thunder and danger, "how very lovely to see you out and about. And with your whole club too. My invitation to this party must have been lost in the mail."

All joking aside, even from my half-dead position on the ground I still saw the swamp witch pale at the alpha's words. Raphael LeRoux was *not* the sort of man who joked around. Nor was he one to walk away from a fight.

His wolves were vicious, bloodthirsty and merciless. The rougarou stood no chance against a pure blooded pack.

"Raphael," the swamp witch tried again, licking her lips nervously. "Leave us be. This is nothing to do with your pack."

"I disagree, Rosinée. This *very much* concerns my pack. I'm giving you one chance to leave with your pathetic pets intact, and then I let my people off the leash … so to speak." There was no mistaking the threat in Raphael's voice as his burning red eyes speared Rosinée.

For once, I stayed quiet. The wolves were saving my ass, but why? What interest did they have in whether I lived or died tonight?

The swamp witch clenched her fists at her sides and for a hot second, I thought she might actually be stupid enough to challenge the strongest alpha wolf this side of the Veil.

"Fine," she eventually ground out from behind clenched teeth. "But I'm not fucking done with you, *fairy*." This last part was directed at me as she turned her venomous glare to my face.

"I look forward to it, bitch," I sneered back at her, unable to rein in my smart mouth for even a second longer.

"Ticktock, Rosinée," the Alpha rumbled and the witch snarled. Throwing her leg back over her bike, she flicked a hand signal to her club and they all peeled out of there with the throaty growl of engines and exhausts.

In the resulting quiet, as the sound of the swamp

queen's MC faded into the distance, no one spoke. My bones were broken in several places, and I was bleeding profusely where I lay on the gravel, but Raphael LeRoux just stared down at me. His face was blank, totally unreadable, as were his enforcers on either side of him, still in wolf form.

"Uh, thanks, I guess." I broke the tense silence with my pained voice.

"We didn't come to help you," the wolf's alpha replied in a carefully neutral tone which made it damn near impossible to work out if I had just jumped from the frying pan and straight into the fire.

"Well …" I winced, pushing myself up to sitting and feeling the ache and burn of all my many injuries. "Thanks anyway."

Those old legends about never thanking a fae only applied to humans, and my mama had raised me with manners.

"Keep your thanks." Raphael shrugged. "Saving you from that old hag served a double purpose. One, it pissed her off. And I do love to piss her off."

He paused and I watched him curiously. "And the other reason?"

"Wait for it …" The scary ass motherfucker lifted a finger, his head tilted like he was listening for something. Seconds later, the familiar sound of motorcycles came rumbling from down the road toward us, pulling up where the rougarou had *just* departed from.

"Arlo!" a distinctive sultry sounding woman's voice

exclaimed, and that damn Veil Keeper collapsed to the ground in front of me. "What the hell happened here?"

My lips tightened and I considered just saying nothing. Why should I? I owed this girl nothing. Goddess or not, she was no one to me.

Yet when my eyes met hers, and her vivid sapphire blue gaze screamed of such pain, and desperation and *fear* … How the fuck could I contribute to that?

"Rougarou lured me into a trap; the wolves here showed up just in the nick of time." I nodded to Raphael over Ciarah's shoulder. It had not escaped my attention that the second my boys had shown up, the wolf alpha had eyes for no one else but our *Gardien du Voile.*

"Oh." Ciarah turned her head as though she'd just seen the handsome silver-haired man and his two accompanying wolves flanking him. How she could have missed them though, was totally beyond me. Those wolves were the size of large donkeys, not to mention their inhumanly handsome leader.

I wasn't blind. Just as I could appreciate my own good looks, so too could I appreciate them in other men. And women.

Once again my attention had been drawn back to Ciarah. She picked herself up from the ground, wiping dirt off on her jeans and pushing her long hair over her shoulder.

Whatever she said next was lost as Killian took her place in front of me and clasped his palms on either side of my face.

"Hold on tight, brother. This will be a bumpy ride." He met my gaze with his own cold blue eyes and the familiar sensation of his magic began crawling through me, blocking out the world around us and deafening me to whatever was happening between Ciarah and Raphael.

Chapter Eight

CIARAH

The man standing between the two enormous fucking wolves was watching me like … well … like a wolf might watch a piece of meat.

"Um, Reece?" I asked, flicking a quick glance over at the huge red-haired biker, but not wanting to take my eyes off this guy for too long.

"Raphael LeRoux." Reece nodded to the silver-haired man respectfully and I raised my eyebrows in curiosity. The name rang no bells in my sketchy at best memory, but that meant nothing. "What's da Pack doin' in N'awlins den?"

"Reece," the man nodded back but his red eyes were still locked on me. His voice rumbled like an angry dog and it sent shivers of fear and … something else, coursing through me. "Heard *Le Gardien du Voile* had resurfaced.

Needed to see for myself whether the rumours were true."

"*Trè bon,* Alpha. Now, you've seen. Ciarah, *allons*." Reece tugged at my elbow to draw me back to his bike, but I was transfixed by the beautiful man and his gigantic wolves.

"Hello." I smiled at him, not really knowing why. Something inside me, something *instinctual,* told me he was one of the good guys. He'd barely spoken, yet those words he did utter had glimmered with *truth.*

Unlike Arlo's explanation for his injuries. That hadn't been a *lie* as such, because fae couldn't lie. But it carried a jarring uneasiness that made me sure he was hiding important details.

"Ciarah, was it?" the handsome man inquired, his words polite but his voice threaded with danger and *power.* "Allow me to formally introduce myself. I am Raphael LeRoux, Alpha and President of the Louisiana Wolves. This here is my beta, and VP, Marcel." He laid a hand on the slightly larger, chestnut brown wolf to his right. "And my delta, my enforcer, Amelie." He indicated to the jet-black wolf on his left and it—*she*—bobbed her head to me in greeting.

"It's, er, lovely to meet you?" I didn't intend for it to come out as a question but it somehow did nonetheless. One corner of the Alpha's mouth pulled up in what *I think* was meant to be a smile and he finally blinked.

It was as if I had been freed from some sort of trap, and I could suddenly breathe again, while he snapped his fingers at the two wolf-ponies. At his command, the two of them *shifted* in one fluid movement until they were in their human forms.

Marcel, to Raphael's right, was a Spanish looking man with close-cropped chestnut brown hair and mean looking eyes. Amelie, to his left, was a stunning woman with willowy curves and jet-black hair tightly woven into hundreds of thin braids.

“So you will know them in both of their forms,” Raphael informed me and I nodded slowly. That was *true* … but there was something else … I cocked my head to the side, frowning at the handsome wolf Alpha while I tried to work out what could possibly be hiding in that statement.

Or maybe I was reading him wrong.

“That's a cool trick,” I commented, indicating to the fact that his wolves had just shifted fully-clothed. “I imagine it would be pretty annoying to carry clothes around with you everywhere.” Beside me, I felt Reece tense. His hand on my arm tightened a fraction and I wondered what I'd said wrong.

“Yes.” Raphael nodded and this time, both sides of his mouth pulled up in a smile. “It is a *cool trick*.” His bloodred eyes narrowed at me, causing his smile to turn into something more predatory.

“It's been a very long time since *Le Gardien du Voile* was seen. A *very* long time. Have you come to fix the Veil, then?” All three wolves watched me in hungry curiosity and I frowned.

What did he mean *fix the Veil*?

"*Allons, bebelle,*" Reece interjected, tugging at my elbow more firmly this time. "Kill is almost done healin' Arlo. We need to get goin' outta here."

"Of course, I didn't mean to keep you." Raphael snapped his fingers once more and his companions melted back into their wolf forms. "It was lovely to make your acquaintance … *Ciarah*." As he said my name, he flicked a glance at Reece, who tensed even further.

"Ah, sure. Nice to meet you too, Raphael." I nodded and he quirked another small smile.

"Please, *cher*, call me Rafe." At this parting remark, he too shifted into wolf form, a glorious moonlight colored creature with burning bloodred eyes that stared straight through me before the three of them disappeared into the night.

Reece tugged at my elbow once more, but this time I let him lead me back to the bikes where he wrapped his huge hands around my waist and swung me onto the seat of his hog.

"Dat was mighty foolish of you, *cher*," he spoke quietly, but with *truth*. "Dat dog wasn't here for polite hellos, so he wasn't. Nah, *bebelle*, he wanted *lagniappe*. Somethin' extra."

"Like what?" I asked, confused as all hell. But that seemed to be my constant state since waking up in that dark and dirty alleyway. Confused.

"Now dat, ma little *minou*, I don't know." He swung his leg over the seat to settle in front of me while we waited for Arlo and Killian to mount their own beasts.

"But we sure soon to find out."

My new bedroom left much to be desired, but it was also a far cry from the place I'd spent my last five years. And possibly even my nineteen years before that? But still, even though the sheets were clean, rustling in a warm breeze from the open window, there was a sense of desperation, a flicker of feeling *lost* that settled over the room.

I swung my feet out of bed and felt the heaviness of my wings dragging behind me. I *could* reign them in, but I wasn't sure that I particularly *liked* to.

Nor did I like this room.

I swept my hands down my face and paused as a tiny creature landed on my windowsill and bared fanged teeth at me in a hiss. It had shimmery wings, like a dragonfly's, while the rest of it looked vaguely human.

"Hello little sprite," I said, even though I had no idea *how* I knew what the thing was called. "No need to be so upset. I won't infringe on your territory."

It looked at me with solid black eyes, the shape of sideways almonds, and then it hissed again, its mouth splitting its face seemingly in half. I frowned. The sprites were very particular over what other fae were welcome in their territory, but not only was I the Veil Keeper, but I was also *not* in their land whatsoever.

Veil Keeper? Sprites? How the fuck do I know this stuff?

I waved my hand at the sprite's mottled green body—its species was one who took after their own environment—and it *bit* me as hard as it could, drawing blood from my hand. It swelled in fat ruby drops and plopped to the old hardwood floors.

"Release me at once," I said, and magic swept into the room, swirling the curtains, knocking over a dusty vase filled with dried flowers. The *other* me buried deep inside was appalled at the sprite's lack of manners. "Release me," I repeated, my voice … husky but *dangerous.* Not my own. Not my own voice at all.

I felt my hands twitch, as if they were no longer under my control.

"Let go!" I snarled, and then my other hand was coming up and grabbing the creature around its tiny naked body. It was the size of a Barbie Doll, but even more alien, more exaggerated in its appearance. My fingers squeezed tighter, and it finally released its hold on my hand.

But I didn't let go.

My grip tightened, and I felt the magic in the room coil around me, ancient and old and sleepy. But angry, too. Furious.

With a sharp gasp, I released the small creature and stumbled back, leaving its crumpled form on the windowsill. After a moment of trying to catch my breath, I eased forward and poked it gently.

It was dead.

My heart dropped into the pit of my stomach, and I turned, fleeing the room, my wings sweeping along the wood floor as I ran.

Straight into Arlo's room.

The door was locked, but a flick of my finger and a dusting of magic *un*locked it.

How I did that, I wasn't sure. But the same part of me that had killed the sprite had done it, that much I knew for certain.

Padding across the wood, I lifted up the corner of Arlo's blanket and slid into bed with him.

He was already growling and groaning under his breath, turning to face me, his naked body pressing up close to mine.

"The fuck are you doing in here again?" he snarled, but I was already reaching out and curling my fingers around his shoulders, putting my head in the crook of his neck. He smelt of mint soap and earth, fresh and wild.

In sleep, he'd shed his glamour so when he lifted his head to look at me, I looked into the emerald eyes of a god. His white horns curved up and away from the tousle of curled dark hair on his head.

He was magnificent, even if I was a bit pissed off at him, too.

"I killed something," I whispered in low tones, "and also, I don't like that room. I much prefer this one."

Arlo just stared at me for a long moment, dropping a

hand to my hip.

My sleeping shirt had ridden up, revealing the pale curve of bare flesh, and his palm rested directly against it, teasing me.

"You killed something?" he asked, but his voice was husky, too, like he didn't much care about that part of my story. Maybe he cared more about the fact that he was naked and I was not wearing panties, that he was an earth god, all male and desperate to breed, and I was a very willing female.

I reached out and put a palm on his chest, my lips parted to ask him about the sprite, when the door opened and Killian appeared.

"Ciarah," he said, voice soft, lifting up the tiny creature by one of its minuscule little feet. "I found this in your room."

"That is not my room," I corrected, sitting up and loving the feel of Arlo's palm sliding down my hip to rest on my thigh. "This one is now."

"The fuck it is—" Arlo began to growl, but I stifled him by reaching out and curling my fingers around the base of his rigid shaft.

"This is my room now," I repeated, squeezing him almost as hard as I'd squeezed that poor creature. *Shit, why had I done that? And how fucking terrifying was it that I didn't know how to stop?*

"I find it disturbing that a sprite even thought to come to the clubhouse," Killian said, his voice buttered with just the slightest hint of a French accent. His words were mellifluous and inviting, a siren's song. I wet my lips and blinked past the feeling. "They come in swarms, you know. Thousands upon thousands of them. They can strip a person of flesh in less than a minute." He wrinkled his nose at the little creature, and sneered with distaste. "I'll give this to Reece to feed to that gator of his," he added, turning to go and then pausing, seemingly stopped by the expression on my face. "Don't feel bad about this, *mon cher.* Sprites are less than rats. They eat everything and every*one* that comes into their corner of the swamp."

I lifted the hand with the bite on it, still bleeding and still *hurting,* and Kill frowned.

"I'll come back and heal that," he started, but I was already shaking my head.

"Just go," I said, the morning sunshine reflecting off the steel toes of his boots. "And I'll come down when I'm ready."

"The president is here," he said carefully, "and so is his wife. If you take too long, they'll come looking for you." With a sinful slash of smile, Killian turned and left, closing the door behind him.

"You want to take your hand off my dick?" Arlo growled, but he made no move to stop me, and it was clear what he wanted from the expression on his face and the vibrant heat in his words.

"No," I said, frowning and then turning toward him, throwing one leg over his pelvis and settling myself on top of him. My hand was still in front of me, wrapped about the base of his cock. "Why did you leave last night?"

“None of your damn—” Arlo started again, but I abruptly released his shaft and crawled forward, straddling his hardness with the nakedness between my thighs, looking down at him with that same wild stare I'd given the sprite. Magic was still in the air, riding me hard, and I didn't know what to do with it.

Whatever man I want is mine, the voice inside my head told me.

The *other* part of me said that was a tad archaic, a little sexist … but even *she* didn't really care. No, both sides of me found the thought intriguing.

“Did you kiss her?” I asked, leaning toward his stubbled jaw and pressing my lips against the side of it. I didn't *really* know if there was a *her* at all, but then … isn't there always?

“You need to get the hell off of me and out of my room before …” Arlo started, putting one of his big hands on either side of my hips. My tongue flicked across my lower lip, drawing his attention.

“Did you? I'd know if you fucked her. I would've smelled it.”

“You creepy bitch,” Arlo said, but then he was reaching between us and taking hold of himself in one hand, guiding the head of his shaft to my opening. Our eyes were locked as he found the glorious wetness between my thighs and cursed under his breath. “Motherfucker …” he breathed, just as I sat back and slid down the length of him, taking the velvety girth of his shaft deep inside of me.

"Did you kiss her?" I asked one more time, sitting on him, feeling him trapped inside of me. After so many years of being powerless … I quite enjoyed the switch.

"No," Arlo ground out, putting pressure on my hips and holding me in place. "Not that it'd be any of your business if I *had.*"

"It is *all* my fucking business," I said, putting a hand against the side of his face and curling my fingers so that my nails dug into his skin. "Everything that happens with the Wild Hunt is my business. And everyone in it? They belong to me."

"Fucking hell," Arlo snarled, but then my mouth was pressing against his, and he was lifting a hand to put pressure on the back of my head. Our kiss … it was violent and primal, an uncomplicated meeting of the masculine and feminine aspects of nature. Our tongues slid together, twisted in a rush of vibrant heat, and my hips began to move, both soothing and claiming the beast beneath me.

My fingers lifted up and curled around of Arlo's horns, sending a shiver through his body. Once again, I knew things I shouldn't have known … like how Arlo's horns were erogenous zones. I had never met a man with horns … never met a faerie … as far as I could tell?

It was all so confusing, living with two personalities inside my head.

But as I began to move, I realized those feelings were drifting further and further from me, replaced with the bestial pleasure of a good rut, a wild mating.

Arlo moaned against my mouth as my body rocked on top of him, taking everything and demanding more. My lips left his and my back arched, tilting my hips until I could feel the tip of him sliding and scraping against my sweet spot, sending lightning bolts of pleasure shooting through me.

The heavy drape of my wings blanketed his thighs as I leaned back further, shivering as the new nerve endings lit up.

His hands slid up from my waist, pushing up my sleep shirt and cupping my breasts in his hands. My breath sucked in sharply as his fingers found my nipples, pinching them and rolling them roughly. He probably intended it to be a show of power and control, but it just made me chuckle low in my throat. Silly man, had he not learned by now? I was his *goddess*.

Not to mention the stinging bite of his fingers on my sensitive flesh only served to arouse me further.

Somewhere in the edge of my memory, a shadowy figure spoke to me of pain *far* outweighing this. Years on years of torture and despair. But when I tried to grab ahold of the memory, to examine it closer, it melted away like mist.

"Veil Keeper, don't go thinking this means you own me," Arlo growled, his unglamoured voice rich and husky. When his hands returned to my waist and he began to thrust up into me, his eyes locked on mine with a wild intensity that gave me chills. In a good way.

My only response was another sultry laugh, because

we *both* knew that was exactly what this meant. I owned him, body and soul. And right now, that body needed to learn a damn lesson.

Bracing my hands on his hard, muscled chest, I rode him like the wild thing he was, building my own climax and not hesitating for a second before giving into the euphoric haze of orgasm. My fingernails dug into his skin, hard enough to draw blood, while I cried out my release then *immediately* sat up and let his *hard-as-fuck* cock slip from my cunt.

"What are you doing?" Arlo panted in confusion, his huge hands gripping at my hips.

"Listen carefully, Cernunnos." My voice was both mine and *hers*; every time we spoke our voices mixed just a little more and I knew it wouldn't be long until we were one. "If you ever so much as *think* of putting this inside another woman." My hand grasped his slick shaft in a tight grip once more. "You'll have a hell of a lot more to deal with than just a case of blue balls. Am I clear?"

Arlo glared back at me, his bright green eyes furious and disbelieving. As his lip curled, no doubt preparing to tell me where to shove it, my fingers tightened around his dick and I let *her* meet his gaze.

Slowly, ever so slowly, he nodded his agreement and I released him one finger at a time.

"Good," I nodded without blinking, but swung my leg off him and stood. My wings brushed across his midsection as I moved, and he sucked in a sharp breath.

"Your president and his wife are waiting downstairs," I

reminded him, "we shouldn't keep them waiting."

Arlo glared at me for a long moment, but I held his gaze unwaveringly. Amnesia or not, I knew what I was doing here.

"Fine," he ground out, pushing up from his bed and deliberately crowding me with his enormous frame. I didn't so much as bat an eyelid though, and he moved to his dresser to throw on a pair of low slung black jeans and a thin looking t-shirt. He made a very deliberate show of stroking himself, as he tucked his still erect shaft inside his jeans, and my mouth watered.

What did he taste like? I could smell his pent-up desire from across the room, and it was almost enough to make me change my mind.

"Do you plan on wearing pants?" He challenged me, as I stood there with my head cocked, watching him.

"No," I replied, "come along."

Before I could give in to the primal urge to tear the fabric clean off his body, I turned and led the way back down the stairs to the main room where I'd first met Reece.

It didn't bother me to be totally naked under my loose sleep shirt. There were ragged slits in the back for my wings, which I still wasn't inclined to put away, and I was comfortable.

Of course, knowing I was without underwear and still slick with arousal would be driving Arlo to near distraction.

"Fucking creepy bitch," he muttered again. His

glamour was back in place, and he'd tugged on his leather vest displaying the Wild Hunt patch.

As he passed me, though, his fingertips trailed over the tips of my wings and an involuntary moan escaped my throat.

Bastard.

Two could play at that game. If he didn't want to roll over and take this punishment like a man—*fae, god, whatever*—then this meeting with his president was about to get *very* uncomfortable.

At least, I hoped it would. *Come on patchy memory, don't fail me now.*

I padded down the stairs and into the common room, finding Reece, Killian, Donal, Fionn, and a woman I didn't recognize waiting for me. I could've felt something like shame or embarrassment at my undressed and aroused state, but I didn't. Half of me said I should; the other half was confused as to why I'd even *consider* something like that.

Arlo came up behind me where I was blocking the doorway, and growled low in his throat, reaching down to put his hands on my shoulders and move me out of the way. I let him, watching the woman's back carefully.

Her leather jacket said *Property of Fionn mac Cumhaill,* but when she turned to look at me, red lips curving up in a smile, I got the feeling that that was just a front. This woman … didn't belong to anyone but herself. In fact, the more I looked at her, the more the words on her back felt like a joke.

"Hello Veil Keeper," she said, her voice this husky purr that made me shiver. There was power in that voice. "My name is Sadhbh." She pronounced it like the number *five,* but with an S. I tried it out on my tongue.

"Sadhbh," I repeated as she made her way toward me in leather pants, motorcycle boots, and hair as red as blood. Her green eyes bored into mine as I looked up to meet her much taller gaze.

"Dis here is my Mère," Reece said, lighting up a cigarette. I could feel both him and Killian watching me the same way I could feel Arlo doing everything in his power to *not* watch me. He wanted to look and it was *killing* him to avert his gaze.

That made me smile.

"His Mère, my old lady," Fionn said, rising from his chair and moving over to the bar. He gestured with his chin in Arlo's direction. "Pour me some Scotch, boy," he told the horned god, and I saw Arlo's jaw clench. He was an alpha male through and through, and he didn't like being told what to do by anyone—not even his president. Maybe he had an easier time of it when he wasn't coming down from a scolding?

I smiled a little wider.

"Old lady," Sadhbh said with a scoff. "You best shush, old man, before I get angry."

She flicked her eyes in her husband's direction before looking back at me. But my eyes had wandered over to the two hound dogs in the corner, watching me with a certain level of intelligence that was far above your average Irish wolfhound. There was something almost … human about those eyes.

I tore my attention away from them and found Killian watching me, his sinful lips twisting into an inviting sort of smile. His blue eyes locked onto mine and I found that my heart rate sped up, my palms sweated, and I was distinctly aware of the fact that I wasn't wearing panties.

Lifting my wings up off the floor, I moved over to the edge of the cracked leather sofa and sat down, letting the heavy limbs rest along the back side. The muscles in my shoulders and back didn't feel strong enough to hold them yet.

Sadhbh sat down on the other side of the couch and snapped her fingers.

With a growl, Reece flicked his cigarette into an ash tray and moved over to the bar, grabbing her a drink and placing it into her outstretched fingers. Hmm. Yes, definitely a different dynamic than a typical motorcycle club. I couldn't remember a lot from … before, whatever *before* all of this had been, but I knew that there was often a displaced power dynamic, with women on the bottom and men on the top.

Neither the ancient voice inside of me nor my own thoughts imagined that'd be much fun.

I liked *this* dynamic.

"So, Veil Keeper, how are you faring?" she asked me, her voice tinted with a hint of a Cajun accent, but more like she'd absorbed it from living here for so long rather than being born here. I just looked at her, but I didn't know how to answer. I could talk now, but so many years of *not* talking seemed to make natural conversation slightly more difficult.

How was I faring?

I didn't know.

So far, I'd slept with two men, torn a man's soul to shreds, and grown wings.

Was that a sign that I was doing well?

"I don't know," I said, licking my lips carefully and looking around the room at the bearded Donal and his president. They were watching me with a certain level of interest … and expectation. Not sexual, I didn't think, more like … they expected great things from me. Important things.

"I see you've been getting to know some of the men here," Sadbh said, but her words didn't sound judgmental, just curious. "I hope you found my son pleasing to take to bed."

Reece laughed and shook his head, tossing back a drink and muttering something under his breath. I guess it didn't matter how old or tough a man was, when his mother set out to embarrass him, she could do it with a certain amount of flair.

"He was lovely, thank you," is what I said, because I wasn't sure *what* else to say. Sadbh laughed and Fionn made a rough sort of coughing sound like he was trying to remind her of something. She snapped a green glare in his direction and then turned back to me, reaching out to take my hands in hers. Her eyes were sparkling as she looked into mine, full of hope. Hope for what, I wasn't sure, but it shone so brightly that I had to look away to catch my breath.

"I imagine this is all very strange to you," she said carefully, and I nodded because fuck, I couldn't lie. I felt like at one time in my life, I had that ability, but not anymore. "But you're in the right place at the right time, my friend," she continued, her words ringing so brightly with truth that it made my breath catch. "You were meant to come here and find us. This," she gestured a hand at the men standing in the room with us, "this is your Wild Hunt, and your destiny."

Truth, truth, truth ... everything this woman said was *true.*

"Do you know what you're here to do? Do you know who you are?"

"The Veil Keeper," I answered her, but the words were somewhat empty because I didn't entirely understand what that description entailed. I *was* the Veil Keeper; I could feel it in my bones. But … how did I keep this Veil? What was it? Where was it? Or was it a who? I didn't even know that fucking much.

"I wish I could tell you this was going to be easy or that there was some way to bring all your memories rushing back but … I can't do that. Ciarah, you were chosen by the last Veil Keeper to be reborn into this body." She paused and reached out a single finger to touch my chest. "This is the same body that's been the Veil Keeper for millennia. The soul inside changes, but the memories and the feelings and the knowledge of power, those stay the same."

Her words were true, I knew that beyond a shadow of doubt, but they didn't make sense.

How could what she was saying be correct when I had so few memories to speak of? And those few that I had retrieved from the murky darkness of my mind, were they mine? Hers? Did it even matter?

"I can see I have confused you, and this worries me," Sadbh frowned, cocking her head to one side as her intense gaze raked over me. "Why don't you tell me more about that?"

My gaze flickered around the room, landing briefly on Reece and Arlo, two men—two sidhe—I'd so recently allowed inside my body. Her body. Fuck, this was a mind trip. Killian watched impassively, his face smooth and unreadable. Beyond him, Donal and Fionn, two huge, bearded men who clearly ran this show.

"You can trust everyone in this room, Veil Keeper," Sadhbh informed me, seeming to read my mind. "We are all invested in your well-being. We have wanted for nothing, these past hundred and eighty-six years, than for the Keeper to resurface and the Veil to be restored."

I nodded, cautiously. Again she spoke the truth.

"I don't…" My voice cracked a little and I cleared my throat before trying again. "I have few memories, and no knowledge of power. Why?"

"We don't rightly know." Sadhbh's voice was quiet, saturated with pain and sadness. "But I understand you have regained … *something*?"

"Barely. Fractured shards of memory at best. Echoes of pain and torture, of despair and desperation. My knights did as they were commanded, and preserved the secrets of the Veil." As I spoke, my voice had shifted into that lower, sultry tone that I was growing accustomed to. She was both her and me, but we were not yet joined enough to share one mind. "Knowledge is power just as dangerous as power itself, and the risk was too great."

Sadhbh nodded, pursing her vibrant red lips while the five enormous fae watched me with unblinking stares.

"That makes sense why you are this way. How can we help you retrieve the secrets?" She raised her eyebrows and the *hope* that reflected in her clear green gaze made my heart hurt because I already knew the answer to her question.

"You can't," I replied softly, my voice once more my own. "Only I can unravel a spell of her—*my*—creation. Only me, and my knights."

"Dem Fae Lords," Fionn muttered, "dey long since gone from dis world, almost as long as you yerself, *Gardien*."

"Not them." I frowned, chasing the soapy bubbles of memory in my mind. "They were *hers* and when she ceased to exist, so too did they."

"Ahhh," Sadhbh nodded and gave me a knowing smile before she sat back and grinned at her husband. "Fionn, *mo grá*, get us some drinks would you? You're being a terrible host. If we're to aid our *Gardien,* we can't be expected to sit here with dry mouths, no?"

The red-haired MC president raised an eyebrow at his wife's order and flicked a hand at Donal, who obediently disappeared into the kitchen.

"Now then, I suspect you have already claimed my son to be your Lord of Autumn?" Sadhbh narrowed her eyes at me shrewdly and words escaped me. *She* had withdrawn completely, leaving me vacant minded and sweating under this intimidating woman's stare.

"Um." My eyes wide, I glanced over at Reece but he seemed just as interested in the answer to this question as his mother did. Shit.

"Boss." Donal interrupted our Mexican standoff as he came back into the room. How I knew what a Mexican standoff was, but not how I'd come to be in this body, I had no idea.

"What is it?" Fionn snapped, looking annoyed at this intrusion into my decidedly awkward moment.

"Someone's here to see *Le Gardien*." Donal scratched at his bearded chin and shrugged his leather clad shoulders. "Want me to tell her to fuck off?"

"Her?" I asked, despite the question not having been directed at me. They were talking *about* me and that seemed far more rude than me butting in.

"Yeah." Donal nodded, acknowledging my question. "The Louisiana Wolves Delta, Amelie."

"Let her in," I ordered, with a steely note of *command* in my voice.

Donal hesitated, glancing from me to his president and

back again. When Fionn said nothing to contradict me, Donal shook his head slightly.

"Naw, girl. You don' get it, see? The Louisiana Wolves are a club all in of themselves, ya? It's not good manners to be goin' turnin' up at each other's clubhouse uninvited." Donal clicked his tongue, like I was the stupidest fucking thing alive.

Maybe I was.

But one thing I knew for sure … this Hunt *belonged* to me. How dare he question my orders?

"*Let her in*," I ordered once more, pressing a careful mental finger against the little glowing orb that was Donal.

That was all it took. Just the reminder that I *was* the Veil Keeper. Memories or not. And I was *never* to be disobeyed.

"Of course, *Gardien*, right away." Donal dipped his head in obedience and retreated back out of the room. His face beneath his beard was pale, and his gaze skittered across the floor like a horse in a thunderstorm, but instead of regretting my actions, I felt almost a sense of satisfaction.

"Good." Sadhbh murmured, watching me with the intensity of a falcon on a mouse. "The unity between old and new is still happening. It's slow. But it's happening. There is hope for us all yet."

This time, I knew exactly what she meant. I could feel it happening. Feel my mind … *shifting*. With every word we spoke, every magic we used, we became closer to one.

"Delta." Fionn stood as the dark wolf-woman entered the room with an animalistic grace.

"President." She nodded in return, then turned her golden brown eyes to me. "Veil Keeper."

She flashed a bright grin at me, moving into the room and past Reece's scowling face. Arlo growled at her, but Killian just watched impassively, like he didn't much care either way. I saw right through him. Nobody in this room liked the werewolf.

"Can we help you?" Sadhbh asked with a cocked brow, pushing red hair over her shoulder and turning to face the newcomer. "You're breaking every rule in the book right now."

"Rules?" the girl said with a laugh, scooping her waist-length braids forward and moving around Sadhbh to take a spare seat. "What rules? The Veil Keeper's back; there are no rules."

"Like hell dere ain't," Reece snarled, but his mother lifted a hand to shush him. He growled low under his breath and I flicked my eyes his way, watching as his snarl shifted into a slight grin. "We don't need no wolves prowlin' around da clubhouse, Miss Ciarah."

"Why are you here?" I asked, because I wanted to hear for myself. That, and I was intrigued by the alpha we'd met outside the bar. "What do you want?"

"What do I want?" the girl asked me, her honey-brown eyes locked onto mine. Her skin was the color of roasted pecans, her clothing not dissimilar to what Sadhbh was wearing, only more colorful. Underneath her leather jacket, she had on a bright pink shirt that she'd paired with holey jeans and brown boots. "I want what everyone here wants," she said, and I tasted the truth in the air as she spoke, wetting my lips for a moment. "I want back across the Veil," she said, like her voice was strained to the point of breaking. "I want to see what else is out there beyond this *shit* ..." She trailed off, snapping that last word off the end of her tongue and scowling as she turned away.

"You're a child, too young to miss the Veil," Fionn said, but the Delta girl—Amelie—ignored him.

"You're not the same Veil Keeper," she said, chewing her lower lip. "That's good because we need someone modern to deal with the modern world, not some old bag of bones."

"That's enough!" Fionn roared, but Sadhbh reached out and put her hand on his belly.

"That *is* quite enough," she whispered and I swear, for a moment there, I saw his glamour crack. Either that, or I could simply … see through it to the man underneath. I turned back to Amelie.

"Rafe has sent me as his representative, to ensure that our pack isn't left in the dust when the time comes."

"How arrogant," Killian said, his arms crossed over his chest, his leather trench coat hanging down past the seat of the bar stool he was perched on. He leaned forward, putting an elbow on either knee and steepling his fingers together. "The fact that your alpha thinks you even *deserve* a representative. This is gentry business."

"The Veil is everyone's business," Amelie ground out,

flicking her eyes briefly to Killian and then turning back to me. "The last Veil Keeper didn't think so, but maybe this one is different?" She scooted toward me. "Are you different, then? You feel different. You might be in *her* body, but you've still got a mind of your own, don't you?"

"I …" I started to say, but Arlo interrupted, clearly still upset at not having been able to finish mating. I had the bull by the horns so to speak.

"Let's toss this bitch out on her ass," he growled, stalking across the room.

Amelie was up and out of her seat, spinning around to stand behind the couch.

"You touch me and it's war," she snapped, her teeth much longer, much sharper than a normal human's. But then, she wasn't human, was she? She was werewolf.

"Touch you? You come in here and try to manipulate the Veil Keeper? I should rip you to pieces and feed you to Reece's goddamn gator."

"Try me," Amelie snarled, but I was already rising to my feet.

"She stays," I blurted and saw Arlo's green eyes flicker over to mine, the color of wet leaves after a rainstorm. He looked ready to kill the wolf girl. "I want to know what else she has to say."

"What *else?*" Arlo snapped, gesturing wildly in the girl's direction. "She doesn't know *shit.* Killian is right—this is gentry business."

"You mean *faerie* business," Amelie purred, a menacing note in her voice.

"I mean *gentry,*" Arlo growled right back.

It took my fractured mind a moment to put the pieces together. *Faerie, fae ... any creature born on the other side of the Veil, sharing one intrinsic quality ... they cannot lie. And gentry? The elite, the ruling class, like the sidhe.*

"I can't take anymore shouting," I whispered, because shouting brought to mind other things, endless nights of torture and pain, of iron teeth and claws, being berated for memories that I didn't have, that I didn't know. This was almost the same as that—everyone wanted to know what I knew, and they wanted me to do something about it.

I didn't know a fucking thing.

And I also knew there was a damn good reason for that.

I rose from my seat at the same moment I heard a car pull up outside the clubhouse, tires loud against the gravel driveway.

"Fuck me, that'll be Caley," Arlo said, glancing at an old clock on the wall, its plastic face cracked right down the middle. The room went silent for a moment as Arlo's sister entered and then went completely still.

"I was just checking in …" she began as Arlo rolled his eyes at her.

"Caley," I said, because I felt like I needed to get out of there. "I don't have any clothes."

"Clothes?" she asked, still dressed in her waitress uniform, her dark hair in a messy bun atop her head. "You want clothes?"

“I’ll give you some money,” Sadhbh said, nodding in Caley’s direction. “Take our new friend here shopping and get her some outfits.”

“I just worked a double!” Caley whined, and paused when Arlo whipped her a violent look.

“When the president’s old lady asks you to do something, you say *yes ma’am,* and hop to it,” he snarled and his sister sighed, tucking a few loose strands of hair back with her blue painted fingernails.

“Yes, sir,” she said, but there was a hint of sarcasm in the way she said *sir* that I liked. “Alright, *Gardien du Voile,* why don’t you, um, clean up a bit and I’ll take you out?”

I nodded and rose to my feet, glancing over at Amelie.

“Would you like to come, too?” I asked, because I had vague memories of girlfriends and shopping and … my brain was craving something that resembled normalcy, whatever that was anymore. I couldn’t decide if shopping for clothes was normal … if fucking a horned god was normal … or if they both were.

What I did know was that I had a whole eternity of secrets to unravel and no surefire way to go about it except …

Except maybe one …

Chapter Nine

KILLIAN

Arlo and Reece were too hotheaded to be of any use today, so I tagged along with *le Gardien* to a small boutique at the edge of the swamp. It was a trashy little place on the outside, but the clothes sold inside weren't so bad. And anyway, it was the *only* shop this far outside the city limits. We could've driven into town, but ten minutes in Caley's car and Ciarah was already starting to feel sick from the effects of the iron.

One positive of growing up in the modern world, most of us alive now had twice—if not three times—the tolerance to iron that our ancestors did. But *Le Gardien du Voile?* Even if her soul was young and fragile, her body was ancient and used to the old ways. Iron was poison; iron killed.

I stood outside on the porch, next to an old man in a rocking chair who was singing old blues songs and smoking a tobacco pipe. He was blind, his eyes milky and white, but I sensed the power in him. I didn't know what he was, but I was keeping an eye on him, just in case. Although he did seem more inclined to stay draped in his old chair, watching a sunny day in the bayou that he couldn't see.

"Hello." Ciarah spoke from beside me and I startled. How had she just snuck up on me so quietly? When I glanced down though, it wasn't me she was speaking to.

The old man paused in his song and his head tilted in Ciarah's general direction.

"Who dat?" he asked, his milky eyes staring out at nothing between our heads.

"What are you?" The living goddess beside me spoke with genuine curiosity, ignoring the man's rhetorical question. Undoubtedly if I could smell the power on him, so too could she. His old blind man routine wasn't fooling anyone here.

"Dat be a verra rude question for an ol' man, cher." He hedged Ciarah's question like a pro, so he had to be some form of faerie. "Come see, girl." His gnarled fingers beckoned Ciarah closer to him.

An unfamiliar surge of concern swept through me as she took a step closer, and my hand closed over her thin arm to prevent her moving toward the strange fae.

"Kill," she murmured, glancing up at me through those lush black eyelashes of hers. "I'm fine."

Gently, she detached my hand from her arm and bent down close to the 'old' man.

This girl, this waif-like damaged creature, she was my goddess. My *Gardien du Voile*. When she gave an order, we had no choice but to follow her wishes.

Although she had not ordered me to back off, the implication was there and I had no desire to feel whatever Donal had when he dared question her.

Before my eyes, the unknown fae creature engaged *Le Gardien* in a rapid whispered conversation, none of which I was able to pick up on despite my fae hearing.

"Pleasure to meet you, sir," she finally said in a normal volume, as she straightened and held out her hand for the man to shake. "I better go back inside before Caley and Amelie pick out too many racy outfits." She smiled at me then, an open, excited smile that transformed her whole face, and I swear to the Veil, my heart straight stopped.

I wasn't all together sure how long I stood there with that same dumbstruck expression on my face after Ciarah disappeared back into the store, but my trance was broken by the coughing laughter of the old man fae.

"*Seigneur de L'hiver,*" he nodded to me in greeting, and I shifted uncomfortably.

"Not yet," I ground out from behind clenched teeth. "She has not yet named a Lord of Winter."

"Ah, but soon. *Ça c'est bon.* The wheel be turnin' once more, an' we must all decide if we want on, or off." He peered at me with those milky eyes. "Best you be on, *boi*."

Trying my best not to snarl at the man, I nodded

tightly. "*Je connais*. I know."

"Word o' warnin' then, *Seigneur de L'hiver*." The man drummed his fingertips on the arm of his chair in a staccato rhythm. "Dem dat held her all deese long years. Dey ain't gonna give her up wit'out a fight, y'hear?"

The conviction in his words made me narrow my eyes in suspicion. "Do you know something?"

"Ol' Blue know a great many thing. On dis, you can trust. Trouble is a'comin' and dat girl be it's target." The man, Old Blue, shook his head and clicked his tongue, and I found it increasingly difficult not to rip his riddle-filled head clean off his shoulders with my bare hands.

My teeth creaked as I ground them together. Hard. "Do you have any advice?" I asked, as politely as I could possibly manage.

"Only one thing y'can do, *boi*. Get dat girl her thoughts back. Quick smart, y'hear?" Old Blue sighed heavily and rapped his walking cane on the wooden slats beneath our feet. "What's dat over dere?" he asked, gesturing with his stick at something behind me.

Turning toward where he was pointing, I saw nothing but cypress trees.

"What's what …?" I started to ask, but quickly realized I'd just fallen for the oldest trick in the book. When I turned back to the storefront once more, not a trace of Old Blue remained except the gentle sway of his recently vacated seat.

Almost as though I'd imagined the whole damn thing.

Chapter Ten

CIARAH

My skin tingled with the intensity of Killian's glare as he entered the little boutique, but I didn't turn to look. Instead I cooed and nodded in the way that seemed socially appropriate for when another girl tried on a cute outfit. Or, that's what I was guessing based on my observations of Caley and Amelie.

Whether it was yet another sinkhole in my personality and memory, or whether none of the manifestations of me had really been into shopping, it didn't matter. I was a quick study, and could learn how to act by emulating others.

"*Gardien*," Killian's lightly accented voice growled in my ear, and his huge hand closed over my upper arm once more.

A wild shiver ricocheted through me at his touch, his hand almost big enough to totally encircle my arm, and ice-cold despite the balmy weather.

"Yes, Kill?" I blinked up at him, the picture of innocence. Of course, I knew he wanted me to fill him in on what the seer had told me. But something about his cool, calm, collected vibe made me badly want to ruffle his feathers.

"Tell me," he ordered, but his eyes pleaded. Here was a man who knew his damn place in the pecking order, whether he liked it or not.

"Not here," I replied with a tiny shake of my head. I wasn't totally sure, but I could have sworn I'd seen a sprite lurking around the front door just moments ago. Lower than rats, they may be, but they could still understand us when we spoke. And relay that information to others, if they chose to.

Killian stared down at me a moment longer, then nodded tightly and looked over to Caley and Amelie.

"Ladies, are we almost done here?" he asked impatiently. "We have important shit to sort out back at the clubhouse."

"Almost." Caley grinned back at him and I rolled my eyes. I'd barely known the girl a couple of days, but I knew her. Which was why I wasn't terribly surprised at her next suggestion.

"Ciarah just needs to pick out some underwear and try them on. You don't mind helping her, do you Kill? Just to hurry things along?" She batted her mascaraed eyelashes at the huge biker man and his eyes narrowed at her.

"It'd be my pleasure, *mon chéri*." He smiled at me a little wickedly. Where for the most part, the guys around here used *cher* in the Cajun way—pronounced *sha*—Killian sometimes slipped into true French which made me curious about his background. My toes curled at the sexy way his mouth delivered those syllables.

Kill swept his ice-blue gaze over my body, sizing me—literally—before turning to the racks of brightly colored lace, satin and silks. His long fingers flipped through the coathangers with confidence, and before I knew what the hell was happening, I had both hands full.

"Changing room," he prompted, giving me a small push toward the curtained alcoves at the back of the store.

Much to my curiosity, when I entered the small cubicle and hung the hangers on the little hooks, Killian followed and pulled the curtain shut behind us.

"You can tell me now," he said, crossing his arms over his chest, his leather jacket creaking with the motion. I cocked my head at him and then reached down to put my fingers underneath the bottom edge of my borrowed t-shirt. "No, *mon chéri*," he said, the edges of his knuckles playing against the warm skin of my belly as he reached out to take hold of the fabric. "Not until I leave the room."

My belly ... or her belly? Because ... this isn't the body I was born to, now is it? But then, birth was relative, wasn't it? A soul entering the child of an infant, newly taken of its first breath, or me … entering the body on a last dying scream …

I blinked away the memories and started to pull my shirt up anyway. Killian stubbornly fisted his hand in the fabric and kept it from riding up, and I frowned.

"Call me confused," I said with a slight smile, "because I may very well be the most confused living thing on this planet or any other, but isn't modesty a human invention? Isn't nudity as natural as breath amongst the fae?"

Killian's teeth and jaw clenched tight, and I knew then that I was right.

He let go of the shirt and I pulled it off, exposing my breasts to the cool air of the shop, the old air conditioner blasting, the ceiling wet with tiny drops of condensation. I dropped it on the floor and reached for one of the bras, my fingers playing against the cream colored satin for a moment. I didn't have bras like this before … in either before, really. In one of my befores, there were no such things. This was a human invention, something of this world. The Veil Keeper's ancient skin had never once felt the caress of undergarments like this. And my other self … the self I was starting to realize was the *me-me* part, the *soul* as Sadhbh had said … she couldn't afford things like this.

"Put it on for me," I told Killian and heard him suck in a sharp breath. I looked over at him and found his ice-blue eyes lit up, the pulse in the side of his neck thundering.

"You want me to put your bra on for you, *la petite chose*?" he asked, and while the words were calm enough, the fire in his gaze was unmistakable.

"It'll go faster if you help me into it," I said, lifting the small scrap of fabric from the satiny hanger and passing it his way. He took it on a single, inked finger, letting it dangle there between us as he sucked in a deep breath and cursed in French.

"As you command, *Le Gardien,*" he said, his voice dropping to a low whisper as I turned away and faced my reflection in the mirror. It was the first time I'd really done that since waking up in the alley, and for a moment, I forgot to breathe.

There was nothing about the face that stared back at me that was familiar … those eyes … that hair … The Veil Keeper was beautiful, even in her glamoured form, with milky white skin, sapphire eyes, and long dark hair with a green streak near the front. It trailed down her … *my?* … body in gentle waves, curling around my ass in the borrowed white leggings I'd taken from Caley.

"This isn't me," I said as I lifted my hands up and palmed my own breasts. They were small but perky, full for their size with erect pink nipples. As I ran my thumbs over them, sensation swept through me and made me shiver. "This isn't what I look like."

"It's what you look like now," Killian said, leaning down toward me. He was so much taller. I could see him in the mirror, towering over me, his eyes as blue as mine but pale, like a winter sky. Mine … hers … ours were a deep, rich color, like a lake in summer, all the way at the bottom where the sun just barely shines. "Rebirth is never easy. Why do you think most souls choose to *forget* who they once were?"

"I'm much taller than this," I said, standing on my tippy toes as Killian leaned over my shoulder, his raven dark hair sliding across his forehead, his tongue running over his lower lip. For a moment there, I thought he might slide it down the side of my neck, make my skin pebble with goose bumps. I thought he might take me by the hips and pull my ass toward him, shove my leggings out of the way …

But Killian wasn't Arlo or Reece—he was a gentleman.

Carefully, he extracted my fingers from my breasts and slid the bra straps over my hands, up my arms, trailing his fingertips against my skin and making me sigh.

"I'm much taller, and I have bigger breasts," I told him, and he chuckled against my ear, the sound low and deep as he slid the bra up to my chest and then dragged his fingertips across my rib cage to my back, making my breath catch. "And I'm blonde, I know that for sure."

"You *were* taller, and you *were* blonde …" Killian said as he leaned back, and I watched in disappointment at our mirror selves as he pulled away and clasped the bra for me. "And the breasts … Well, I find it hard to believe this is much of a downgrade."

"Ey!" a voice called from outside the changing room, the sharp rapping of something against the wood frame of the little cubicle. "You two better not be up to anything nasty in dere! You stain it, you buy it!"

Killian's face wrinkled up with distaste, and he

sneered, but I just smiled and turned toward him, pushing him through the curtain and into the store.

"I'll be out in a while," I said, because having him help me with the bras … well, now I could see his hesitation in not wanting me to take off my shirt.

I tried a few of the bras, but decided I didn't quite like the feel of most. I made myself choose two anyway, just in case I felt like I wanted to wear them later, and let myself out of the dressing room.

"Damn near thought you died in there," Amelie said, sitting at the bar in the corner—yes, there was a bar in the corner of the clothing shop. I didn't remember much about my previous life, but I remembered New Orleans, and I knew the bayou, and that seemed about right. She held a bright blue drink in her hand and was sipping it slowly, watching me with honey-brown eyes. "You find something you liked in there?" she asked with a long, exaggerated wink.

I ignored her and put the bras and underwear I'd chosen on the counter. There were other things in there, too, lingerie and the like. I didn't *need* those things, but I wanted them. And Sadhbh had said to buy me what I wanted.

I didn't think Killian would mind when he saw what they were.

I headed back into the racks and noticed that Caley was missing.

"Dressing room," Amelie called out to me and I smiled, taking my moment free from the influence of both girls to grab some items that made *me* feel more like … well, fucking *me.* I chose low-slung skinny jeans, black t-shirts, and a varied assortment of other casual items from the used section of the store. Not that I had anything against the new stuff, but … there was something about a faded pair of jeans and an old tee that said … Ciarah.

Because whoever I was then, at least I knew one thing.

I knew my name.

And there was power in that.

Unpacking all my new clothes into the closet hadn't been too difficult as there were already several empty hangers just waiting for me to use. The drawers were somewhat more populated with Arlo's things, but I did a little rearranging to empty out a drawer for myself.

"Jesus fucking Christ, you weren't kidding," the green-eyed man muttered as he stopped abruptly in the doorway and stared.

"About what?" I blinked at him, trying to keep my eyes on his face rather than his toned upper body. He was shirtless. Again. Was he deliberately testing me? Probably. I deserved it after leaving him high and dry earlier.

A grin curved over my face, remembering his shocked outrage when he realized I wasn't finishing him off. I bet there had been a long cold shower after the girls and I had left with Kill.

"This is *my* room, Ciarah. There are plenty of others you can choose from that won't have sprites lurking in them." He sighed and rubbed a hand over his face as he flopped down onto the bed.

"So, you go choose a new one. I like this one." I shrugged a shoulder at him and turned back to my bags of shopping.

"No," he snapped back, his eyes narrowing.

"Well then." I smiled. "Looks like we're sharing. Roomie."

Not totally sure why I said that … A small frown creased my brow as I inspected my memory for what the hell a 'roomie' was, but came up blank.

There was a long pause before he responded. "Kill says you had a run-in with someone at the clothing store?"

"Uh-huh." I nodded. "Curiosity eating at him, is it?"

"Something like that." Arlo tightened his lips as his huge arms folded under his head. His eyes on me didn't seem to blink, but I didn't mind. In fact, I *liked* being watched.

"Are Reece and Amelie downstairs, too?" I tipped out the contents of the next bag onto the foot of the bed to sort through.

"Why?" he questioned, his eyes narrowed in suspicion.

"Because I believe the information I gained concerns Reece too." My fingers threaded through the price label of the garment I'd picked up and snapped it off.

"And Amelie? Why does she need to hear this?" The way he said her name left no doubt what his—and really *all* of the *sidhe*—thought of wolves.

"Because I like her." I had no further reason than that. She was nice, and seemed genuinely friendly. Whoever I had been, before coming into this body, I got the hollow sense that I hadn't had many friends.

Arlo made a noise under his breath that I couldn't decipher so chose to ignore. For another few moments, I worked silently, folding my new clothes and placing them carefully in my drawer or on hangers.

"Done." I beamed at the surly biker when just one top was left in my pile.

It was a vibrant red halter-neck thing, with a low, almost non-existent back and a ribbon tie around the neck. The color reminded me of Sabdh's lips and the cut was *perfect*.

Grasping the hem of my t-shirt, I pulled it over my head in one clean movement and my sharp hearing picked up on Arlo's breath catching.

"What the fuck are you doing now, Veil Keeper?" he growled, but his voice held a note of curiosity and eagerness that made me chuckle.

"Changing. Is that acceptable?" I met his gaze, not blinking, and also making no move to cover up my nakedness. Like I'd said, *this* wasn't my body. *These* weren't my tits. Wherever the fuck I'd been since my earthly death, it hadn't been anywhere that modesty was considered so even if this body hadn't been a stranger to me, it wouldn't have phased me to have his hungry eyes on me like they were.

Arlo made another noise; this time I took it to be approval. Not that I *needed* his approval on anything. But I shrugged one of my bare shoulders and slipped the ruby red fabric over my body, then turned my back and perched on the edge of the bed.

“Do me up?” I asked innocently. This time, unlike when I'd asked Kill to help me dress, I knew *exactly* what I was doing.

So did Arlo.

His rough fingertips trailed up my naked spine to my neck where he took hold of the trailing ribbons and ever so carefully, tied them into a bow.

“Why the need to change?” he asked, his voice husky and thick with desire, and I could see the hard evidence straining his jeans when I turned back around. I'd already exchanged Caley's borrowed leggings for a pair of secondhand, ripped skinny jeans while I'd been unpacking my shopping, but I'd been *aching* to have my back bare all day.

Answering Arlo in actions instead of words, I released my wings and moaned aloud with the sheer joy of freeing those heavy appendages.

It seemed strange, on some level, how *complete* I felt when my wings were free. As far as I could tell, my former body had not had wings. Hell, I didn't think I'd even been fae. But now, I couldn't imagine life without them.

"Fuck," Arlo hissed, his chest rising and falling rapidly as his dilated pupils watched my wings shudder and stretch. "Why did *Le Gardien* need to be so Veil-damned beautiful?"

His words were quiet, almost reverent and I wasn't altogether sure he meant for me to hear them.

"Come on." I held out a hand to him. "I'll tell you all what the seer said. Then we can start working on how to fix the Veil."

He took my outstretched hand, tugging me up from the bed until we were face to face. Or, as much as we could be given my diminutive size and his … considerable one.

Reaching over my head, he stroked a finger over the top curve of my wing, and I groaned. Tingling warmth seemed to shudder through me from his touch, and the scent of springtime filled my nostrils. Fresh grass, wild flowers blooming, and the heady aroma of Arlo's arousal.

From where my face was directly in front of his chest, all I could see were the detailed, swirling patterns of his ink, and my fingers grasped instinctively at his broad waist.

"Let's go, Keeper," he rumbled, withdrawing his touch from my wings almost reluctantly, and brushing past me to the door. "The sooner we get this fucking Veil fixed …"

He trailed off with a strangled sort of sound, and the sour taste in my mouth told me he'd been about to lie.

That was the first time anyone around me had come even close to lying, and I didn't look forward to the time when someone did manage it.

But it did beg the question, what *exactly* had he just been about to lie to me on?

Chapter Eleven

CIARAH

Downstairs, Arlo didn't lead me through to the living room as I'd expected, but instead into what looked like a dimly lit bar, complete with pool tables where Reece and Killian were engaged in what appeared to be a heated debate.

Their words died off before I could catch anything of substance, but I cocked my head at them curiously.

"Boys." Arlo greeted them with a smirk. "Arguing over who breaks again?"

"Something like that," Killian replied with a glare, and again the sour taint implied there was much more going on than a debate over their pool game.

"*Filles*, can you give us a few?" Reece asked Caley and Amelie, who had been sitting at a high table and sipping on drinks.

The rest of the bar was totally deserted, which was probably a good thing given I had my enormous wings on full display. Then again, the entire Wild Hunt MC were fae, so it wouldn't have shocked anyone.

"No." I shook my head. "They can stay."

"Whatever's goin' on here ain't none of their damn business," Reece said, standing up and frowning, the massive muscles in his arms straining as he tightened his fist around the pool stick, all those swirls of … I wasn't sure if they were tattoos or some sort of fae marking … but they twisted around his skin and disappeared underneath the sleeves of his shirt.

"Caley especially doesn't need to stick around and hear this shit," Arlo snorted, lighting up a cigarette and kicking open a back door. The raggedy old thing swung wide, letting in the sounds and smells of the bayou. I could hear the distant call of birds as the sun set on the horizon, warning calls and hello-chittering alike. It mixed with the distinct grunt of gators, the call of an eagle, and far away but not far enough … the whir of an airboat engine.

"Who is that?" I asked, my wings perking up in alarm. I made my way over to the door as Arlo smoked and leaned outside, watching the sun reflect off the murky water, huge clumps of Spanish moss dangling from branches, trailing their mossy green fingers in the gators' domain. Water sloshed against the edge of the old dock as I peered outside and squinted into the sprawling mess of trees and swamp and mud. It was a landscape unlike anywhere else in the world, a tangled paradise of times past, both ancient and surreal. And the smell? It had this deep, earthy quality to it, like there was magic hiding underneath that shallow water. "The airboat."

"That'll be the boys taking care of business," Arlo said, and the way the word *business* snapped off the end of his tongue, I didn't much care for. I turned my sapphire gaze on him, but he wouldn't look at me.

"Okay, Arlo is right …" Caley said, sliding off the stool and sucking down the last of her drink before placing the glass back on the copper surface of the bar. "I'm not a member of the club, and I don't want to be."

She snatched her purse up and slung it over her shoulder, throwing a soft smile in my direction before bending down to pick up her shopping bag from earlier. Not only had I found myself a few outfits, but so had Caley and Amelie. She patted the plastic bag and grinned.

"Sorry in advance for my brother's attitude," she said, "and thanks for letting me piggyback a few outfits on your shopping trip."

"Get the fuck out of here," Arlo said, exhaling and curling up his lip. He gestured rudely in her direction. "Don't you have to get some sleep before your next shift?"

"Thank you *Dad,*" Caley said with an exaggerated roll of her eyes. "But yes, I'll be heading upstairs for some *quality* sleep. Now that the Veil Keeper's here and all the groupies have been kicked out of the building, it's a hell of a lot quieter …"

Arlo picked up an empty beer bottle and chucked it in her direction as Caley squealed, dodged it, and then slipped out of the room through a pair of old-timey swinging doors.

"You need to learn to treat that sister of yours right," Amelie said, and Arlo snarled low under his breath.

"What business are the boys taking care of?" I asked, because whatever business it was, it wasn't *my* business and it should be, shouldn't it? Ciarah … she was never anyone of much importance, I knew, but the Veil Keeper? She was more important than every soul on this planet combined. She *should* know everything that was going on, shouldn't she?

Arlo scoffed under his breath and Killian whispered something in French.

"Feedin' bodies to the gators," Amelie said, and when I turned to look at her, her white toothed smile was bright in her face, almost … wolflike. "How inconvenient to drag 'em out there like that. Back home, we just eat 'em ourselves."

"Dat's about enough o' dat," Reece said, lifting his hand up and massaging his temple. He glanced over at me and some of the anger leaked out of his expression, making way for a lascivious smile, a magnanimous grin that spread across his tanned face and made my heart thunder. "And girl, why you wanna shack up wit' Arlo dere? Old Reece'd be *more* than happy to let you share his bed." He winked at me and smacked his lips, making me bite my own. "That'd be a huge honor to share with da

Veil Keeper. Wouldn't hear none of dat bitching and whining from me, no."

"You're more than welcome to change your mind," Arlo said, finishing his cigarette and flicking it out the back door to lie in a pile of other discarded butts. "I'll even move your clothes for you, free of charge."

"The more you protest, the more determined I am to stay," I told him as Killian moved over to the bar and poured two drinks, bringing one over to me. I took it in steady hands and stared into the glass, my mind flashing with distant memory. As I closed my eyes and took a sip, sounds and sights came rushing back to me … *a crowded bar, a man's warm mouth trailing down the side of my neck, big hands on my hips.* I blinked a few times and the memories flittered away like sprites in the wind.

And speaking of …

"There's another one," I said as I looked over and found a mottled-skinned little monster crouching on the windowsill. As soon as it caught me looking, it opened its wide mouth in a hiss, flashing sharp teeth, its see-through pixie wings thrumming as it tried to take flight.

"The fucking *audacity,*" Killian said, and with a flick of one, long tattooed finger, he had the sprite coughing and choking, wings fluttering as it tried and failed to fly away. It fell back to the windowsill, stumbled forward and collapsed inside the bar.

Moving over to it, I lifted it into my hands and found that its breath was frosted and cold, pluming in the air with little shards of ice clinging to its lips. As I held it in my palm, it took one, last shuddering breath and … died. I felt its spirit flee its body and then, I grabbed hold of it. It stuck for a few seconds and then shattered, flittering away like leaves in the wind.

"Its spirit …" I said, feeling my mouth water and sweat drip down the side of my face. I'd been about to *eat* it, that spirit energy. Hell, I felt like I was starving all of a sudden. And it wasn't food or even sex that I was starving for …

"Sprites share one spirit," Killian said, moving over to me, the steel toes of his boots appearing in my vision before he bent down to take the corpse. "Thousands of them make up one being. The punishment of being reborn as a murder of sprites is reserved for the worst of the worst."

He stood back up and I followed, watching as he passed the tiny creature's body over to Reece. The big Cajun man moved outside and paused with his foot on one of the dock's extended legs.

"Hey, Meme!" he shouted as I stepped out after him and paused. Fireflies had gathered above the water, dancing in the early evening shadows. I watched them, curling my fingers against the legs of my jeans. "C'mere girl!"

Reece tossed the tiny carcass into the water and not ten seconds later, a gator's head was popping up and grabbing it, dragging the mottled creature into the dark depths.

"Taking care of business …" I whispered, but it made sense. And gators needed to eat, too.

"Nice and clean, no dirty hands 'round here," Reece said, glancing over and noticing the expression on my face. Something about those fireflies … I shook my head to clear it and looked over at him.

"There could be more sprites around here," I said, glancing up at the last fading orange and yellow lights of evening. "Listening in …" And the things I had to tell the boys, I didn't want anyone else to hear. Except Amelie, of course. Somehow, deep down, I had a sick feeling about the sprites and whatever their agenda might be …

"You'll have to cast a spell," Kilian said with a long sigh, coming up to stand beside me. "There're already several no scrying spells on the clubhouse, but the sprites are like … birds … or gators … just a part of the natural landscape. Or at least, they *were.* I don't much like what I'm seeing from them now." He glanced down at me, his ice blue eyes sharp in his handsome face. "You'll have to cast a new spell."

"Me?" I asked, because casting a spell seemed like a huge jump for someone who'd barely been able to remember her own name … and yet had called a Wild Hunt, gobbled up a soul, and grown wings….

"*Oui, chéri.*" Killian scuffed his shoe on the planks of the dock, sending some dried leaves skittering into the water. "We could, but with the sprites acting up…"

"It'll be stronger from you," Arlo finished for him.

Glancing over my shoulder—past my wings—I saw him on the end of the dock with his huge arms folded over his chest and a scowl set on his face. He hadn't even bothered to put a shirt back on when we came downstairs, and his jeans hung low on his hips, drawing my eye.

"Would you like me to help?" Killian asked softly, pulling my attention away from the half-naked asshole and back to the task at hand.

"You can do that?" I was genuinely surprised. It wouldn't have shocked me in the least if they'd simply said, "*Do a spell, Ciarah!*" and just expected me to know how to work it out.

"*Oui*," Killian confirmed, holding out his hand to me, palm up. "The fundamentals of magic are similar, if not the same for all *sidhe*. What changes the outcome depends on our individual levels of magic." Placing my hand in his, I stifled a shiver at his cool touch. Not that it was unpleasant, not in the least. Just, unusual.

"My own magic allows me to connect with your mind. From there, I will be able to guide you," he continued, tugging me lightly until I stood toe to toe with him on the end of the dock.

"Like when you healed me?" I asked in a quiet voice, genuinely curious.

"*Oui*, just like that." His other hand slipped into the heavy hair at the nape of my neck, and his ice-blue eyes met mine. "Ready?"

"*Oui*," I replied, mimicking him in a way that echoed of familiarity. Maybe either *she* or I had spoken French at some point in time?

Kill wasn't one to fuck around, and before my brain even finished the thought, my vision was ensnared in the chilly depths of his eyes.

Just as before, the rest of the world faded away and all I could see for miles was blue. Frozen tendrils of Killian's magic snaked around me, caressing and soothing, telling me without words that I was safe.

My mind watched with eager fascination as Killian's mist-like magic showed me the correct way to place a spell. Feeling confident that I'd understood, I repeated what he'd done.

"Did that—" I started to ask, but my words were cut short by Killian's lips on mine.

The hand he had on the back of my neck pulled me in closer, and I sucked a surprised gasp. Confidently, his tongue slipped past my lips, meeting mine with a gentle, languid stroke that made me want *more*.

"Kill." Reece's voice broke into our private moment like a hammer through ice, and Killian reluctantly pulled back from my mouth, just an inch.

"Yes, Reece?" he replied sarcastically, his eyes still locked on mine, but his magic retreating.

"Da spell be workin'. Thought you might wanna know." My gaze still held captive, I didn't attempt to look over at Reece, but I could hear the grin in his tone. Bastard.

"How polite," Killian remarked in a dry voice, blinking a couple of times and releasing me. "You're a natural, Ciarah."

"At, um," I floundered, feeling my cheeks flush, my lips still tingling from his kiss.

"Spellcasting," he clarified and I nodded.

Spellcasting. Of course that's what he meant. Not that I wasn't a natural at kissing, too. Some things required no memories, they were just ingrained in your soul. Or body too, I guessed.

"Is it always like that? Your magic?" I asked, realizing he'd ended up kissing me after healing my wounds, too. "I don't remember seeing you kiss Arlo after healing him?"

A broad, somewhat wicked grin split Killian's face and his tongue ran over his lower lip, like he was savoring the taste of me.

"Why, would you have liked to?" he teased and my mind went to dirty places.

"*Mo Dhia,* Ciarah he is taking liberties. His magic don' require dat, his cock does." Reece snorted a laugh and even Arlo snickered.

My gaze dropped down, peering at the appendage in question and I shrugged. "Good."

"So what did you have to tell us about this seer, Keeper?" Arlo prompted, still standing at the end of the dock with his legs spread wide and his muscular arms folded.

"That's what the old guy was?" Amelie asked, raising her eyebrows at me. "I could smell the magic on him but couldn't for the life of me work out what he was. Hmm. Seer. How curious."

My wings flexed as a cool breeze teased at them, and I noticed how sore my back was getting. If nothing else, it showed me I needed to keep them out more often if I wanted to build those muscles up. Or, *back* up. I had to assume that the Veil Keeper had always had wings, and the amputation was a recent thing.

"Reece, if I sit, will the gators have a go?" I indicated to the bubbles on the surface of the water, a promise that there was more than just Reece's Meme down there.

"Naw, dere ain't enough meat on you, sweet t'ang." He winked, and sat down himself before tugging me down to sit with him.

My feet dangled over the edge of the dock, but I was so short in this body I was still nowhere near the water.

"'sides," he continued, "even gators know better dan chewin' on da Keeper, ya know?"

Amelie sat her ass down beside me and flipped her long braids over her shoulder. The many glass beads made a pleasant clicking sound as they moved and I smiled.

Something about this wolf girl … she felt kind.

Which was odd, given Rafe had introduced her as his enforcer.

"So, spill it Veil Keeper." She bumped me with her shoulder. "What did the old creeper say?"

"He wasn't creepy," I defended the old seer, "and he didn't say much that I didn't already have a feeling about. He just helped me catch some bubbles."

"Catch … bubbles?" Arlo asked, having come closer. He and Kill were now standing just behind us, looming over me like gargoyles … or knights.

"Yes." I nodded, glancing up at them briefly before turning back to the swamp. "I have these … thoughts.

Memories, I think. They're like soap bubbles, and every time I try to catch one, they slip just beyond my reach, or else they burst."

"So, dis seer … he helped you catch a bubble?" Reece repeated and I nodded.

"My … *her* memories. The knowledge of the Veil, it was taken from her … me … whatever. But it was taken for safe-keeping by her knights." My teeth worried at my lower lip while I clung to this one scrap of information that the seer had helped me regain. "They split it amongst themselves and then stored their individual pieces for safe keeping."

"Do you know where?" Killian questioned, but I shrugged again, my heavy wings shifting with the movement.

Yes, no, maybe? I should know the answer to his question. The knights had left valuable pieces of information in the last Veil Keeper's memory that *should* have made it easy to recover all the shards.

"No …" I murmured. "Or, not exactly. The breadcrumb memories that were left … whatever happened to me after I took this body …" I trailed off with a sigh. Chasing *this* bubble hurt. It radiated pain and anguish, desperation and *fear,* and I just wasn't all too sure I really wanted to catch that one.

"Whatever happened … it's broken me. Her. Us. We're fractured in a way the Veil Keeper never should have been." My fingers picked at a splinter on the dock beside me, and I flicked the little bits of wood into the water as I spoke. "But I know this … it all begins with the Spear."

As I said this, I glanced back up to Arlo, and found his blazing green gaze locked on me, full of emotion I just couldn't read.

"It's gone," he repeated himself, saying the same thing he'd said when I first asked where the Spear was. I hadn't known, then, what the significance was.

His words still rang *true* but …

"Gone doesn't always stay gone, brother," Killian said quietly.

Amelie made a noise in her throat, flipping her braids to the other side and peering up at Arlo. "You want to tell me *you're* Cernunnos?" Her voice was flavored heavily with disbelief. "*And* that you lost the Spear of Lug? Oh, Rafe is going to lose his shit over this."

"*I* didn't lose it," Arlo snapped, taking a step forward like maybe he wished he could snap Amelie's neck and feed her to Meme. "It was either the father or the fucking sage."

"The father or the sage …" I began carefully, closing my eyes and humming.

"The three aspects of the horned god," Amelie explained carefully, reaching down to the dock and putting her hand over mine. Arlo growled again, but she ignored him. "Just like there are three aspects of the goddess—the maiden, the mother, and the crone. We don't worship the horned god back home …" she began, glancing over one shoulder as though Arlo was the sole reason for that. "For *obvious* reasons," she added, and I almost smiled. "But we do pray to the goddess."

"I thought you crazies howled at the goddamn moon," Arlo said, and when I followed Amelie's gaze back over to him, I found him scowling.

"Yeah, dumb shit, as a physical manifestation of the goddess — the waxing, full, and waning moon, the three aspects." Amelie turned her attention back to me and smiled. "So, figures it'd be the masculine aspect of nature that lost the spear, right? A woman would never make that mistake."

"You little bitch," Arlo grumbled, but as I kept staring at him, he simply pulled out a cigarette and started smoking again. I turned back to the water and watched the fireflies hovering lazily over the surface. As I stared at them, one drifted closer and closer, increasing in size until it was at least double or triple that of the others.

I held my palms up and it settled above them with a sigh, like it was coming to rest.

"Will-o-the-wisp," Reece said from beside me and Arlo let out yet *another* snarl. The man was, quite frankly, bestial as all hell. I loved it. "She got an invitation from the sage."

"Speak of the devil," Arlo said with a tired … and an almost frightened? … sort of sigh.

"The sage?" I asked and Reece chuckled, reaching out and teasing the edge of the will-o-the-wisp's light with his rough fingertips. I could still feel those fingertips on my head, encouraging me to take his cock, on my hips as he lifted me onto the counter … I shivered and glanced away.

There'd be time for sex later.

"The sage is Arlo's Paw-Paw," Reece explained, hauling himself to his feet with a groan and lifting his arms above his head with a yawn. "He lives in da bayou and he don't just invite anybody to come pay him a visit, 'specially not his own grandson."

"I don't have any want or need to visit the crazy old coot," Arlo said, as if he didn't much care either way if we went. I let Reece take my hand and haul me to my feet, managing to look over and catch just a brief glimpse of Arlo's hands shaking as he smoked his cigarette. He tossed the still burning butt into the water and made me frown before turning and heading for the open door of the clubhouse. "Goddess' tits, I need a fucking drink."

"You shouldn't litter," I warned him, calling out from my tippy toes. He ignored me as I turned and plucked the butt from the water, dropping it into a rusted, dented coffee can near the door. It was clearly intended to be used as an ashtray but was overflowing onto the dock. Somebody needed to get out here and sweep. "He shouldn't litter; it goes against every aspect of his nature."

"He does it on purpose, just to see if he can," Killian purred as the will-o-the-wisp danced around my head like a halo. "Now, should I get the airboat ready?"

"I thought the *boys* took the airboat for their business?" I asked, watching as both Killian and Reece smiled.

"Girl, dis is da bayou, and there's only *one* way to get around out dere and let me tell ya—it ain't on the back of no hog."

I sat at the front of the airboat with my mouth closed tight, my head whipping every which way as I tried to take it all in. It was dark out, but the Veil Keeper's eyes had mighty fine night vision, at least ten times as good as anything I'd experienced as Ciarah. I tried not to think how that was a boon now … and had been a horror before.

Even trapped in the dark, I'd been able to see things I hadn't wanted to see. At least … when my eyes had still worked … They'd been seared and blinded … healed and seared again …

I clenched my jaw tight and held a hand over my stomach. I couldn't throw up right now, not with the small rickety metal boat gliding as fast as it was. It would all come back on us, and I didn't think me or a single one of my four companions would appreciate that. Besides, the reason my mouth was clenched so tight was because I'd already learned a very important lesson about how many insects made their home out here in the bayou. We'd also driven through some *very* impressive spiderwebs, and I felt like my hair was crawling. Not that I had a problem with spiders though, because I distinctly did not. Everything out here had its place. If anything, *we* were the intruders.

Reece killed the boat's engine at the edge of some swampy marshland. At first glance, it looked solid but as we drifted, I saw in shafts of moonlight that it was nothing more than mud on water. Yanking my ear muffs down to my neck, I stood up and the entire boat rocked violently.

"Careful there, *Gardien*," Reece said with a chuckle, "you don' wanna go swimmin' in the bayou at this time o' da night."

"We're here?" I asked and I swear, his grins were so big, so full of emotion, that I could just *feel* the expression behind me.

"We're here," he said, and then used a rope to tie us to the gnarled limb of a nearby tree.

As I watched, Reece stepped down with one massive boot and sunk about an inch into the muck before it seemed like he settled on something solid.

"C'mere, girl, and you best watch old Reece if you don' wanna end up takin' a swim with Meme and her brudders."

He reached out for my hand and helped me from the boat. I found my footing easily enough in the motorcycle boots the boys had encouraged me to wear, the thick soles perched on what seemed to be a sunken block of cement?

Reece led me through the tangled mess of tree limbs and clumps of hanging moss, taking out all the spiderwebs for me, like a real gentleman. Killian followed close behind, and then Amelie, and lastly, Arlo. I was pretty sure I could hear him cursing under his breath as we walked through the muck, massive lily pads slapping me in the calves as we moved, stirring up the water. I felt something slither between my legs, and I was almost certain it was a snake.

"Here we go," Reece said, pulling me up onto the edge of a small island. It was so small, in fact, that I could easily see the entire thing from where I stood, even in the darkness. It was hardly large enough to hold both our group *and* the bald cypress tree that stood sentinel over it.

"Sir," Arlo spat, like he'd rather chew on a piece of dried shit. "What do you want?"

A creaking sound echoed through the woods and chills skittered down my spine as I felt a movement of great power, *ancient* power, almost as old as I was. She was? Ciarah had been nineteen when she died. Those years of torture had felt like a hundred years, but my best guess estimate for how long I'd suffered … was five. So, I was twenty-four then?

"You young fool," a man's voice croaked, hoarse and brittle with disuse. At first, I thought the tree was speaking to us, but then the gnarled roots spread and a man appeared, curled on his side with horns as white as his grandson's. Unlike his grandson however, his face was ancient as time, dressed in wrinkles, and puckered with distaste. His beard was made of moss and his eyes were the sage green of dried leaves.

He sat up and yawned, his old body covered in ink and faintly glowing. His skin was as silver as Arlo's was without his glamour and as I watched, the will-o-the-wisp flitted over to him and settled itself on a nearby branch.

Well, as much as a glowing ball of light could settle itself …

"You do wise to show respect, young buck," he cautioned Arlo, who simply ground his teeth together and glared.

"Keeper," the ancient fae greeted me, rising to his feet and *towering* over both me and my companions, "at last."

"Hello," I squeaked, more than a little intimidated by this creature. Somewhere inside me, though, I sensed he was one to trust. The Sage had not always been on the side of *good*—whatever that was—but *this* one was.

"It has been a very long time," the Sage hummed and scratched at his moss-beard, causing little bits of greenery to flake off, "since your pretty face has graced this world. How have you been adjusting?"

Arlo snorted but I ignored him, my interest locked on the Sage and his fascinating appearance. "I've been… confused," I admitted, and the moss covered man nodded … well … *sagely.*

"Understandable, given your ancient knowledge has been stripped from your very being." He tapped at his lips with a finger that vaguely resembled a twig.

I frowned. "How do you know that?"

"Irrelevant." He flapped his hand in the air and the *will-o-the-wisp* flittered around as though startled. "I've been holding some information for you for over one hundred years, waiting for you to reappear so that I might put you on your path to restoration."

"Why *you*?" Arlo snapped, and the Sage swung his

ancient eyes over to his grandson with a look that could strip bark.

"Because your papa knew he wasn't long for this world, and he needed to keep this scrap safe, should the Veil Keeper reappear." The Sage gave Arlo a long stare until the younger man—fae, god, whatever—looked away first, and the old fae turned his stare back to me. "Your knights stripped you of any knowledge pertaining to the Veil, in an attempt to preserve the magic until such time as your earthly body might be recovered. They had left you with small clues of where to begin looking, but I suspect those crumbs may have gotten lost?"

Pursing my lips, I nodded. I knew they were there, I could sense them just out of reach, but when I tried to get them I became bogged down in *pain*.

"As I thought." The Sage waved a hand at his tree, and it obligingly bowed down two branches to create seats, to which he indicated I sit. "Your former Lord of Spring entrusted his portion of your memories to my son, *The Father*, and requested they be hidden."

"Within the Spear of Lug," I whispered, my vision blurring and fading as I slipped into a dark and shadowy memory.

Faces like nightmares, shrouded in heavy hoods, gleaming white fangs from between leering lips. Another silent scream tore from my throat, my voice long since destroyed by years of wailing in agony. The Nightmare yanked again on my wing and I felt it tear from my flesh a little further as wet tears slid down my face.

My body hung limp and useless from the shackles on the roof, my wrists dead to feeling where the iron held them high, and my toes barely reached the ground. Every vicious tear of my wings sent my half-dead body swaying on the chains, the musical chime of metal on concrete my constant companion.

The Nightmare wrapped its filthy claws around the base of my wing once more, and tore it a little further from my back, and this time the agony was so sharp, so blinding, that my mind slipped from my body as it had done on a thousand occasions before.

"Stick with us, mo ghaol,*" my lover begged inside my pain-filled brain, "the spell is almost ready. We have but one treasure left to find and then we can complete the transfer, starting with the Spear of Lug."*

"Please," my mind's voice begged, "please hurry. I need to know the knowledge is safe. After that, they can do as they please to this form and never succeed."

"Tha gaol agam ort, *Gràinne," my lover, my Lord of Spring, whispered with reverence. "Please hold on a little longer. For us. For the Veil."*

"I love you too, Curadan," my mind sighed, as agony dragged me back to consciousness, "all of you."

"Curadan," I repeated, this time in my own voice, and I felt the syllables slide over my tongue, both foreign and familiar all at the same time.

"Yes, your former Lord of Spring, Curadan Mac

Daibheid. He and my son were close, and as the protector of the Spear, trusted no one else to hide such valuable information." The Sage cocked his head, watching me with eyes as old as time itself. "Would you like to know where to begin, young Keeper?"

Still lost in the memory I had just lived through, I nodded slowly. *Gràinne*. Another name. Was it mine? Hers? Ours? Did we have one name that carried with our body or did we keep our own name from our former life? These were questions I needed to ask, but first…

"Yes, tell me. Where do I begin?"

"The spear is guarded and heavily spelled. To access it, you will need a key." The Sage propped his bony elbows on his knees, his twig-like fingers steepled together.

"Of course she will," Arlo muttered under his breath, but I ignored him and his grand-daddy issues.

"Do you have it?" I asked, both eagerly and reluctantly. Did I really *want* to recover all my memories? If that small flashback was a taste of what was to come… perhaps I might be better off *not* knowing?

In the memory, it had felt like I—*Gràinne*—had been almost ready to give up, but I *knew* she hadn't. That memory was old, maybe over one hundred years, and I was confident I hadn't suffered more than five under the *care* of those Nightmares.

A startling noise coughed from the Sage and I jumped, before realizing he was *chuckling*.

"Naw, Keeper," he grinned, and a small woodworm wriggled from the corner of his mouth and down his beard. "That'd be too easy, see? The key is held by someone strong enough to keep it safe. Papa Cocodril."

Reece made a noise that drew my attention, and I found him with a confused and bewildered look on his handsome face. "Papa Cocodril?" he repeated, and the Sage nodded. "Dat ol' voodoo man ain't real. He nutin' more dan a story *ma Mère* told us as *chevrette*."

"Don't you know, boy? All the best stories are based in truth." The Sage turned his wise old eyes back to me. "Papa Cocodril is very real, and he has your key."

His words were said carefully, and each one rang with the clean feeling of *truth*.

"He ran afoul of the Swamp Witch some years past, but you can still find him on the apex of the bayou, when the moon is full. You'll need to go alone, Keeper, as he won't show for any but you." The old tree man held my gaze for a long moment, before his eyelids drooped. "Now, get you gone. This old man has had enough excitement for one year."

My mouth opened to ask more questions, but Killian's hand closed over my wrist, pulling me gently to my feet.

"Come along, *cher*, the Sage has said enough. Your answers can be found along our quest, I have no doubt." His voice was calm, and reasonable but still I wanted to argue with him. Why couldn't I just ask now?

But when I glanced back to the Sage, I found him still, like he'd been petrified. The tree was moving slowly, wrapping its limbs around him once more and pulling him back into its depths bit by bit until no sign of the Sage remained visible.

"Now what?" Amelie asked, leading the way back to where we had left the airboat.

"We can't do jack shit until the moon is full," Arlo growled, and I shivered at his bestial tone. "Which ain't tonight."

"We'll head back to da clubhouse," Reece decided, hopping onto the airboat and holding out a hand to help me on. "Don't know 'bout you, but I could sure use a drink, me."

Amelie made a noise, and pushed Arlo out of the way to take the seat beside me in the front of the boat. "Ciarah, babe. I don't want you pissed off or thinking I'm double-crossing you, I'm *not*. But Rafe will need to know at least some of what is going on here."

"No fucking way," Arlo snapped. "You breathe a fucking word of what you just heard—"

"And what, Arlo?" Amelie cut him off, her eyes turning hard as stone, and her teeth sharpening to deadly points. "What will *you* do to *me*? Do not forget who you speak to."

To my genuine surprise, Arlo backed down, sliding back into his seat in the row behind us and saying nothing. His jaw was clenched tight though, and I could see a muscle in his cheek jumping with anger.

"Anyway," Amelie, turned back to me without a trace of the terrifying enforcer she'd just presented to Arlo, "I wanted to be open with you, babe."

My head tilted, and I pondered this information. Of

course her loyalties lie with her Alpha; I couldn't be mad about that. And I was sure his interests were in restoring the Veil for his own people's good.

"Actually, I would like to meet and discuss this with your alpha myself," I announced, and her eyes widened a fraction.

"No," Reece snapped, and I jerked around in surprise to find all three biker men glaring with hardened expressions.

"We can't risk you entering pack land, Ciarah," Killian explained, "it's too dangerous. Too uncertain where their loyalties lie."

Amelie's lips tightened but she gave a tiny nod. "He's right. I wouldn't risk your safety, Keeper."

Part of me, maybe the old part? I wasn't sure. But part of me flared hot with outrage that my *subjects* thought to tell me what I could or couldn't do. *Truth* shone through their words of concern though, and my better judgement prevailed. This time.

"Fine, then they will need to come to us." I met Reece's gaze, unblinking, making it *clear* I wouldn't be budged on this.

He stared back at me a long, tense moment before sighing heavily and scrubbing a hand through his red-brown hair. "Fine. Kill, organize a gathering with the Louisiana Wolves."

"*Laissez les bons temps rouler*," Killian murmured, scratching at his dark stubble and watching me with his ice-blue eyes.

Arlo grunted a noise that I couldn't decipher the emotion behind, and looked away into the distance as Reece kicked the engine on and steered us out of the shallows we'd been stopped in.

"I hope you know what you're doing, Ciarah," Amelie said as the wind picked up and began whipping our long hair around like a frog in a blender.

I hoped I did, too. But something I was *sure* of, was that I would need all the allies I could get in the coming times. Why not start with the wolves?

Chapter Twelve

KILLIAN

My favorite part of any day were those first few moments when the sun kissed the edge of the horizon, banishing the shadows of night in a centuries old feud with no end. There was no winner, no right or wrong. It simply … *was*. How peaceful, to exist in a state with no good, no evil, no moral qualms or questionable judgments. There was a cycle and a routine, and that was that.

"I know you don't like me, so what am I doing here?" Raphael LeRoux asked as he melted from the shadows, his silver fur rippling into sun-weathered skin, his nakedness marred with dozens upon dozens of random scars. He didn't have to be nude to shift, so I had to wonder if he was trying to make a point.

I didn't even bother to turn around the rest of the way to look at him, keeping my elbows on the wood railing and flicking my eyes back to the bayou. That first glorious crash of orange and yellow sunshine on the water made life worth living. And let's be honest—there weren't a lot of things left in the world like that anymore.

"I'm inviting you to a party," I said as I tapped my fingers against my sleeve and listened to the wild sounds of nature, a constant symphony of living and breathing and dying and fucking. It was like the complete opposite to the dance the sun and moon made, a random spattering of merciless choices. Eat or be eaten. Breed and then die. Get lucky or starve.

I sighed.

I knew I was being way too goddamn introspective today, but seeing the Veil Keeper … it was stirring all sorts of strange, primal memories and feelings. What did I know of life on the other side of the Veil? *Le rien*. Fucking nothing. I'd been born here—like most of my peers, like Arlo and Reece. It was only the old-timers like Donal or Fionn that had any idea what we were all missing out on.

The way they carried on, one would think it was paradise on the other side.

I figured it couldn't be any *worse* than what we had here. This world was mad, but it was also beautiful.

"You called me all the way out here to invite me to a party?" Rafe growled, coming to stand beside me. I'd let the boys know he was coming, so nobody tried to kill him on his way into the clubhouse. Frankly, there was a good chance whoever challenged him would've been the one to end up dead.

"This is an important party with an important purpose. Our Veil Keeper wants to speak with you herself."

"So I was told by Amelie," Rafe said, his voice rough and husky, the voice of an animal. He stared over the railing and into the water like he could see things that I couldn't. Maybe he could? He was a wolf, more animal than human. And I was fae. I was neither of those things. "I got the memo on the Sage and the spear. What else does she want?"

"Careful, wolf, or someone might think to find you ungrateful." I stood up and stretched my arms above my head in a yawn, casting my blue eyes over to his bloodred ones. "I called you here because the Veil Keeper seems to trust you."

Rafe scoffed a laugh and stood up, curling his fingers around the wood railing and shaking his head.

"She's a fool then. She shouldn't be trusting a damn soul—least of all me. Have you told her about—"

"No."

The word was short and sharp, and Rafe sighed..

"You people and your weird hang-ups. I'll never understand any of it. Fine. We accept your invitation—but don't make me regret it. If I bring my wolves here and a damn hair on a single one of their fine furry asses is out of place by the time we leave, it won't be a good day for you and yours."

I smiled and dropped my arms to my sides.

"*Bien*. Ciarah will be pleased to hear it."

Raphael gave me a strange look and shook his head.

"Next time, motherfucker, just call me on the damn phone."

He started to shift as he turned, his palms falling to the deck. By the time they hit the old, rough wood, they were paws. Rafe cast one last bloodred glance at me and took off at a slow jog. I followed at a careful distance behind him, around the corner and toward the edge of the woods. Using magic, I cloaked my approach, crouching down in the brush just outside the new wards Ciarah had erected.

Sure enough, there was a sprite, watching and waiting.

Raphael glanced up at it as he passed and seemed to cock his head a little. The sprite just hissed and took off into the trees as he shook his silver pelt out and kept moving.

That wasn't a definitive answer to my question on whether the wolves were involved with the sprites or not, but it helped.

The Louisiana Wolves … if they chose to turn on us, the battle would be brutal and bloody.

One side would *crawl* away from that fight, but there'd be no victor.

Now I just had to hope that whoever the sprites *were* reporting to … that they couldn't slaughter us both.

“Doesn’t it take time to plan a party?” Ciarah asked as she stood inside the front entrance of the clubhouse and watched Reece hollering at a few hang-arounds to put some white lights up outside. That was about as fancy as we ever got around here.

Kegs were brought in, special order, too. Regular beer was close enough to water for humans. If we wanted to get drunk out here, we’d need something with an extra kick to it. Fortunately there was no shortage of suppliers for faerie wine in the state. We could get it anywhere.

“Not this kind of party,” Arlo growled, looking ticked off at having to spend the night in the same bed as a beautiful, willing woman. What an idiot. Just looking at him right now made me seriously consider freezing all the useless cum in his balls. Not only would it hurt, but it’d be more suitable if he were nut-less considering the way he was acting. “Booze, tobacco, pot, maybe a little coke, and a bunch of beautiful girls and that’s about all we need to have a good time.”

Ciarah’s back got stiff as she turned around to look at Arlo, her eyes flashing with that beautiful otherness that made my hands curl into fists at my sides. I’d never seen anything more … *perfect* in my life. They were endless, depthless … *ancient*.

"Didn't we already have this conversation, Arlo?" she asked, her voice as cold as ice. That made me smile. There wasn't a damn person on this planet that knew cold and ice quite like I did. "Your cock belongs to me until I say otherwise."

"I'm not your *pet*," Arlo snarled back, getting up close to the small woman like he wished he could fight her the way he'd do to any other man in this clubhouse. The only problem with Ciairah was … he knew he would *lose*. "You've taken my room, and now you're what? Trying to swipe my fucking dignity?"

"You're the horned god and I'm the goddess and I'll have my males as I please."

Arlo laughed, a strange caustic sort of sound. The odd thing was, he was clearly sporting a rigid dick inside his jeans. The hard tent in his pants made that ridiculously obvious. He wanted this girl and yet, he was playing games.

What bullshit.

"You can have my cock if you want it," I said, and the room went quiet. I heard Caley chuckling behind the bar, wiping down glasses and pretending not to be involved in the conversation when she was soaking up every word.

Ciarah turned slowly to look at me, her face ferine and liquid, a mask of power and old memories and want.

"I'm claiming the men I want before the party," she says, and her voice was only half Ciarah. The other half, echoing beneath it with undeniable authority was clearly the Veil Keeper.

"As is her right, Arlo," Fionn said as he stepped in the back door with Donal following close behind him. They'd had an officers only meeting at church today, but god only knew why. Ciarah should've been invited to that, welcomed into the chapel with open arms. In a traditional MC, women weren't allowed anywhere near the club's most important meeting place. But we weren't a regular club, and we knew better than to relegate women to whores and housewives.

Feminine power was mighty.

And I could see an endless amount of it pouring from Ciarah's face.

"The Veil Keeper chooses her lovers from within the Wild Hunt. If you don't like it, then leave. Walk out dat door right now and hop your ass on dat bike, see if dere's somewhere safe from a goddess' bed."

Donal and Fionn both laughed, and I could hear Reece guffawing from outside.

Arlo was so pissed that his glamour flickered, and I could see the horns on top of his head as clear as day. He squeezed his hands into fists by his sides and closed his eyes for a long moment before opening them again.

"Fine, I'll keep my hands off the Willing Hunt," he said with a rude smirk, using the derogatory name for the clubwhores that the boys liked to toss around. "But you better give Reece a talking to if you're interested in him. The man doesn't know how to keep his dick in his pants."

Ciarah's nostrils flared as she ignored Arlo's nagging

and turned to face me.

"I'll accept your offer; I want your cock."

"I'll bet you do," Arlo said with a sneer, and then Ciarah was turning and sweeping her arm wide. The magic behind the movement sent the Lord of Spring flying toward the back wall, through the window, and outside. I could hear his body hit the water and raised both brows in response.

Ciarah was panting, almost shaking as she stared at her palm in awe and I heard a barrage of wild cursing from outside. Damn. The man had finally found a woman that could bite back. I wondered how he might take it?

Chapter Thirteen

CIARAH

What the fuck ... I stared at the palm of my hand, unsure if I was in awe of myself or horrified that I'd just so casually tossed a man—a *god*—through a window. Surely that qualified me for anger management classes or something.

If I could remember what the hell they were, maybe I'd know.

"Um." I tucked my trembling hands under my armpits and tried my best not to chew my lip nervously. I was the damn Veil Keeper. The Veil Keeper should *never* show weakness to her subjects. "I think I might go change." After all, the Louisiana Wolves were coming with their mysteriously handsome alpha and something told me I wanted to look good.

No, not good. Hot.

"Should I …" I frowned in the general direction of the swamp where Arlo could be heard swearing and cursing me like an enraged voodoo priestess.

"Nah, *bebette.*" Reece shook his head, having just seen the tail-end of my, er, *discussion* with Arlo. "You go on, let old Cernunnos cool down a tad, see?"

Still shaking slightly, I nodded and beat a hasty retreat back to Arlo's—*my*—room. Slamming the door behind me, I leaned my back against it and let out a long breath.

This dual personality was beginning to frighten me, and by the echo of unease I could feel inside my mind, it worried *her* too. We needed to get ourselves under control. Fast.

A light tap on my door startled me out of my thoughts and I jumped, spinning to open the door a crack.

"Hi." Killian smiled at me with his arctic blue eyes and ran his hand through his scruffy black hair, almost as though he was nervous. Of what? Surely not me.

Then again, I had just tossed his friend with little more than a flick of my wrist.

"Hi, Killian." I smiled back, opening the door wider.

"I thought you might need a hand picking out an outfit for tonight? I know you don't remember much of your former life, of *any* of your former lives, but I doubt any of them partied with bikers." He said it with a small smirk and I wondered just what exactly a *biker* party entailed.

I'd soon find out though.

"Really?" The worry and fear I'd been feeling a

moment ago slid off me like a rattler's skin. “Are you *sure* that's why you followed me up here?”

Killian shrugged. “Sure, that sounds like a plausible reason. Don't you think, *ma petite chérie*?” His eyes sparkled with wickedness as he advanced into my room, coaxing me to back up until my legs touched the bed.

“I think you followed me up here to offer me your cock in a more literal way.” I grinned, my tongue darting out to wet my lips as I ran my gaze over his form. He was huge, like all the fae bikers seemed to be, but of a slightly slimmer build than both Arlo and Reece.

“And if I did?” He quirked a black eyebrow over one of those glacial eyes. “Would you accept once more? Would you take me as your own and name me *Seigneur de L'hiver*?” The French words rolled off his tongue, but I understood the meaning without struggling. Lord of Winter.

“Is that what you want?” I asked, genuinely curious as I sat on the edge of Arlo's bed and looked up at the darkly handsome biker who loomed over me. “To be my Lord of Winter? To bond to me for as long as my soul shall inhabit this body? This is no small decision to take lightly.”

My voice had dropped lower, but it wasn't *all* her. It was us both. While she spoke with knowledge, I spoke with caution. Killian didn't know me at all, and this was not a job one could quit from.

“Does it matter?” he retorted, but without heat. “*Le Gardien* chooses who she chooses; the men of the Hunt have no say in the matter.”

"This is true," *we* said softly, "so why should I choose you, Killian? Show me what makes you a better choice for my Lord of Winter than any other man in the Wild Hunt."

"Show you?" he repeated, raising his eyebrows. Clearly, this was not the reaction he'd expected. Oh well.

"Yes." I nodded, my lips pulling up into a sultry sort of smile. "Consider this an interview." My eyes dropped to the waistband of his black denim jeans, where his hand rested over a skull-shaped belt buckle.

Killian said nothing for a moment, and was probably looking at me, but I couldn't seem to tear my eyes off his long fingers. His thumb was hooked under the rough fabric of his pants and it was consuming me while I waited for him to make a move.

"Interview," he murmured, half chuckling under his breath. "Very well then, *méchante fille*. I tell you once more, you can have my cock … if you want it."

As he spoke, his hands made quick work of his belt, sliding it through the loops of his pants then coiling it around his fist and setting it on the side table. Next, his fly. Flicking the button from its hole then dragging the zipper down, he exposed the straining fabric of his black boxer-briefs.

Then, he paused, and my gaze flickered back up to his face to find him watching me almost expectantly. It took me a moment or two to realize he was waiting for an answer.

"Yes," I said. *We* said, our voice full of magic as I accepted his offer. "I want it. Give it to me … *now*."

The possessive, almost desperate tone to that ancient voice startled me, but I had no time to question it as Killian responded, putting a palm on my chest and gently pushing me back onto the bed.

I lifted my arms up and crossed them above my head, closing my eyes as his cool hands slid up underneath the long, dark skirt I was wearing. Kill's palms had scars and rough spots from years of riding his bike and doing … well, whatever it was that a motorcycle club did, but they were also soft in a way, like he cared for himself. I liked that, a man who took pride in his appearance.

"Do you know what temperature play is, *mon Gardien*?" he asked, curling his long, inked fingers under the waistband of my new panties and making me gasp. I stared up at the ceiling, biting my lip, listening to my heart thunder inside my chest. No wonder I liked sex so much—it was *fun.* It was invigorating. It was *exciting*. And maybe … after all those years of being trapped and chained, beaten and abused, it was nice to be reminded what pleasure felt like, that this was *my* body to do with what I pleased.

"No," I whispered, wracking my brain for that term. *Temperature play.* If I had known what it was before, when I was Ciarah O'Rourke, I no longer remembered. "Are you going to tell me about it, Killian?"

"I'll do more than just *tell* you about it," he purred, sliding my panties down with an achingly painful slowness, like he was painting a picture of the pleasure he planned on giving me, each careful stroke of his brush adding a new layer to the image. But it would take time to build on it, hours maybe before I could see what all those shadows and highlights were coming together to create. "I'll fucking *show* you."

The panties slid over my feet and I raised my head up just enough to see Killian toss them aside. A moment later, the door to the room slammed open and Arlo entered, pausing to glare at me and Kill before he scowled and headed in the direction of the bathroom.

"Not enough to take my bedroom, you gotta fuck in it, too?"

"Clearly throwing you out the window wasn't lesson enough," Kill growled, the sound like that of a cat, low and unassuming but full of threat. I wondered what it might be like if he were to show his claws? "Show some goddamn respect. Or if the thought of a powerful woman frightens your alpha male sensibilities so terribly, then leave."

"Leave? I can't *leave*," Arlo roared, wet and dripping from his swim in the bayou. "She's already named me her damn Lord of Spring. I'd rather not have the Wild Hunt on *my* ass." He stormed past us and tore the bathroom door open, slamming it shut behind him.

"I haven't officially named him," I told Killian, leaning up on my elbows, the sharp scent of Arlo's anger … arousing me even further. He was like a beast that needed taming. Or mating. I would do either and both with him if he would only calm down. "Shall I let him go?"

Kill snorted.

"He doesn't want you to let him go," he told me, pushing my thighs apart and dropping his head between them. Since my legs were dangling off the end of the bed, I hooked my knees over Killian's strong shoulders for support, gasping in surprise when the firm, wet heat of his tongue flicked over my clit.

Reaching my right arm up, I blindly grasped for the first pillow I could find and yanked it to my face. Good thing Arlo and I had left the bed messy this morning or else I wouldn't have been able to reach it.

Biting down hard, I curled the fingers of my left hand into Killian's silken locks, the thick ebony strands of his hair smooth against my skin.

"Is this temperature play?" I choked out, swallowing hard and groaning as Kill locked his fingers around my hip bones to hold my thrusting pelvis in place. I couldn't help myself—I wanted to be pressed up against his face. I wanted *more*. "Because your mouth is fucking hot. Almost too hot."

"This isn't the trick, *mon cher*," he whispered. "*This* is."

Killian pulled back as I yanked the pillow from between my teeth and stuck it under my head so I could relax my neck. As I watched, he twirled his fingers in the air, pulling water from the humid atmosphere and drawing it into his palm in a swirl of blue light. *Magic.*

My breath stuttered as I watched him collect and then *freeze* the water molecules into a long, thick ice cube.

"The cold is where my expertise lies," he said, his blue

eyes locked on mine. "Some people despise the cold but when you pair it with heat … it makes things *scalding.*"

Kill took the ice cube and, his eyes still locked on mine, slid it along my heated folds, making me gasp and cough with the sheer rush of sensation. He stroked me several times, drawing little screams from my throat, and then he replaced the cube with his hot tongue.

And oh.

Oh.

Temperature play.

I quite liked that.

Killian warmed up all the places he'd just cooled and then … slipped the ice cube inside of me.

My scream of pleasure drew Arlo out of the bathroom, still wet and dripping but this time with hot water from the shower. Steam rose from his skin as he stood there and watched Killian follow up with his fingers inside of me, chasing the cool slide of the ice cube.

"Don't butt in—not today," Killian growled, just before he leaned down and kissed my clit with gentle swirls of his tongue. His left hand held my bucking pelvis down as I thrashed and turned my head, biting the pillow *hard*. "I won't share today."

"Like it's your choice to make," Arlo snapped, but he didn't come any closer, watching from the doorway to the bathroom, leaning his big muscular form against the frame. Without his glamour on, his skin was brilliantly silver, his eyes green as emeralds, his horns shock white and wicked sharp.

His eyes met mine and he threw on this infuriating smirk, wrapping his big hand around his cock and giving it a squeeze. He worked himself nice and slow as Killian brought me to the edge of an eye-watering orgasm and then pulled back, breathing against my heated cunt with hot … warm … then *cool* breaths. Ah, a true Lord of Winter.

The ice cube was melting inside of me, cool water trickling out of my pussy and dripping down my ass. The sensation was almost enough to drive me to climax all on its own.

"Killian," I gasped, and I felt his laughter against me as he stood up and looked down, an imposing figure with dark hair and pale eyes, stubble guarding the slight smirk on his lips. "Finish me."

"I wanted to make sure you got a taste of the full package before you made your decision," he said, stepping between my legs and taking hold of my ass in his long fingers.

The two men exchanged glances and Arlo growled low in his throat, pumping his shaft with tense knuckles, the ink on the back of his hands dancing with the violent motion of his fingers on his cock.

"Let's see what it is you're so frightened about," Killian taunted, turning back to look at me, meeting my gaze with a look that was both ice-cold and red hot. I couldn't explain it, but the duality was beautiful, like the sun and the moon, summer and winter, light and dark. "*Le Gardien*?"

"Fuck me," I whispered and threw my head back in the burst of a brilliant white-hot orgasm as he entered me, his long hot dick thrusting against the cool sensation of the ice cube. I came around him, squeezing tight, water trickling down my cheeks as I flailed and thrashed against the bed, digging my fingers into the blankets.

Killian waited for me to finish before he started to move, thrusting against the cool ice cube with his scalding cock, melting it faster, mixing up all the new sensations together into this bundle of energy that coiled tight and ready in my belly, waiting to explode again. I wouldn't be long to a second orgasm.

The fae man buried between my thighs spoke low, sweet words in French, their gentleness at odds with the violent nature of his thrusts, the frenzy of his body as he buried himself deep within me. His face blurred in my vision as I struggled to hold back tears of sheer unadulterated pleasure. I'd never felt anything like this before … not as the Veil Keeper … not as Ciarah … just never.

"Fuck," Arlo snarled, moving over to the edge of the bed, his member quivering with need as he grit his teeth and looked down at me. "I know you've cast a fucking spell on me. Take it off."

"You're a …" I tried to choke out the word fool, but it wouldn't come out right. I was too busy enjoying the pleasure rippling through my body. No more words would come, so I spoke with my body, reaching out a hand and snatching Arlo's thick, hard shaft with an iron grip.

He sucked in a sharp breath, his eyes widening as his hips thrust forward into my hand.

"I swear to the Keeper, this has to be a spell or some shit," Arlo muttered with a strangled moan as my hand slid the length of his dick and knocked his own fist out of the way.

"*Frère*," Killian growled, pausing and glaring at Arlo while I writhed underneath his strong hands. Damn it, don't stop now! "Shut your trap or leave. Your words don't even make sense. You swear to the Keeper? Here she is, with her perfect hand wrapped around your cock. Don't be a damn *imbécile*."

There was a tense moment between the two fae men, as they remained locked with their angry eyes on one another, Killian's dick buried deep inside me and Arlo's hard shaft in my grip. The moment didn't bother me at all, though. I found it … fascinating. Despite still teetering on the edge of my second orgasm.

Curiously, I watched Arlo's face as he seemed to be wrestling with himself. Kill's words had forced him to accept the choice he'd already made. That we all knew he'd made. He was my Lord of Spring, through and through. He just needed to get used to it.

With lazy motion, my hand stroked up and down his rock-hard length while I studied the two of them. Killian was just a fraction taller but Arlo was a lot broader across the chest. They were both … perfect. *Mine*.

I saw the moment Arlo cracked, breaking his staredown with Killian and casting his angry green gaze over my body, pausing on my tight nipples straining against the light cotton of my tank top.

"*Très bon,*" Killian grunted, adjusting his grip on my ass before thrusting back into me.

The breath puffed out of me and I felt a sultry smile creep over my face as I settled in for the ride, not for a second letting go of Arlo.

Killian murmured something more under his breath in French, too quiet for me to make out, before exhaling a long, ice-cold breath as he leaned in close to kiss me. The air between us sparkled with frost and my body shivered violently as his hot mouth descended to mine.

Arlo, for his part, did as he was told. Kept his trap shut. Aside from the occasional moan, he simply stood there and let me jerk him off while his wild, angry eyes remained glued to the in and out of Killian's cock in my cunt.

Killian kissed me like I was the only woman on earth. Like I was the center of his universe. Like I was his fucking *goddess*.

I loved every damn second of it.

Delicate lines of ice crept from Kill's fingers where they gripped my flesh, coating my skin like lace and provoking another shiver from me as Killian groaned.

"*Ma déesse*," he breathed as I clenched around him, that second orgasm back with double force. This time though, I wanted to drag him with me. Arlo too. Nothing would make this moment more satisfying …

Kill touched a frigid fingertip to the searing heat of my

clit and I gasped aloud, pleasure rolling through me as I let myself go. My muscles fluttered and tensed around his hardness, holding him captive and *demanding* he join me.

"*Merde*," Kill swore, fighting to hold on but eventually giving in with a few hard thrusts.

Meanwhile my hand milked the climax from Arlo, whose hot seed splashed across the icy cold of my exposed belly as he came with a primal sounding grunt.

The sounds of our labored breathing filled the room for a long moment before Killian, almost reluctantly, withdrew from me and tucked his junk back into those pants that had never made it past his ass.

"We should get downstairs." He frowned. "I can sense the wolves have already arrived."

"Fuck," Arlo spat, picking up a towel from the floor and wiping off his dick before shimmying into a pair of jeans. "Shower's yours, Keeper. You'll want to wash well. The smell of sex on a woman drives the wolves a little … *wild*."

Well, for the Horned God to be calling someone else *wild,* it almost made me curious to see. But I could already feel the slickness of Killian's come dripping down my ass and if there was one thing both my selves agreed on, it was that *that* was not a sexy sensation.

Killian bent back over me, snaking a hand into the back of my hair and claiming my lips in a passionate kiss. His tongue met mine in a torrent of emotion and desire, until I was breathless and more than a little tempted to demand an encore performance.

"So," he whispered when he broke our kiss. "Do I get the job?"

Cheeky boy, one of the me's in my head chuckled and my lips lifted in a grin. "I'll consider you for a callback."

Killian narrowed his pale blue eyes at me and trailed another line of ice down my bare thigh as he stood back up, as a promise or a reminder, it didn't matter. He'd made his point.

I lied there on Arlo's bed a little longer, watching Killian retreat out the door, then turned my attention to the bestial asshole again. Somehow in that short time he had replaced his glamour and now stood there with his massive, ink stained biceps crossed over his chest as he glared at me.

"What?" I demanded and he rolled his emerald eyes.

"Shower, Keeper. Now. Before those mangy mutts catch your scent." He jerked his thumb to the bathroom door.

"What would happen if they did?" I asked, standing from the bed and making my way over to the bathroom.

"I'm no *seer*, so I can't predict the fucking future. But in the *past* …" Arlo shrugged his toned shoulders. "Well, suffice it to say the result wasn't *good*."

His words rang with truth, and none of the usual aftertaste that implied a deliberate deceit. There was a lot more to the story, for sure, but I guessed the past didn't matter when compared to the future. After all, my past was nothing more than a shattered mirror. It was my *future* that would find those missing pieces though.

Or, at least I hoped so.

Raucous sounds of male laughter filtered up the stairs to me, and I smiled. I recognized Reece's laugh without question. It was like the rustling of autumn leaves and it warmed my soul to hear.

The little tryst with Killian and Arlo had ignited something within me, and I felt a burning need for more. Oh, that callback for my Lord of Winter was going to come much sooner than he realized. For my Lords of Spring and Autumn, too. My body felt as though it was just now awakening from an endless slumber and it demanded to be worshipped.

"*Gardien*," Fionn greeted me as I pushed through the swinging door to the bar area where the party was already in full swing.

"Fionn." I nodded to him and accepted the red plastic cup from his hand. There was something familiar about that cup. The cherry red of its exterior, its white interior, the foamy amber liquid it held. It flittered across my mind like so many other memory bubbles before it, but I didn't care enough to chase after it.

"I hear y'all had a productive day, meetin' da Sage?" Fionn enquired politely, but his eyes were tight and pinched, like he was poised on the edge of a breakdown.

"I did," I murmured, taking a sip of my drink and being pleasantly surprised by the taste. My sketchy memory had warned that it would taste bad, like old socks steeped in dishwater, but this drink was delicious. Like honey, and jasmine, and *sunshine*?

"Fairy wine," Fionn supplied when I hummed my approval and licked my lips.

"Ciarah," Reece grinned, coming up beside his father and raking his gold-brown eyes over me. "You look—" Whatever he'd been about to say was cut off by Fionn's sharp elbow to Reece's gut.

"You mind your manners around *Le Gardien du Voile* boy," Fionn warned. "She ain't like these Willing Hunt girls, y'hear? She be our goddess and you damn well better treat her such."

"'course." Reece seemed unphased. "But even goddesses must want t'hear how smokin' hot dey are, no?"

Fionn's eyes bugged out at what I could only assume was what he considered impertinence on his son's part, but in that moment I was just *Ciarah*, and as far as I could tell, Ciarah loved hearing how smoking hot she was.

"Reece." I greeted him back with a grin. "So this is a fae-biker party, huh?"

The whole Wild Hunt was in attendance—I could tell without needing to count—along with just as many scantily clad women and at least two dozen wolves. Don't ask me how I knew they were wolves, I simply did.

Across the dimly lit room, a pair of bloodred eyes

locked on mine and a shiver ran down my back. If my wings had been out, they would've trembled under Rafe's intense stare, but I wasn't ready to show all my cards just yet.

Still, I'd been careful when selecting my new clothes to ensure all of my tops had a bare back, just in case I needed to free my wings unexpectedly. Not that I had any issues baring my breasts, but my fuzzy memory spoke of modesty and reminded me that humans weren't comfortable with casual nudity.

"Dat it is, sweet t'ang." Reece nodded, sliding an arm around my waist and leading me over to the pool tables where Amelie stood leaning on a cue while she watched Rafe's beta try and fail to sink a ball … What was his name again? Marcel?

"Your dogs, *Gardien*," Reece announced with a glint of disgust in his eye as he looked at Rafe, "as you requested."

Those *dogs* in question all rumbled a growl at Reece and I laid a hand on his rock-hard midsection to stop him from retaliating. Amelie caught my eye and winked, a small smile playing at her lips like she was enjoying the animosity.

"Thank you, Reece." I smiled up at him and he scowled down at me. He knew full-well he was being dismissed, but he didn't like it.

Too damn bad.

Something inside of me was urging me to make friends with the wolves and that wasn't something I could do with a scowling autumn fae hovering over my shoulder and tossing insults at them.

"I'll get you a fresh drink," he muttered reluctantly, taking my surprisingly empty cup from my hand. I hadn't even noticed myself drinking it.

Loud music filtered into the room through metal speakers placed at the four corners near the roof. It sounded tinny and garbled to my sensitive ears, but there were several people dancing and swaying to the noise, so I let it go.

"Some party," Rafe said, leaning down, silver hair falling over his forehead, like beams of moonlight turned locks. "If this is how the fae celebrate their big victories nowadays, then maybe we'd best leave the Veil up and keep this taint away from Faerie?"

"What did you expect?" I asked him, watching as he sent the colored balls pinging across the green surface of the table. "What did you think coming here and insulting me would win you?"

"I'm not here to win anything," Rafe continued, lifting his bloodred stare to mine. We locked gazes and I felt the pack members around me rippling with concern and agitation. I couldn't remember much about myself or who I used to be, but I *did* have a general idea of the world around me. Dogs stared one another down in displays of dominance.

Neither Raphael nor I would look away first—I knew that instinctively.

"Okay," Amelie said, covering my eyes with her

palms. "That's about enough of that, you two. Rafe, you did not come here to start trouble, did you?"

"Who says *I'm* the one starting trouble?" he continued as Amelie released me, and he leaned down to study the pool table as his beta took a shot. "And anyway, I didn't expect to get a damn thing from this party. What I did expect was to see some of that fire, that *spark* that made the fae so goddamn great once upon a time. But maybe that's all those legends are … faerie stories. They don't mean shit anymore, do they?"

"Back in the day, my people would decapitate the heads of *your* people and roast them on spits. We'd play games and we'd make bargains. We'd torture and kill for fun, and we'd drink the tears of the weeping. If that's what you came here to see, you'll be sorely disappointed."

"Don't have the guts for it?" he asked, standing up to his full height and towering over me. He didn't seem like a bad man, just a man who knew what he wanted and how to get it. I wasn't sure if he was intended to be friend or foe.

"Maybe I just don't have a taste for cruelty?" I retorted, turning back to survey the room and hearing the alpha male sigh behind me.

"I didn't come here to insult you or get in an argument—I came to offer my help."

Glancing over my shoulder, I found Rafe watching me with a severe expression, one that spoke volumes as to the type of man he was. Stern, set in his ways, a leader, but also … an asshole. Both Ciarah and Gràinne knew what an asshole was.

And both of us loved … and hated them.

"In what capacity?" I asked, ready to walk away from the situation. I could feel that Rafe wasn't used to dealing with equals. He was used to being the one and only boss. But he wasn't going to boss *me* around.

"The full moon. You'll need an escort to find Papa Cocodril."

"I have many choices of escort," I said, realizing that the room around me had devolved into drugs, drinking, swearing, and fucking. It didn't much bother me, just a more modern version of what a faerie court used to look like.

A bacchanalian affair.

A den of debauchery.

I liked it that way … so long as *my* men knew to whom they belonged.

"Full moon. Werewolf," Rafe continued, moving over to stand next to me. He smelt like earth and wild magic, like beast and burden. And he positively *reeked* of need, like he hadn't mated recently and was in dire need of a warm body to soothe his. "You won't find a better man for the job."

"I'll take Amelie then," I said as his eyes narrowed on me. "A better man, perhaps I won't find. But a woman? We both know what the wiser choice is here." I turned away, shoving dark hair over my shoulder as I made my way to the open back door and found Reece standing on the dock, smoking and chatting with a group of other men.

He glanced over his shoulder as I stepped outside, waving his hand and sending the other men scattering.

"Wat you doin' dere girl?" he asked me as I paused next to him, close enough to feel the heat of his body.

"Wondering why your father seems so bent out of shape?" I hedged, glancing up at the big man as his eyes roamed over the bayou, studying the distant shapes of sprites in the evening air. They hovered just outside the edge of my wards, waiting, watching.

"Some of da old-timers," he started and then coughed, shaking his head and lighting up a cigarette, gray smoke curling over the thick curve of his lower lip. "They done gone and got used to bein' in charge around here. They're either too stupid or too slow to realize what your presence here means."

A girl's rowdy shout echoed from inside the building and I narrowed my eyes. There were more than just guests in there—there were strippers. I didn't know who had hired them, but I let it go. For now. These men had been trapped out in the swamp for so long, they'd developed their own way of life. I wouldn't break that in an instant, steal away their culture—even if it *was* foreign to me.

"Here's dat drink I meant to give ya," Reece said, picking up a red cup and handing it over to me. "But I saw you chattin' with da alpha and I didn't want to disturb you, me."

I took the cup and held it in my hands, drinking down a sweet mouthful and feeling my head spin in the most pleasant way possible. I liked this faerie wine … very much so. And I liked the tingling feeling in my body, this promise of release from all the torture and pain of my own mind. The wine would set me afloat on a river to a different place, a different state of being.

"Are they planning something?" I asked Reece, studying the sprites in the distance and wondering what I would do if I found out my own men were plotting against me. But then, when a fae broke the rules, I should *feel* it—*especially* with my own hunt. And I could sense lies. I waited for Reece to speak to see if his voice would ring with truth.

"Dunno," he told me, and I felt the honesty in that one word roll over my skin like a fresh breeze. "I don't think so. Fionn is old, but not fucking senile … yet." Reece chuckled and shook his head. "I just think as much as they moan and complain about missin' da old world? They kind of like the shit they got goin' on in this one and you being here? You change everything they come to know, you."

"Once the Veil is open … what happens?" I asked, because although I was slowly regaining Gràinne's memories, slowly regaining my own, I didn't know the answer to that question. "We go home?"

"We go home," Reece said, but his voice had that slight *off* quality to it, like he was telling the truth so far as he knew it … but maybe he didn't believe it in his heart? Maybe, like me, Reece didn't feel like he had a home.

Home.

I wasn't sure if I'd ever had one.

Not as *Le Gardien du Voile*, not as Ciarah.

Not now.

But I could make one, couldn't I?

Glancing over at Reece, I felt this warmth inside my chest. He was still a stranger to me, but he also had this … comforting presence to him. For such a big, gruff man, there was a tenderness and a gentleness inside of him that made his alpha male attitude and strength that much more appealing.

"Strippers, pot, coke, and alcohol. Sounds familiar. Am I certain I wasn't a biker before all this?"

Reece grinned, his teeth white in his tanned face, and knocked back the cup of alcohol in his hand.

"You forgot to mention sex, gambling, and fights. But girl, you too sweet to be a biker or one of dem clubwhores."

I smiled and it felt like a dark shadow passing across my face. Reece noticed and cocked a questioning brow at me.

"Don't be so sure about that," I said, and took another sip of wine.

The door to my bedroom flew open and I hopped out of bed, fully-clothed and ready to fight. But it wasn't one of my mother's boyfriends, not this time. It was the bitch herself.

"Get up," she screamed, obviously drunk. I actually prefered it when she was on heroin. Then all I had to worry about was whether she would die on the couch and stink up the house. When she was guzzling tourists' discarded hurricanes from the trash can outside (like, she actually went out and stole souvenir fish bowls that thirsty tourists had left in the garbage with leftover alcohol in them), she was a raging bitch beyond comparison.

She screamed obscenities at me. Insults. She hit me. She pulled my hair and threw stuff at me, broke my things and tried to break me. But she never did, never could. Because every time I looked in her eyes, I saw what a broken person looked like and I knew I'd never let that happen to me.

Never.

"Get a fucking job, you piece of shit, worst mistake I ever made ..." Laura—because I wouldn't call her Mom—drawled, sloshing alcohol across the already stained carpet.

"Why don't you get a job!" I screamed back at her, because I had been working for the last few months, down at a bar on Bourbon Street, slinging drinks for tourists with a fake ID I got from my last boyfriend. It was quality, good enough to pass intense inspection. But I wouldn't tell her that. If I did, not only would she steal my money, but she'd come down to the bar while I was working and harass me for free drinks. She'd gotten me fired at places *before and I didn't doubt her ability to do it again. "You're the mom—it's YOUR job to work. It's your job to pay the rent and buy the food and clean the house. I've been doing all those things by myself for YEARS and I'm done."*

I grabbed my backpack off the old, scratched metal desk under my bedroom window. I might've only been seventeen but I could live at the library and shower at the school. Fuck this. I was done putting up with Laura's crap. I was supposed to love my mother, but I hated her. I hated her. I fucking HATED her.

Pain exploded in the back of my skull and I stumbled forward, dropping my bag with a grunt, curling over the edge of the table as white spots danced in my vision. The shock of pain came again and again and again, curses exploding from my mother's mouth like the violent shrieks of a dying crane, torn apart by a fucking gator.

That's how little I meant to her—as little as a decaying carcass in a swamp.

She was hitting me with her liquor bottle and as I fought to turn around, she got me right in the temple and sent me crashing to my knees, darkness sweeping over and consuming me.

I wasn't out long, not even long enough to feel my face hit the floor because suddenly, I was not lying on the ground anymore ... I was sitting.

In a chair of spikes.

When I tried to relax and take some of the pressure off my arms, pain spiked through me and I gasped. Laughter echoed in the dark room around me and I knew I was not in my room anymore. I was not seventeen and I was not just Ciarah now.

I was the Veil Keeper, too.

'Ciarah, this is a dream,' *someone said to me.* 'Wake up.'

But I couldn't wake up because there were eyes everywhere, eyes and smiles glinting in the darkness, looking at me like they couldn't decide if they wanted to violate me or eat me. Or both. I screamed, but my voice as so ragged and broken, no sound came out.

That was how low I'd fallen.

First, a carcass to my mother.

Now, a broken doll without a voice.

They'd stolen away my words, my opinions, my emotions.

They'd silenced me.

They wanted to break me.

But I'd already promised I wouldn't be broken. By anyone.

'Ciarah, can you hear me?' *the voice asked again, the sound a cool breeze against my heated skin.* 'You need to wake up, *mon cher.*'

It was Killian, I realized as the sharp gazes and the awful smiles came closer.

My arms hurt so goddamn badly, I knew I was about to give in. I was about to let go and be impaled on so many spikes, the weight of my own body crushing me into the blades.

And then ... my mouth bloomed with a kiss that was both cold and hot at the same time, scalding, searing, aching.

And I woke up.

Chapter Fourteen

CIARAH

"Killian." His name sighed from my lips like a prayer. "Thank you."

"Nothing to thank, *chère*, you were dreaming and it didn't look like a particularly pleasant dream, no?" His face blocked my view of the room, his lips still close enough to mine that I could feel the heat from them.

"No," I replied in a small voice, still trembling from the horrors of my *dream*. My soul knew it was no dream though. Those had been flashbacks. Memories.

What a horrible life I must have led. Maybe those memories were better left gone, after all?

"Sorry, Kill." I smiled into his gentle blue eyes as his thumb stroked my jaw. "I must have drunk more than I realized."

The sounds around us indicated we were still in the communal clubhouse, and the party was nowhere close to its natural end. Dimly, I remembered having crawled into a booth to take my little nap, so we were out of the way a bit.

"Faerie wine, Ciarah," Killian grinned, releasing my face and shifting to sit back a bit further, allowing me to see the rest of the room. "It sneaks up on you if you don't expect it. How's your head? That stuff can be known to leave a nasty hangover, too."

Cocking my head, I took mental stock of any lingering effects but all seemed fine. "I'm okay, Kill. Just a bit shaken from those memories. They were …" I trailed off as I shuddered, rubbing at my arms to reassure myself that they were whole.

Not far from where we sat in the shadowy booth, there was a woman perched on the edge of a table with her legs spread, the bandanna-clad head of one of my Hunt buried between them. Her own head was thrown back, and her hands clasped at the man's scalp while he serviced her.

Killian must have noticed I was distracted and glanced over his shoulder.

"Oh." He turned back to me as the woman moaned louder, clearly approaching her climax. Her skin was rippling with glittery scales so she can't have been human. "Sorry, that's sort of normal around here. Does it bother you?"

"No." I shook my head slowly, still watching the scaled woman while she orgasmed onto the heavy-set man's face.

"Will you tell me what your dream was about?" Kill asked, changing the subject and drawing my attention back to him. "How do you know it was a memory?"

"Memories," I corrected, my eyes still darting back to the couple as the biker got to his feet and kissed the woman passionately before lifting her off the table and pushing her to her knees in front of him. "There were two … or at least, I'm pretty sure. One each for Ciarah and Gràinne. Neither of my former lives were very gentle."

Killian's mouth tightened as I finally wrenched my attention from the scaled woman, who was now enthusiastically returning the favor on her partner, and back to my Lord of Winter. Or … prospective Lord of Winter at any rate. I was still yet to formally accept any of my Lords.

"Tell me, *ma belle fille,*" he urged. "Let me share the weight of those memories for you."

His gaze was so intense, so sincere, it tightened something in my chest and I almost accepted his offer. How would it feel, I wondered, to share the burden of my fragmented horrors?

"No," I whispered, even as my hand cupped his cheek gently.

Killian held my gaze for a long moment, his emotions clear in the crystal depths of his eyes. He was frustrated, desperate, and in pain. I understood. He wanted to help, he wanted to *heal*. But some agonies were not halved when shared; instead they doubled.

"Very well," he accepted, his jaw tight with anger *knowing* he couldn't question my decision. There was no doubt I was in charge around here, memories or not. Now the old-timers simply needed to accept it.

My attention flickered back to the couple near us. The woman was still on her knees, her hand wrapped around the bearded biker's slick cock, working it up and down while her mouth was busy with his balls.

The quick foray into temperature play with Killian prior to the party starting had ignited something inside me, awoken a *need* that had not yet been satiated. A rogue memory bubble burst, allowing me insight into my former life—*Ciarah's* former life, that was—and I knew that I'd liked sex. Loved it. And I wanted more.

Right now.

"Killian." I turned his face back to mine as he too had become distracted by the live-action porn show we were being treated to. When I had his attention back on me, I dropped my hand to his lap. It wasn't difficult to locate his cock, already halfway hard through the heavy fabric of his jeans, and I grabbed it firmly.

"Ciarah, *mon amour,*" he grinned. "Are you sure? You're not one of the clubwhores, so if you want to go somewhere private …"

My lips parted to respond, to tell him privacy meant nothing to me. For countless years I'd been afforded no such luxury as my ruthless captors had done as they pleased, so I saw no reason why I couldn't do as these *clubwhores* did.

These men were *mine*, and if I wanted them in front of ten times this many spectators, then who was to stop me?

Before the words could pass my lips, the song playing over the speakers ended, shifting into something new, and the group of girls who'd been dancing near us moved.

In their absence, I could see straight across the room to a pool table where a voluptuous woman with violet hair undulated to the sexy beat of the music.

As I watched, she reached up, slowly, sensually, tugging at the neck-tie of her bikini top and releasing her full breasts from their fabric confines. She tossed the scrap of material at one of the men surrounding the table, staring up at her with adoration, and seemed to laugh at whatever he said in response. They were too far away for me to hear, but as he leaned forward into the light, tucking a folded note into the girl's fairy-floss underwear, my blood turned to ice.

"*Merde*," Killian swore, seeing exactly what I saw. "That foolish boy. Ciarah, *chère*, he is just pushing the boundaries, trying to get a rise out of you."

"It's working," I snarled, climbing over Killian and out of the booth, not for a second taking my eyes off *my* fae-damned Lord of Spring.

Perhaps I hadn't made myself clear enough, when I'd laid my claim. Perhaps he needed a fucking reminder, right here and fucking now in front of my *entire* Wild Hunt.

"Ciarah." Killian snatched my hand, halting me as I was about to storm over there. "Ciarah, he is not foolish enough to let her touch him. He's just trying to make you mad."

My ire turned to Killian in a single glare, and he wisely dropped his hold on my hand. Thank the Veil *one* of these stupid fae men respected my power.

Well, Arlo was about to learn that lesson the hard way. I'd had enough of his insolence. It was time he made a choice. Accept his position as Lord of Spring or forfeit it permanently.

Even as ancient as I—the Veil Keeper—was, I would not force a man against his will. It would be his choice, but if he chose badly it would also cost him his position in The Wild Hunt. After all, this was *my* Hunt and all the men in it *belonged to me*.

My black patent leather heels clicked across the hard floor as I approached the stripper and her audience, and Arlo watched me, his jaw set stubbornly and his glare hard.

This was going to be enjoyable.

"Do you not speak English?" I asked him as I approached and stood in front of him. The big man towered over me, covered in ink and bullshit, glaring with defiance. I understood—he was the typical alpha male type. And he should be. I needed him strong and powerful to fight for me, defend me, *pleasure* me, but I also needed him to be a willow branch.

He could bend and not break.

I knew that firsthand.

I had been twisted, tortured, all the best attempts to

tame had been thrust upon me.

I'd bent … but I hadn't broken.

I'd do the same to Arlo.

"The fuck are you talking about?" he growled down at me, every bit a god. There was this arrogant gleam to his eyes, this set to his jaw. Upstairs, he'd almost succumbed. Hell, I thought he had. But I should've known better. It takes more than a hand job to bring a god to his knees.

"Do you not speak English?" I repeated, putting my hands on my hips. Several of the people gathered around us were staring now, men sipping beers, women running their fingers through their hair and licking their lips.

This was going to be a spectacle.

How fun.

Vague memories told me fae court was all about spectacle.

We might be in a dirty clubhouse in the middle of the bayou, the air humid and smelling of swamp, the music loud, the drinks in plastic cups … but this was still court. Her court. *My* court.

"Because I know what I told you not once, not twice, but three times. I warned you, Arlo. Now." I paused and my nostrils flared at the same time he gritted his teeth. "Shall I repeat my warning in another language? Sidhe? Gaelic? Because if I have to, I will tear my memory apart until those languages come back to me, and I will repeat myself. One. More. Time."

"What are you getting at?" Arlo asked, low and quiet. Dangerous. He would be a dangerous man to anyone but me. His green eyes shone with a brilliant light and his tongue slid over his lower lip. “I haven't broken any of your rules.”

“Toeing the line is close enough. It's willful disobedience,” I snapped as Rafe came out of the other room and paused, raising a silver eyebrow and leaning against the wall with one shoulder to watch the show. I ignored him.

“Disobedience?” Arlo scoffed with a shake of his head. He lifted his chin and looked down at me. “I'm not really the type to be disobedient, Veil Keeper. Because I ain't the type to be obedient in the first place.”

Laughter rippled around the room—male and female alike.

This was going to turn into a battle of wills, wasn’t it?

Well, *I* wasn't going to lose.

“You have two choices now. Take off your cut and walk out those doors, climb on your bike and leave the Wild Hunt. Or, you can be my Lord of Spring. In that case, leave your cut on but take off your pants.”

More laughter swirled around me as the spectators stood and sipped their faerie wine, glamours flickering in and out. With a wave of my hand, I shattered them all like glass. A collective gasp went up from the crowd and then … silence.

Arlo now stood above me with his horns curving over his head, his silver skin gleaming, his eyes like rare jewels. His rage was a palpable fucking thing.

“You want my dick?” he asked with a bit of swagger,

but this time, nobody laughed.

"Leave the Hunt. Be my Lord. Those are your choices."

I stared him down, feeling every moment of helplessness and torture from the past five years pushing against me like an iron weight, burning my skin and crushing me to the floor. It felt like my ribs would break, my skull would crack, my insides would ooze across the floor. Because for years, they did. For years, I was barely a person, nothing but flesh and blood and meat. And for years, I had no choice in the matter. It wasn't a matter of fighting hard or fighting smart or being clever—I was trapped.

This time, today, here, I had a choice.

I would not be bullied or abused. And maybe, if I had to assert myself more than usual to make up for all that time, then Arlo would have to learn to love me despite it, for it … or else he could leave. The only vulnerability I would show in this moment was me picking *him*.

"Oh, come on, brudder, don't be a damn fool, you," Reece said, appearing at Arlo's side and then turning his eyes to mine. Without his glamour, they were the color of autumn. Without his glamour … he was pure sex. His magic flowed in the room like honeyed wine as he reached out and brushed his fingers down the other man's inked shoulder.

Arlo shuddered and grit his teeth, lifting his hands up to his hair like he was about to go insane. I understood. It wasn't easy to give up control. But to be here, with me, he'd have to learn. I couldn't be subjugated or dominated or crushed under male feet for the sake of pride. Whatever the Veil Keeper was like in the past, I couldn't speak to her rules, her wants, her desires … I could only speak to mine.

"Fuck," Arlo choked, reaching up to his vest and slowly removing it. "I'm out then. I can't do this, be treated like a …"

A single tear rolled down my face and Arlo paused as I dashed it away, his nostrils flaring.

"Are damaged things not worth being loved?" I asked him, and he went completely still and then stopped, letting go of his cut and reaching out to me. "No. If you couldn't accept me when I was strong and only when you saw weakness, maybe I don't want you as a Lord. Maybe you're not right for it."

I spun away and headed for the exterior doors, Arlo following after.

I made it out to the railing, leaning over the water and choking on a sudden rush of *pain.* Tears streamed down my face, but from where or why, I wasn't sure.

"Don't touch me!" I shouted when Arlo put a big hand on my shoulder and I spun around, throwing him off. Killian and Reece stood nearby, and the crowd watched through the open windows and doors. "Don't touch me," I repeated with quiet menace.

"Keeper—" Arlo began to say in a strangled sounding voice but Reece cut him off with a smack to the head.

"Our goddess has a name, best be usin' it at times like this, no?"

Arlo turned to glare at Reece, but once again was cut off by the older fae man. "She be more dan jus' some bedtime story yo mama told. She be here, a real damn woman and you been actin' a real damn fool."

Turning his cheek to Arlo, Reece speared me with his autumn gaze, so sharp it made my breath catch.

"Ciarah, this *couillon* need a lesson, see? He need ta understand, you more dan jus' a goddess, more dan jus' *Le Gardien du Voile.* You still be a woman, an' a woman sore in need of some love in her life. Now, I don' know what you been through, me. But I do know when a woman need love. It's in my magic, see?" Reece stepped closer to me and the world around him faded into obscurity. Nothing mattered except me, and him, and the words he was saying.

He was *dia gnéas*, a god of sex, and it rolled off him in waves as he stepped closer still. His magic reached me, touching my skin cautiously, then creeping over me in comforting ripples that lit up my nerve endings and flooded me with the *truth* behind his words. Reece meant every damn word he was saying and I could already feel more tears rolling down my face as he continued.

"More dan dat, Ciarah. You *deserve* dat love, and Ol' Reece be more than willin' to give it." His eyes still locked on mine, he sank gracefully to one knee and a flash of something older transposed over him, some*one* older, of a different time, and I realized I was seeing a flash of the last Lord of Autumn in this same position, about to pledge his fealty to the Keeper.

"Ciarah, *ma déesse*, *Gardien du Voile*, I offer me as your Lord of Autumn. From now til forever, Ol' Reece will be by your side. Knight, Protector, Confidante, and me hopes Lover." He threw a saucy wink at me. "Dis pledge be given free and un-coerced. My life be yours, *'tit fille*."

His head dipped, breaking our intense stare, but I knew what I needed to do as sure as I knew how to breathe.

"Reece," I sighed, my voice husky and low with magic as I surrendered to *her* lead. I already knew what we needed to do, but she knew the words, knew how to activate the magic behind those words, so I'd take a backseat and learn. "A pledge freely given I humbly accept. Let it be known, my Lord of Autumn has been appointed."

As *we* spoke these words, magic snapped out from my body and into nature, carrying my words and spreading them to all fae creatures this side of the Veil. All now knew of my Autumn Lord, and that alone was cause for celebration.

It had been hundreds of years since the last Lords were chosen, so many of *these* fae would never have experienced what would happen next … but so long as they lived now, they'd never forget it.

Reece's head lifted once more, his eyes shining bright with my magic as it seeped into him, beginning the magical bond which would only be completed with the sharing of pleasure. The look on his face though, was more than lust. It was sheer rapture, unadulterated joy, and dare I say even the stirrings of true *love* behind those rust gold eyes.

I held out my hand, intending to raise him to his feet and seal our bond, but paused when Killian stepped forward into the little bubble of magic surrounding Reece and me.

"Ciarah," he said quietly, speaking my name with reverence, and I withdrew my hand, waiting to see what he, too, would say.

Despite my previously spoken claims to their cocks, I hadn't truly expected them to formally offer themselves as my Lords so soon. Could I be this lucky? Was Killian about to pledge fealty as well? Surely not …

Killian held my gaze, and slowly sank to one knee beside Reece while fresh tears ran down my face. For so many years I, and Gràinne before me, had known nothing but the touch of unkindness. Of hate, pain, fear, and despair. We'd been *bent* though not broken, and inside me *she* was falling to pieces remembering the all-consuming love of her Lords, her Knights, already gone from this world.

"Ciarah," Killian said again, his gaze serious and solemn, "I too offer myself, freely and un-coerced as your Lord of Winter. My soul to join with yours, forever to support, never to betray or deceive. My life is yours to keep. This is my pledge, if you will accept, *mon chéri*?"

Kill ended his words with an uncertain edge, his clear blue eyes showing his fear and self-doubt, his obvious worry that I may not accept him. But his fears were unfounded, and the tears I cried were those of such joy that it hurt my heart.

"Killian," I whispered, this time taking the lead from *her*, as she wept for her lost loves in the shadows of my fractured mind. "A pledge freely given I humbly accept. Let it be known, my Lord of Winter has been appointed."

The magic snapped out from me once more in a tsunami, and I dimly heard cries of joy and celebration from the clubhouse where so many fae were already gathered. The party tonight would be one of legend, to be told from father to son, mother to daughter, for centuries yet.

Never had more than one Lord been appointed at one time before.

I raised my head to look at Arlo. Finding more than one lord in a single night was something that may never happen again in the history of this world or any other. But standing on an old deck outside the clubhouse of a motorcycle club, listening to the frogs and the gators, the distant chatter of sprites, this was not a conventional knighting ceremony.

New guardian, new world, new traditions.

"Even butterflies without wings deserve flowers," I said as Arlo gaped at me and I closed my eyes, letting my head fall back as my wings unfolded behind me. Butterflies. I remembered butterflies. Sometimes, my captors would bring big cages full of them and then slowly and without mercy, they would present them to me one by one … and tear their wings off. *Shadowy fingers stained with bright colors, thrashing insects, my own body screaming in violent melancholy as I remembered the pain of losing my own wings.*

"Even without wings," I repeated, opening my eyes and looking at him, reaching up to rub the tears away. "Go inside and find yourself a clubwhore," I continued, making a split-second decision. If Arlo accepted my proposal now, it would be because he didn't want to leave the Wild Hunt and not because he actually wanted me. "I won't bully you. If you want to stay, stay. But I no longer wish to have you as my Lord. Reece, Killian."

"Yes, ma'am," he murmured in that beautiful accent of his, keeping his chin lowered in deference.

"*Oui, mon cher.*"

"When we're done here, you'll move my things out of Arlo's room and into an empty one. We'll be sleeping in there together from now on." I crossed my arms over my chest and beat my wings in a slow, easy motion. Just feeling them on my back made everything okay. I didn't need Arlo. Fuck, I didn't want him if this was his attitude. I was worth more than this. But I also didn't want to bully or pressure him either. "I set you free—go on now."

"Ciarah," he started, but I shook my head.

"I apologize for the way I've treated you, Horned One. You deserve more respect than that. But I am telling you now to go; please respect my wishes."

I curled my wings around me like a shield, a blanket, their warmth and smell so soothing after so much time without them. Yes, every once in a while, my captors would drag fae before me, fae that *reeked* of pain and death and corruption. In my weakened state, it was impossible to resist the pull, and I'd take their souls … heal … and then feel myself torn apart all over again.

Those few moments of being whole made being torn apart hurt so much worse.

The purple and turquoise colors of my wings blended together, as if the two shades were dancing a waltz across the surface, the edges a rich velvety black like the night sky, dusted with silver that reminded me of stars. I remembered my wings as different shapes, different colors over the years, and old knowledge locked away inside my head whispered that each time a new soul took over the Veil Keeper's body, her wings changed to reflect the spirit inside.

These wings didn't just belong to *Le Gardien du Voile*, they belonged to Ciarah, and the person *inside* of Ciarah, the spirit that made me, me.

"Thank you for your service, Arlo," I told him, nodding my chin and turning away, focusing on the two men offering their *souls* to protect me. The last guardian's knights … had not been very lucky. And these two, they knew they were promising themselves to a queen who would end up in the middle of a war.

One that they might not survive.

When I didn't hear footsteps, I looked back and found Arlo staring at me with a hardened expression, his body trembling in either rage or lust, I wasn't exactly certain.

"I'm the fucking horned god," he growled out, his

words colored with truth. "You're the maiden aspect of the goddess."

"So if I am?" I asked, because I knew that to be true. The Veil Keeper always held the title of maiden, the youthful and energetic manifestation of the goddess, the feminine aspect in nature. Out there somewhere in the world, the mother and the crone would be watching me.

"We're meant to be mates," he snarled, and that, too, rang truthful.

"I'm not interested in fated bonds or destiny. What I'm interested in is freedom of choice and dedication. Don't feel obligated to me, Arlo. I don't want that burden."

With a violent snarl, Arlo dropped to one knee and dipped his head. Every impulse in me cried out for my fingers to reach forward and curl around one of his horns. But I didn't. I stood stone-still and stared at his dark hair, the leather vest draped over his back with the words *The Wild Hunt*.

"I pledge my life to you, Veil Keeper," he growled, more beast than human.

"I need more than a life, Arlo," I said, and I wasn't trying to be greedy. It was just pure and simple truth. I needed knights with passion and not just obligation.

"Take everything I have then," he snarled, "but it's not much. I don't have a lot to give."

It broke my heart to hear those things—especially because the truth in them was more vibrant than anything he'd said to me thus far.

"But if you want it, it's yours."

Arlo was panting now, his eyes downcast. I could see the shadows of demons tracing across his skin, dancing behind his eyes. I knew what they looked like because I had so many. I'd been beaten, torn apart, put back together, and then ripped to shreds all over again. I couldn't remember the faces of my enemies, only that they had eyes that gleamed like fresh blood under cold moonlight, and disembodied smiles.

"I want it," I blurted, before I could stop myself. My breath hitched and I spread my wings wide. The moon caught on the edges and cast shadows over my knights. My lords.

My wings were different, like no other creature on earth, with three distinct segments on either side, their colors as vibrant as fresh paint, their shimmer as bright as stars.

Three knights, offering themselves to me at once.

This would be a … messy fucking ritual, wouldn't it?

Sex was to everything to the fae. Currency, threat, promise, love, hate … and the ties that bound.

Glancing up, I saw Rafe watching me through the window, his red eyes flashing with something primal as he stared out at us. I looked back at him, my gaze full of defiance. Another staring match would've ensued if Amelie hadn't covered *his* eyes with *her* hand this time. She really was the perfect righthand woman. I wondered if she and Rafe were an item?

"Arlo," I said softly, turning my attention back to my third Lord, "complete the oath. I need to know you're sure."

Also, the *magic* needed to know he was sure. It simply wouldn't work if he weren't invested in this decision with his whole heart.

Arlo's glittering emerald eyes held mine, and he spoke without hesitation. "Veil Keeper. My body, my soul, my life, my heart; these I offer up to you freely and un-coerced. Will you accept my pledge as your Lord of Spring?"

"Arlo," I breathed his name, "a pledge freely given I humbly accept. Let it be known, my Lord of Spring has been appointed."

This time when the magic snapped out of me, an almost overwhelming rush of euphoria hit me and I staggered. I would have fallen too, if not for Arlo's strong hand on my waist, steadying me while I blinked away the dark spots from my vision and rolled my shoulders.

My wings flexed and stretched, spreading wide before settling once more against my back and I sighed blissfully as I surveyed my three Lords. My knights. Sworn to guard me with their very beings until the end of our combined existence.

Inside my broken mind, Gràinne sobbed with joy, her love and hope flooding my body as a small smile curved my lips. The ritual was not yet complete …

"Reece," I prompted, and he needed no further encouragement.

Rising to his feet, he slipped one huge hand into my dark hair, cupping the back of my head and pulling my face to his. As our lips touched together, his magic flared to life between us and I groaned.

My nipples tightened, straining against the thin fabric of my top, and I pushed my body against Reece as our tongues danced with one another, spurred on by the raucous cheers radiating from the clubhouse. We had spectators, as was the way of our kind.

The appointment of a Lord was a joyous occasion, and the completion of that ritual was a glorious thing to behold. I couldn't have denied my people the honor of watching. Instead, I owed them a damn good show.

Reece needed no guidance, *dia gnéas* that he was. His fingers tugged firmly at the fabric ties which held my halter top to my body, freeing my naked breasts and palming them in his rough hands.

"*Ma déesse,*" he groaned, rolling my hardened nipples between thumb and forefingers before dipping his face to kiss me once more. His kiss wasn't possessive nor wild, it was *worshipful.*

The black pencil skirt I wore was embellished with a gold zipper, running the entire way from waist to knee, and given how tight it was I'd opted to go *sans* underwear. Thus, with a deft movement of Reece's fingers, the fabric dropped away from my body, leaving me totally naked except for my four inch stiletto heels and my glorious, glittering wings.

To my left, Killian whispered under his breath in French, while to my right Arlo's eyes burned laser-like patterns as they trailed across my skin, but my attention was solely on Reece. For now. Their turns would come, as was required to complete the magic of the bond.

"Reece." I pushed him back a couple of steps toward the old wooden picnic table sitting on the side of the dock. "Pants. Now."

Given his hands were already at work unbuckling his belt, I really hadn't needed to say anything, but after so much tender emotion from their pledges, it felt good to reassert my dominance.

Reece's big beautiful penis had barely been freed from the denim confines of his pants before I pushed him to sit on the bench, not bothering to strip him any further before taking what I needed from him.

Placing my knee on the bench beside his hip, I balanced my hands on his shoulders, bringing my other knee up so that I straddled his waist. My wet heat pressed against the rigid length of his shaft and his lips captured mine once more in a kiss of worship.

Ever the gentleman, Reece's calloused palms slid around my waist, lifting me slightly and allowing me room to reach between us and line the head of his cock up to my opening.

No foreplay was needed. Not during a ritual like this and certainly not with the god of sex radiating his magic over me. My cunt was already wet and throbbing, *begging* to be filled and I wasn't about to wait a second longer.

"Fuck me runnin', Ciarah," Reece gasped as I pushed down firmly onto him, sliding him inside me inch by inch until my bare ass touched his denim clad thighs and I was *full.*

The sensation was exquisite, and knowing he had just pledged his very soul to bond with mine made the experience so much sweeter. Words could do no justice so instead I moaned, sealing my mouth back to his and beginning to move.

Starting slowly, I slid up and down on his rock-hard length, letting my pussy stretch to accommodate his size while grinding my clit against him at the end of every *downward* thrust. Memories or not, I was secure in the knowledge that I knew how to work this body, and I intended to *work it.*

Reece's hands held tight to my waist, moving with me and urging me faster, just as his hips rode up from the bench seat to meet me thrust for thrust. It wasn't long until I gave over to his subtle cues and began riding him hard and fast.

"Oh for the love of the Veil," Reece panted, sucking my lower lip back into his mouth and delivering a nip. Near us, I could hear the slightly heavier breathing of my two *other* Lords as they stood and watched, waiting patiently for their own turn.

The Wild Hunt clubhouse party was raging again, the sounds of cheers and laughter spilling out to us, but I wasn't in the least bit surprised that when I looked over Reece's shoulder, I found Rafe's bloodred eyes glued to me.

Amelie stood to his left, a bemused smile on her face as she watched me pleasure both myself and my Autumn

Lord, but to Rafe's right, his beta glared with a thinly veiled *hatred* that sent a shiver down my spine.

I didn't have time for such a nonsense, so with a simple flick of my fingers in Marcel's direction, I blinded him with a temporary glamour and heard him howl in wild rage. One would think I'd fucking gouged his eyes from his skull … like what'd once happened to me.

My throat clenched with remembered pain, but I used the savage pleasure between my legs to push it back into the shadows of memory. I knew in my heart I wasn't going to be able to recall the memories I needed without absorbing the ones I did *not.* It was a price I was going to have to pay, whether I liked it or not.

Fortunately, sex was not tainted for me. My captors … whatever they were, were too alien, too foreign to get off on rape. They did their best, with hot iron between my thighs, by castrating me, rending my flesh until it hung in ribbons. But they didn't have either the will, the knowledge, or the equipment to take me against my will for sexual gratification. Certainly, if I'd ever let on how much that would hurt me, they would have found someone to do it.

Instead … they did other things.

But at least for now, I could find salvation in sex, here with Reece in the silver moonlight with fireflies and will-o-the-wisps flitting around my head. I could curl my arms around his neck and press my cheek against the stubbled surface of his, feel his warmth sink into me—both literally and figuratively—and breathe in the crisp autumn scent that clung to his skin.

My fingers curled into Reece's bloodred hair as his cock sunk deeply into me, igniting the fire in my belly, the raging heat that coiled inside of me and begged for release. When I let it go, though, the whole world would *know.* Every insect, each flapping bird, each grunting gator … The Veil Keeper was as much a part of the natural world as the sun or the moon, the earth itself, the stars above.

Rafe caught my gaze one last time before I turned away and ran my tongue across my lower lip, letting Reece cup the back of my head and pull me in for another kiss. His beautiful gold skin shimmered in the dim light leaking from the club, a beautiful complement to the pale blue color of my own. Without my glamour, I was an exercise in cool colors, jewel tones. A streak of turquoise in my dark hair, wings of purple and silver, skin the color of a stormy sky just before the clouds clear away.

Reece and I danced an ancient dance with our bodies, the sounds we made mixing with the whispers of the bayou and turning the entire night into a brilliant symphony of sex and revelry.

This feels like home, the old whispers inside of me crooned.

This feels like a fucking frat party, Ciarah replied snarkily, but I wasn't just either of those women anymore—I was both. And really this was nothing like else.

In court, our sex would be empty and frivolous.

In a party, our sex would be bland and clumsy.

Here … it was transcendent.

"Don't try to impress me now," I whispered in Reece's ear and he chuckled, the deep warmth of his voice radiating through me and making me groan. He had a voice to match his heart—endless and full of possibility. Yes, I could tell that Reece was the type to have many lovers—well, at least he *used* to be because I wouldn't allow that anymore—but that's because he was brimming with emotion. He had so much to give. I wasn't sure that I'd met a man in either life with such a well of feeling buried inside.

I quite liked him.

Oh, I totally have a fucking crush, I thought as I bit my lip, flipping between my two brains. Half of my being was taken up by a nineteen year old girl with a snarky attitude. The other half was an ancient goddess who wasn't used to being told no. In between, there were five dark years that made my stomach turn over.

"Finish yourself," I growled in Reece's ear but he just laughed again, lifting me up and making me yelp in surprise. I did *not* like the feeling of him pulling out, leaving me empty and cold.

"Bend over dere, girl, and Ol' Reece will do exactly what you want, you."

"Quit showing off, you Cajun fuck," Arlo growled, but Reece just threw his head back and laughed, the sound echoing off the water, scattering the fireflies and will-o-the-wisps. But they didn't stay gone for long. They were skittish, but there was nothing frightening about Reece, not right now.

In fact … his magic seemed to be seeping into the clubhouse. I could see naked bodies writhing together in pleasure as wolves and fae alike coupled in strange pairings. I wondered if they would regret what they were doing in the morning?

"If I put my all into dis, our poor little Veil Keeper would think you got a limp noodle in those slacks o' yours. Better hold back, me, or else you won't be able to please our girl here." He laughed again as Arlo snarled, his green eyes flashing as I turned around and put my palms on the rough surface of the table, my knees on the bench.

Reece took his place behind me and curled his fingers around my hips, *slowly* sliding himself into me with an accompanying chuckle that made his cock feel like a vibrator. Cool air teased the swollen heat of my cunt as he took me again from behind, making my nails curl against the wood of the table, my wings curving back to tease his face.

My mountain of hair seemed to slide over my shoulders like a waterfall, tangling around my arms and hands as my breasts swung with the motion of Reece's hips against my ass.

"*Merde*," Killian cursed under his breath, his cool presence at odds with the bright and violent need coming from Arlo. And to think he'd only just made me cry. We were going to have an interesting relationship, him and me. I could already tell.

Reece took a handful of my too-long hair and pulled my head back, forcing me to arch my body in just such a way that his balls slapped my clit. My vision speckled with flecks of white, clouded with pleasure as the sex god let out a deep, guttural groan and spilled his hot seed inside of me.

When he pulled away this time, I almost choked.

I was in *no* way done.

"Fucker," Arlo snarled, stepping up close to me. Our eyes caught as I glanced over my shoulder, but Killian stopped him with a palm to the chest.

"The ritual *must* be followed in order," he said and I swear, it looked as if Arlo was going to kill the other man with his bare hands.

"You son of a bitch, you better be quick," he snapped and Killian's face … well, it was painted with a sinful smirk that was as cold as his hands when he placed them on my hips. I knew he was using his magic to turn them to ice, teasing my heated skin with a sharp temperature change. It was like he was waking up every nerve ending in my body.

"I'll take as long as *Le Gardien* wants me to take," he purred as Arlo curled his lip, crossing his inked arms over his broad chest and lifting his chin in defiance.

"Stop it," I snapped, tossing my hair over my shoulder and turning my face toward them, "You'll get your turn *Cernunnos,* but the ritual must be followed in correct order. Killian, if you please?"

Killian threw a triumphant smirk at Arlo, who

glowered and stepped back, barely.

“I'd be my absolute pleasure, *mon chéri*,” Killian responded, shifting his grip with his Arctic hands so that the tip of his scalding hot cock rubbed between my slick folds and teased at my clit.

The breath rushed out of me as my eyelids fluttered shut. My hands braced against the rough wood of the picnic table while my hips pressed backward, encouraging Kill to enter me. From what I could tell, Ciarah had never done something like this before, never fucked three men in such quick succession, but there was an air of familiarity to it. Doubtless, the previous souls of the Veil Keeper had done this and more, so it simply felt … natural. As natural as breathing, or flying.

My wings fluttered at the thought, and I knew I'd need to try it out. Later though, as the moonlight caught on the shimmering glitter of my newfound appendages and cast sparkling light out across the darkened bayou.

“So beautiful,” Killian murmured, trailing one frosty hand up my spine and then across the arterial support of my top wing segment. The incredible feeling of his fingers on my hyper-sensitive wings made me moan with arousal and I could feel my cunt flush with heat and damp once more.

“Kill,” I begged, “I want your cock.”

The echo of the words I'd spoken to him earlier was not lost on him, and he sucked a gasp. Repositioning his hands on my hips, he withdrew his teasing length from where he'd been rubbing at me, and then slammed into me with one smooth movement, all the way to the hilt.

Lord of Winter that he was, he'd changed the temperature of his cock to become cold. As cold as the cube of ice he'd slid inside me earlier when we'd had sex on Arlo's bed. The exquisite cold against the searing heat of my oversexed pussy made me climax instantly, screaming my release into the moonlit bayou.

Gentleman that he was, Killian waited me out while I writhed and moaned through the intense orgasm. His fingers held tight on my hips and his body coiled with tension as my muscles clenched and fluttered around his ice-cold shaft, the temperature so extreme it felt like it was burning me from the inside.

It was nothing even remotely like the burn of iron that I'd been impaled on so many times during captivity, this was something exhilarating, blissful and intoxicating and it was driving me *wild*.

This was pure sex, and I fucking loved it.

“Move, Kill,” I gasped, coming down from yet another wave of orgasm aftershock and pressing my ass back against him in desperation. This body was fae, it was immortal, pure *magic* and I knew I was only just getting started.

Killian did as I asked, sliding his dick out of me almost entirely before thrusting back in so deep I could feel him touch the end of me as his balls slapped against my clit. A startled gasp shocked out of me at this, my clitoris already so swollen and sensitive from the intense climax I'd just experienced, and I felt Killian chuckle.

"More," I groaned, bending lower over the table until my nipples brushed against the rough wood.

"Ah, see now? Maybe Ol' Reece shouldn'a gone first, eh?" Reece chuckled from somewhere to my left.

Sweeping my long dark hair with its turquoise streak over to my other shoulder, I turned my face to look at him. He'd sat himself on the bench where I knelt, his pants still open and his long golden dick standing straight to attention in his firm grip while he watched Kill take me from behind.

"*Ferme ta bouche,* Reece," Killian snarled, his fingers digging painfully into my hips—in a good way—as he picked up his pace. His frozen shaft pounded into me, and his balls slapped at my clit in a rhythm that made me moan in ecstasy as another intense orgasm began to build.

"Both of you shut up," Arlo snapped, "and hurry the fuck up Kill. This isn't the time for your fancy ice moves and shit."

Reece chuckled in a dark sort of way, reclining against the table beside me and meeting my feverish gaze with a grin. "Dat boy need a lesson or three in patience, no?"

I couldn't help myself, I grinned back. Arlo *did* need a lesson in patience and I greatly looked forward to being the one to teach him. Another night. For now, the magic *required* we all share in the pleasures of our flesh and it wouldn't be satisfied until *all* of us were spent.

Killian slipped a hand back up my spine, rubbing over the sensitive muscles of my wings to my upper back and then pushing me down until my upper body was pressed flat against the table top.

He bent over me, changing the angle of his cock, pounding into my burning hot pussy and planting his lips against the arch of my left wing.

"These wings," he murmured, his lips sucking and kissing at the glittering skin, "are the most stunning I have ever seen on a fae this side of the Veil."

Reece grunted something under his breath that sounded like agreement, but it made me realize, other than the sprites I had yet to see *any* other fae with wings. Did they not have them? Or did they simply choose to keep them hidden due to the nature of the human world?

I knew I held a scant ten percent or less of my memories, but even so I could hardly comprehend what a struggle it would be to keep my wings hidden permanently. They just felt too damn good to be out, to be able to stretch them and feel the light caress of the wind. Not to mention the incredible feeling of Killian's caresses … My wings contained so many nerve endings, they were even more of an erogenous zone than my nipples and damn near close to my cunt.

"Kill," Arlo growled, sounding pained, and Killian chuckled.

"Patience, my brother," my Lord of Winter groaned as my walls tightened around him; another orgasm was close and we both knew it. "Our *déesse* is worth the wait, I promise you."

"Finish, Killian," I urged, panting with need but wanting to hold off my climax until I could have Arlo inside me. "Come for me."

He needed no further encouragement; instead he bit down lightly on the sparkling skin of my wing and thrust deeply into me once, twice, and then a third time as his seed spurted hotly against my cervix.

"Move," Arlo commanded, and from the corner of my eye I saw him clap a heavy hand on Killian's shoulder.

Reece clicked his tongue, scolding Arlo's impatience even as he sat there working his cock with his hand, slick beads of pre-cum already glistening on his tip and his cheeks flushed with arousal. It made sense that he'd have such a quick refractory period though, what sort of *dia gnéas* would he be otherwise?

Killian withdrew from my now *very* slick sheath and trailed gentle kisses down my spine, deliberately taking his sweet ass time and making Arlo wait. I almost laughed, but it just wasn't the time.

Instead, I waited for Killian to move and flipped around to face Arlo with a slight smile. It was hard to pull off cheeky though, when all I really wanted to do was arch my back like a cat in heat and beg him to fuck me.

"The magic is not particular as to *how* we … *get our rocks off*."

"Get our rocks off?" Arlo growled, nostrils flaring as he looked me over, sweaty and wanting, my tits exposed, my thighs clamped together against the wetness between them. I *lounged* on that bench seat, daring him to touch me. But he knew better than to force our interaction. "The fuck are you playing at woman?"

"Respect," Kill snarled from beside him. "Show some, fool."

Arlo ignored him, staring down at me with narrowed eyes.

"This magic," I continued, putting a palm on my belly and staring up at him. "It isn't gender specific. It doesn't *judge*."

"Meaning. What," Arlo ground out as he glared at me.

"It's designed to work the way a person does—two bodies coming together to create pleasure. It isn't specific to a cock in a pussy," I challenged and Arlo made this sound in the back of his throat, like a wild animal. "As long as we both get off, it doesn't matter how."

"You're kidding me, right?" he asked, but I wasn't. Not exactly. Mostly, I was trying to gauge his reaction. And … I did have something *other* than his cock in my pussy in mind. I just didn't think he'd be opposed to my suggestion—so long as he kept his fucking temper long enough to hear it. "What do you want me to do, *your majesty*?"

"I want you to get on your—" I barely got those words out before Arlo was dropping to his knees and pushing mine apart. With a gasp, I felt my head fall back, tucking my lower lip under my teeth as Arlo put his mouth to my wet cunt and licked it, with the other mens' seed and all. This wasn't actually what I had in mind. I'd expected protesting and a fit, but then I was going to invite him to fuck me … in the other aching opening between my legs.

But this was … this was *perfect*.

My fingers curved around the gleaming ivory of his horns, squeezing them in tight fists as he curled his big hands around my ass cheeks and gripped them mercilessly. The way he used his mouth was nothing short of savage and I *loved* it. It woke up every basic instinct I had inside of me, gave rise to this bestial feeling of possessiveness, this need to *mate*.

Behind me, I felt my wings quiver, desperate to be touched. They seemed so fragile at first glance, but crushed against the picnic table, they didn't hurt. It was like leaning back on my elbows. It made me realize how much force would be needed to rend them from my flesh …

With a choking gasp, I grabbed a handful of Arlo's hair —much as I was enjoying him between my thighs—and lifted his head.

"Touch my wings," I whispered, feeling tears threaten again. But I wasn't about to cry a second time. No, not tonight. I'd found *three* of the four men I wanted as Lords *and* claimed them all in one night. This wasn't an event I'd allow to be tainted by those years of darkness and torture. This was *my* night. "Touch them," I said again, pushing his face away and rising to my feet.

Arlo stood up, too, towering over me and smelling like the earth. I could breathe that scent in forever and never tire of it. It was a smell I wasn't permitted in that never-ending darkness. The sweet bloom of fresh flowers, the easy muskiness of new shoots, the pungent whisper of decaying leaves. The place where I was held … it was a void. An endless blackness with no stars and no moon, just shadows without texture or meaning. And eyes. Glowing eyes. Mouths with no face.

"Please," I said again, and I felt that odd sense of fragility that neither Ciarah nor *Gràinne* truly understood. "Touch them."

"Goddess' tits," Arlo grunted, but he reached out and cupped my face in two big, warm hands. His teeth were clenched and he flicked his eyes away from mine. "You're not the only damaged one here. I know what it's like to be … scarred up and fucked up. So don't think that has anything to do with why you piss me off so damn much."

He turned his gaze back to mine and the power in it … was breathtaking.

"I'm just a fucking badass bitch," I said and he raised both brows. "What? I *am* a modern woman … of sorts. I mean, in my previous life I was." I sucked in a sharp breath as Arlo ran a thumb over my lower lip. "You're just not used to having an alpha female in your life."

"Arlo ain't used to having any female in his life, eh boy?"

"Shut your fucking mouth, *Reece*," Arlo snarled over at him, curling his lip back like an animal. "You have enough *females* for the both of us, you goddamn whore."

"I just love women, me," he said, running his tongue over his lower lip and stroking his cock with sure, easy movements. "And it ain't like you a vestal virgin. You just keep your cock warm and your heart cold is all. I get myself into trouble, yeah, because I don't know how to separate the two." He winked at me as Killian let out a small sigh and moved to sit on the bench on my other side.

"And Killian?" I whispered, even though it was getting cold out and my body was wet and aching between my thighs. I wanted to know more about all three men, all their hopes and dreams and fears, their pasts, their *past*times, their habits.

"*Ah cher,* done nobody know the answer to that," Reece chuckled, but Arlo got this smirking expression on his face that made Killian go stiff.

"You tell her about the time you got spelled by that witch? Spent a whole year as a woman and started fucking that wolf—"

"I will kill you where you stand," Kill purred, his voice ice-cold and full of shards.

I was intrigued as hell now. That wolf? He couldn't possibly be talking about Raphael, now could he? But also … maybe that explained why Killian was so good in bed? If he'd spent time as a woman, he'd know how a woman's body worked. I liked that.

"Now, what do you want, Veil Keeper, and let's get this thing done?"

The night was perfumed with sex and laughter as I looked up at Arlo's face, curled my fingers around the back of his neck and stood up on my tip toes to kiss his warm mouth. His tongue slid against mine, wet and hungry, and he let out another bestial sound that made my skin ripple with goose bumps.

"I was going to invite you into my ass," I whispered

and this time, it was his turn to shiver. “But maybe we should just keep going the way we've been going tonight and save that for another day.”

“Either way, this is one command I won't fight,” Arlo said, his voice huskier and warmer than I'd ever heard it. “Tell me what you want.”

“Just … I want to look at the bayou … and I want you to hold my wings while you make love to me.”

“Make love?” Arlo asked, shaking his head. “Well, fuck. I'll see what I can do.” He took me by the hand, his huge one engulfing mine with inked fingers as he pulled me over to the railing and took up a position behind me, leaning over and kissing the side of my neck. His stubbled jaw teased my smooth skin and made me bite my lip in pleasure. “Bend over, Veil Keeper, and let's do this.”

I put my hands over the railing and stared out at the dancing fireflies, the twirling will-o-the-wisps. They made this soft sighing sound that I found as pleasant as music, and I closed my eyes momentarily as Arlo gripped my hips in his hands, bending down and spreading my ass cheeks wide. At first, I had no clue what he was doing, but then his hot tongue flicked out and teased across the sensitive nerve-endings in my ass.

My lids flickered as I stared across the waters of the bayou and let Arlo tease me into a warm, weak-kneed frenzy. He might not be as gentle or careful as the other two men, but his mouth was hot and his tongue seemed to know exactly where to go to get me wet and warm and ready for him. When he stood back up, I was almost limp and curled fully around the railing.

Sliding his palms across the surface of my wings, Arlo took hold of one in a tight fist and yanked it back like he would a handful of my hair. I expected the move to hurt, but in reality, it just felt good. Really good. Exquisite. I *loved* the pulling sensation between my skin and wings. I thought I wouldn't, that it might remind me too much of having them torn from my body, my flight and freedom stolen from me. But it only served to remind me that they were there, they were mine, and I could finally fight back. Freed from my shackles and my prison of darkness, I could figure out who had taken me and why.

And I could kill them.

With vengeance riding hot and hard in my blood, I growled out to Arlo, "*now.*"

"Yes, *mistress*," he said with a smirk in his voice. I couldn't see it, but I knew it was there. In that moment though, it wasn't important. Completing the ritual was. Feeling Arlo inside of me was.

The Horned God teased me with the hot tip of his cock, rubbing it along my cunt and pushing in just enough to make me gasp before pulling away and slicking the full length of his shaft between my folds. Just when I was certain I was going to kill him, he pulled the edge of my wing to his face, kissed it with a certain level of reverence I hadn't expected, and then thrust into me.

My body hummed with pleasure and I let out a small scream, scattering a few unfortunate night birds and making the will-o-the-wisps flicker through the air like shooting stars. It was a scream of pure ecstasy though and they soon quieted, leaving room for the grunting of gators and the slick slide of Arlo's body thrusting into mine.

"'ey Meme, you leave them alone now, you." Reece appeared on my right side, pants undone, but his cock tucked safely back into them, and then chucked a few marshmallows over the edge of the railing. The gator popped her head up, snapped them from the surface of the water and then glared at us with two round eyeballs above the surface, like we were disturbing her by being there. "Go away now, get on wit' ya."

I closed my eyes and felt a smile ripple across my face as Arlo grunted and moaned, clearly enjoying my body, our connection, even if he said I pissed him off. My breasts bounced with the motion as Kill took up my other side and both he and Reece watched as my body contracted, muscles fluttering naturally and locking down on Arlo, freezing himself with a snarl of primal rage.

He exploded inside of me at the same time I felt my orgasm unfurl like the petals of a flower, opening up and unleashing a ripple of power that trailed the metaphorical surface of the world like a ripple on a lake.

It was so wildly powerful, so raw and full of promise, that I knew they'd feel it, my captors. They'd feel it and they'd come for me again. But this time, I would be ready. This time, I had my knights, my lords, and *nothing* would stop me from taking my revenge.

Chapter Fifteen

ARLO

"First time I ever see you introduce a girl to your mama, you," Reece chuckled as I swung myself off my bike and glanced over to see Killian helping Ciarah off of his. Behind us, Caley's rusty shit bucket of a car pulled up with a screech of old brakes, and I heard her car door slam as she got out.

"Yeah, well." I heaved a sigh, glancing up at the old plantation style house apprehensively. "First time I ever pledged my soul to a girl for all-time too, so …" I shrugged, trailing off as I scratched my chin.

"I hear dat," Reece agreed with a wry grin. "Still funny, d'ough."

"Shut up, Cajun, you won't be laughing when your cock gets the message it's tied to one pussy for all eternity." I snapped the words at him quietly, not wanting Ciarah to overhear me. In truth, I was surprised I was able to say those words at all, what with our inability to lie. Maybe it was just a strange enough metaphor that the magic got confused?

"Is this where you grew up?" That *one pussy* in question sidled up beside me smelling like jasmine and sunshine, her curtain of dark hair offset by a green streak draped over her delicate shoulders.

Christ. She'd have been a whole lot easier to deny if she'd been a troll. Not that I was so shallow I was only attracted to her because she was hot, although that certainly helped.

No, what sealed the deal for me was when I saw her tough chick façade crack, and the haunted damage show in her tears. She said she didn't want me if all I cared for were her unbroken parts, but she didn't understand.

"Sort of," I grunted in reply, following her gaze up to my Mama's house. "I was about five when my blood-mama died. She was a wood-nymph and some asshole, a drunk tourist, accidentally set fire to her tree. Anyway, my Daddy had been seeing Linda on the pretty regular so after my blood-mama went up in smoke, he decided he needed a woman to raise me. So he set her up here, knocked her up with Caley, then clean disappeared off the face of the earth."

"So Linda is …" She blinked up at me with those

stunning sapphire eyes and I needed to look away to keep from bending her over my damn bike and slamming my dick into her again.

"His mama," Reece replied for me, clapping a heavy hand on my shoulder and giving me a smirk. Of course that horny bastard knew exactly what I was thinking. "Or damn near as close as he's got."

"She's also going to tear him a new one for not telling her about you sooner," Caley snickered, linking her arm into Ciarah's and tugging her toward the house with her.

Shit. She wasn't wrong either. Mama was *not* going to be pleased.

Despite being a former Willing Hunt—or rather, a clubwhore—my mama had a temper that could rival even the meanest of fae. She knew about our kind, how could she not? But she was human through and through. It made me love her all the more for having the nuts to live amongst us so long.

"Arlo!" The woman who raised me hollered from the verandah as Caley dragged the Veil Keeper inside with her.

Reece and Killian snickered, following the girls and leaving me to handle my mama alone. As usual. Linda had been known to give me and the boys an earful a time or two in the past and those two always seemed to disappear pretty damn quick.

"Hi, Mama." I tried to paste on my very best smile in the hope that she'd be so excited to see me she'd drop the angry act.

No such luck, though, as I reached the top of the balcony steps and she grabbed me by the ear like I was five years old again.

"Boy, you got some explaining to do," she growled at me, yanking me along behind her into the kitchen. How she had the strength to do it, I could never work out. She was barely five foot two and weighed less than a wet cat but somehow she was able to tow me around by my ear like she were fae.

"Goddamn it, that hurts, let me go!" I wasn't playing up for her ego; it really did hurt.

"Well maybe you ought to think before you go messing around with the Keeper-damned *Keeper* without telling your damn mama, no?" She was mad as hell, I could tell, and I groaned when she let my ear go.

"Mama, you're human," I said defensively, rubbing at my ear as she glared at me with her hands on her hips. She'd dragged me into her kitchen but I could hear the others waiting in the sitting room.

"So?" She scowled, despite knowing full-well she wasn't privy to fae business. The fact that she knew about us at all was more than most humans were permitted, and it was the reason why she'd been told to keep away from the clubhouse these past few days.

I sighed heavily, again, and turned to start some coffee. I was tired and could seriously murder a cup of joe.

"Mama, you're being childish. You know why you've been kept out of the loop. The Veil Keeper returning is big business for us fae, and everyone's magic has been going all kinds of screwy over it. Hell even my own glamour has been broken more times in the last few days than my entire life combined." I pulled out some cups from her cupboard and then hunted her pantry for baked goods. Linda baked like a demon, and there were always some sweet treats to be found.

"So what? I've seen you unglamoured before, boy. Don't forget who used to wipe your snotty nose and bandage your skinned knees." There was a tightness to her mouth that said she knew she was being unreasonable but wasn't backing down.

"Yeah, but what do you think would happen if you happened to see Donal, or hell even Fionn? They wouldn't take lightly to being seen by a human without their glamour. You really wanna test their kindness? Because let me tell you now, Mama, it wouldn't end well." Turning back to her, I leaned my ass against the counter and folded my arms. "No, best you stay here out of trouble until this is all … over."

Over? What would *over* even look like? Does that mean the Veil restored and all the earthside fae allowed to return home? In which case, what happens to people like Caley? Half-human, half-fae, would she crossover or stay here?

"Over," my mama repeated with a scowl, "and then what? This girl takes you for herself and I never see you again?"

There was a hitch in her voice that betrayed how upset she was feeling. She was one tough bitch normally—she had to be to live amongst The Wild Hunt MC for so many years—so this was as close as she really came to properly crying.

"I don't know, Ma," I groaned, wrapping her tiny frame in a hug. She practically disappeared under my arms she was so small, and I felt her shaking slightly with unshed tears. In all my years I was yet to see this tough little broad *actually* cry and I doubted it would start now.

"We'll just take it as it comes. But … she's not some evil witch come to steal me away. She's the Veil Keeper. She is the only one that can save the fae …"

"I know," Linda muttered, pushing back from my hug and busying herself making up a tray for the coffee, "but you still could have damn well introduced her to me before you went pledging yourself, you know?"

A hot flush of shame heated my cheeks. "It wasn't really something I planned to do."

My mama narrowed her eyes at me and sniffed in irritation. "Right, well then. Let's meet the girl that stole your heart."

My cheeks heated even further and I cast a furtive glance toward the sitting room, praying my mama's voice didn't carry through to the damn Keeper. That girl did *not* need a bigger ego than she already had.

Feeling sufficiently chastised, I followed the little human through to the sitting room, carrying the tray of mugs for her only to find my Keeper missing.

"She went to use the bathroom," Caley informed me, obviously seeing my look of confusion. Damn chick was more observant than she let on sometimes. But she also had an evil look in her eye that said she was up to no good.

"Caley …" I growled, narrowing my eyes at her as her grin spread wider.

"I sent her to the one upstairs," she snickered and I groaned for what felt like the thousandth time since getting here. I swear, visiting Mama and Caley fucking *aged* me.

"Fucking hell," I muttered, placing the tray down on the table and stalking up the stairs. Caley couldn't have just directed Ciarah to the half-bath downstairs; no she needed to send her upstairs to where mama had literally *hundreds* of embarrassing photos of me and Caley framed and hung on the wall of the hallway.

Sure enough, when I got to the top of the stairs, Ciarah stood there inspecting a particularly amazing snap of me as a six year old, stark naked and running through a sprinkler on the lawn.

"Did you get lost?" I snapped, folding my arms over my chest and glaring. She jumped at the sound of my voice, obviously not hearing me arrive.

"No." She turned to face me, her sapphire blue eyes alight with mischief that made me want to drag her into my childhood bedroom right there and have my way with her. "Just admiring the décor. Do you have a brother as well?"

I frowned. "What? No. Why do you ask?"

"Oh, I just wondered who the cute little kid was in all

these pictures." She shrugged and tossed her silky hair over her shoulder. She was dressed in a low-cut white tank and the most delicious looking leather pants I'd ever seen on a chick … so damn sexy.

"Very funny," I sneered, lest she catch me checking her out. "You know full-well that's me."

As if the picture of a grinning eight year old with shimmering silver skin and white horns wasn't obvious enough for her.

"Hmm," she hummed. "Maybe if I'd ever seen you smile it might have been clearer."

"What?" I scowled. "I smile all the time."

She raised an eyebrow at me, her lush rose red lips pulling up at the corners slightly, like she wanted to laugh.

"Seriously?" she asked, wrinkling her nose in the cutest fucking way I'd ever seen.

Fucking Veil Keeper.

"Whatever, come on. Coffee is getting cold and I found some cupcakes that Linda made." I rolled my eyes, knowing perfectly well that my current facial expression was confirming her theory that I never smiled.

She cocked her head to the side in a way I'd come to realize was her searching her scattered memories.

"I don't know if I like cupcakes. How weird is that?" She blinked up at me and my heart constricted painfully. Damn it. Her question was innocent enough, more of an observation than anything really, but it only served as a reminder of the horrors she'd endured before finding us.

Finding *me*. I'd never forget the fact that I was the first man to find her, after she'd shown up in the alleyway outside Caley's work. That surely wasn't a coincidence. Right?

"Come on, you can find out now." I jerked my head back toward the stairs and she nodded thoughtfully. As I began down the steps, she fell into stride alongside me and slipped her small hand into mine, twining our fingers together.

The move surprised me enough that I almost tore myself from her grip.

Holding hands?

When was the last fucking time I held anyone's hand?

I scowled again, but I didn't mean shit by it. It was just sort of my thing. It didn't really work for a man's reputation to walk around grinning like an asshole all the time—look at fucking Reece. He was a goddamn caricature.

"Well, look at that," Mama said as we rounded the corner and our ridiculous hand-holding suddenly seemed like so much more. "You really did capture my boy's heart and his cock, didn't you?" she asked, rising to her feet and looking way too goddamn young to be anyone's mother—let alone mine. Problem was, when my dad knocked her up, she was only sixteen years old, so in reality, she *was* too young to be my mom.

Didn't stop her from acting like it though.

"I doubt I've captured either of those things just yet," Ciarah said, in that strange lilting voice of hers. Half goddess, half snarky ass young adult. It was weird as fuck, a combination I didn't know quite what to make of.

Thing was, she was only half right.

At the sound of her voice, the feel of her fingers on mine, I felt my cock rising to attention.

Even my damn mother didn't miss the bulge in my pants.

"At this point," Ciarah continued, dragging me over to the sofa and sitting in the center cushion with Killian on her left. I took up the right side and for a moment, we just listened to the frantic whir of the air conditioner. "I seem to have captured his *interest*, but that's all I can really speak to."

"Seems to be enough for him to have committed his life to you," Mama said, glancing over at me with her blonde hair curling around her shoulders, her face still stunning despite the fine lines around her eyes and mouth. She was young, sure, but this was a hard fucking life. Being a biker's wife was tough enough, but to have to hide her children from the world? To keep a secret as big as the fae … it'd damn near sucked the life out of her. "You understand I'm not happy about any of this."

"Why not?" Ciarah asked, tilting her head to the side, shiny dark hair sliding over her shoulder. She looked at my mother with genuine curiosity, beams of buttery yellow sunshine cutting through the white shutters on the windows, cutting across my mother's face like stripes.

"I wanted Arlo to find a nice girl and settle down, have a family, not get mixed up in all of this shit. He'll never have those things now."

"Why not?" Ciarah repeated, head still tilted. "I'm a nice girl. If he wants to settle down, nobody is stopping him, and the Veil Keeper can bear children if she wants." She smiled and flicked her eyes over to mine. "If *she* wants. You haven't come close to earning that privilege. Besides, I swore I wouldn't have babies until I was thirty. Maybe thirty-five. Hell, now that I'm in this body, I can wait as long as I want." Ciarah put her hands on her waist. "These hips aren't going anywhere."

"You'll give my Arlo babies?" Mama asked and I swear to fuck, there I went scowling again. If these people wanted me to smile, they best give me something to smile about.

"I don't want babies, Mama," I said with a long sigh. The last goddamn thing I needed were rug rats running around and getting underfoot.

"Nonsense. You're the Horned God. Fertility and the natural order are your domain. You spit on the earth's spirit itself if you refuse to breed."

"It's his body, his choice," Ciarah said, blinking like she was coming out of a haze and glancing over at Killian. He looked like he was trying ridiculously hard to hold back a smirk. "Well, it's true. I wouldn't want to be forced to have babies, even if I were just a man."

"Just a man?" Reece asked, throwing his head back with that awful guffawing laughter of his. The shitty thing about it was that it made Mama blush which drove me up the fucking wall. I knew she'd bed him in a New York minute if she had the chance, too. Well, maybe that was another reason she didn't much like the Veil Keeper. "Oh, *'tit fille,* you a real cutie, you know that?"

"Well, it's not like men do any of the work with the baking," Ciarah said and this time, Reece, Killian, Caley, *and* my mother laughed. I was the only idiot in that room that wasn't chuckling.

"Not like you could make babies without us," I said and Ciarah turned a glare on me. "What? You have your role and we have ours."

"Your *role*," she said with a roll of her eyes, "is to thrust a few times and come. We have nine months and a hard labor we have to put in, you dick."

"Arlo, don't be an asshole," Mama said, reaching over and smacking me on the back of the head. "You're speaking to a goddess. Show some of those manners I worked so hard to beat into you. You know better than anyone else that a man's role isn't in the baby making—other than a literal sense. It's his job to pleasure his lady."

"Damn straight," Reece said with a bright grin. Once again, everyone but me was smiling. Bunch of assholes. "We just gotta pleasure dis girl straight to da full moon, and then we make some progress, no?"

"We have less than a week," Killian said, a darkness in his voice that said he suspected trouble.

"And what happens on the full moon?" Caley asked, leaning forward in her chair. She was genuinely curious, but she wasn't privy to club business. The Veil Keeper and all her secrets, most definitely club fucking business.

"Nothing you want to know about," I said, reaching

down and avoiding the mugs of coffee—fuck if I even knew why I'd bothered making it—and grabbed a tall, cold glass of iced tea instead, the ice cubes clinking pleasantly, the sides of the drink sweating in the oppressive humidity. The AC was working at full capacity, but even with the dehumidifier chugging away in the corner, it was fucking moist as hell in here—and in a bad way. "Now try this tea and see what you think."

"That's my famous sweet tea," Mama began, leaning back in her rocking chair, her lips painted as red as the day she waltzed into the clubhouse and captured my father's … well, his *interest* and his cock, if not his heart. "That won the over the entire Wild Hunt MC, every last man from President to hang-around."

"Are you sure it wasn't your cunt?" Caley giggled, receiving a proper swat on the knee for being an asshole.

"You'll love it," Mama declared, crossing her arms over her chest. She truly believed there wasn't a person in the world that couldn't be charmed by her famous sweet tea recipe.

We all waited in silence for Ciarah to sip the drink slowly and carefully, like she was putting a lot of thought into something as stupid as cold tea. But shit if it wasn't important to my mother.

"It's fucking amazing," she said and Mama, Caley, and Reece all flashed big grins. Killian smiled like he was in a frigging underwear ad or some shit, and I sat there … scowling again. Jesus H. Ciarah was right. "I wouldn't be a proper Southerner if I disliked sweet tea, now would I?"

"Once had a girl from New Zealand show up at the clubhouse wanting to be a part of the Willing Hunt. She was pretty, curvy, big tits. But one of the boys offered her up some of my sweet tea and she refused, said cold tea was downright gross. Well, I'll tell ya what, they kicked her ass right to the curb, sent her outside to spend the night with the gators."

A laugh bubbled out of Ciarah at this, sounding like the wind chimes on Mama's upstairs veranda, and fuck it … I smiled.

I couldn't frigging help it.

Fucking Veil Keeper was wearing me down. Hell, I was already worn down. I was *hers,* whether I wanted to admit it or not.

Chapter Sixteen

CIARAH

As I laughed at the mental image of some poor girl left out in the bayou at nighttime, my eyes flickered over to Arlo, my Lord of Spring, and my heart almost stopped.

No wonder that man never smiled. Fucking hell, he'd be causing car crashes and breaking up marriages everywhere he went if he smiled more often. The sight of it was nothing short of dazzling. Heart-stopping. Panty-dropping.

"What?" he snarled at me, his stunning smile fading back into his trademark scowl, but it was too late. I'd seen it.

"Nothing," I replied with a smirk, and he glared.

Too late, Cernunnos, I've seen what you're hiding and

now I want more.

As I grinned, and Arlo glared, I wasn't focusing on what was going on around us, so didn't see the small dog coming until it was too late.

It leaped into my lap in a fluffy bundle of white … er … fluff, knocking the glass of tea out of my hand and saturating my white tank top.

"Shit, Linda I am so sorry," I apologized, placing the now empty glass back on the tray and frowning at the brown liquid seeping into the couch cushion around me while Arlo manhandled the small dog out of the way.

"Not a worry at all." Linda flapped her hand. "I'll grab a tea towel for that if Caley can grab you a clean shirt?" She gave her half-fae daughter a pointed look and Caley nodded her blond head.

"Sure thing, come on Cia," she agreed, hopping up from her seat and holding out a hand to me. "Arlo can take Noodle outside to play with the chickens or something."

The idea of Arlo playing with both the excited fluffball that was Noodle *and* chickens made me want to laugh, but I bit my lip to hold it back and followed Caley down the hall to her room.

"Here." She grabbed a t-shirt out of her top drawer and passed it to me. "Sorry if it's a bit small, I keep most of my clothes at the clubhouse because it's closer to work."

"It's got to be better than this." I smiled, taking the garment gratefully and glancing down at my soaked top. I'd gone bra-free *again* seeing as this body had smaller tits than I was used to in my former life. They were perky enough that they really didn't need anything more than the support of a good halter top, but that now meant the dark circles of my nipples were showing though the wet fabric.

"Uh, yeah," Caley snickered. "I'm pretty sure all three of the guys cracked a fat one the second your top went see-through, so like … be quick changing or one of them will *hunt* you down."

She chuckled at her own joke, then headed back to the living room, leaving me alone to peel the tea-soaked fabric from my skin.

Caley hadn't been kidding when she'd said the top was small … it was literally a cropped t-shirt which barely covered the lower curve of my breasts and left my flat stomach totally exposed down to the low waist of my pants. I'd worn a pair of tight, acid washed jeans, since I'd been on Kill's bike coming out here, and a quick glance in the mirror suggested the tiny top was actually kinda sexy on me.

Totally useless for my wings, but I supposed it would do for now.

As I wandered back down the hallway to rejoin the others, Arlo stepped through a door that must lead into the backyard.

For a moment, we both froze and his eyes raked a burning path over my body as he took in my borrowed shirt.

"Arlo," I whispered as he took two steps closer to me and laid a finger over his lips, indicating I be quiet. My eyebrows shot up, but I did as he said and closed my lips as he advanced closer still, backing me up until I was pressed against the wall just outside the living room.

Arlo's huge frame crowded me, and his intense green gaze held mine for a long, charged moment before his fingers reached out and skimmed the flesh below my tiny t-shirt.

My breath hitched, and he raised the fabric up, exposing my naked breasts to the cool evening air which blew in from the open doorway he'd just entered through.

Carefully, deliberately, he palmed each of my tits, rolling my nipples with his fingers sharply and I felt my knees turn slightly to jelly. He leaned in close, placing his lips on my ear.

"Shhh," he breathed, dropping my breasts and flicking open the fly of my jeans.

Before I had more than a moment's notice, he'd already yanked the tight denim of my pants down to my knees.

With his green eyes locked on mine, Arlo put his boot on the crotch of my jeans and shoved them down to the floor, stepping close and whispering against my ear.

"Get your foot out," he growled, and I listened, yanking my right foot free as he bared his own rock-hard erection from his jeans. Arlo clamped a hand over my mouth with one hand and curled the fingers of the other under my thigh, lifting my leg up and savagely thrusting his massive cock into me with one quiet grunt.

My fingertips clenched on his biceps as he pounded into me, my toes barely reaching the floor.

Arlo was wild and fierce in that moment, but he wasn't

the Horned God, a primal beast of fertility and desire. No, he was a man, a *biker* and he was ramming me into the wall like a clubwhore.

And I *loved* it.

Letting my heavy lids flutter shut, I let him drive into me with needy fury, heat and pleasure ricocheting through my body, making me feel weak, dizzy, vulnerable. And I hated that, that vulnerability. But I let Arlo have it in that moment because it felt good and because … he seemed like he needed it.

With a deep, low grunt and a final few thrusts of his hips, he spilled himself inside of me with a shudder, pulling away suddenly and leaving me hot and bothered and shaking. I slumped down the wall, my legs unable to keep me standing.

“Get up,” Arlo growled as his mother's voice echoed down the hallway, calling us back into the living room. I sat there on the floor, panting, still wearing my heels, jeans tangled around my legs. After a moment, he mumbled something under his breath and leaned down, scooping me up from the floor.

The idea of getting rammed into the wall by some random biker was hot, but I also liked that random biker showing a bit of tenderness by picking me up. He carried me a room just off the hallway and heeled the door shut.

“There's a bathroom just in there,” he said, pointing at the cracked door in the corner of the room. “Don't take too long back here. We should get going anyway.”

“I'm not finished,” I said, but Arlo just smirked at me.

"So what? *I* am."

"And I'm *not*," I snapped back, but he was already shoving the bedroom door open and then slamming it behind him. I sat there on the edge of his bed for a moment, probably leaving a suspicious stain on the comforter—which he *deserved*—as I looked around the room. There were posters on all the walls, most of them of women, cars, or motorcycles. The room itself didn't tell me a damn thing about Arlo. It was generic, empty, like all the good stuff had been cleaned out a long time ago.

I was about to give up and head into the bathroom when the door opened again and there Arlo was, shoving his jeans down his hips and flipping me over. He clamped his hand over my mouth again as he thrust his thick, hard cock inside of me. Oh. The Veil Keeper was *very* proud of her male, coming back to service her. The human part of me was surprised he was ready to go again … both parts were glad it was happening.

Arlo's childhood bed creaked beneath his massive weight as he filled my body with the velvet wrapped steel of his shaft. And this time, he used the fingers of his free hand to reach underneath me, the rough pad of his thumb teasing my clit and bringing me to such a rapid orgasm that I really did scream, the sound muffled by the warmth of his massive palm.

He continued his rapid thrusting until a grunt escaped his throat and he had his way with me a second time.

"Don't even *think* about snooping around in here. There's nothing to find. If you want to know something about me, ask." Arlo pulled away from me and fixed his pants, crossing his arms over his chest while he waited for me stand up, plop down on the toilet, and clean myself up.

By the time we got back to the living room, everyone was staring at us and it was fairly fucking obvious that we'd been … well, fucking.

"Jesus H.," Arlo's mama said with a long sigh, looking up at the two of us like we were crazy. "To be young and stupid again."

"I am older than the universe in which you sit," my voice said automatically, almost without my permission.

"Maybe," the blonde said, glancing over her shoulder at me, "but the girl in those eyes is young, dumb, and crazy. You watch yourself with these fae, little girl, because they'll as soon break you as they will take care of you. Life in a motorcycle club is a double-edged sword—the finest protection … at the highest price. Fail to pay, and watch it all fall apart."

Shadows swept around me, monsters without name, decades without hearing the sound of another's voice. Everyone thinks they have a breaking point, but in reality, that's just the first marker of the race. Once it's shattered, another goal will show itself, another landmark to measure time by.

After that, another. And another. And another.

Each time that breaking point is reached, the mind, the heart, the soul, and even the body can reach new heights.

But then ... your head hits the sky, far beyond the point where you thought you'd take your last step, breathe your last breath. That's when you know you've truly reached it and everything falls apart.

My soul ... was tired. My knights, dead and gone. I was alone in blackness with nothing but pain for company. And I needed a way out.

The only way was for me to give up this body, this life, these memories that I loved so much. Some were mine, some were from previous Veil Keepers, but they all held a special place inside my heart. I didn't want to leave. No, I wanted to believe that at some point, salvation would come.

It never did, and I needed a way out.

But even then, my stubbornness persisted and I stayed. Even then, I made myself fight for one more breath, one more day.

It was only when their torture reached new heights, needles digging into my brain, the very depths of my soul ... that I knew I needed to leave. If I didn't, then one day I would break and they would know.

They would know everything and they would murder the world.

I couldn't let that happen.

I wished I could say it was fate, destiny, that I chose

her because she was meant to be chosen. In reality, it was a simple coincidence, a collision of circumstances. She died the moment I fled. I gave her my body and she freed my soul.

Becoming the Veil Keeper, it seems like it should arrive with pomp and circumstance.

Sometimes ... it's just a gasp and a scream.

The six days until the full moon seemed to disappear in a mere moment and before I knew it, I was on the back of Reece's bike on our way to pack land. Arlo and Killian were with us, on their own bikes and looking every bit the bad boy bikers they were.

We rode in silence, tense from the ongoing arguments about this mission to visit *Papa Cocodril*. It wasn't so much visiting the magicked gator that was an issue for my Lords. It was that *they* couldn't be present.

"This is foolish, *cher*," Reece muttered as we pulled to a stop on the border between Hunt land and pack land. Rafe himself had come to meet us, along with Amelie and Marcel.

"This is necessary, Reece," I replied with firm authority in my voice. Over the past week, *she* and I had been meshing more and more to the point now where our voices had blended into something halfway between our individual pitches.

Without bothering to argue the issue further with him, I swung my leg off his bike and ran a hand through my windswept hair. It was so much longer than I remembered *my* hair had been, and was taking some getting used to.

"Keeper," Rafe greeted me, his bloodred eyes burning under the bright moonlight.

"Rafe," I replied, a small smile curving the corners of my mouth. I couldn't help it. Something about the wolves, or *this* wolf, made me happy.

"Raphael," Reece snapped, climbing off his bike and coming to stand beside me. His arm snaked around my waist and he held my hip in a decidedly possessive manner. "We would like to ask permission to enter pack land."

Behind me, I felt Kill and Arlo climb from their bikes and take up positions around me, like the Knights they were.

"Denied," Rafe replied without a moment's hesitation, then he held out a hand to me. "Keeper? The night won't last forever and you have a hard task ahead of you."

Giving Rafe a short nod of understanding, I peeled Reece's fingers from my hip and turned to face him.

"Reece. Relax. The wolves have no reason to hurt me. They want the Veil restored just as much as we do." I raised myself up on tiptoes and placed a quick kiss on his tight lips.

Releasing Reece, I turned and did the same to both

Killian and Arlo.

Of course, Arlo wouldn't let me off with the quick peck I'd given the other two and seized my hair, demanding entry into my mouth and kissing the *shit* out of me. Clearly, he was putting on a show of dominance for the wolves, but hell. Who was I to complain?

"My Lords," I purred in a voice that was far sexier than I'd intended thanks to Arlo's kiss, "wait for me."

Flipping my green-streaked hair over my shoulder, I turned my back on the three of them and crossed the invisible line between territories. The *second* my foot touched tarmac on the wolf side, a smile curved across Rafe's face that sent a shiver of anticipation through me.

Whatever he was up to, it wasn't of totally pure intentions.

I'd lied to my Lords—apparently, I was the *only* fae who could lie—when I'd said the wolves had no ulterior motives for this. I'd felt it on their words every time they spoke of this quest, but nothing they'd said had been an outright untruth so for now I was content to let it play out.

"Hey girl," Amelie greeted me, the beads in her braids clinking together as she hip-bumped me on my way past her. "Ready for a swim with the gators?"

"Of course," I smiled back at her. Maybe she was the reason I liked the wolves so much? She'd spent *most* of the past week with us, only returning to her alpha a few hours ago, and I really wanted to say we'd become friends. Whatever that meant.

Sketchy memories or not, I knew I'd never had close

girlfriends in the past as *either* Ciarah or the Veil Keeper.

"You can ride with me if you want?" she offered. "But it is totally time you made those boys get you a bike of your own. You're our damn goddess—you should *not* be riding bitch to any man."

"She rides with me, Amelie," Rafe ordered in a voice like smoke and shadows. To me, he nodded his head respectfully. "If that is acceptable to you, Veil Keeper?"

"Ciarah," I corrected him, for some reason not liking such a formal title from this impressive man, "and that is fine. It's not that far, I understand?"

The silver-haired man just cocked his head to one side, then repeated my name.

"Ciarah," he murmured, and the sound of my name on his lips made me shiver. "No, it's not far."

Marcel, the caramel-skinned man with eyes as black as death made a noise under his breath that sounded oddly like disgust, before climbing onto his own bike and revving the engine.

"Let's go, Boss. We're wasting moonlight." His voice was low—*angry*—and I made a note to keep a close eye on him. Something … something wasn't feeling right with him.

But there were more pressing issues at hand, such as finding *Papa Cocodril* in the Louisiana Bayou *and* convincing him to hand over the key to my memories. Or, to part of them anyway.

This is going to be a long road.

Chapter Seventeen

CIARAH

The sound of frogs and crickets echoed through the still night as I stood on the mossy dock, looking out over the bayou water. The moon was full and round, bathing the whole scene in a cool silver glow better than any artificial light could ever provide, and in a word, it was *magical*.

"Peaceful, no?" Rafe murmured, standing slightly behind me but close enough that I could feel the warmth of his body.

"It's beautiful," I sighed, not wanting to dive in and disrupt the glass-like surface of the water.

"You going in fully-dressed?" he asked, and I could hear the edge of amusement in his voice.

"You know," I said, as I touched a hand to the white tank I was wearing, buried beneath a leather trench coat I'd stolen from Killian's closet, "back in the day, in human times, they'd swim in outfits baggier than this." I stripped the trench off and threw it to the mossy ground.

The tank was ribbed, and tight, and just *barely* thick enough to hide the circles of my nipples. I was finding I wasn't a particular fan of bras. And with the Veil Keeper's magic, I could go without as much as I wanted and never have to worry about sagging breasts.

In the right light though, and with my nipples pebbled from the cool breeze coming off the water, I figured Rafe could probably see them through the fabric.

"In Victorian times, they basically wore dresses into the water, with leggings underneath." I put my palms flat on the hips of my skintight leather pants. "So perhaps I *am* going in fully-dressed? My suit would be more revealing than anything humans would've worn a hundred years ago."

Rafe snorted and looked me up and down, already shrugging out of his own coat and reaching over one shoulder to tear his tee over his head.

"Right, but you're not human anymore—you're fae. And fae *despise* clothing that isn't intentionally decorative or provocative. And *especially* if it hinders whatever activity you folks are up to—which, let's not kid ourselves—usually involves *sex*."

"You think you can just say the word *sex* and I'll fall at your feet in acquiescence or adoration?" I asked as I stood there and blatantly watched him undress, his silver hair catching the beams of moonlight. It shimmered like the stars in the velvet sky above our heads and made my throat feel tight. He really was a beautiful man, Raphael LeRoux. "I bet that happens a lot, doesn't it?"

"Maybe," he said as he kicked off his motorcycle boots and then *slowly* opened the button on his leather pants, dragging the zipper down with agonizing intensity. "But that's not what I expect from *you.* No, I like a little sass in my women."

"Your women?" I asked with a scoffing laugh.

"I said what I meant," he continued, pushing his pants down his hips and revealing the full, erect length of his cock. "Now, are you *truly* going swimming in that getup? Or do you want to get naked? It could take a while to find Papa Cocodril and if the full moon goes down, you'll have to wait a whole other month to find him."

"You're acting like your dick isn't hard and leaking pre-cum," I challenged, tearing my white top over my head and revealing my breasts. Rafe's eyes dropped to them immediately and his breath hitched. He glanced away for a moment and cursed under his breath in a strange language I didn't quite recognize.

"I'm not *acting* like anything. What does it matter if my cock is hard? Your nipples look like rocks and I can *smell* your arousal from here."

"What can I say?" I replied coolly, pretending like the idea of him smelling me wasn't at all weird … or sexy. "My Lords' kisses make me wet."

I kicked off my own boots and then reached for the button on my pants, just as slowly and teasingly as Rafe had. He watched my every movement, his red eyes gleaming, his tongue flicking across his lower lip.

"Your women," I said with another snort. "Please. Do you think to make me one of those?"

"You're missing a Lord of Summer," he told me, like he full-on expected to get the job, and I laughed.

"Only a fae can hold that position," I told him, "someone born of Faerie. Even if distant in blood, a relative who lived on the other side of the Veil is an unbeatable requirement."

"I am part fae," he told me, and I raised both brows as he crossed his arms over his chest and smirked at me, his dick pointing straight at my face. It was just *asking* to be grabbed in a tight fist. "But once upon a time, I had the Swamp Witch make me an unshakable glamour. Not even *you* could see through it. It's permanent, can never be shed. But my faerie blood is still in there somewhere."

"A permanent glamour?" I echoed, searching the Veil Keeper's memories. Mmm. It was a hell of a lot easier to make a strong, beautiful glamour that *stayed* than one that could be removed at will. But the price was high. Whatever Rafe had paid to the Swamp Witch would've been costly, dangerous, and probably required a serious amount of bloodshed. "Why would you want to hide that side of yourself?" I continued, detecting nothing but truth in any of his words. It seemed that the more someone was truthful to me, the less my powers sung inside, as if it didn't need to alert me until … they weren't.

Then it was like white-hot needles ripping through my soul.

Fortunately, Raphael LeRoux wasn't stupid enough to try to lie to me.

"I couldn't become alpha if I were part fae. Purebloods only. You're the only person that knows my secret now except for Amelie."

"Is she your mate?" I asked and Rafe grinned with bright white teeth.

"Hardly. We've never even fucked. She's more like … a sister. Why? Are you jealous?"

I shoved my pants down my hips, purposely turned away from Rafe, and then bent over to take them off, knowing that I was flashing the perfect plump shape of my cunt in his direction. *Take that, asshole,* I thought as I stepped out of them and stood up, flicking my dark hair over my shoulder at the same moment I opened my wings.

They spread wide through the silver moonlight, catching the shimmering beams and radiating with their own inner glow.

Rafe's jaw was clenched so tight, I expected to hear the cracking of teeth.

"Not jealous," I said as I turned back around, letting the rest of my glamour go. My skin shimmered a pale blue-white color, like I was lit from within, and I knew my eyes could catch and hold the attention of any man—even an alpha. "I just wanted to know if I should set Amelie up with one of the men in The Wild Hunt. Fae make excellent lovers, you know."

"Yeah, fucking and killing, the two things your people excel at."

I ignored him—and the *my woman* comment—as I made my way over to the edge of the water, tilting my head back to take a deep breath of the night air. I hadn't practiced flying yet as my back and shoulder muscles weren't strong enough to hold me, but even if I could have, I wouldn't do it now.

The bayou was too messy, too twisted and tangled to fly through. I'd have to soar above it and even then, I might miss Papa Cocodril

I had to swim.

And Rafe … he'd shift and run beside me.

"Be careful out there," he growled, his hot breath fanning against my right ear. I hadn't even felt him move, he was that quick. "I'll be watching you from the shadows, but you never know what we might run into."

He lifted a hand up and hovered it over my arm, moving around me and shifting at the same time, his body melting into a wolf the size of a fucking pony.

His bloodred eyes blinked at me from his moonlight silver wolf form, and I couldn't help myself. My hand reached out and slipped through the fur of his neck, feeling the silken warmth of his pelt against my skin.

A noise rumbled from his throat that sounded almost like a purr, then he was gone, dashing into the cypress in a blur of silver.

My wings stretched and fluttered once more, and I

sighed at the glorious feeling of the night air against the sensitive tissue. They weren't practical for swimming though—I'd just wanted to tease the alpha—so I retracted them into my back before diving headfirst into the inky bayou waters.

The Sage had said I would find Papa Cocodril at the *apex of the bayou* which the guys had explained was a very literal place here on pack land. Apparently, once upon a time, he had lived out here in a small shack, surrounded by nature. He'd run afoul of the Swamp Witch though, and she'd cursed him into gator form until he apologized for whatever indiscretion had triggered such punishment.

He sounded like a stubborn old bastard, because he was still here in gator form, many, *many* years later.

The apex of the bayou was anywhere along the stretch of water that I swam, and I let my magic guide me. Inside, I could feel all the bright lights of my Wild Hunt, with my three Lords shining the brightest. Past them, I could sense *all* fae creatures, as I was their Goddess. Their souls were tied to me as sure as the water was wet.

In the immediate vicinity, I could sense Rafe, a burning light that confirmed he was indeed more than mere wolf. But past him, I could sense another.

Papa Cocodril.

Humming to myself happily, I followed my magical senses closer and closer, until I felt I was practically on top of him. Rafe was loping along the banks of the water, darting between trees in flashes of silver, but I knew he had almost caught up to me.

"Hello?" I called out, treading water and sweeping my dark, wet mane off my face, "Papa Cocodril?"

He was here … somewhere. I could feel him watching me. Watching *us*.

"Rafe," I said in a careful voice, knowing his wolf ears would hear me, "I need you to back off. The Sage said he would not reveal himself to anyone but me." From the trees there was a snuffling and then the Alpha of the Louisiana Wolves let out a howl, before doing my bidding.

"Papa Cocodril?" I tried again, looking all around me. "It's just the two of us now. Just you … and the Veil Keeper."

For what felt like a *long* time, the bayou was still. Quiet. Then I felt movement in the water and something scaly brushed my legs. My breath hitched, but I reminded myself this was no ordinary gator. This was a fae-blooded voodoo priest in a gator's form. He wouldn't eat people … would he?

A chirping noise sounded near the banks of the bayou, and bubbles rose to the surface as Papa Cocodril emerged. First his eyes, then his snout, then slowly, with his gaze locked on me, his enormous gator form exited the water and staggered up the muddy incline. All the while … chirping.

"Papa Cocodril," I breathed with a healthy level of apprehension. Ciarah's human life had been here in Louisiana, and a sensible level of respect for the deadly beasts was ingrained in my soul, so to see *this* mighty creature … "Are you … laughing?"

The chirps grew louder, and his jaws opened in the semblance of a grin while his massive tail swished back and forth behind him.

"Yea, girl," a deep and powerful voice rumbled from the reptile, "I be laughing at you. Veil Keeper, p'shaw."

"Well, that's not kind," I scolded with a frown, "what have I done to deserve your laughter, Papa Cocodril?"

"It's of none importance, young one," he chuckled, his scaled head swinging back and forth in a hypnotising rhythm. "Are you gettin' out, now? De moon be almost at it's zenith an' Papa Cocodril been cravin' som rum somet'ing fierce, no?"

"Rum?" I repeated, feeling like a bit of an idiot. I wasn't totally sure *what* I'd expected from Papa Cocodril but … it wasn't this.

Swimming over to the edge of the water, I took a moment to inspect him a little more closely. Even if I hadn't known he were a magical being, it'd be clear just by looking at him. Normal American alligators grew to a maximum of around fourteen feet—how I knew that, I had no idea—but this guy … he was an easy twenty-five or thirty feet long and wore a necklace made of what seemed to be gator teeth.

"Dis way, girl," the gator ordered, swinging his massive body around and leading the way through the cypress trees and deeper into the darkness.

In near total silence, I followed the talking gator for

some time, my naked skin glistening and shimmering in the moonlight without my glamour on, until we reached a run-down old shack on stilts with a burning kerosene lantern hanging from the eaves.

"Ah, *bon*," Papa Cocodril nodded his huge gator head, "she be 'ere already. One moment, young one."

Curious, I stepped back and watched as he stepped his stumpy, reptilian legs onto a circle of symbols that looked freshly scratched into the dirt. He paused there, looking up at the full moon, then as the cloud moved and the silvery light bathed his brown and green body, he *shifted* into a man.

"Much bettah," he sighed, grinning at me with teeth as white as rice against skin as black as coal. "Now, let us see what my woman 'as prepared fo' us. Come see, come 'side, girl."

He nodded his head to the shack and I raised my eyebrows, thoroughly intrigued.

"Your woman?" I asked, and he laughed a hearty belly laugh.

"Yea, *cher*. My queen, my lover, my jailer, Rosinée." The way he said her name was like he spoke of a fine wine, or perfectly aged cheese that he *craved.*

"I heard that!" a woman's voice snapped from inside.

I stayed where I was, near the waters of the bayou. It was dark out, the silver moon casting her long arms across the surface of the water, but it was far from quiet. I could feel little bugs skimming across my skin, mosquitoes swarming in buzzing circles around my head, unable to bite my enchanted skin or drink my magicked blood.

"I didn't expect you to have a visitor," I said, adding silently in my head, *and most especially not the Swamp Witch.* Lover? Jailor? How could a person be both one in the same? I could *never* be around my jailors again, not without trying to kill what I wasn't positive could even *be* killed. But sharing a bed with someone willing to steal another's freedom? I couldn't wrap my head around it.

"Yeah, well," Papa Cocodril said, his irises gleaming yellow in the darkness. I wasn't sure if that was from the enchantment, his magic, a failed glamour, or something else. "I only get one night a month, girly, and I ain't about to waste it if you know what I mean." He flashed me another grin and a wink, reaching up to tug on the gold ring threaded through the center of his nose. "Get outta dat swamp and come on in."

He gestured at me with a hand covered in rings and then started off toward the wooden shack, perched on stilts and hovering above the soft, mossy ground. The man was nude and erect, but I didn't sense that his hard cock had anything to do with me—no, he was clearly *very* interested in seeing Rosinée.

I waited until his bare butt disappeared into the house and then started across the wooden platform toward the front door, wondering why he was nude but still wearing jewelry. Interesting. I added that mental note to my index of questions to ask Rafe later. And trust me, I had a lot of them. *I should invite the man out for beignets and coffee and pick his brain.* There were so many things I wanted to know about the wolves, their customs and culture, their shifting abilities (especially the whole clothes/no clothes thing), their relationship to the fae and the Veil Keeper.

The night air kissed my skin, along with the hot burn of Rafe's red eyes, watching me from the shadows.

I ignored him and moved across the ground on silent feet, listening to the chattering of night birds, the grunting of gators … and the distant buzz of sprites' wings. Pausing in the center of Papa Cocodril's island, I noticed one watching me from a nearby branch, its sharp white fangs bared in a hiss.

“Don't worry,” a woman's rich voice called from the doorway. I glanced over to find the Swamp Witch, Rosinée, standing in the golden glow, wiping her hands on her apron and gesturing with her chin for me to come up the long wooden ramp to the house. “I spelled this island against unwanted visitors. One of those little buggers try to fly over my wards? They'll be incinerated faster than these bloodsuckers in the Zap lamp.” She tapped her knuckles against a light hanging near the door before turning around and heading inside, not even bothering to see if I would follow.

Sweeping my wet hair over one shoulder, I quickly arranged it into a fishtail braid, and headed up to the front door. Well, the tattered curtain hanging over the doorway, but same thing.

The air was thick with the savory smells of gumbo—I recognized the spicy burn of andouille sausage, the salty scent of crab meat, and the richness of … gator meat?

Hmm. Was that cannibalistic for Papa Cocodril to be eating? I had no idea.

"Take a seat," the witch said, her dreadlocks swinging forward as she leaned over the bubbling pot and inhaled sharply, letting out a satisfied sigh. "And do you want a robe or something to cover up with?"

Taking a quick look around the shack—which, really, was just a single room—I noticed a small bed, a dresser, and the tiny stove Rosinée was working over. There was nothing else but an old metal screen in the corner, Papa Cocodril's smooth, velvety tones echoing out from behind it as he sang a low, sad song under his breath.

"I don't need a robe," I told her, comfortable enough in my nakedness to sit in a chair in a strange room with full confidence.

"I thought that new soul o' yours was human?" the president of the rougarou said, dressed in heavy skirts that jangled with beads and bone as she moved. She seemed so different than the woman in the story I'd been told, the one about her straddling her motorcycle, lording over Arlo's crumpled form.

I squeezed my hands into fists and Rosinée noticed, letting out a deep, chilling bellyful of laughter.

"I might be human on the inside," I snarled, before she could comment further, "but just remember, this new body is fae. This new body belongs to a *goddess*. I could rend your head from your shoulders before you had a chance to add the okra to that gumbo."

"So you think," the woman said as Papa Cocodril

made his way over to the table and took one of the other two mismatched chairs, settling into it with a top hat lilting on his head, a cane across his lap, and a blue and white bowtie at his neck. "But you don't know everything, girly. In fact, you don't know a lot from what I hear."

"You hear?" I asked, immediately on edge. "You sent the sprites."

It wasn't a question, but Rosinée laughed and answered me anyway.

"No, I have other methods, you silly girl," she said, chopping up some `okra and tossing it into the pot. "You best reign in that arrogance or your immortal head will end up in a glass jar, staring at shadows for the rest of eternity."

My throat tightened and I had to blink several times to banish the sudden rush of memories.

Dark shadows surrounding me, claws raking my skin, rending my flesh. My mouth opens in a scream and those nails dig into my tongue, severing it, taking my voice away for the hundredth, the thousandth, the millionth time. I can't remember. It doesn't matter; I don't care. I just want to have a voice again; I want to feel human.

"Tell me about those lords of yours? The whole world took a gasp and a breath when you claimed three of them at once. You sure you want to go committing to all that dick for the rest of your soul's stay in the Veil Keeper? Or maybe you plan on jumping ship like the last one and so your commitments don't mean shit to you?"

"I can have other lovers," I growled out through gritted

teeth.

It was true—I could. The Veil Keeper was not bound to mate with just her Lords, *but* it was very rare for her to stray outside of them.

"P'shaw, Rosinée," Papa Cocodril scoffed, rapping the head of his cane against the table, "Dat's enough o' dat gossip, eh? Dis young Veil Keeper didn't come to listen to you prattle on, and nor did I, see?" He turned his eerie white irises back to me and scratched at his chin. He still wore the same bone necklace as he'd had on as a huge gator, which was interesting.

"So, girl. You come for da key? Took you damn long time, no? Dat key been not'ing but trouble *por moi*, see?" He narrowed his eyes at me and I couldn't help my curiosity.

"How so?" I asked. "Does it have something to do with you being turned into a gator?"

My eyes flickered to Rosinée and back to Papa Cocodril. The story *said* it had been the Swamp Witch who'd cursed him …

"Yeh, you could say dat," he chuckled heartily and even the dreadlocked witch cracked a smile. "See my woman here, she ain't never had the best of morals and values. Only good t'ing she ever do was fall in love with a *fils-putain* like me. Anyway, dat last Horned One, he entrust yo' key to me, for safe keepin', see? But Rosinée, *ma chère*, she want dat power fo' herself."

Startled, I glanced at the swamp witch in question and found her scowling at Papa Cocodril, looking every bit the pissed off wife.

"Ah, don't cha give me dat scowl, woman. Dis be old news, dis." The ageless man scolded his lover then turned back to me with a flash of bright white teeth. "Ah, da rest be history. I refuse, she turn me into gator. One day a month, we meet, we eat, we fuck, and she ask me to apologize and give her yo' key. Every month, I say no, and off I go as a huge ass gator."

"Ah …" I wasn't totally sure *what* to say to that. The whole reason he'd spent so many years in gator form was because he was protecting *my* key? From the woman standing mere feet away?

"But you here now, you can take dat blasted t'ing off my hands and my woman an' I can be done wit dis stupid fight, no?" He raised his brows at me but when my attention flickered to Rosinée, there was *something* I didn't like about her smile.

Everything Papa Cocodril had said was true, but she had noticeably not contributed to his story. Why? For fear of being caught in a lie?

"Yes, I suppose I can." I squinted at the swamp witch, but until she spoke I wouldn't be able to sense any deception. "So, may I have it? I'm sure you have better things to do with your night than entertain me."

"'course you can, girl." Papa Cocodril tugged his gator tooth necklace off his head, removing his top hat to do so then replacing it on his curly dark hair. He then took the middle tooth and inserted it into a groove of his intricately detailed cane and popped it open to reveal a hidden compartment.

A hidden compartment, that was totally empty.

"How … no …" The ebony skinned man stared up at me, then at his lover with pale eyes wide in shock. "Dis isn't possible."

"Of course it's possible, you old fool," Rosinée snickered with a cruel edge to her voice, "Did you really think I'd just *give up* on accessing the power of the Veil when it was so close to my reach? I found your little hiding place some fifty odd years past, *cher.*"

"What?!" Papa Cocodril thundered, slamming his cane down on the floor and actually shaking the structure we were in. "Fifty years? *Fifty years?!* Why I still been swimmin' around dat dere bayou like an overgrown lizard if you had da key all along?"

"Because you haven't apologized!" she screamed back at him, throwing a glass and smashing it against the wall. "You should have given me, *your wife,* what I damn well asked for in the first place!"

"Woman, I aught to—" Papa Cocodril was looking like he was gearing up for a hell of a screaming match so I decided to butt in early.

"Sorry, hi. Can you finish *this* later? Where is my key, Rosinée? I assume you weren't able to use it or we wouldn't be here right now." I gave her my very best *don't fuck with me* glare and she shuffled her feet a little awkwardly as her bluster deflated.

For a long moment, she said nothing, just inspected her fingernails with a tight mouth until Papa Cocodril made a low, menacing growl in his throat.

"Fine!" she snapped, glaring at the enraged voodoo priest and then snarling at me. "No, I couldn't use it. Damn thing is fucking useless in the hands of anyone but the Veil Keeper." A sly look crept over her face, despite her words ringing true. "I do know *where* you need to use it though."

"Let me guess," I sighed, "it'll cost me."

"As anything worth having does in Faerie, no?" The Swamp Witch smiled and tossed her long dreadlocks over her shoulder as she regained her confident stance.

"What's your price, witch?" I demanded, growing *very* tired of these games.

Her eyes darted to her lover then back to me before her chin tipped up stubbornly.

"A baby," she said decisively, and I thought I must have heard her wrong.

"Uh," I frowned, "you want ..."

"I want you to cure me of infertility. I have asked your good for nothing Horned God *multiple* times, and even tried my very best to *persuade* him, but it seems he is more stubborn than ... well... than this bastard." She nodded her head to Papa Cocodril, who had groaned as he sat back down to rub at his eyes. "It's simple enough to do, for you. All I require is a sample of your bodily fluid after the height of passion."

"My bodily fluid?" I asked, the human side of me roaring to life. Ciairah O'Rourke burst out of my mouth in a shower of profanity. "What the fuck sort of bodily fluid are we talking here?" I snapped before the goddess' eternal patience took over and I found myself sucking in a sharp breath.

"I need the wetness of a god or goddess—specifically one whose powers extend to fertility. My magic can do the rest."

"How do I know you won't misuse what I give you?" I started, trying not to think *too* hard about what she was asking for. She wanted the sweet nectar from between my thighs, the slick easy arousal that I made for my Lords. I couldn't even *imagine* 'giving' that to Rosinée or anyone else. It wasn't a commodity; it was a privilege I bestowed on my lovers.

But I needed that goddamn key.

"How do I know you won't use it against me?" I repeated as Rosinée spooned the gumbo into a wooden bowl and passed it to me. I stared hard at the food. It smelled like heaven, but I wasn't about to eat anything this woman gave to me. I supposed I could just ask though, couldn't I? "Is this poisoned?"

"This here is regular ol' gumbo, my Mami's recipe, and if you don't want it then I'll eat it or give it to that stubborn ass of a husband over there." She gestured at me with the bowl and I narrowed my eyes. "It ain't gonna kill ya, hurt ya, maim ya, or put ya to sleep. How does that sound?" Every word she spoke was thick with truth.

"It won't transfigure me?" I asked, and the swamp witch snorted.

"Good goddess girl, you a paranoid little thing, aren't

ya? No, it won't do nothing to you except fill your belly with good wholesome food. Here." I took the bowl with a small sigh and set it on the table, breathing in the spicy smell as my mouth watered.

"So, are you going to take this deal or not?" Rosinée asked, serving up another bowl of gumbo for her husband. She served herself last and joined as at the table as I tried to figure out what to do here.

"How do I deliver this … fluid?" I asked, goosebumps crawling across my skin. This whole idea was making me uncomfortable, but I needed that key. I fucking *needed* it. My whole people, the entire hunt, the very fabric between *worlds* relied on me getting that key.

"You just bring two fingers dipped in the sacred waters and you touch them to this here charm." Rosinée lifted up a necklace by the string, a dried chicken foot dangling from the end of it, decorated with beads, bits of bone, and tiny gems.

"I could just kill you and try to search out where you've hidden the key," I said and both Papa Cocodril and Rosinée laughed at me.

"You could try," she said as her husband muttered something under his breath.

"Would be a bloody battle, no?" he asked, shaking his head like he was disappointed with the whole situation. Well he should be considering he lost the key he was meant to protect in the first place. I shouldn't *have* to make a trade. And I also wasn't so sure I wanted the Swamp Witch to reproduce. She'd had her club attack Arlo, so she could, what, steal *his* bodily fluid for her spell? "You got that werewolf out there. He seems like a fertile sort of folk? Go mate him when you finish your gumbo and we can be done with this exchange."

"I'm not mating *him*," I said with a wrinkled nose. *Not after his comments just now.* The arrogance … Rafe truly believed I was going to choose him as a Lord. What a fool. "You'll have to wait until—"

"No," Rosinée said, her fingers tightening around the wooden spoon she was using. "I won't wait." She paused and looked over at her husband. "Wipe that fool smile off your face," she growled at him as I spooned a bite of gumbo in my mouth and had to resist the urge to groan in pleasure.

Truly, it was one of the most delicious things I'd ever eaten in my life.

But I wasn't about to tell the Swamp Witch that.

"If she be needin' a lover," Papa Cocodril said and before he could get out another word, I reached over and slapped him across the face *hard*. "No, no, not me!" he said, dropping his spoon in his now empty bowl and holding up his hands, palms out. The look of fear he cast in his wife's direction spoke volumes as to how their relationship must play out.

I didn't want that with my Lords.

I'd need to be careful in the future and stop doing things like tossing Arlo out a window and into the swamp. I wanted us to be equals; I did *not* want to lord myself over them the way Rosinée was doing with her husband.

"Not me, girly, I meant you can be your *own* lover. As long as you get that special little shiver of pleasure," Papa Cocodril wiggled his eyebrows at me, "then the spell will work."

"I can masturbate?" I clarified and the old man chuckled.

"*Oui*, you can be your own lover and the universe will love you just as good."

I finished the last few bites of my gumbo and turned to look Rosinée in the dark brown of her eyes.

"Make me a fae's bargain," I said and my voice radiated with power. I wasn't even one hundred percent sure *what* I was doing.

"A fae's bargain," Rosinée ground out through clenched teeth, but like she knew she didn't have a lot of choice in the matter. "Fine."

"Two fingers of liquid from my cunt," I said blatantly, "in exchange for the key that was entrusted to Papa Cocodril by the previous Lord of Spring, the one that unlocks the Spear of Lug *and* the location of said spear, delivered no later that one hour from now."

Each word I spoke perfumed the air with the sweet scent of flowers as my wings burst from my back and uncurled over the back of the chair. A glow suffused the room as power took hold of my lips.

I held out my hand and Rosinée offered hers.

"I agree," she said as I sliced her palm with a fingernail and her breath hissed out in pain. I let her do the same to me and we clasped hands, smearing our blood in an ancient ritual of power and promise. If one of us were to break the bargain … we'd drop dead.

Not even a goddess like the Veil Keeper could escape the pain and punishment of a fae's bargain.

Standing up, I wiped my palm on my naked hip and stared down into Rosinée's ice-blue eyes. I didn't trust her, not with the fae's bargain, not even with my truth telling powers, but bringing myself to orgasm with a little masturbation was not a high price to pay for that key.

And if she somehow managed to wiggle out of our agreement with careful words and well-placed tricks … I would kill her. Or my Lords would. Fuck, I wouldn't be surprised if *Rafe* tore her throat out. The two of them couldn't be the best of friends since he'd jumped into the fight with the rougarou to save Arlo. I hadn't seen that part of the conflict with my own eyes, but Reece had told me all about it.

"I'll be back," I told the odd couple, leaving the hut to stand in the middle of a tiny island in the Louisiana bayou. If I was going to do this with the allotted hour time slot, I'd have to do it here, and while outside seemed like a much less palatable option for most people, I was fae. I was Veil Keeper. I was *divine.* The Horned God was my consort and the earth was our bed, so I had no problem finding a mossy patch of ground and relaxing against the trunk of a large tree.

Scanning the trees and the rippling waters around the island, I looked for a pair of red wolf's eyes but couldn't find them. Wherever Raphael LeRoux was hiding, he was laying low. It was below me to call out and ask him not to peek. Fuck, that would only *encourage* him to look, I bet, asshole that he was.

So I decided instead to close my eyes and think of my three fae Lords, waiting for me at the edge of pack property. I could feel them, tethered to me by magic, and I reached out on silent wings as I dropped my hand to my inner thigh and trailed my nails along my skin, imagining that it was Killian's long fingers approaching the wetness of my cunt.

"Mon cher?" I heard him ask from miles away, his voice as warm and silken to my ears now as it was when he was actually standing beside me.

"It's me," I told him … *them*. I wasn't exactly sure *how* I was communicating with them, but I didn't care. That knowledge was buried somewhere deep in the Veil Keeper's psyche, and I was accessing it through sheer need. That's how much I wanted them. *"I need your help."*

"Girl, you don't gotta ask Old Reece twice for help wit' dat."

A surge of violent heat shot through my body making me gasp, taking my pathetic clumsy attempts at teasing my inner thigh and squeezing my own breast and turning them into impossible acts of erotica. My thumb tracing across the hardened peak of a nipple became Reece's thumb, the fingers dipping inside my heat became Killian.

"Arlo?" I asked, but he was silent when I called out to him. His refusal to answer me seemed purposeful, almost

defiant. *"My Lord of Spring?"*

"I'm not helping you impregnate that fucking swamp witch whore," he growled out, making my skin ripple with pleasure. Even though he was being a complete ass, the sheer desire and possessiveness threaded through his voice turned me on even more, a feat I didn't think possible with Reece's sex magic poisoning my veins.

"We need the key, Arlo," I whispered with my magic, biting my lower lip as I traded out two fingers for three … then four, the power rolling between the four of us convincing my aching body that it was Killian's cock instead. My hand on my breast became Reece's, and the sound of my own groaning turned into Arlo's as it hit my ears.

"Fuck," he growled, and I could just imagine him reaching down to take hold of his own cock, stroking himself to the vision of me lying naked and prone in the swamp, fucking myself with my hand, teasing my own nipple into a hardened pink point. *"You're going to be the death of me."*

I worked my body with the help of Reece's magic, my magic, the careful dance of my thumb on my clit, my fingers buried in hot wetness. The orgasm rose inside me like a phoenix from the ashes, brilliant and flaming, cast red-hot arms of pleasure across my skin as I arched my hips toward the sky and opened my eyes, tears blooming at the edges.

As I did, I caught a glimpse of a man in the trees, his hand wrapped around his cock, his red eyes half-lidded and heavy with desire. I didn't mean for it to happen, but our eyes locked at just the right moment and the magic swept through me, convincing my body that it was Raphael's hard, muscular form atop my own, driving me to the precipice of pleasure and over the other side.

I came screaming, my voice echoing around the crowded bayou and stirring up turtles, gators, birds … and sprites. But fuck them. If they saw, I hoped they enjoyed the damn show.

Rafe however … I was fucking *furious* with.

Panting and shaking, my body trembling with the aftereffects of my climax, I rose to my feet and felt the whisper of the magic I'd shared with my lords drifting away in the musty bayou breeze. Catching Rafe's eyes had cut my connection to the other three.

"You fucking piece of shit!" I snarled as I stormed through the bushes toward him and cracked him hard across the face, not caring that his cock was half-hard and fresh seed glimmered in the palm of his right hand. I'd taken him straight to orgasm right along with me, and I hadn't even meant to do it. "Who gave you permission to watch?"

"You called to *me*!" he screamed back, gritting his teeth and putting his clean hand up to the palm print on his face. "I was patrolling the area and *you* whispered that you needed my help."

"I never called to you," I said, wondering if I'd somehow made a mistake and project my need to every person in the immediate vicinity. Ugh, if that was the case then Rosinée and Papa Cocodril would've felt it, too.

"You did," Rafe repeated, but I didn't have time to argue. I'd gotten what I needed and it was time to make a trade—a baby for a key. At least this trade was a fair shade better than the fairytales—I didn't have to give my own firstborn up, simply help another have her own. That much, I could do.

"Forget it. Go home, Raphael LeRoux, I can find my own way back from here." Without waiting for a response from him, I whirled on my heel and stalked back to the swamp shack that held *my damn* key.

It appeared my magic *had* bled out a little more than intended, as Rosinée and Papa Cocodril were frantically mauling each other when I stepped back through the door. She was straddling his lap and his hands were buried deep inside her voluminous skirts while their tongues wrestled one another.

Pausing a moment, I cleared my throat.

"Quickly, girl," Rosinée panted, arching her neck and holding the amulet out to me. "Quickly while the magic is still fresh."

My eyes narrowed at her as I stretched my wet fingers forward. "The key?" I reminded her, pausing before touching the decorated chicken's foot.

"On the table. Now *hurry up* so me husband can put a baby in my belly." She shook the charm at me even as Papa Cocodril's lips made their way down the line of her throat.

With my free hand, I snatched the key from the table

where she had left it for me, then touched my two fingers, wet with the product of my orgasm, to her charm. Magic visibly sparked and hissed as my juices met the chicken foot and then it was done.

"Yes," Rosinée groaned in ecstasy, "yes, I can feel my body come alive again. Go, Veil Keeper. You'll find your Spear in the old Saint Louis Cemetery. Look for an angel watching over the dead; she be holding your treasure."

"Wait, then where do I use the key?" I demanded, but it was too late. The swamp witch and her magical lover were rapidly shedding clothes and I knew there would be no more discussion until they were done copulating.

It could take hours, and that was time I didn't have. Hopefully, the keyhole would be obvious when we got there.

"Pleasure doing business with you," I muttered, leaving the shack and closing the door firmly behind me even as the distinctive grunts and moans of their babymaking followed me out into the bayou.

Placing the key tight between my teeth, I dove headfirst back into the water and began making my way back to the point I'd entered. Hopefully Rafe had followed my directive to leave as I was in *no* mood to speak with him. It'd be a long walk back to Wild Hunt land, but it could be just what I needed to clear the anger I felt toward him. He had intruded on a private moment with my Lords, regardless of their physical presence, and it was an offense that could not be lightly forgiven.

When I arrived back to the dock where I'd left my

clothing though, I found Amelie waiting for me.

"Successful trip?" she asked with an easy smile, and I let her help me out of the water. I took the key from between my teeth and held it up, grinning.

"Nice work, girl. You really are gonna save us all, huh?" Amelie chuckled and handed me my clothes so I could dress. "Rafe came running through here with his tail between his legs a few minutes ago. Asked me to see you safe back to the faery boys. Everything okay there?"

"No," I replied, "it's not. But I will deal with your alpha another day. Tonight, I have a Spear to find and some memories to retrieve."

As much as I wanted to feel excited, or even simply optimistic about the retrieval of one-fourth of my lost memories, I simply couldn't muster anything more than a grimace.

Was I really prepared to take the bad with the good? From the shards of memory I had regained on my own, there was no shortage of bad.

Was I strong enough to endure it all over again?

Chapter Eighteen

CIARAH

The boys must have sent a message ahead, because when the four of us arrived back to The Wild Hunt clubhouse, my entire Hunt was ready and waiting.

"Keeper," Fionn greeted me with a respectful dip of his head, "lead us and we shall follow."

I cast my eyes over my Wild Hunt, all sat ready on their gleaming bikes, dressed in their club patches and bandanas. The older ones scowled, while the younger ones looked excited, but I knew in my heart that they would not betray me. Not tonight, anyway.

"Good," I replied from the back of Killian's bike. "Let's go then."

There was no real reason why we needed to go immediately, no reason except the burning urgency in me that something bad was coming.

My powers did not extend to the gift of prophecy, as far as I was aware, but the gnawing feeling in my gut warned of impending danger.

Without any further words, Killian turned his bike and lead the way out of the driveway with the rest of the club falling into position around us. No discussion was necessary. I'd told my Lords where we needed to go, and it was the rest of the Hunt's job to simply follow.

It wasn't until we were roaring down the I-10, on our way into New Orleans proper, that I was hit by a wave of *agony* which caused me to cry out.

Killian stopped his bike immediately, leaping off and grasping my face in his hands.

"What is it, *mon amour*? Speak to me," he urged. Around us, I sensed the rest of my Wild Hunt had stopped their bikes also, but only my Lords got off to surround me.

"Ciarah, *'tit fille*," Reece murmured, "what happenin'?"

I wanted to answer them, I did, but I couldn't. Pain, sorrow, and *fear* wracked my body and it was all I could do to sob and moan while my hands clutched at my head.

Come on, Ciarah. Get a grip, this pain is not your own. You have felt the cold sting of those claws rend your own flesh and survived. You can survive this ... this shadow. This echo.

Gasping for air, I forcefully loosened my grip on my hair then ground my teeth together as I looked to my Knights.

"Death," I croaked. "Fae are dying. Lots of them. They need my help, *our* help. If not to save their lives, then to save their souls. The creatures …" A violent shiver shuddered through me at even mentioning them. "The creatures responsible won't stop at killing their bodies. Once they achieve that, they will consume their souls and there will be nothing left to regenerate."

A shocked gasp rose from the club. It was the most unspeakable of punishments, for a fae soul to be consumed. Our race relied heavily on the recycling of old souls as very few new souls were ever created in Faerie.

It was my job, and my job *alone* to pass judgement on those who did not deserve to be recycled.

"Where?" Arlo growled, his glamour shimmering in and out of focus, betraying his heightened emotions.

"The Saint Louis Cemetery," I whispered, my eyes unfocused as I sought out the location of death and destruction in my mind. "They're waiting for me there. This is a trap."

"Then we can't go," Killian frowned. "These are the creatures who held you? Who tortured you for more than a century?" I smiled softly at him, even through the secondhand fear and agony I was plagued with. My Lord of Winter was a sharp one—nothing got past him.

"Yes." I nodded and he scowled, folding his leather clad arms over his muscular chest.

"Then we must get to the spear another way. It is too much of a risk, to let them near you again." His jaw was locked stubbornly and I felt a little bad for what I needed to do next.

They were concerned for my safety, and they had every right to be. These creatures had bested the Veil Keeper once before, and look how that had turned out …

But that was Gràinne, *not* Ciarah. Ciarah was the one who'd escaped them.

"I cannot, *will not*, abandon those fae to those vile bastards." I met Killian's defiant stare calmly as I threaded powerful, ancient magic into my words. "You will do as I command, and continue on this quest with me. Our duty demands we do everything in our power to save fae lives, and I will not accept retreat. Am I understood?"

Kill's eyes flashed with ice-cold fury, but I had layered so much magic into my voice that he was powerless to respond with anything but a curt nod. The same went for my other two Lords, as well as their comrades in arms.

As one, their eyes glowing bright with Keeper magic, the bikers kicked their rides back into gear and we proceeded towards the cemetery. This time, though, the silence of our ride was broken by Fionn's rough voice.

"And so we ride," he growled out, his voice carrying through the still night, and the rest of the Wild Hunt echoed him in unison.

Guilt sat in my throat like a grapefruit, making it impossible for me to respond. My Lords' anger was so palpable I could feel it radiating off them in waves.

Had I not just told myself that I would treat them with respect? Not to rule over them but to rule *with* them? And yet here I was, imposing my will on them and taking away their ability to choose for themselves.

I was no better than the Swamp Witch.

Hell, I was *worse*.

The first thing I noticed as we navigated the narrow streets of New Orleans on our way to the Saint Louis Cemetery, was the lack of people. Humans. They were nowhere to be seen.

Of course, it was several hours before dawn yet, but this was NOLA, a city which took 'never sleeping' to whole new heights, so the eerie lack of drunken humans was both a relief and a concern.

Could they feel the danger? I wouldn't have been surprised if they could … it was thick in the air like an impending hurricane.

From inside the walls of the burial ground, screams of dying fae echoed out to us, rattling my body and making me tense.

Not your body, not your pain, not your fear, Ciarah. You're strong. Powerful. They will not win, not this time.

The words repeated over and over in my head, and I wasn't even sure who spoke them. Me, or one of the previous Keepers. Whoever it was, I was thankful.

Those words helped me cling to sanity. They were the

life raft I needed to keep my focus and do what needed to be done.

Killian rolled his bike to a stop alongside Arlo, and I swung my leg off without waiting for his assistance. He was furious with me, and I didn't blame him, so I wasn't going to push the issue until we were safe.

"These creatures," I started, in a low voice intended for the ears of my Hunt only, "*feed* on fear. They cannot be harmed with human weapons, so do not waste your bullets shooting them." I eyed a couple of the older bikers who were loading and checking their handguns. "They will stop at nothing to make you afraid, and then they will prey on that emotion. *Don't let them*." I wove the magic of command into my voice once more. Whether it would work, I had no idea, but I *had to* hope.

Because without hope, those bastards may as well have won already.

The cemetery walls stretched out on either side of us, giants made of stone and topped with barbed wire. I remembered from my life as a human that there were numerous break-ins at this particular cemetery, looters and hoodoo practitioners defiling the sacred tombs of the dead. The city had this place on fucking *lockdown*.

As I stood there and peered up at the bright silver eye of the moon in the sky, my nostrils flared with the distinctly metallic scent of blood. Glancing to my left, I found the body of a policeman with his heart torn out, red splattered across the white walls of the cemetery and just *barely* visible in the shadows cast by the street lamps.

I remembered that, the sensation of having my beating heart torn from my chest. As the Veil Keeper, an immortal and invincible goddess of Faerie, it wasn't a death sentence … but it was *pain.* A heart is more than just an organ that pumps blood. It's the core of a person's being, the place where all their hopes and dreams, their love and their hate, their fears and their desires coalesce.

It was even worse than having my voice stolen from me and that was almost insufferable.

I glanced away from the comatose police officer. He was already dead, his soul gone, his flesh a shell of meat and blood that could do nothing for us now.

"The Wild Hunt *rides,*" I snarled and the men rushed the gate, snapping the heavy chains on the front with a pair of bolt cutters and pushing their way into the cemetery. I lagged behind, unfurling my wings from my back and tasting the air.

They were here.

They were fucking *everywhere.*

My body is unchained from the wall for the first time in months and I drop to the floor on my knees, weeping at the blessed feeling of being able to cross my arms over my chest, duck my head, curl my legs close.

It doesn't last.

The shadows swarm around me, dragging my head back in a fistful of claws, laying my body out on the floor with sheer force. They don't know the meaning of rape nor understand the appeal, but they fill every orifice I have with iron. It scalds and burns, makes my skin bubble and my body convulse.

I can't breathe; I can't speak; I can't even remember my own name anymore.

Blinking the vision away, I swiped my palms over my face and shook my head to clear it. *Fuck.* I'd been there all of two minutes and they were getting inside my head, summoning my worst nightmares to the surface.

"Psychological torture," I whispered as the boys followed me into the cemetery, weaving through the mess of mausoleums.

The pain of the fae wracked my body with violent tremors, made my teeth hurt, my throat tight, my muscles sore. But I was having a hard time finding anyone but the members of the Wild Hunt.

"They're here somewhere," I promised as I felt my men getting tense, amping up for violence that wasn't coming. They were dangerous beasts, these bikers at my back, dark fae with a thirst for blood. Once promised, it had to be sated. "I promise you—they're here."

I continued on, looking at all the locks, feeling the key in my hand and wondering which one. Because the sooner I could solve this puzzle, the sooner the spear was mine, and the sooner we could leave. My captors, they weren't the type to be easily conquered. I knew right away that we'd be better off *running.*

The men might not like it, but once I gave the order, they'd have no choice but to submit.

I kept walking, my Lords to my right, my left, one of them behind me. In the front, I had Fionn and his officers to guard me. Franky, I didn't care *what* happened to my physical body so long as I got the spear. Pain was nothing but currency to me now, and I could *horde* it like the world's richest businessman.

Rounding a corner, I felt my heart contract in my chest as I gazed up at an angel statue with a spear clutched tight in her stony hands, face raised to an unhearing god.

Hah.

What a concept.

There were no gods above, only those that walked amongst men.

Nostrils flaring, I continued forward as if I hadn't seen a damn thing, as if any stone weapon in that cemetery—and there were lots of them—would do to satisfy me.

As we approached the base of the mausoleum, I turned and abruptly flapped my wings behind me, rising into the air and finding myself face to face with a lock made of iron. *Fuck.* But I wasn't about to give up now.

Instead, I thrust the key into the lock and turned it, freeing the stone hand from its eternal grasp as my right hand lashed out and curled around the base of the spear.

"Seems we didn't condition you quite enough," a voice said, but before I could even recognize who it was that was speaking, a wave of power washed over me, hot and scalding, like tiny fires were melting my skin like wax.

I fell from the sky, wings curling around me in pain, the spear rolling across the grass. I glanced up as Killian lunged for it … and found himself wrapped in *talons*. A massive spread of dirty wings filled the sky as my Lord of

Winter was lifted off the ground and tossed across the cemetery, his body slamming into the stone wall of a crypt, blood spurting from between his lips.

It was a fucking harpy.

Rolling onto my stomach, I pushed to my feet as shadows danced around me, not memories this time but the creatures from my endless torture, my captors, my jailers. Their voices so foreign, they may as well have been alien, these strange scraping sounds like nails on the inside of a coffin, like a corpse being dragged across cement.

Clamping my hands over my ears, I struggled to fight back the rush of emotion, bile rising in my throat as shadowy fingers played over the curve of my wings, tugging and threatening, bringing to life memories of them being rent from my flesh.

With a gasp, I shifted them off and fell forward onto my knees. Those shadow creatures wasted no time swarming me once more, kicking me while I was down. The only advantage was that they needed to take physical form to attack me, even if it was only their limbs and teeth.

Gritting my own teeth, I steeled myself against the fear of memories and focused on the fight at hand. There was simply too much at stake to let these bastards win.

The next time one of them swiped at me with razor-like claws, my hand snapped out and I seized its wrist. They had no genders, no individual identities, or at least not so far as I could tell. They were all simply *it*, so when

I grabbed *it* by the wrist and slammed my magic into it, I was shocked to hear the almost feminine scream that tore from the hood shrouding its face.

The surprise was just enough that I loosened my grip for just a second, allowing the thing to wrench free and another of them to sink a long, dagger-like claw deep into my side.

My scream echoed through the night, in harmony with the grunts, curses and cries of the battling fae around me.

So far as I could tell, there were only a handful of the nightmare creatures here; the rest were all harpies. Good, in a way. Harpies could be hurt, *killed.* If only my Wild Hunt weren't so outnumbered …

Some distance from me, at the base of the mausoleum which I had just liberated my spear from, Arlo was locked in a bloody fight with three harpies and bathed in blood. Desperately, I hoped it was harpy blood, but in my heart I knew it was his.

My men were being overpowered by sheer numbers and I could do little to help them while being attacked by the five nightmares who'd come to retrieve what they failed to extract from me for *so many* years.

"Who is behind this?" I demanded of the creatures, as I clutched my bleeding side and rolled to dodge another knife-sharp claw swipe. "Who is pulling your strings?"

"I think we liked you better without that tongue," a hissing, raspy voice replied from one of the shadows, and I just barely reacted quick enough to avoid my throat being sliced. "Stand still and we can rectify that."

"Not on your fucking life," I growled, letting my instincts take over as I conjured a ball of burning magic and lobbed it straight into the black, moth eaten fabric that clothed a nightmare.

The thing screeched, but evaporated into smoke, only to reappear some dozen or so feet away. Judging by the heavy wave of *fear* it hurled back at me, it was *pissed.*

My jaw clenched hard, my teeth grinding together as I steeled myself to weather the onslaught of memories. Some real, some fabricated. That was how this torture worked: they took your worst fears, your worst terrors, and made you relive them over and over, each time making them *worse*.

Not that my memories needed any enhancement. The torture I'd endured at the hands of these creatures was as bad as it could physically get, and I really only remembered a fraction of it all.

Sharp needles of iron littered my naked flesh as I hung useless from the wall shackles. Glancing down at my body through heavy, pain addled eyes, I saw them bristling from my skin like some sort of sick porcupine.

"This is just the beginning, Keeper," a smoky, raspy voice hissed at me from the depths of a black hood. "We do not age, we do not die, we do not measure time in the ways of your people. This pain will be forever lasting, and this is just a mere taste. It will become worse. Oh, so very much worse for you ... just wait until we start on those pretty, pretty wings of yours." The laugh the creature barked out was pure sadism and I was powerless to

prevent the wash of fear flooding through me.

Not my wings! How can I survive if they harm my wings?

"Mmmmm," the creature moaned, "sweet, sweet fear. This will be fun for us, until you hand over the information our mistress requires."

The memory faded out as I fought back, blinking my eyes rapidly to regain my vision of the cemetery. The battle still raged, but my men were alive—for now—so it can't have been more than a split-second.

That particular memory had been an early one, from not long past Gràinne's initial capture, but it had given me a little clue …

"Your mistress," I panted, climbing back to my feet and narrowly avoiding another nightmare creature. A small part of my brain told me they didn't have very accurate vision so if I kept calm, I should be able to avoid their attacks for the most part. It was why they kept their captives bound so tightly.

"Who is she?" I demanded, but got nothing back except maniacal laughter.

This battle needed to end; I couldn't allow it to continue any longer for fear of losing any *more* fae. None of my Hunt were dead—*yet*—but I could sense several of them were injured *badly* and around a dozen fae had been slaughtered here before we arrived.

My men fought in the narrow corridors between above ground burial sites, so I couldn't see them, but I could sense them. More than that, I could sense my spear.

Now that my hand had come in contact with it, it was *bound* to me and I knew beyond a shadow of a doubt that I could *not* let these bastards hand it over to their mistress, whoever the fuck she was.

Ducking and weaving between shadow creatures, I made my way back to where I had last seen the ancient artifact and sucked in a gasp when I found it.

"*Drop that spear immediately*," I bellowed at the harpy who had it clutched in her claws and was using it to stab Reece repeatedly in the gut.

My Autumn Lord was pinned to the ground between two crumbling tombs with a harpy on each arm while the third was perforating his torso with the Spear of Lug. Blood was *everywhere,* but I could still sense his light. It wasn't *as* bright as it had been but it was still there.

Distracted as I was by the sight before me, I wasn't paying attention to the shadows which had followed me, and I cried out when five deep gashes opened down the length of my back, slicing through my fragile wings. *When had I shifted them back on?* It hadn't been a conscious choice. No, the shadows had spurred me to it with those memories, those nightmares.

It didn't matter though. This was an immortal body and would heal in time, and with enough power from the souls of sinners. Their attacks no longer meant anything to me, all I needed was to retrieve my spear, and save my Lords.

Sucking a deep breath into my lungs, I gathered magic into my core, then sent it snapping out of me in a pulse which threw the shadows a good distance away from me and would hopefully leave them stunned for long enough.

The harpies paused when my magic pulse washed over them, and looked up at me in terror. It had only been designed to take out the shadows, so hadn't thrown the winged bitches in the same way but it was enough to give them pause.

"*I said, drop that damn spear,*" I ordered them, my voice booming through the cemetery and shaking some bricks loose. To my satisfaction, they seemed afraid.

Chittering something in their own language, the two holding Reece down took to the sky and quickly disappeared, leaving the one clutching my spear to face me alone.

She froze under my glare, holding her twisted claws in the air and releasing the spear, which dropped to the ground with a metallic sounding clang. She chittered something that was probably along the lines of "*please don't hurt me*" but this bitch had been stabbing *my Lord of Autumn* and that did *not* go unpunished.

Letting my wings flap painfully, I closed the distance between us in the blink of an eye and seized her ugly face between my palms.

"You have been found guilty of the most heinous crimes against Fae. The attempted murder of the Keeper's Knight is a crime punishable by death and consumption. May your soul never find peace." My voice was that of the Keeper. Ancient and *powerful*.

Placing my lips close to her bloodied fangs, I ignored her frantic thrashing and screaming as I *sucked* her soul straight from her body without first killing her physical form. This was the worst pain a fae could ever endure, and a skill I *alone* possessed.

Within moments, her thrashing ceased, and her body fell limp in my grip as I consumed every last scrap of her rotten soul and let it fuel my own healing. Once finished, I tossed her empty husk aside and watched it crumble to dust against *Jean Baptiste Arlington*'s burial plot.

"Ciarah," Reece gasped, blood bubbling from his lips and I crouched over him.

"Shhh, love," I whispered, not allowing myself the tears that I cried on the inside, "I will help you soon. First we must end this fight."

I could feel waves of terror flooding the cemetery and knew the shadows had recovered from my magical pulse. But I had a feeling I also knew what would beat them.

Wrapping my bloody fingers around the Spear of Lug, I stood and turned to face them as they approached, rushing down the narrow corridor of crypts.

Maintaining my calm, despite my almost overwhelming fear for Reece, I hefted the spear in my hand and let my magic trickle down its length. My eyes narrowed, and I took aim at the shadow closest to me … then *threw.*

The Spear of Lug, shimmering with the magic of the Keeper, flew true and impaled the nightmare creature, pinning it to a concrete wall.

It did not matter that they were made of mist and shadow, of fear and death. The Spear of Lug transcended the laws of physics and when combined with my own ancient magic … the shadows stood no chance.

The empty looking black robe howled and thrashed against the tomb wall where it was pinned, the sound of its death grating against my ears like nails down a chalkboard until eventually … it died.

"Not possible," one of the other creatures hissed, but every one of them had frozen to watch their companion expire.

"And yet …" another whispered.

I raised an eyebrow at the remaining creatures, *daring* them to try me again, but as one, they faded to smoke and disappeared completely from the cemetery, taking their oppressive fear magic with them.

A long, loud howl rose up from somewhere nearby, followed by several more. The wolves were here, and in perfect timing to help us dispose of the harpies.

The shadows may have left, but we still had several dozen of those vicious winged bitches tearing into my men and they required sentencing. Fae law was brutal, but necessary. Each and every one of them had broken that law when they sought to harm The Wild Hunt, and each and every one of them would pay the price in blood.

Not one would leave the sacred burial grounds alive.

"Were you looking for backup by chance?" Rafe asked, kneeling on the top of a nearby crypt. My gaze flicked to him and I frowned slightly. I wasn't going to forget what happened in the swamp anytime soon. Even if he had heard my call, that didn't give him the excuse to watch me. Papa Cocodril and Rosinée hadn't come running. If he'd had needs to take care of, he could've taken care of them without watching me.

"I'm not in the mood to see or talk with you right now," I said, turning back to the open space in the center of the tombs, this grassy area that gave us a battleground amongst the dead. Bitching at Raphael LeRoux sounded like a good time, but I had more important things to worry about.

Like winged demon women.

And …

My heart thumped in my throat as I glanced over at the dead shadow.

Thump, thump … freeze.

I couldn't breathe anymore, one hand flying to my chest, my eyes widening as I thought I saw something that I couldn't possibly be seeing.

The black shadows around the creature I'd killed with the spear disintegrated, drifting away in the cool breeze like mist, the silver moonlight catching in the supernatural fog and glimmering brightly. As the swirling darkness dissipated, I found myself looking at a familiar face …

"Mom?" I whispered, the sight of her gently wrinkled face, disheveled brunette curls, and thin, wide mouth … It shook me deep inside. I could hardly remember who I was or where I was.

Suddenly, I was just Ciarah O'Rourke, nineteen year old loser with nobody and nothing. I had a mom who beat me, who blamed me if her boyfriends tried to fuck me, a heroin addict and a drunk …

She was an all-around horrible human being.

But … had I just killed her?!

Stumbling forward, I put my hands on the belly of the woman I'd just stabbed, my fingers curling around the handle of the spear, sweaty and shaking, my grip weak and trembling.

“Mom?” I asked again, squinting up at her face, blood draining down from my scalp and into my eyes. Standing this close, my fingers tangled in a dirty white t-shirt with the name of the bar where I'd used to work—Sweet, Sweet Times. The low slung jeans, a pair of boots that I recognized as being my own, as being Ciarah's.

Even the smell of her perfume was familiar: Kim Kardashians' Fleur Fatale. I'd *always* hated that smell. When she was fucked off on heroine, she didn't get dressed to go out, didn't even shower and she *reeked* of BO.

I'd always thought *that* was the worst smell I'd ever breathe in my life.

But then I got older and she started going out more, and when she went out she drank. When she drank, she brought home men that tried to touch me. That, or she hit me herself.

So fuck that perfume.

Yanking on the handle of the spear, I stumbled back and into Killian. He caught me in a flutter of black leather, the musky scent of male, and the sharp metallic reek of blood. I dropped the spear, knowing he would grab it, and lunged forward, grabbing my mother's body before it could hit the ground.

I laid her out before me, the screeching and cackling of the harpies a distant echo behind me. I was too busy gazing at the woman I'd hated my whole life … a piece of my broken past chasing me into my new one. Reborn in a new body, I *shouldn't* have my fucking human memories. That was not the way rebirth worked. Centuries of shattered memories, of love and loss and pain, stacking on top of one another, life after life … that was not something many souls could endure without sinking into perpetual madness.

But the previous Veil Keeper had had no choice. To lock *her* memories away, hide the knowledge of the Veil from me and thus from my captors, she had to give me a mind to keep, an identity.

I'd been gifted Ciarah.

So new body, new life … still Ciarah O'Rourke, native New Orleanian and *human*.

Human, human, human.

Weak.

Putting my fingers on the side of my mother's neck, I felt for her purse. Killian was beside me, kneeling down, desperately trying to draw my attention.

But I couldn't look at him right then. In my confused state, I almost forgot who *he* was.

"*Mon Dieu, Le Gardien,*" he whispered, reaching out and trying to take my arm. I jerked away from him, this little voice in the back of my mind *screaming* for me to get up and go find Reece, find Arlo, make sure my Lords were alive.

I couldn't.

I couldn't move, couldn't think straight, couldn't remember what I was supposed to be doing.

"Mom, I'm sorry," I whispered, tears rolling down my cheeks as I reached out and covered her wound with both hands, smearing blood everywhere. *Like, why am I in a cemetery? What was I doing with a fucking spear?! And my mom ... she can't be dead. She just can't. I didn't get a chance to say goodbye, to tell her I hated her ... to tell her I loved her, too.*

"We need you out there," a voice growled from beside me, a man's hand curling around my bicep. My gut reaction was to jerk away from him violently, tearing my arm from his grip and simultaneously sending him flying with a surge of power I didn't understand, knocking him against the side of a crypt with a hard crack.

The red-eyed, silver-haired man I just threw came at me again, but this time, as he did, he became a wolf, knocking me away from my mom's corpse and onto my back. I hit him, punched him, clawed at his face while I screamed.

"*Wake up Veil Keeper!*" he roared, hot wolfy breath in my face.

"Get off of her!" a man in a black trench coat screamed, shoving the wolf.

"Look, dude, I don't want any trouble," I said, grabbing the fucking ancient ass looking spear off the ground. *Who the hell carries around a spear in this day and age?* I wondered, eyes wide as I flicked my gaze around the St. Louis Cemetery. How the *fuck* did I get here? And how had I ended up stabbing Mom? "You come near me again and I'll kill you!"

My attention flicked to the right and I found some big dude in a leather jacket getting ripped in *half* by two women with wings instead of arms?!

WHAT THE FUCK?!

Taking the spear with me, I turned and ran as strange ripping sensations tore through my soul. "*Fae are dying!*" something whispered in my ear and I screamed as a woman with long dark hair tackled me and knocked me on my back, the teal streak in her hair sliding forward and brushing over my face. She had huge, vibrant butterfly wings on her back and a face with wide green eyes.

"Get the fuck off of me," I growled, swinging the spear up to hit her. The weapon went right through the woman's body, making her image ripple like a reflection on the surface of a lake. "What the …?"

"*You need to collect yourself, Ciarah O'Rourke. Get up and fight for your Wild Hunt—you are their Queen!*"

"No, I'm nobody's queen," I breathed, trying to push the woman off of me. But my hands went through her again.

"*Yes, you are. The Wild Hunt belongs to the spirit who inhabits this immortal vessel.*"

"Who are you?" I asked, but it was starting to come back to me …

My own death.

My rebirth

Years of pain.

An alleyway with zero memories to draw from.

My Lords.

The hallucination of … Gràinne? myself? the essence of the Veil Keeper? … disappeared. Panting, I shoved myself to my feet and ran straight into Killian and Rafe. I hit Kill's hard chest and bounced off, his arms steadying me as I held the spear out to one side.

"Ciarah's mother is here," I said, choking on the words. "She … I killed her." Blinking at Killian and then flicking my eyes briefly to the silver wolf at his side, I managed to get out the question whose answer I was afraid to here. "It's not really her, right? A hallucination?"

"Oh, *cher*," Kill breathed and I knew. I knew without him having to say it.

It really was my mother.

"Those shadows are wraiths, *Le Gardien.* They only have a physical form if they attached themselves to a human's body. It's the only way they have any influence on people or objects in *this* realm."

I stared at him and wondered how it could possibly be a coincidence that Ciarah's mother would show up here.

There was no chance.

This was not a coincidence.

A shock of agony rippled through me as another faerie met their match at the hands of the harpies … and the shadows, they were back.

My Lords.

Both Arlo and Reece were on the roof of the tallest crypt, their blood dripping down the sides of the cement structure.

A woman was with them, a bemused smile on her face.

"Hello Veil Keeper," she said, her long red hair hanging down on either side of her face, pooling on the roof of the mausoleum beneath her feet. "Or should I call you Ciarah?"

Jogging over to the base of the crypt, I swept my wings out and snapped them close, rising to the roof of the nearest building. The horde of harpies had fanned out behind the woman … and the shadows that'd retreated … they took up all the dark places around her, every nook and cranny, every bit of dark covered and protected from the silver moonlight.

"You brought my mother here?" I asked, and she smiled.

"She's no longer your mother. You understand that, don't you? You are no longer the human girl you once were, you're a fae woman now. A fae woman with awful memories and the poison of torture clogging your brain. You have responsibilities you never asked for, duties you never needed."

"Give me my lords," I told her, my voice surprisingly calm. I was so focused on the woman standing on the nearby crypt that I didn't bother to look when the sound of nails crashing around the roof next to me echoed through the cemetery.

Raphael was no ordinary wolf—he'd just *leapt* up to join me.

Killian appeared on my other side, teeth gritted in frustration, blue eyes narrowed.

"Who is this?" I asked him because I had the feeling the woman wasn't about to introduce herself.

"Queen Medbh," he whispered, pronouncing the name *Mayv.*

"Honored you remembered, Lord of Frost," she said, her voice soft, at odds with the hardness in her face. But she didn't *look* like a bad guy. No, she looked soft and sweet and strong—despite the fact that my men were bleeding on the ground in front of her. And *she* was looking at *me* like I was the one at fault here. "I'd thought perhaps my memory might be lost with time, but it seems like your parents have passed along the knowledge of me?"

"Give me my lords," I repeated, because I wasn't about to stand here and have a conversation with this woman while two of my men bled.

Several of the harpies dropped down to the crypt roof, one of them turning Reece over with her massive bird's feet, black talons shimmering as she stood over his body, straddling him.

My throat tightened and my fingers squeezed the spear so hard that if it hadn't been a magical artifact, I most certainly would've broken it.

"If she touches him …" I warned because harpies had reputations for rape, torture, and disease. Even a sex god wouldn't hold up to the rancid diseases she could pass on.

"You'll what, Ciarah?" the woman said, still staring at me like I was the filth of the earth. "You don't exactly seem to have a lot of options right now. If you want these men back, if you want to leave the cemetery with the rest of your hunt, you'll listen to my proposition. Give me the Spear of Lug, and we'll leave you and yours in the exact condition you are now."

She paused and her mouth got wide and tight.

"Resist and we'll have to see how your man fares under the pussy of a harpy."

I stood there for all of a millisecond.

And then I attacked her.

Chapter Nineteen

KILLIAN

The False Queen had barely finished her words before Ciarah was flying at her like a harpoon. Her wings beat one powerful push and she was hurtling into the red-haired fairy with the force of a damn freight train.

The two of them disappeared from sight behind the crypt Ciarah had just propelled them off, but the sounds of their battle could be heard clearly.

The Alpha wolf and I exchanged a worried look, then both scrambled off the crypt to help Ciarah. Stupid woman still didn't have her memories, so she had *no idea* what she was up against in Medbh.

The one thing going for her, was that Medbh likely expected a magical attack and would have been totally caught off guard by Ciarah's brute force style.

Huh, I guess there was something to be said for her

lack of memories after all.

"Ciarah!" I called out, reaching the place where I would have assumed they'd landed, but finding nothing there. "*Chère?*"

"Cheap tricks," Raphael LeRoux growled, shifting halfway back to human and raising his nose to the air to sniff. "The Pretender doesn't have her full power in this realm, so she's using her host's magic to hide. They're still here somewhere, I can smell them."

"How do we help?" I asked him, furious that I had no idea myself. Every fibre of my being cried out to help my Lady but how could I when I couldn't find her?

"Check on your faery friends," the wolf snarled back at me. "Keep them safe from those harpy whores. If anything happens to them … well we're all as good as dead because the Veil Keeper's grief will tear this world in two."

I nodded tightly, but still didn't leave. How could I leave? *Mon amour* needed my help, I could feel it.

"Go!" The Alpha barked at me. "My wolves and I will assist the Keeper as best we can until Medbh's magic wears weak, which it will soon enough."

As he spoke, a half dozen more wolves skidded around the corner and trotted toward us and I nodded again. He was right, of course. Medbh's true form was still trapped in Faerie; she was only inhabiting the body of the witch she was in, and the amount of effort it would require meant she couldn't maintain it forever …

"When they reappear, yell for me," I commanded. My voice was thick with frost magic as was expected when the Lord of Winter gave an order, and Raphael dipped his head in respectful acknowledgement even as his lip curled with a snarl.

Not bothering to spare any more time discussing our best course of action, I raced back to where Arlo and Reece had been held by those disgusting bird women.

Using my ice magic, which I'd felt grow stronger since Ciarah had accepted me as her Lord, I built a short staircase which allowed me to run straight up to the crypt roof where they lay bleeding and unconscious.

Most of the harpies had taken off and were flapping around above us like the bunch of confused vultures they were. Without their Mistress guiding them, they were clueless fucking birdbrains. The only one still following their directive was the leader, the grotesque bird-woman who was straddling Reece's pale form while licking blood off the side of his face.

Not wasting my breath on words, I threw myself forward and ploughed a fist into the side of her face. Fucking harpies were stupid bitches though, and she simply held on to Reece's body with her claws and took the punch like she were a sand bag.

"Let him go," I demanded, standing over Arlo's prone form even as I formed little daggers of ice in my palms and stabbed them into the harpy's torso.

Those bitches were insanely hard to kill, they needed to be totally decapitated and I didn't want to risk hurting Reece when he wasn't able to get out of the way. Not to mention, I seriously doubted my ice would be sharp enough to sever a harpies head.

Whatever Medbh had hit the guys with had to have been strong to keep them down this long, but I could only hope it sapped a good chunk of her borrowed magic and she wouldn't have much left to fight Ciarah.

"Kill!" Fionn yelled from the ground below us. "Catch!"

Glancing down to our club president, I held out my hand and snatched the heavy iron sword he tossed up to me.

"Très bon, this will do nicely," I nodded, and the harpy squawked something. Her eyes widened at the sharp blade in my hand, and I saw a moment of indecision cross her ugly fucking face.

She was either going to use Reece's body as a shield or …

"Yes," I grinned as she took the other route, dropping Reece and frantically flapping her wings to try and get high enough that I couldn't reach her.

Like I said, harpies were stupid bitches.

Pushing off the roof of the crypt, I jumped and caught her by the scaly ankle, yanking her back down to the concrete surface with me. Her talons raked deep gouges down my arm, but I ignored them.

Throwing the vile creature down on her back, I wasted no time on pleasantries before slamming Fionn's ancient blade down across her scrawny neck.

Rancid fluid sprayed out across the roof. It was the harpy's version of blood, but instead of metallic scented redness, it was black and putrid, as thick as oil. The other harpies screamed their rage as both Reece and I were bathed in the foul-smelling liquid.

As soon as this was all over, we'd both have to get some seriously powerful shots.

Harpy blood was *almost* as pungent and diseased as harpy pussy.

Their male counterparts … were even *worse.*

Thankfully there were none here. Male harpies were weak as hell, but the diseases they carried were *magical* in nature and virtually impossible to get rid of.

Reece muttered something in French that I couldn't hear as he struggled to his feet, bloody as hell and covered in enough wounds that I knew for a fact he was going to need about a *dozen* shots to get over the rush of harpy bacteria.

"Beck moi tchew," Reece snarled, his glamour cracked to pieces, gold skin glimmering under the moonlight—even with the blood and the harpy fluid. With a single wave of his hand, he sent sex magic coursing through the sea of harpies. The screams they let out … were sickening, like they were being ripped apart from the inside out.

I had no idea *what* he was doing to them, but whatever it was, it kept them away from Arlo long enough for me to turn him over.

He wasn't breathing.

"Fuck," I cursed as I felt that first flicker in the ripple of the Wild Hunt's magic that said he'd *just* stopped breathing, that he was dying. We'd already lost at least five members, maybe more. I wasn't the Veil Keeper so it was hard to say for sure, but I could feel those losses to our numbers like knives to the gut. "Arlo, you *caca boudin*," I growled, calling him a *shit sausage* and praying like hell to the Veil-damned Keeper that he was going to wake up and start insulting me right back.

He didn't move.

In fact, he was so mutilated below the belt that I wasn't sure he *could.*

It looked like the harpies had … torn his cock off. It was hard to tell with the mess of blood and rent flesh. Putting my hands on either side of his face, I closed my eyes.

"Watch my back, Reece," I growled and then I dropped into Arlo's body to heal him.

His injuries were … extensive.

"*Merde,*" I cursed, and then I sunk so deeply into him that I forgot I had a voice, a body. I *became* the magic, curling into my brother's body like mist rolling over the bayou. All the places he was injured burned like bright flames in the distance, beckoning me.

When I'd healed Ciarah that first night, I'd seen a lot.

There were twice as many now. Three times.

Starting in the worst place—Arlo's mutilated genitals—I healed him, funneling my magic into his body and realizing as I did so that I didn't have enough to save him. Not without giving something *else* up.

Damn it, Arlo, I snarled inside my own head, knowing what I was going to have to do.

The Veil Keeper had just returned, something my people had been waiting on for hundreds of years. At the tender age—at least for a fae—of thirty-five, I perhaps didn't understand *all* of their elation or what treasures waited on the opposite side of the Veil, but I knew I was witnessing a monumental occasion, something that would live on in legend for centuries or even millennia to come.

And I wasn't going to get to see it.

Gathering up every ounce of power I had, I thrust it into Arlo's body and heard him gasp ... just before my own heart seized violently in my chest and my breathing stopped.

"You fucking idiot!" Arlo was screaming as I tilted to one side, and he caught me just before I plunged off the edge of the crypt to the cemetery ground. "What have you done?!"

You'd have done the same for me, I thought as my eyes slid closed and I felt my spirit disconnecting from my body with a sharp rending, like I was tumbling over the edge of a cliff. As the Veil Keeper was literally the *keeper* of all faerie souls, I found myself drawn right to her.

As soon as Ciarah judged my soul, if she found me worthy, I'd be reborn into the body of another fae, all my memories wiped clean. There was some comfort in that, knowing that perhaps I'd get to see Ciarah's rise to power in another form.

But there was nothing I could do but accept my fate, my consciousness whipped through the air by forces much greater than my own power.

A sea of ghostly faces surrounded *Le Gardien* as she fought with Medbh, a faerie queen I recognized from the stories of older fae. She was known as the False Queen, taking kingdoms without rulers and making them her own.

It seemed she'd also tried to take over the Veil Keeper's rule.

She was pisse-froid—literally piss-cold.

My spirit came to rest in a horde around the Veil Keeper's, blocked from reaching her by Medbh's magic.

"*We need to help,*" I said, and several of the other ghostly faces turned toward me.

I could talk.

I could move.

The others could see and hear me.

For all intents and purposes, I found myself in the form of a … ghost? A lost spirit?

Whatever I was, I wasn't corporal and I couldn't touch.

Ciarah and Medbh rolled right through me, as if I weren't there. Turning to follow their tussle, I saw blood, a knife sticking out of the Veil Keeper's shoulder as she locked her hand around the False Queen's throat and picked her up from the cemetery ground.

"Killian!" she called out, lifting her hand up and beckoning me forward. "Come to me!"

Moving forward, I reached out a hand … and found Ciarah's fingers curling around my own. She yanked me forward and *inside* of her. Not the way I'd enjoyed being inside of her before, but … my spirit melted with her body and ice crackled at her fingertips.

Medbh threw us off and into the side of a crypt, agonizing pain shooting through Ciarah's body. I wanted nothing more in that moment than to heal her. Instead, I felt her draw from me, pulling ice magic out to throw at the fae woman in her stolen witch body.

The other spirits surrounded us, putting their hands on the Veil Keeper's body, sending power and magic surging through her.

The Veil Keeper rose to her feet with me as a passenger and took off at Medbh, channeling all of her borrowed magic into one blow. She hit the woman with a surprising amount of force, sending the witch's body tumbling into a sea of shadows and wolves as Raphael's pack fought for the upper hand.

I supposed *he* would have to tell *Le Gardien* about our strange history together.

Goddess knew I wasn't going to get a chance.

I relaxed into Ciarah's control, the magic that was a part of my very soul traveling from my spirit and into hers. She hit Medbh with one more burst of magic and froze her in place, shackling her to the ground amidst all the fighting. Ciarah then lunged forward and fell to her knees next to the struggling witch, pulling the knife from her shoulder and shoving it into the woman's throat.

A short, brutal time later and her head was separated from her shoulders.

A swirl of power came from the woman's neck, twisting in the air like a snake before it solidified into the shape of a woman.

"Veil Keeper, your time is past. New order reigns in Faerie. Accept that and stay here, rule with your remaining lords over humanity. You could be gods *this side of the veil."*

"We are gods both sides of the Veil," Ciarah yelled out, in a voice that was a mix of both mine *and* hers. With a wave of her hand, she sent the spirits around us away.

None of them came to her, so I knew they'd been sent for rebirth.

"I can restore your Lord of Winter if you enter into a fae's bargain with me," the spirit of Medbh announced, but Ciarah was done and with another wave of her hand, the woman shimmered … and disappeared.

But where the other souls had been quickly judged and sent along, Medbh's 'spirit' was simply a trick of light and magic. The woman herself—body and soul—were safely locked on the other side of the Veil, beyond our reach.

As soon as she disappeared though, the shadows went with her.

"Your spear, Veil Keeper," Rafe said, naked and dripping blood. He handed the weapon over and watched as Ciarah took it in shaking hands. She was so badly injured, it was killing me to know I had to leave her.

I could feel her holding me in place, using her body to keep my soul on earth.

But I couldn't stay here.

The longer I sat there, the less I seemed to remember. Memories leapt away from my fingers, as slippery as the frogs in the bayou that Reece used to catch as a child. It was time for me to go, whether or not Ciarah wanted to release me.

I need to go, Cher, I started, but she was shaking her head.

No, Killian, she growled, turning and bounding up the ice steps I'd left next to the crypt.

But even if she wanted me to stay, I didn't have much choice.

Once my spirit started to fade, she'd have no choice but to judge me and send me on my way.

Goodbye, le Gardien, I said, and then I forced myself out of her body … and away.

Chapter Twenty

CIARAH

"Killian!" I screamed, reaching out for his spirit at the same moment I slammed my fist onto the chest of his comatose form, restarting his heart with a burst of power that seemed to travel from the Spear of Lug, into me, and then out of my fingertips.

My other hand literally *grabbed* his soul and jerked it back, shoving it into his body as he choked and gasped and struggled against my grip. I couldn't blame him—a spirit's natural desire was to move on. He was simply trying to follow the natural order of things.

But I was the Veil Keeper, and I was all about bending the natural order to my whim.

Mine.

The word echoed in my head as Killian rolled to his side and pushed up to his knees, chocking and coughing, his skin rippling as he dug his nails into the cement roof of the crypt.

"How?" he gasped out as I dug my fingers into his hair, leaning close to the top of his head. I didn't care about the blood or whatever the rancid black goo was that covered him.

"I have the power to judge souls," I said as he lifted his blue eyes to mine. "I also have the power to put them back where they belong. You gave all your magic to Arlo to save him—your body wasn't damaged, just too empty of power to keep your soul tethered. All I had to do was give a little bit back."

"A little bit," Killian choked out, exhaling with a shudder. "I feel like I could move mountains, *mon cher*."

"Thank da gods," Reece said, moving over to kneel beside me and Killian. "We for sure knew you'd be able to fight your way outta dis one, you. But Kill? He's as much proof of your miracle magic as anything I ever need to see."

Arlo, Rafe, Fionn, Dougall, and several of the other officers crowded around us.

"Those were your captors," Arlo grumbled—it wasn't a question.

"They were," I whispered, memories gnawing at the back of my mind, worse horrors that I hadn't yet uncovered on my own. But the Spear of Lug knew. It held some of the memories I needed in order to take control of the Veil again. “But they …”

My voice trailed off as I stood up and glanced down at all the bodies littering the ground. Some were mine, the fae of the Wild Hunt. The others were human, innocents dragged into this mess by the creatures of darkness, monsters I had no name for.

Heading down the steps, my Lords trailed behind me, Arlo supporting Killian's weak form. Raphael, Amelie, and Marcel followed after with my officers trailing behind. I made my way over to my mom's body and knelt down, fingers shaking as I reached out and brushed her hair from her forehead.

What an awful, awful trick, the type of cruelty that doesn't require knives or claws, blood or pain or bodies. Cruelty that kicks the heart, that rends the soul.

Leaning forward, I press a kiss to my mother's waxy forehead.

I don't know if she ever loved me, or if I even love her now … but … now I'll never get a chance to figure her out or talk to her or see what became of her after I died.

“Their ultimate act of cruelty,” I said, closing her glassy eyes and glancing back at the sea of bodies behind me. We needed to clean this mess up and get out of here before any humans stumbled onto us. Not that we couldn't handle them—just that I didn't want to.

I didn't want to hurt innocent people.

“We'll get da Veil Keeper back to da clubhouse,” Reece started as I exhaled and stood up. “And the boys'll take good care of your Mama for ya, no?”

"You're not the president yet, boy," Fionn said, standing nearby with his officers surrounding him. I heard Reece growl something under this breath about *bullshit club business,* but I didn't get to see the rest of the argument because a sharp, hot pain exploded from my fingers up my arm.

Glancing down, I realized the Spear of Lug was glowing.

And it was white-fucking-hot.

I tried to drop it, but my fingers were locked, like an electrical impulse keeping my muscles clamped tight. I opened my mouth to ask for help, and then, when the pain ratcheted up, to scream.

The glow from the spear exploded outward, like a bomb going off, killing my vision and blinding me at the same time. Flames rushed across my skin, convincing my mind that I was, in fact, being burned *alive.*

I fell to my knees, thrashing with the spear still clutched in my hands, feeling my body melt away in the raging flames of magic. It tore through my mind, seared my flesh, invaded my muscles. It was the *worst* physical pain I'd ever felt in my life, far worse than anything the shadows had ever done to me.

It made me want to die.

That wasn't exactly a thought I was unfamiliar with. Many times over my years in torture I'd wanted to die. Many times I'd felt cheated that the previous death had done anything but give me peace. And I wanted that, a new life, no memories ...

But now Ciarah O'Rourke was being given a second chance, a new life, an opportunity to make things better.

I wasn't about to lose that chance.

Flicking my eyes open, I used every ounce of strength and power I had left to drop the spear. As soon as I did, the pain stopped and I was left lying on the ground with my breath coming in frantic, wild bursts.

Pushing myself up, I glanced around ...

And found that I wasn’t in the cemetery anymore.

No, based on the lavender color of the sky, the strange trees with vibrant striped fruit ... and the faerie with skin the color of shadows and neon pink irises ... I had a feeling I wasn't even in the same realm.

The man in front of me knelt down and flashed me a smile with two sharp canines.

“Welcome to Faerie, Veil Keeper.”

To Be Continued ...

Coming Soon

Cruel Glamour

The Wild Hunt Motorcycle Club # 2

Flip the page for an excerpt of chapter one.

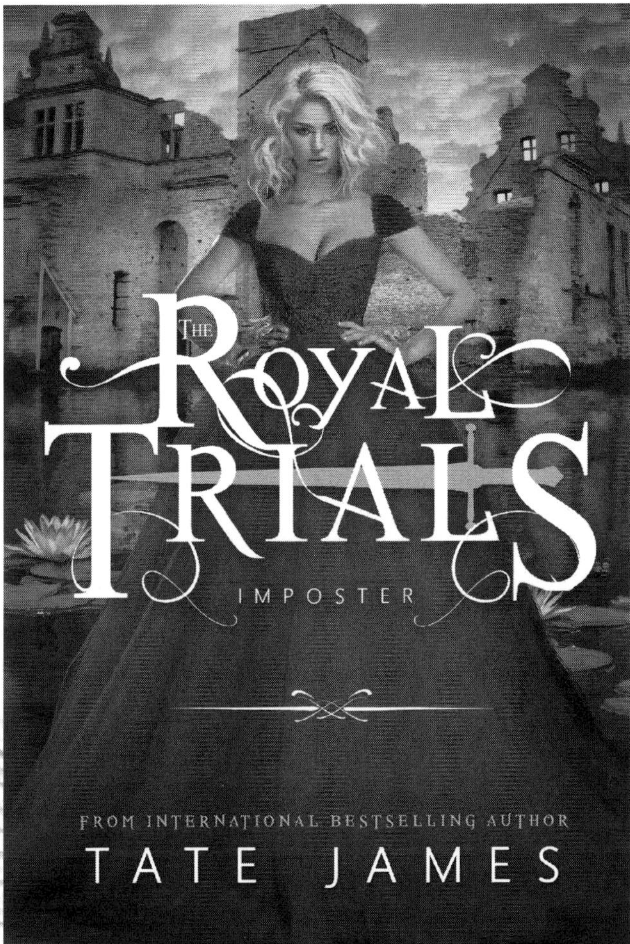

THE ROYAL TRIALS:IMPOSTER

TATE JAMES

1

CHAPTER ONE

"That one," I whispered to the grubby-faced boy beside me. "You see? The one with the beer gut? He's half asleep, an easy mark."

We stared across the crowd to the cluster of guards following the smartly dressed royal steward as he went door to door through the richest part of Lakehaven—capital city of Teich—delivering invitations to the most eligible women in the kingdom.

"Are you sure *now* is the best time to be doing this?" my companion asked with a tremor in his voice. "Surely with the Trials about to start, everyone will be on high alert?"

I rolled my eyes and turned to glare at him. "That's *exactly* why now is the best time. Look at them all, acting like it's Frogs' Feast or something. Trust me, Flick, they aren't focusing on two unassuming kids who have wandered too far from the Pond."

My charge, Flick, screwed up his dirty nose as he inspected me. "You're not exactly a kid, Rybet. If those guards caught you, you'd be tried as an adult now that you're eighteen."

I gave him a bitter smile and chuckled. "So would you, kid. The royals don't give a shit about us dwellers. We've seen loads of Pond kids hung for bullshit crimes, and at well younger than eighteen, too." He blanched white under his freckles, and I cuffed him around the head. "So, don't get caught, okay? Master Bloodeye and I have invested far too much time and money into you to see you hang now."

If anything, this only made him look *more* like he was going to vomit, and I sighed heavily.

"Look," I offered. "Do you want me to go first and show you how easy it is?"

He nodded frantically, his dirty-blond hair flopping in his eyes and making him need to push it away again so he could see me. "What will you take from him?"

Turning my attention back to the guards following the steward, I considered what they were carrying that might make a target both easy enough to take without being caught and hard enough that Flick could prove he was ready to go out alone.

Our boss, Master Bloodeye, was no amateur. He took in orphans of The Pond, gave us a roof over their heads, clothes on their backs, and food in their bellies. In exchange, we stole for him and contributed to making him the unofficial ruler of The Pond.

Once upon a time—though really not all that long ago—the area we lived in had been the richest part of Lakehaven, with marble streets, sprawling mansions and *technology* for the Teichian nobles. That was before our deities had tried to kill us all with the Age of Darkness. Before the years of droughts that took away our water and then storms that plunged us into four years of darkness and rain.

Before the plague that followed.

I shuddered at the memory of bloated corpses lining the streets. Corpses I'd robbed at Master Bloodeye's orders.

Now, that once-wealthy area of the city was a relic, a painful reminder to us all not to piss off our gods.

Streets that had once been walked by women dripping in gold and jewels, escorted by their wealthy husbands and fathers, now lay under a foot of murky water. Technological advancements that the nobles had been first to access were now doorstops and washing lines. Technically, that area of town was supposed to be off limits. The buildings were too damaged to be safe, and the water seemed impossible to drain.

Technicalities never mattered much when you had nothing and no one.

It had taken no time at all for those abandoned mansions to become the new homes for those of us without one of our own... and so The Pond came to be. Our very own waterlogged slum bordering the palace grounds.

"That," I announced, spotting my target. We'd been trailing along the street some distance back from the royal emissaries but keeping them within sight. As they approached each house, one of the guards would withdraw a tightly rolled invitation from his jacket and hand it to the steward, who would then present it to the household.

It was a huge to-do. The girls would come rushing out to receive their invitations and gush and cry as though they had *no* idea they'd be getting one. All within view of the street, of course. What good would it do to be *chosen* by the palace and not rub their neighbors' faces in it? It took ages too; in the time we had observed them, only three invitations had been successfully delivered. No wonder Tubby looked half asleep.

"The invitations?" Flick squeaked in surprise.

"Yup," I nodded. "See how they all keep them in their left, inside breast pocket? Tubby over there at the back hasn't taken any out, but you can see he has some from the way his coat sticks out a little on that side. He's also only bothered to fasten two buttons, so it should be a cinch to slip a little hand like yours in there and snag one."

Flick chewed at his lip in nervous anticipation. He was usually pretty confident every other time I had taken him out, so his anxiousness was out of character.

"Hey, I'm going first remember? I'll show you *exactly* how to do it. Follow me and repeat what I do; you can't go wrong. Okay?" I bopped him on the head and tucked a stray piece of my own straw-blonde hair behind my ear.

"Okay," he nodded. "Let's do this."

"Remember, watch me *closely.* I will meet you at the Pig and Ferret when you're done, yes?" I eyed him sternly to make sure he understood. It was protocol to split up once you'd made a snatch-and-run, that way if you got caught you weren't dragging your partner down with you.

Not that I did this sort of work much anymore. Pickpocketing was for the children, like Flick. He was barely eleven but old enough to earn his keep and pay back his debt to Master Bloodeye.

He gave me a nod of encouragement, and I melted into the crowd. It took me less than two minutes to reach my mark, divest him of one scroll, and then slip back into the excited spectators. Then again, I was one of the best. At age eighteen, I'd already gained quite the reputation for myself in Teich. I was the notorious Rybet, protégé and suspected favorite of Master Bloodeye.

It was no mistake my name sounded like the noise a frog made. Technically, it wasn't my name, it was a nickname given to me at age five when Master Bloodeye saw how easily I could slip in and out of buildings and crowds unnoticed... slippery like a frog. I had no idea what my real name was, since he'd found me as a four-year-old, wandering the streets during the Darkness with no memory of my name or my parents. It wasn't uncommon, though. Years of drought, followed by such severe storms, had an impact on lots of people's mental health.

The guardsman had barely even blinked when my hand slipped inside his coat, lifted the rolled-up piece of parchment out, and slipped it up my own sleeve. That was the benefit to having so many people around, for sure.

When I had made it farther down the street, I glanced over my shoulder to ensure Flick was doing as instructed, repeating exactly what I'd just done.

Our meeting point, the Pig and Ferret, was only a few hundred yards away, but I needed to keep an eye on him to make sure he wasn't cocking it all up. I tracked him with my gaze as he made his way through the crowd and approached the same tubby guardsman, who was yawning heavily.

Flick's back blocked his hand from sight, but I knew he'd be making the transfer from the guard's pocket to his own sleeve, and then... I released the nervous breath I had been holding as Flick moved away. The guard was none the wiser.

Good boy!

Letting the tension drop from my shoulders, I turned my back on him to hurry my ass along to the Pig and Ferret, so he wouldn't know I'd stayed to watch. I wanted the kid to think I trusted him to do it all on his own.

Just as I laid my hand on the heavy wooden door of the inn, a commotion broke out in the street behind me. Dread pooled in my belly, and I turned to see what was causing such a fuss.

"Aana's tits," I cursed, ignoring the gasp of shock from a passerby as I rushed back into the crowd. As if I was the only one to curse using the names of our deities.

I still needed to get closer to see what was going on, but when I did, my heart lurched.

Flick... his wrist was held firm by that same overweight palace guard and the stolen invitation brandished in his panic-stricken face. *Shit!* How?

It didn't matter how, though. I needed to get him free of those guards or he stood no chance. The palace didn't care if he was only a kid. He was a Pond dweller, and they saw it as their civic duty to cull our numbers any way they could.

"Flick!" I yelled, pushing forward faster, only to be grabbed from behind by an arm like steel and dragged into a dark alleyway between two ostentatious mansions.

The fight-or-flight instinct was a powerful thing, and I had both. Thrashing hard, I threw elbows and heels into my captor to try and release his hold on me, but he didn't for a moment waiver. His arms held me firm against a strong body, and a large hand clamped down over my mouth before I could scream.

"Stop it!" he hissed in my ear. "Stop fighting, boy! Does your life mean so little to you that you'd throw it away to save a Pond orphan?"

Of course not, you idiot!

I wanted to scream the words at him, but it would be too hard to explain that I had no intention of being caught... simply of giving Flick time to get away. He'd called me boy, though, which was good.

"You caught a live one," another man chuckled, as if I wasn't already far outweighed by the first one. I didn't stand a chance against *two* grown men in hand-to-hand combat. The last thing I needed was to fight off a rape at a time like this.

There weren't many girls in my line of work. When you grew up in the slums, there was really only one career choice for a pretty girl. Whoring. That had never sat well with me, and thankfully Bloodeye had seen talents beyond the income I might earn on my back with my legs in the air.

I pretty much lived in "boys" clothes—a loose shirt and leather breeches with an oversized tunic to hide my womanly curves. It had clearly been too much to ask of Aana, our Goddess of Fortune, to bless me with a boyish frame. Thankfully, this guy seemed too distracted to notice as he restrained me.

"It's too late for him," the man snapped in my ear, and I got the distinct feeling he thought he was *saving* me. "They've caught him red-handed. There's nothing you can do now."

Sure enough, the palace guardsmen were already binding Flick's wrists and throwing him over the front of a horse to be taken to the royal dungeons. It was a crime to steal in Lakehaven. Hell, it was a crime to steal *anywhere* in the Kingdom of Teich, but it was a whole other thing to steal from the royals themselves.

As the smug guard rode away with my little friend, the man's grip loosened on my face, but not from around my waist.

"You can thank me now, kid," he muttered sarcastically. "I just saved your life."

"You can let me go now, *letch*," I sneered back at him, pitching my voice a little lower than a girl's and peering down at the hand still clamped firm across my abdomen. Any higher and he would have felt the evidence that I was most assuredly *not* a boy.

A gold ring on his pinky finger gave me pause, and I leaned a little closer to make out the crest. Then gasped in horror.

"Your Highness," I breathed with dread and revulsion. I'd just tried to kick one of the royal princes in the balls with my heel...

"Shit," the man—*prince*—holding me cursed, and the other man groaned.

"Seriously? You forgot to take off your ring? I'm never letting you sneak out with me again, big brother." The second man sounded exasperated, but also a touch amused.

I just wanted to get the hell away from them. *Big brother* meant that this was another of the crown princes!

"Please, Your Highness," I whispered, "Let me go; I swear I won't tell a soul that you're here in the city."

The one holding me released his grip abruptly, and I stumbled forward a few steps, letting my hood fall further over my face to hide my features.

"Go, then," he snapped. "But we were *never here*."

Nodding as frantically as I could without displacing my hood, I kept my gaze firmly on the ground to avoid any *further* insult as I sketched a shaking bow and backed out of the alleyway. As I reached the crowd, I couldn't help myself... I glanced back into the shadows to get a look at the princes.

Could anyone blame me? No commoner had ever laid eyes on our princes in over ten years. Not since they'd ended the plague by summoning hundreds of *drachen*—a magical creature that was a small variety of dragon but looked a lot like a frog. The *drachen* had swept through the land, devouring the insects that carried and spread the plague, and within a year, it was extinct. The princes had barely been teenagers at the time but had just come into their magic and found a way to help the people where their parents had failed.

Typical of my luck, though, all I could see in the shadows were three sets of men's boots, and a ripple of fear ran through me. Three. All three princes were just within breathing distance of me... and I'd walked away with my life.

The notorious Rybet Waise didn't rise to such heights of crime in such a short time on luck alone, though. No, I had a natural instinct toward danger. Premonition, Bloodeye liked to call it, but I preferred “instinct.” After all, none but the royals had possessed any magic since the last queen was murdered.

My instincts, the ones I’d trusted all my life to keep me alive, told me that this wouldn't be the last time I'd encounter the three mysterious princes of Teich.

Flip the page for an excerpt of chapter one.

THE FAMILY SPELLS

C.M. STUNICH

1

MY FIRST ENCOUNTER WITH DICKFACE
GRACELEY

As soon as I saw my next customer pull up on a motorcycle, I knew I was going to hate him.

"Entitled ass," I murmured as I went back to browsing spell sites on my phone, trying to get a handle on what sort of look I wanted for the store's web page. There was no point in being Ms. Customer Service with this jerk; he'd just parked his Harley in a handicapped space. Based on the way he swaggered up to my front entrance, I was guessing he was most definitely not qualified to use that spot.

I thought about calling the tow truck service on him, but Passionate Potions and Seductive Spells had had a slow sales week. A dickhead customer was better than no customer at all, right?

The man shoved the doors open, rattling the old glass in their panes, sending the bells merrily tinkling. His boots were loud as he pounded across the ancient wooden floors, heading toward the Sex and Intimacy section at the back of the shop.

"Morning," I said, flicking my finger across the screen of my phone. Magic had come a long way in the last hundred years, but there really was no good substitute for an iPhone, now was there? It couldn't make fire tornadoes and chuck them at bad guys, but it could show me an ad for a pretty amazing witch hat that I just had to have. I told myself I was ordering it for the shop, but … that would be a lie. Some women have shoe addictions, some purse addictions, but me, I had a hat addiction.

My customer grunted at me, his cinnamon and sandalwood smell tickling my nostrils and making my nose twitch. Most people wouldn't be able to pick up on such a subtle scent, not with the layer of incense smoke and the stink of herbs in the shop. But I was a witch, and witches had better noses than werewolves. True story, even if they refused to admit it. My husband, Caine the half-wolf, and I had healthy debates on the subject.

Either way, it was a useful skill to have, especially since I now knew, based on his smell, that motorcycle guy was a witch-demon hybrid.

Goddess, that man smells nice, I thought, entertaining only a niggle of guilt at getting pleasure out of another man's scent. I had three husbands of my own, but according to the Oracle, there was a fourth soulmate waiting out there for me somewhere.

I snorted under my breath, and swiped over to the next page of my shopping addiction.

I had another soulmate, but I was never going to find him. At age thirty-two, married three times over with four kids, finding our fourth was starting to seem like an impossibility. Besides, even if I did find my fourth and final soulmate, the jerk who'd just pulled up on the motorcycle was most definitely not him—even if he did have a sweet ride and an even spicier smell.

"What a delightful dish," my familiar, Bast, purred, sitting on her usual shelf behind me. Every once in a while, I had a customer get the ever living crap scared out of them when she moved. Most people were simply not used to a serval—a thirty pound African wildcat—hanging out in a shop in a Seattle suburb. She sniffed the air as I continued to browse for hats online, and then sighed. "He has a familiar, too, but the poor thing isn't with him. I would've liked to see what he looked like."

I snorted, but didn't bother glancing up, enjoying a quiet afternoon in the shop, and a well-deserved break from the kids. Two of my hubbies had the babies covered, while my third was in the back, taking inventory. I magicked my black-and-gold pentagram emblazoned teacup into my hand, and took a sip, letting the steam tickle my nostrils, the honey soothe my throat.

Ah, pure bliss.

"You don't have any crystallized rose petals?" the prick in aisle one barked out at me, and I cringed, sloshing tea onto the counter. He didn't even bother to pop his head around. I glanced up and found just the top of his orange-streaked black hair showing above the shelf. My eyes narrowed.

"Not in stock currently, but I could order them," I replied, my voice as calm and relaxed as I could get it. I had a tendency to lose my temper before an argument even escalated from cold to warm. Crystallized rose petals, huh? I thought as I swiped through my mental spellbook and tried to figure out what this guy might need them for. Erectile dysfunction spells were definitely at the top of my list. "Did you need red, pink, white, purple or black?"

"I need red," he growled, like I was seriously pissing him off. "There's an empty jar labeled Red Petals. Do you know anything about how to stock a store properly?"

My narrowed eyes began to burn with the fires of a righteous rage, and I gritted my teeth.

"With a store that has as much inventory as ours does, it'd take tremendous amounts of overhead to keep everything we carry in the back, just in case. Like I said, I can special order some and get it here by Friday, or else you can just wait until Monday when the next shipment comes in."

I heard jars and books being slid around angrily on the shelves, and seriously debated storming back there. Chances were if I did, I'd end up tripping on my own display and landing face-first at the asshole's feet. Nah, I'd just stay back here and focus on my shopping.

"If you don't have what I need, I'll go elsewhere. It's clear you're not interested in my business," Dick Face ranted as his boots pounded back around the shelf and toward the front counter. I ignored him. Mostly.

"Good luck finding even half of what we carry in any other store. My coven has a half-vampire, a half-fae, and a half-wolf in it. Nobody has our expertise or our selection." Dick Face continued on toward the door, scoffing under his breath, and I couldn't help myself. I decided to throw out another barb.

That was what changed my fate, lashing out with an aggressive quip. Funny how fate works, isn’t it?

"If you're looking for ingredients for an erectile

dysfunction spell, I've got a recipe that doesn't need rose petals that works twice as well."

The man stopped with his hand on the door, the bells just starting their happy tinkle.

That's when I lifted my face, meeting his bright orange eyes dead-on.

Every witch knows that you can recognize a soulmate by their eyes, that penetrating stare that cuts deep into the heart, those fireworks that explode behind the eyes, that hot heat that travels straight to the loins.

"Oh fuck," we both said at the same time.

Dick Face stumbled back into the door, breaking the old glass pane as I scrambled off my stool and ended up falling against the display shelf with the herb jars on it. They crashed to the floor around me, the pungent smells of dried lavender and mint perfuming the air. Bast raised her back in an arch and hissed like a real wildcat, but I'm pretty sure Dick Face was too busy staring at me in shock to even notice that she existed.

"This isn't happening," he said, scrubbing his tattooed hand down his face. "No fucking way."

"Grace, are you okay?" a soothing baritone asked from the direction of the office. Within a few seconds, I had Spectre staring down at me, his pupils so dilated his eyes were nearly back. Side effect of being a vampire-witch hybrid, Spectre could get … excited sometimes. Slowly, with that extra special touch of the undead, he looked up and found Dick Face staring at me like I'd grown a pair of horns.

Worse.

It was worse.

So much worse.

The entitled asswad on the motorcycle wasn't just a rude customer with a bad attitude, he was my missing soulmate and the last member of my soul-circle.

Holy flipping witch hats.

"I'm as shocked as you are buddy," I whispered as Spectre crunched over the broken glass and helped me to my feet. As always, when our hands met, I felt a rush of heat wash over me, making my nipples pebble to hard points. We'd been married five years now, and I still couldn't get over how aroused I got at just the sight of Spec. Tall, dark, handsome—he was every hottie cliché in the book and then some.

"No, you're not," Dick Face said, and then he was throwing himself out the front doors and heading straight for his motorcycle. But I wasn't about to let him get away, not a chance. There were other factors at play here besides my own romantic fulfillment.

“What the hex is going on?” Spec asked, trailing his nails down the inside of my wrist and making me shiver. I looked up into his lavender eyes, and bit my lower lip. How do I explain without freaking him the fuck out? I can’t just blurt—

“Soulmate.” I choked out the word, and then turned, dragging Spec along behind me as I pushed the doors open and stumbled into the surprising warmth of an October afternoon. There were clouds covering the sun, and a near guarantee that we’d be getting a storm sometime soon.

“Soulmate?!” Spec choked out as I released his arm and moved to stand in front of Dick Face’s motorcycle, curling my fingers around the handlebars, and glaring daggers at the asshole.

"Where do you think you're going?" I asked, because there were spells that only complete soul-circles could cast, spells that I hadn't been able to afford to pay another coven to do for me because they cost literal millions. And sitting right here, on this stupid motorcycle was my best chance to save my mother's life.

"Get out of the way," the tattooed prick growled at me, sounding more werewolf than witch. I might think he were both if I wasn't already married to one of those. Oh, and if he didn't have the very distinct cinnamon spell of demon.

I caught his gaze again, even though it was damn near impossible for me to hold it. Fireworks crackled behind my eyelids, and my stomach twisted into a nervous knot. And my lady bits? Well, those fucking bits were enthralled.

Six foot two or three, dark hair streaked with orange, and tattoos made up of swirling purple skies, glittering constellations, and a whole galaxy of planets. His eyes were almost as orange as his hair—demon eyes.

"After what just happened?" I asked as Spec moved over to stand beside me, dressed in his own ink, black slacks, and a tight-as-hell wifebeater. "You looked into my eyes—"

"I look into a lot of women's eyes," Dick Face said, leaning back on his bike and crossing his arms over his chest. He was covered in witchcraft ink, spells etched into his skin in brilliant color from shoulders to fingertips on both arms. My mouth watered, and my ovaries did a little dance at the thought of this guy being my soulmate. Just because you're fated to be together doesn't mean you're fated to be in love, I reminded myself. My mom had a soulmate she didn't fuck, and that'd worked wonders for them for twenty years. Best friends, coffee buddies, knitting partners.

Dick Face didn't really look like a knitting partner to me though.

"What makes you special?" he asked, tilting his head to the side, his full lips in an arrogant smirk that I wanted to punch right off of his stupid face. He had big eyes for a douchebag, unfairly long lashes, and the sort of chiseled jaw people go under the knife for. It was too much, really. When I'd imagined finding my fourth and final soulmate, I hadn't exactly let myself dream this big—in the looks department, that is.

In the personality department, I was finding myself severely disappointed.

"You're telling me you fell against the door and broke the glass for no reason?" I asked, cocking a brow and challenging the prick. "You didn't feel that connection?"

"I didn't feel a fucking thing," he lied, gesturing with his chin in the direction of the sidewalk. "Now move, so I can get the hell out of here; I'm late."

"You were just trying to buy shit for an erectile dysfunction spell. Where the hell could you be off to in such a hurry?"

"To see my fiancée," he drawled, pulling a pair of shades out of his vest pocket and sliding them on his perfect aquiline nose. When he kicked the engine into gear, I moved off to the side and watched him go. I could hold him here with a spell, and have the upperhand. After all, my soul-circle had four members. Seeing as he was our fifth and final, he had none.

But there was a cruel twist to his mouth when he said fiancée that I didn't like. If he didn't want to stay and get to know me, then maybe I didn't want to know him either?

"Are you okay, Graceley?" Spec asked me, putting his hand on my shoulder and giving it a little squeeze. I stepped backward into his embrace, closing my eyes and breathing in the scent of wet dirt and magic, this metallic tang that bothered some people but always comforted me.

It was the smell of witch.

"I'm okay," I said as I watched the tattooed mystery man peel out of his stolen handicap spot, and onto the road leading back to the highway. "He'll be back."

As soon as I said the words, I could taste a bite of magic on the back of my tongue.

The motorcycle dick would come back.

The question was: would I want anything to do with him when he did?

SIGN UP FOR A
TATE JAMES *or* C.M. STUNICH

NEWSLETTER

Sign up for an exclusive first look at the hottest new releases, contests, and exclusives from the authors.

@

www.cmstunich.com
www.tatejamesauthor.com

SIGN UP FOR A
TATE JAMES *or* C.M. STUNICH

DISCUSSION GROUP

Want to discuss what you've just read?
Get exclusive teasers or meet special guest authors?
Join C.M.'s and Tate's online book clubs on Facebook!

@

www.facebook.com/groups/thebookishbatcave
www.facebook.com/groups/tatejames.thefoxhole

BOOKS BY
C.M. STUNICH

Romance

HARD ROCK ROOTS SERIES
Real Ugly
Get Bent
Tough Luck
Bad Day
Born Wrong
Hard Rock Roots Box Set (1-5)
Dead Serious
Doll Face
Heart Broke
Get Hitched
Screw Up

TASTING NEVER SERIES
Tasting Never
Finding Never
Keeping Never
Tasting, Finding, Keeping: The Story of Never Box Set (1-3)
Never Can Tell
Never Let Go
Never Did Say
Never Have I

ROCK-HARD BEAUTIFUL
Groupie
Roadie
Moxie

THE BAD NANNY TRILOGY
Bad Nanny
Good Boyfriend
Great Husband

TRIPLE M SERIES
Losing Me, Finding You
Loving Me, Trusting You
Needing Me, Wanting You
Craving Me, Desiring You

A DUET
Paint Me Beautiful
Color Me Pretty

FIVE FORGOTTEN SOULS
Beautiful Survivors
Alluring Outcasts

MAFIA QUEEN
Lure
Lavish
Luxe
Lethal

DEATH BY DAYBREAK MC
I Was Born Ruined
I am Dressed in in

STAND-ALONE NOVELS
Blizzards and Bastards(originally featured in the Snow and Seduction Anthology) Baby GirlAll for 1Fuck Valentine's Day (A Short Story)
Broken Pasts
Crushing Summer
Taboo Unchained
Taming Her Boss
Kicked

Violet Blaze Novels

(My Pen Name)

BAD BOYS MC TRILOGY
Raw and Dirty
Risky and Wild
Savage and Racy

HERS TO KEEP TRILOGY
Biker Rockstar Billionaire CEO Alpha
Biker Rockstar Billionaire CEO Dom
Biker Rockstar Billionaire CEO Boss

STAND-ALONE
Football Dick
Stepbrother Thief
Stepbrother Inked
Glacier

BOOKS BY C.M. STUNICH

Fantasy Novels

THE SEVEN MATES OF ZARA WOLF
Pack Ebon Red
Pack Violet Shadow
Pack Obsidian Gold
Pack Ivory Emerald
Pack Amber Ash
Pack Azure Frost
Pack Crimson Dusk

ACADEMY OF SPIRITS AND SHADOWS
Spirited
Haunted
Shadowed

HAREM OF HEARTS
Allison's Adventures in Underland
Allison and the Torrid Tea Party
Allison Shatters the Looking-Glass
Kings of Underland

SIRENS OF A SINFUL SEA TRILOGY
Under the Wild Waves

THE SEVEN WICKED SERIES
Seven Wicked Creatures
Six Wicked Beasts
Five Wicked Monsters
Four Wicked Fiends

HOWLING HOLIDAYS
Werewolf Kisses

OTHER FANTASY NOVELS
Stiltz
Gray and Graves
Indigo & Iris
She Lies Twisted
Hell Inc.
DeadBorn
Chryer's Crest

Co-Written

(With Tate James)

HIJINKS HAREM
Elements of Mischief
Elements of Ruin
Elements of Desire

THE WILD HUNT MOTORCYCLE CLUB
Dark Glitter
Cruel Glamour

FOXFIRE BURNING
The Nine
Tailgame

OTHER
And Today I Die

BOOKS BY
TATE JAMES

Fantasy Novels

KIT DAVENPORT NOVELS
The Vixen's Lead
The Dragon's Wing
The Tiger's Ambush
The Viper's Nest
The Crow's Murder
The Alpha's Pack

THE ROYAL TRIALS
Impostor
Seeker
Heir

Romance

STAND-ALONE
Slopes of Sin (originally featured in the Snow and Seduction Anthology)

Co-Written

(With C.M. Stunich)

HIJINKS HAREM
Elements of Mischief
Elements of Ruin
Elements of Desire

THE WILD HUNT MOTORCYCLE CLUB
Dark Glitter
Cruel Glamour

FOXFIRE BURNING
The Nine
Tail Gam

OTHER
And Today I Die

STALKING

LINKS

KEEP UP WITH ALL
THE FUN ... AND EARN SOME FREE BOOKS!

TATE JAMES

Join my group! - www.facebook.com/groups/tatejames.thefoxhole.

Like my page! - www.facebook.com/tatejamesfans

Be my friend? - www.facebook.com/tatejamesauthor

Instagram me! - Instagram.com/tatejamesauthor

Tweet me! - twitter.com/tatejamesauthor

Sign up for my newsletter that I may or may not ever send! - www.tatejamesauthor.com

Pin me! Or ya know … whatever the correct term is for Pinterest: - pinterest.com/tatejamesauthor

C.M. STUNICH

JOIN THE C.M. STUNICH NEWSLETTER – Get three free books just for signing up http://eepurl.com/DEsEf

TWEET ME ON TWITTER, BABE – Come sing the social media song with me https://twitter.com/CMStunich

SNAPCHAT WITH ME – Get exclusive behind the scenes looks at covers, blurbs, book signings and more http://www.snapchat.com/add/cmstunich

LISTEN TO MY BOOK PLAYLISTS – Share your fave music with me and I'll give you my playlists (I'm super active on here!) https://open.spotify.com/user/12101321503

FRIEND ME ON FACEBOOK – Okay, I'm actually at the 5,000 friend limit, but if you click the "follow" button on my profile page, you'll see way more of my killer posts https://facebook.com/cmstunich

LIKE ME ON FACEBOOK – Pretty please? I'll love you forever if you do! ;) https://facebook.com/cmstunichauthor & https://facebook.com/violetblazeauthor

CHECK OUT THE NEW SITE – (under construction) but it looks kick-a$$ so far, right? You can order signed books here! http://www.cmstunich.com

READ VIOLET BLAZE – Read the books from my hot as hellfire pen name, Violet Blaze http://www.violetblazebooks.com

SUBSCRIBE TO MY RSS FEED – Press that little orange button in the corner and copy that RSS feed so you can get all the latest updates http://www.cmstunich.com/blog

AMAZON, BABY – If you click the follow button here, you'll get an email each time I put out a new book. Pretty sweet, huh? http://amazon.com/author/cmstunich http://amazon.com/author/violetblaze

PINTEREST – Lots of hot half-naked men. Oh, and half-naked men. Plus, tattooed guys holding babies (who are half-naked) http://pinterest.com/cmstunich

INSTAGRAM – Cute cat pictures. And half-naked guys. Yep, that again. http://instagram.com/cmstunich

P.S. We heart the f*ck out of you! Thanks for reading! I love your faces.

<3 C.M. Stunich aka Violet Blaze & Tate James

ABOUT TATE JAMES

Tate James was born and raised in the Land of the Long White Cloud (New Zealand) but now lives in Australia with her husband, baby and furbaby.

She is a lover of books, red wine, cats and coffee and is not a morning person. She is a bit too sarcastic and swears too much for polite society and definitely tells too many dirty jokes.

ABOUT C.M. STUNICH

C.M. Stunich is a self-admitted bibliophile with a love for exotic teas and a whole host of characters who live full time inside the strange, swirling vortex of her thoughts. Some folks might call this crazy, but Caitlin Morgan doesn't mind – especially considering she has to write biographies in the third person. Oh, and half the host of characters in her head are searing hot bad boys with dirty mouths and skillful hands (among other things). If being crazy means hanging out with them everyday, C.M. has decided to have herself committed.

She hates tapioca pudding, loves to binge on cheesy horror movies, and is a slave to many cats. When she's not vacuuming fur off of her couch, C.M. can be found with her nose buried in a book or her eyes glued to a computer screen. She's the author of over thirty novels – romance, new adult, fantasy, and young adult included. Please, come and join her inside her crazy. There's a heck of a lot to do there.

Oh, and Caitlin loves to chat (incessantly), so feel free to e-mail her, send her a Facebook message, or put up smoke signals. She's already looking forward to it.

25191122R00236

Printed in Great Britain
by Amazon